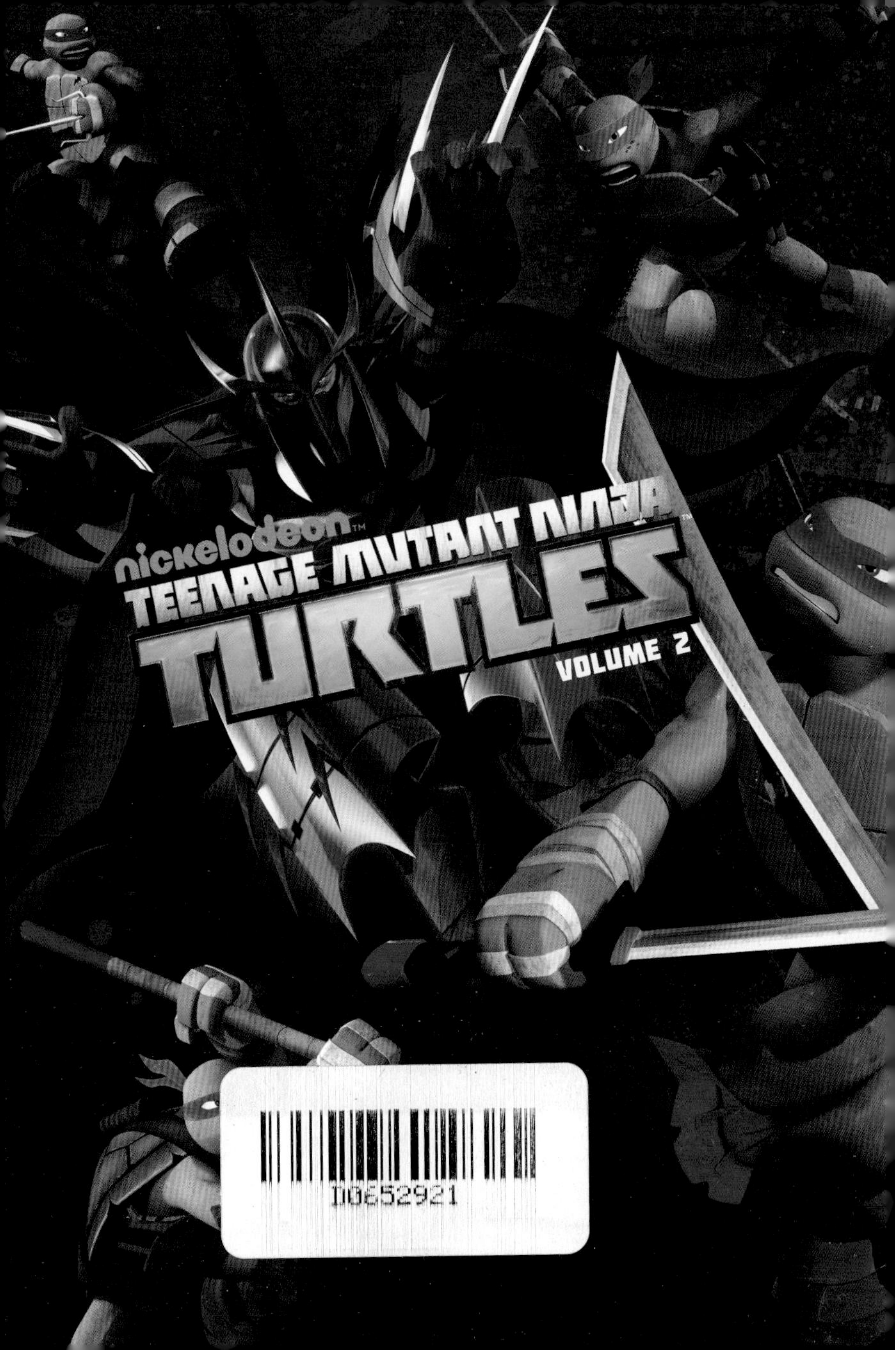
nickelodeon™
TEENAGE MUTANT NINJA™
TURTLES
VOLUME 2

NICKELODEON
TEENAGE MUTANT NINJA TURTLES

NEVER SAY XEVER

Written by
KENNY BYERLY

THE GAUNTLET

Written by
JOSHUA STERNIN
&
J.R. VENTIMILIA

Adaptation by
JUSTIN EISINGER

Edits by
ALONZO SIMON

Lettering and Design by
TOM B. LONG

Special thanks to Joan Hilty,
Linda Lee, and Kat van Dam
for their invaluable assistance.

Based on characters created by Peter Laird and Kevin Eastman.

ISBN: 978-1-61377-753-4
16 15 14 13   1 2 3 4

www.IDWPUBLISHING.com

IDW

Ted Adams, CEO & Publisher
Greg Goldstein, President & COO
Robbie Robbins, EVP/Sr. Graphic Artist
Chris Ryall, Chief Creative Officer/Editor-in-Chief
Matthew Ruzicka, CPA, Chief Financial Officer
Alan Payne, VP of Sales
Dirk Wood, VP of Marketing
Lorelei Bunjes, VP of Digital Services

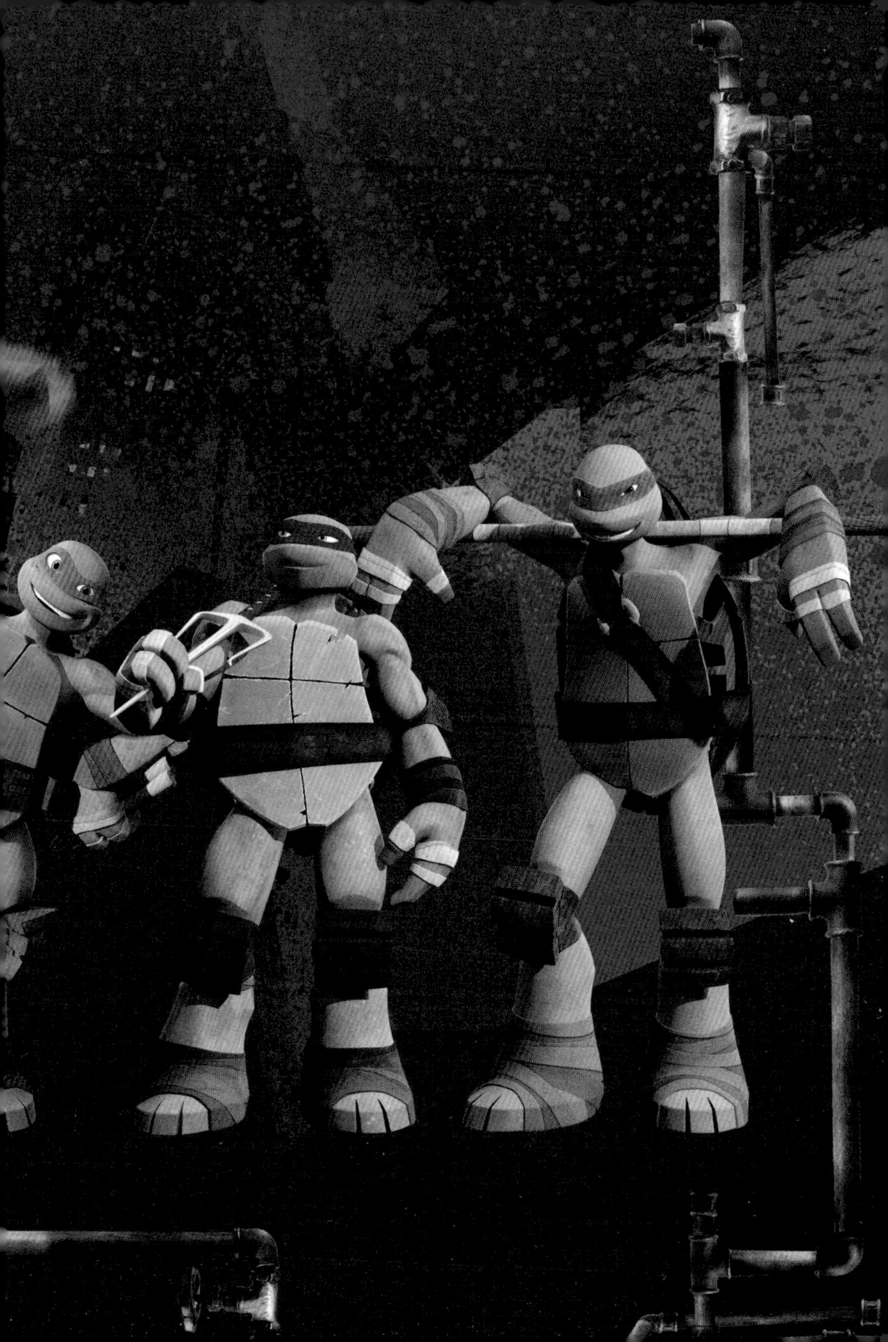

MEET THE PLAYERS

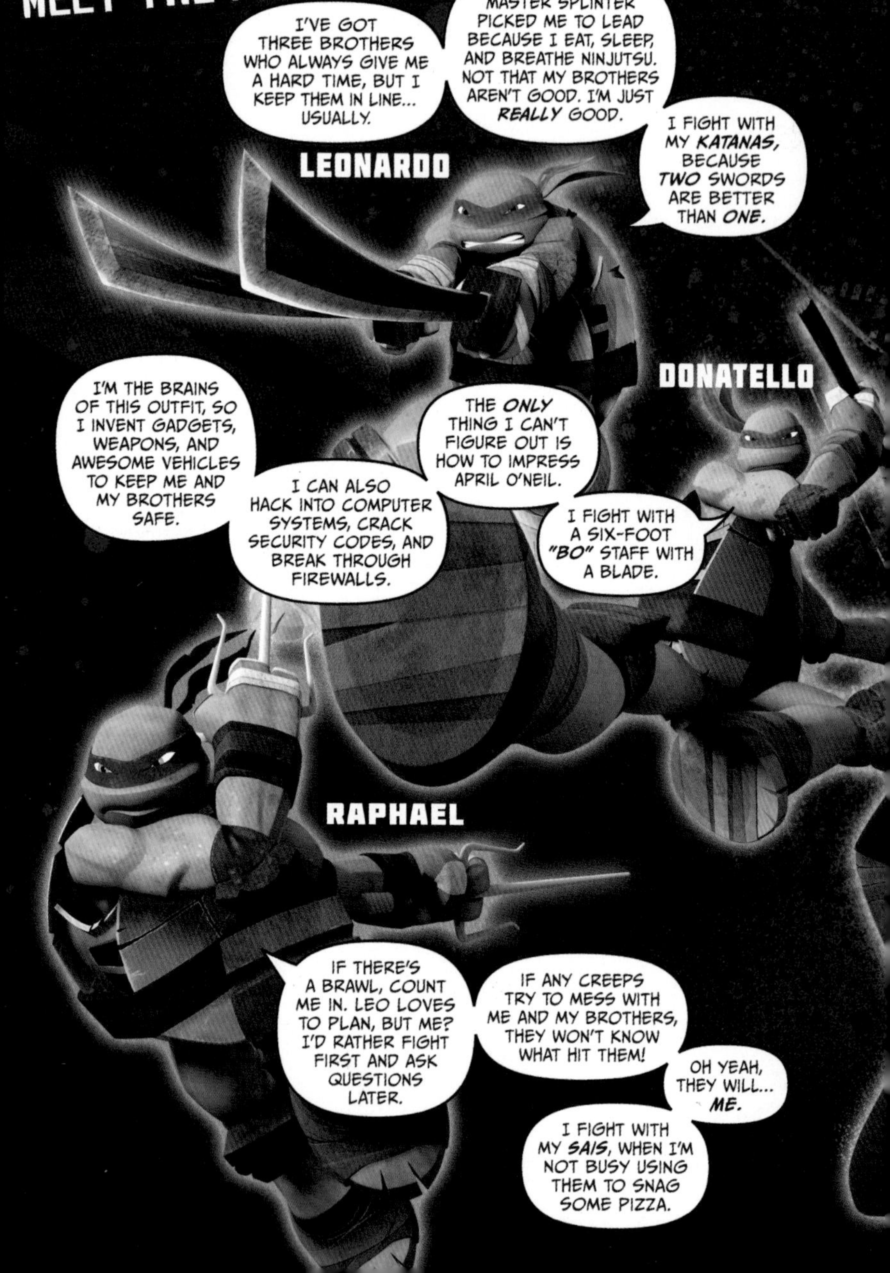

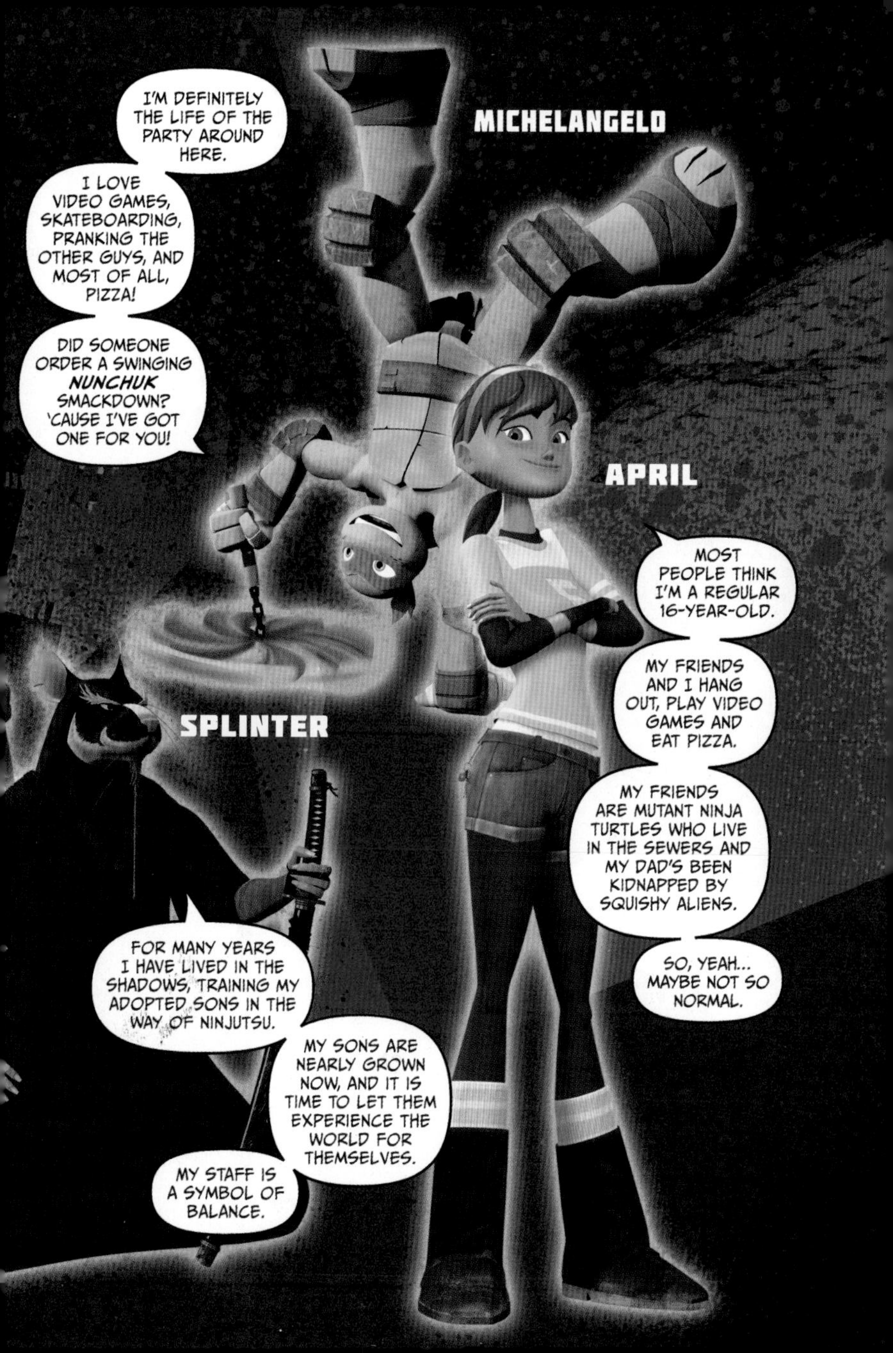
MICHELANGELO
I'M DEFINITELY THE LIFE OF THE PARTY AROUND HERE.
I LOVE VIDEO GAMES, SKATEBOARDING, PRANKING THE OTHER GUYS, AND MOST OF ALL, PIZZA!
DID SOMEONE ORDER A SWINGING *NUNCHUK* SMACKDOWN? 'CAUSE I'VE GOT ONE FOR YOU!
APRIL
MOST PEOPLE THINK I'M A REGULAR 16-YEAR-OLD.
MY FRIENDS AND I HANG OUT, PLAY VIDEO GAMES AND EAT PIZZA.
MY FRIENDS ARE MUTANT NINJA TURTLES WHO LIVE IN THE SEWERS AND MY DAD'S BEEN KIDNAPPED BY SQUISHY ALIENS.
SO, YEAH... MAYBE NOT SO NORMAL.
SPLINTER
FOR MANY YEARS I HAVE LIVED IN THE SHADOWS, TRAINING MY ADOPTED SONS IN THE WAY OF NINJUTSU.
MY SONS ARE NEARLY GROWN NOW, AND IT IS TIME TO LET THEM EXPERIENCE THE WORLD FOR THEMSELVES.
MY STAFF IS A SYMBOL OF BALANCE.

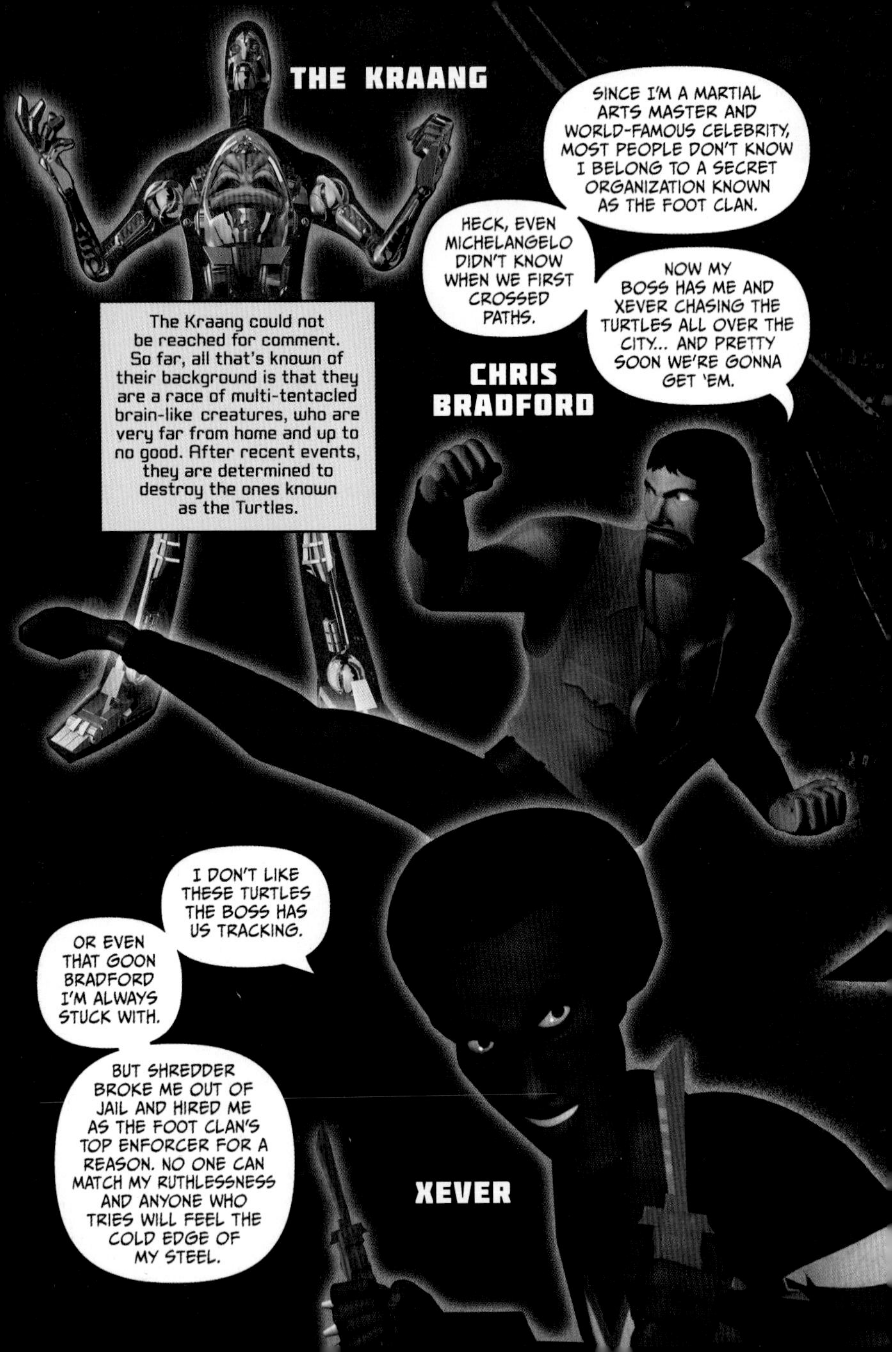
THE KRAANG
The Kraang could not be reached for comment. So far, all that's known of their background is that they are a race of multi-tentacled brain-like creatures, who are very far from home and up to no good. After recent events, they are determined to destroy the ones known as the Turtles.
SINCE I'M A MARTIAL ARTS MASTER AND WORLD-FAMOUS CELEBRITY, MOST PEOPLE DON'T KNOW I BELONG TO A SECRET ORGANIZATION KNOWN AS THE FOOT CLAN.
HECK, EVEN MICHELANGELO DIDN'T KNOW WHEN WE FIRST CROSSED PATHS.
NOW MY BOSS HAS ME AND XEVER CHASING THE TURTLES ALL OVER THE CITY... AND PRETTY SOON WE'RE GONNA GET 'EM.
CHRIS BRADFORD
I DON'T LIKE THESE TURTLES THE BOSS HAS US TRACKING.
OR EVEN THAT GOON BRADFORD I'M ALWAYS STUCK WITH.
BUT SHREDDER BROKE ME OUT OF JAIL AND HIRED ME AS THE FOOT CLAN'S TOP ENFORCER FOR A REASON. NO ONE CAN MATCH MY RUTHLESSNESS AND ANYONE WHO TRIES WILL FEEL THE COLD EDGE OF MY STEEL.
XEVER

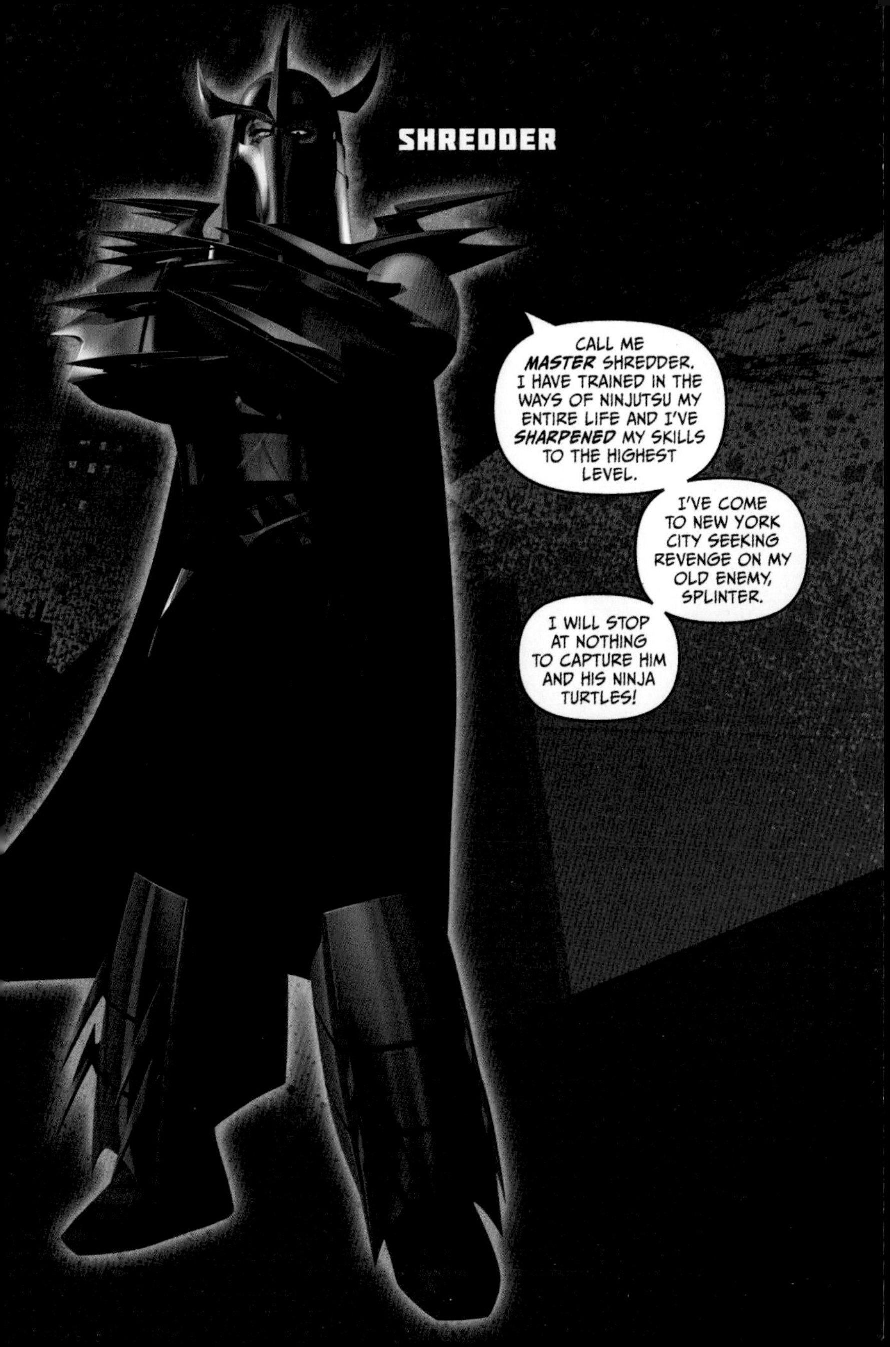
SHREDDER
CALL ME MASTER SHREDDER. I HAVE TRAINED IN THE WAYS OF NINJUTSU MY ENTIRE LIFE AND I'VE SHARPENED MY SKILLS TO THE HIGHEST LEVEL.
I'VE COME TO NEW YORK CITY SEEKING REVENGE ON MY OLD ENEMY, SPLINTER.
I WILL STOP AT NOTHING TO CAPTURE HIM AND HIS NINJA TURTLES!

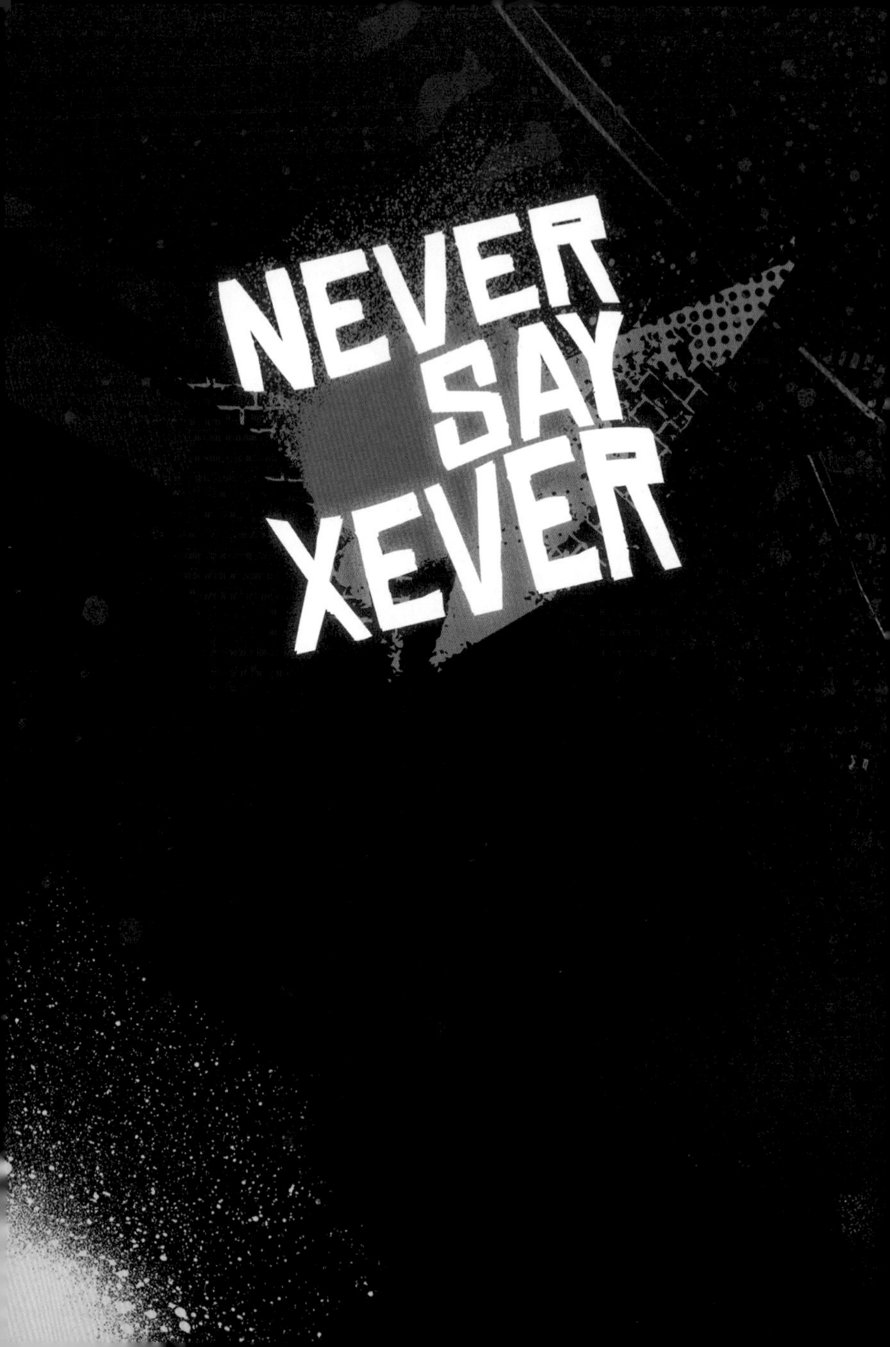
NEVER
SAY
XEVER

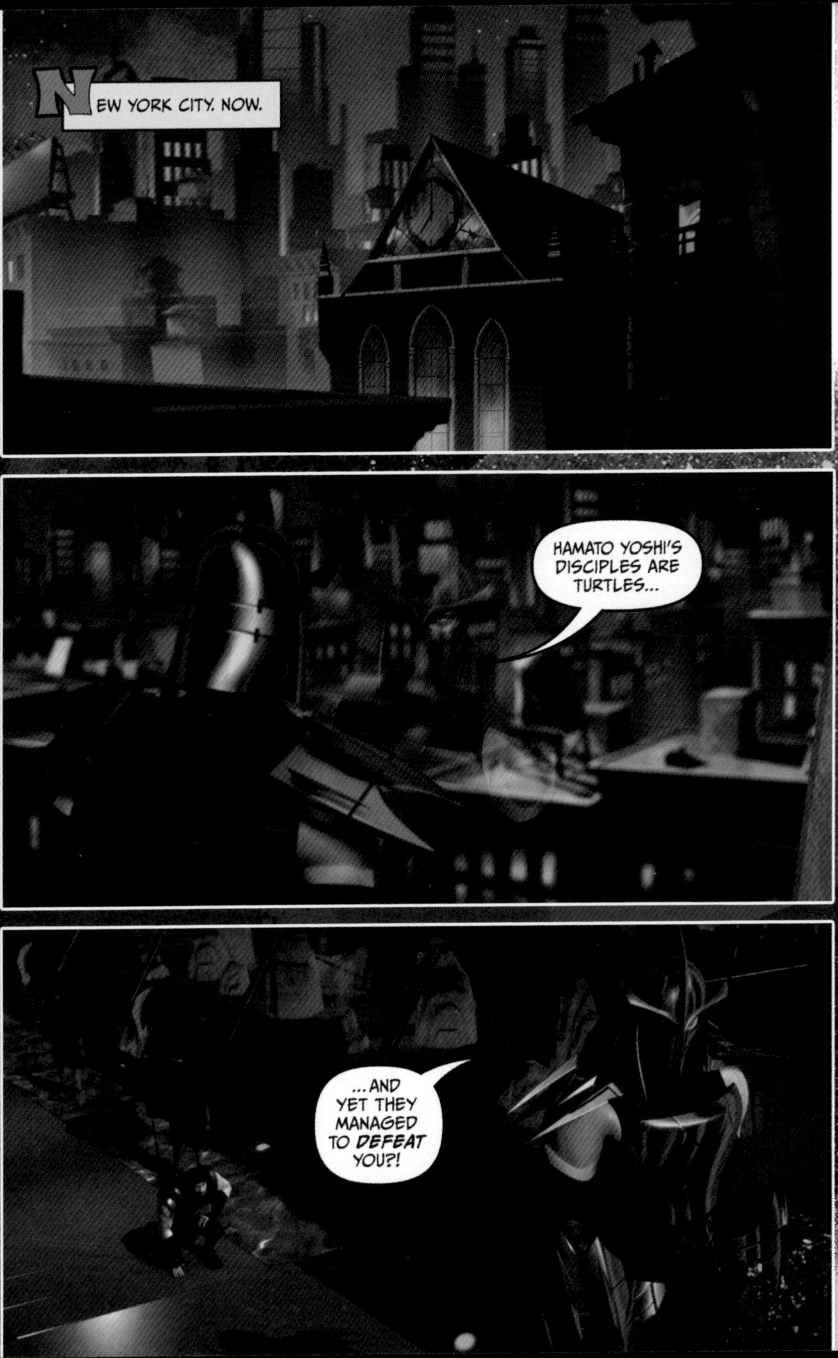
NEW YORK CITY. NOW.
HAMATO YOSHI'S DISCIPLES ARE TURTLES...
...AND YET THEY MANAGED TO *DEFEAT* YOU?!

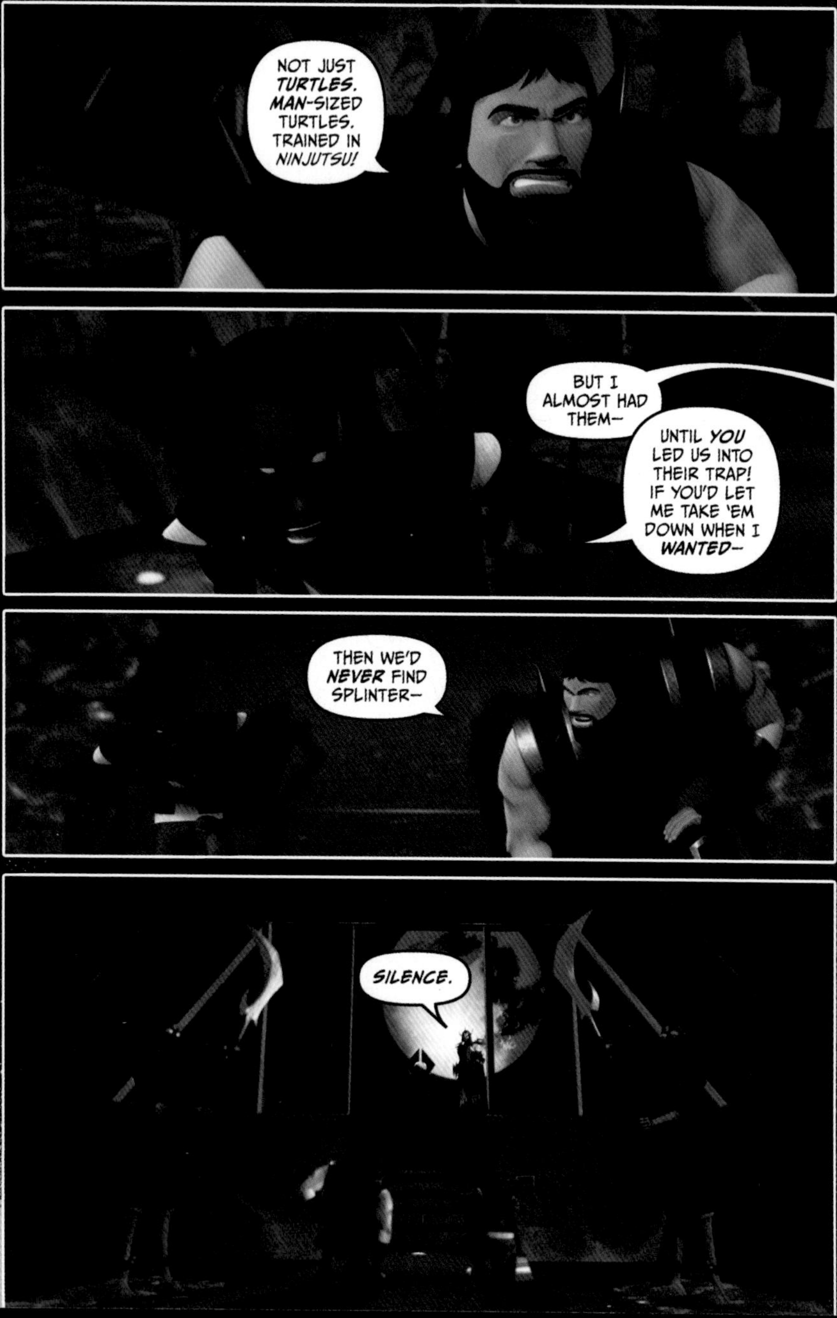
NOT JUST *TURTLES*. *MAN*-SIZED TURTLES. TRAINED IN *NINJUTSU*!
BUT I ALMOST HAD THEM—
UNTIL *YOU* LED US INTO THEIR TRAP! IF YOU'D LET ME TAKE 'EM DOWN WHEN I *WANTED*—
THEN WE'D *NEVER* FIND SPLINTER—
SILENCE.

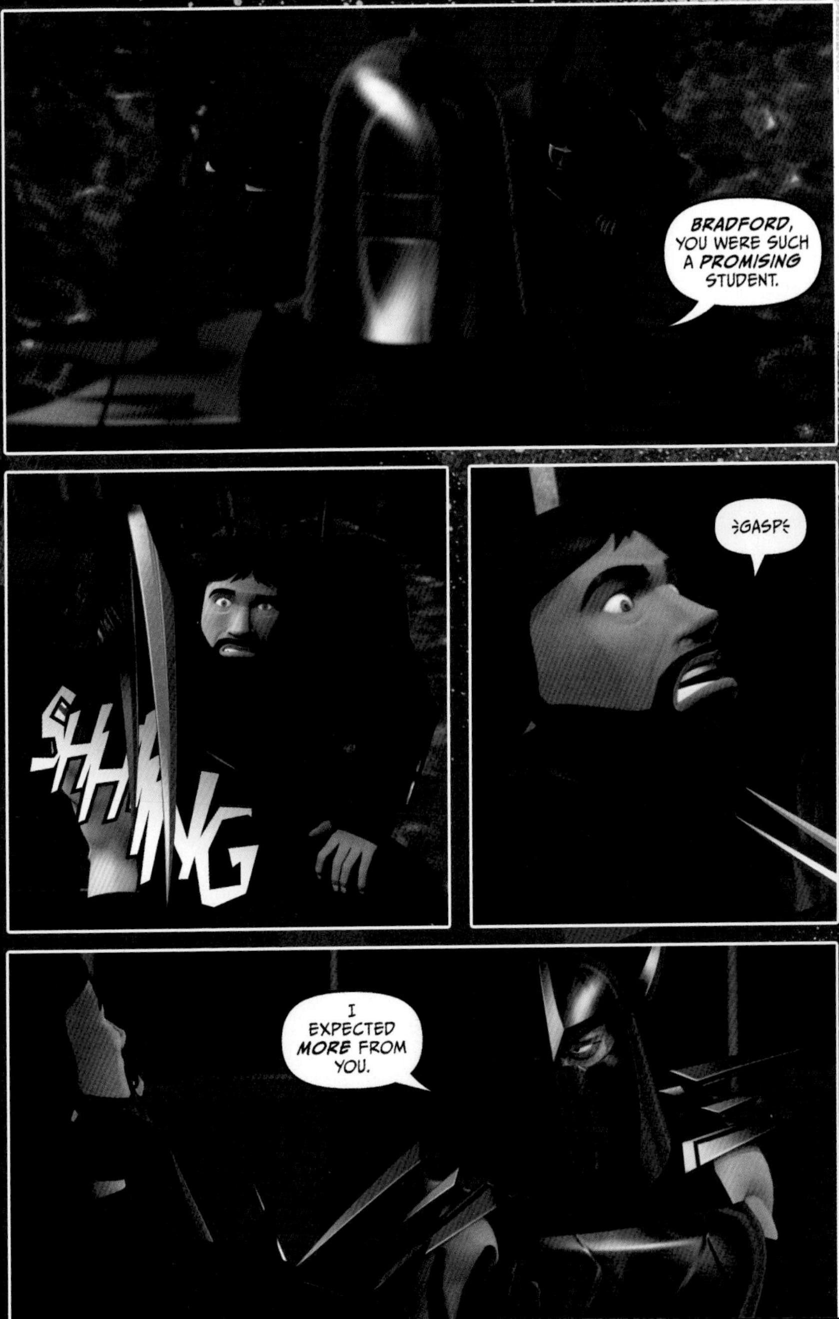
BRADFORD, YOU WERE SUCH A PROMISING STUDENT.
SHHING
GASP
I EXPECTED MORE FROM YOU.

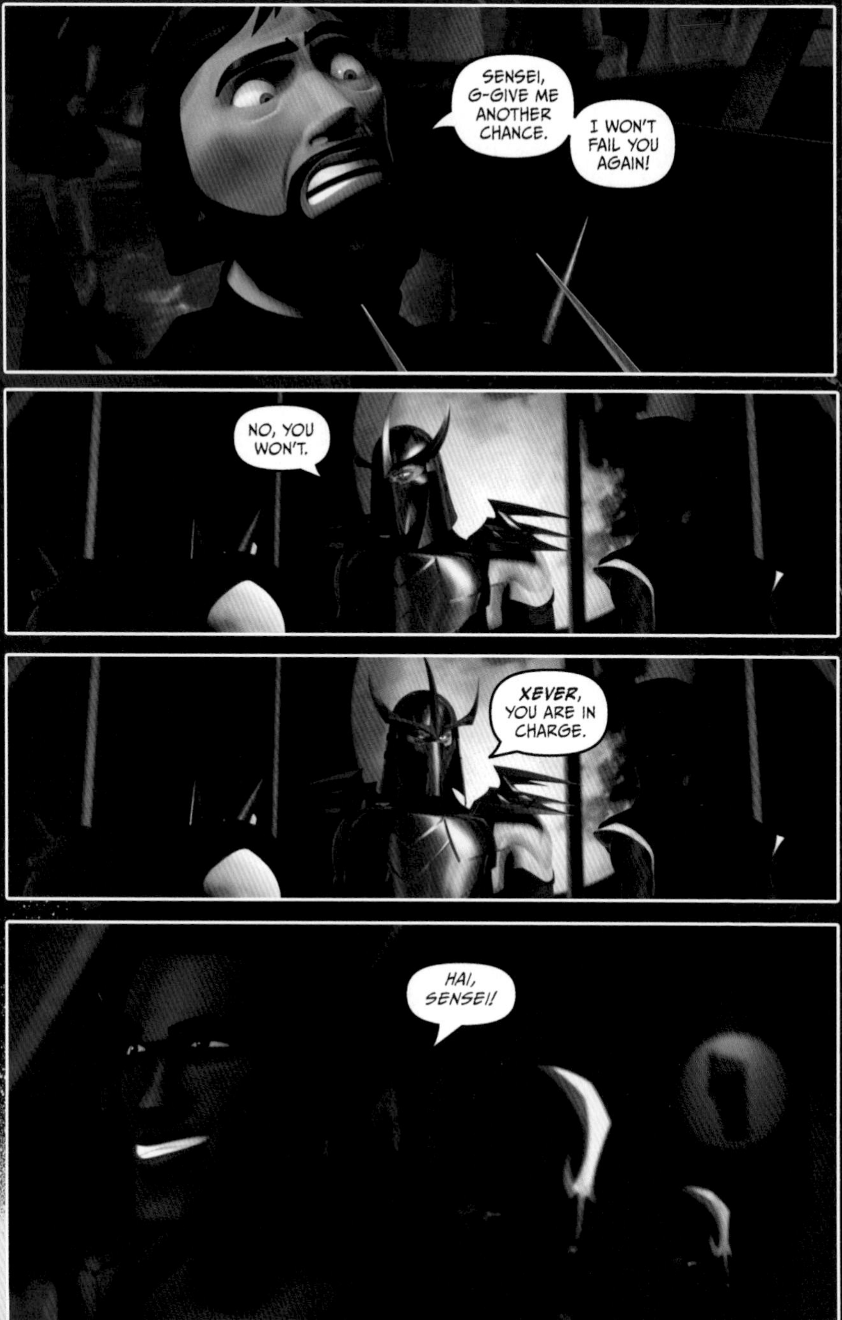
SENSEI, G-GIVE ME ANOTHER CHANCE.
I WON'T FAIL YOU AGAIN!
NO, YOU WON'T.
XEVER, YOU ARE IN CHARGE.
HAI, SENSEI!

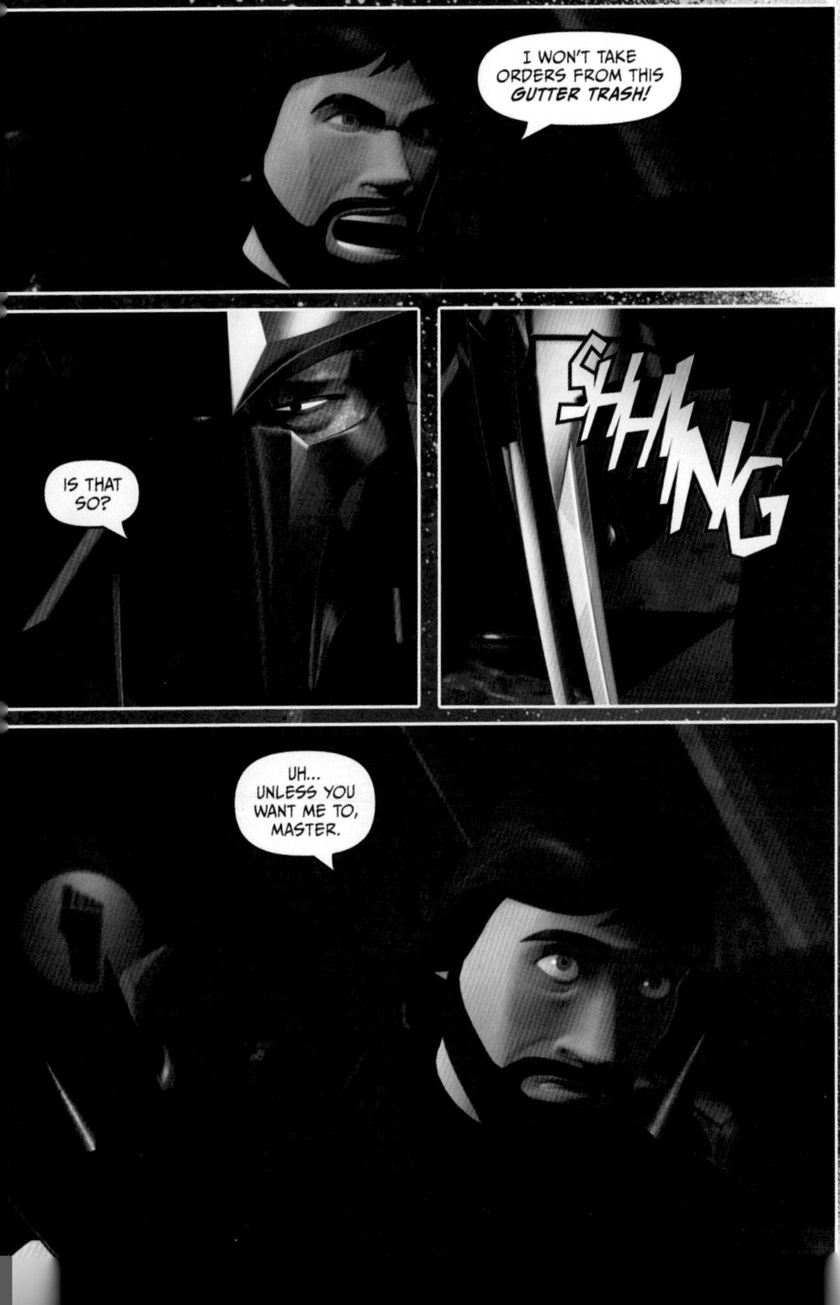
I WON'T TAKE ORDERS FROM THIS *GUTTER TRASH!*
IS THAT SO?
SHHING
UH... UNLESS YOU WANT ME TO, MASTER.

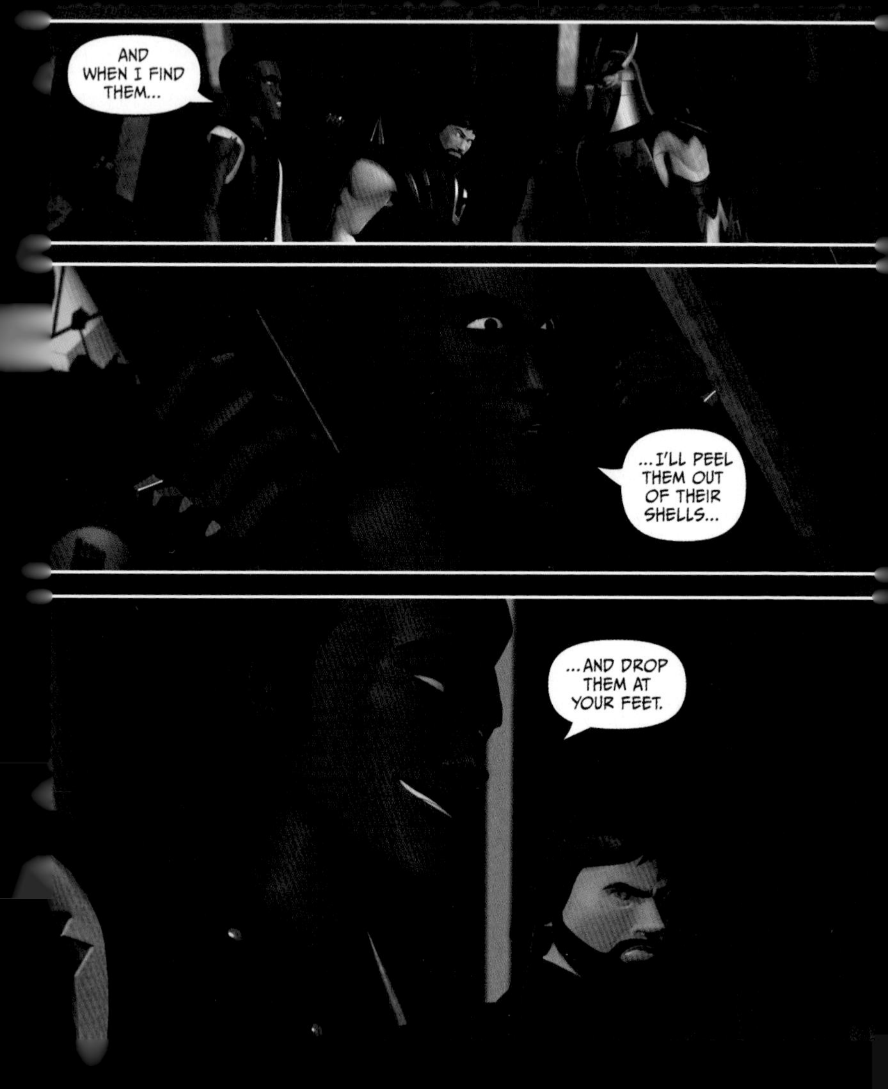
AND WHEN I FIND THEM...
...I'LL PEEL THEM OUT OF THEIR SHELLS...
...AND DROP THEM AT YOUR FEET.

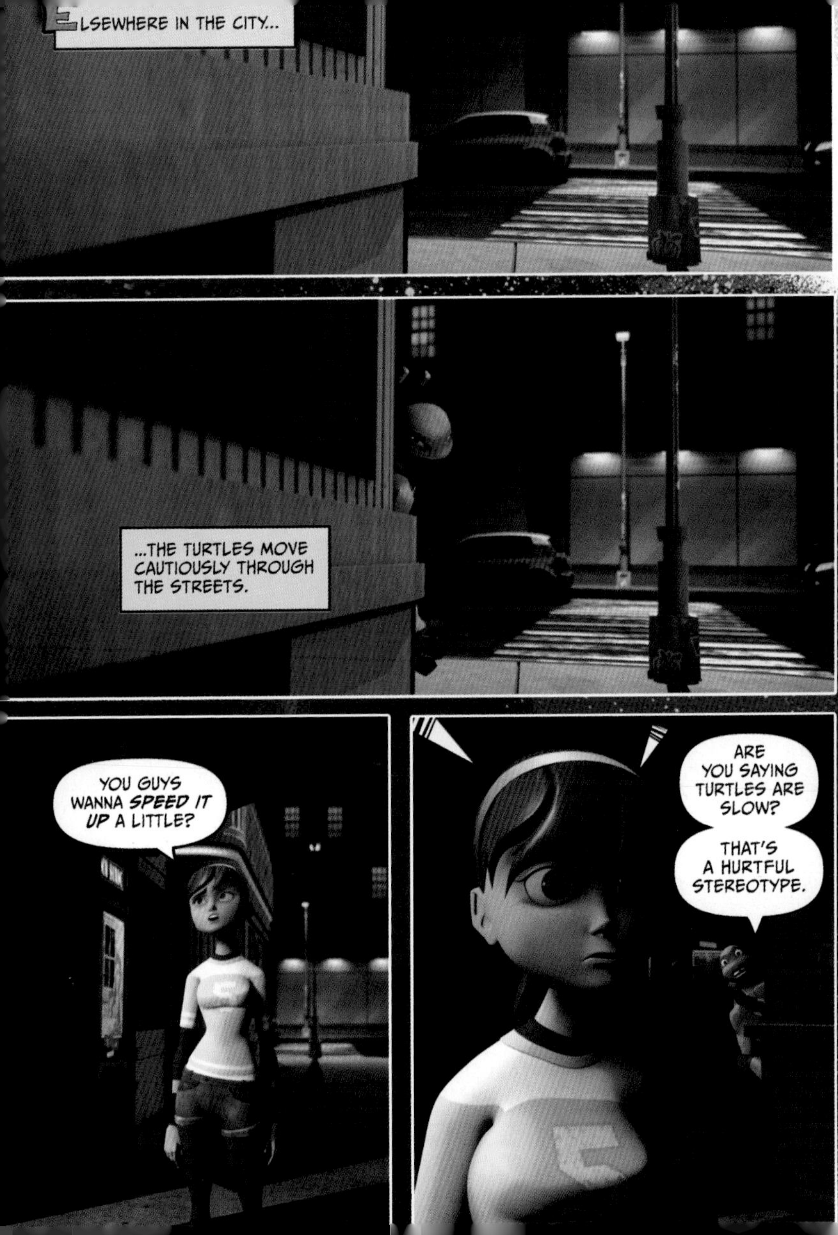
ELSEWHERE IN THE CITY...
...THE TURTLES MOVE CAUTIOUSLY THROUGH THE STREETS.
YOU GUYS WANNA SPEED IT UP A LITTLE?
ARE YOU SAYING TURTLES ARE SLOW?
THAT'S A HURTFUL STEREOTYPE.

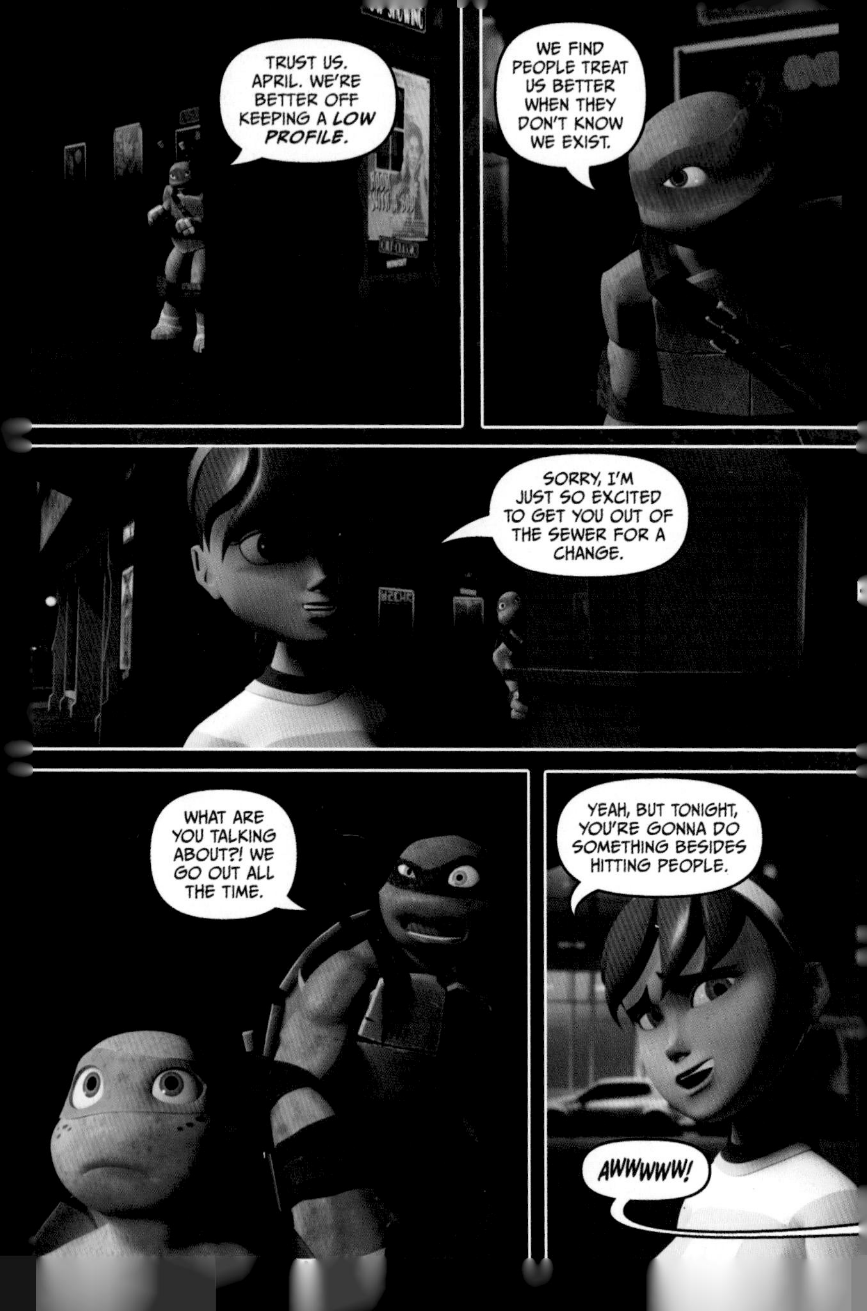
TRUST US. APRIL. WE'RE BETTER OFF KEEPING A *LOW PROFILE.*
WE FIND PEOPLE TREAT US BETTER WHEN THEY DON'T KNOW WE EXIST.
SORRY, I'M JUST SO EXCITED TO GET YOU OUT OF THE SEWER FOR A CHANGE.
WHAT ARE YOU TALKING ABOUT?! WE GO OUT ALL THE TIME.
YEAH, BUT TONIGHT, YOU'RE GONNA DO SOMETHING BESIDES HITTING PEOPLE.
AWWWWW!

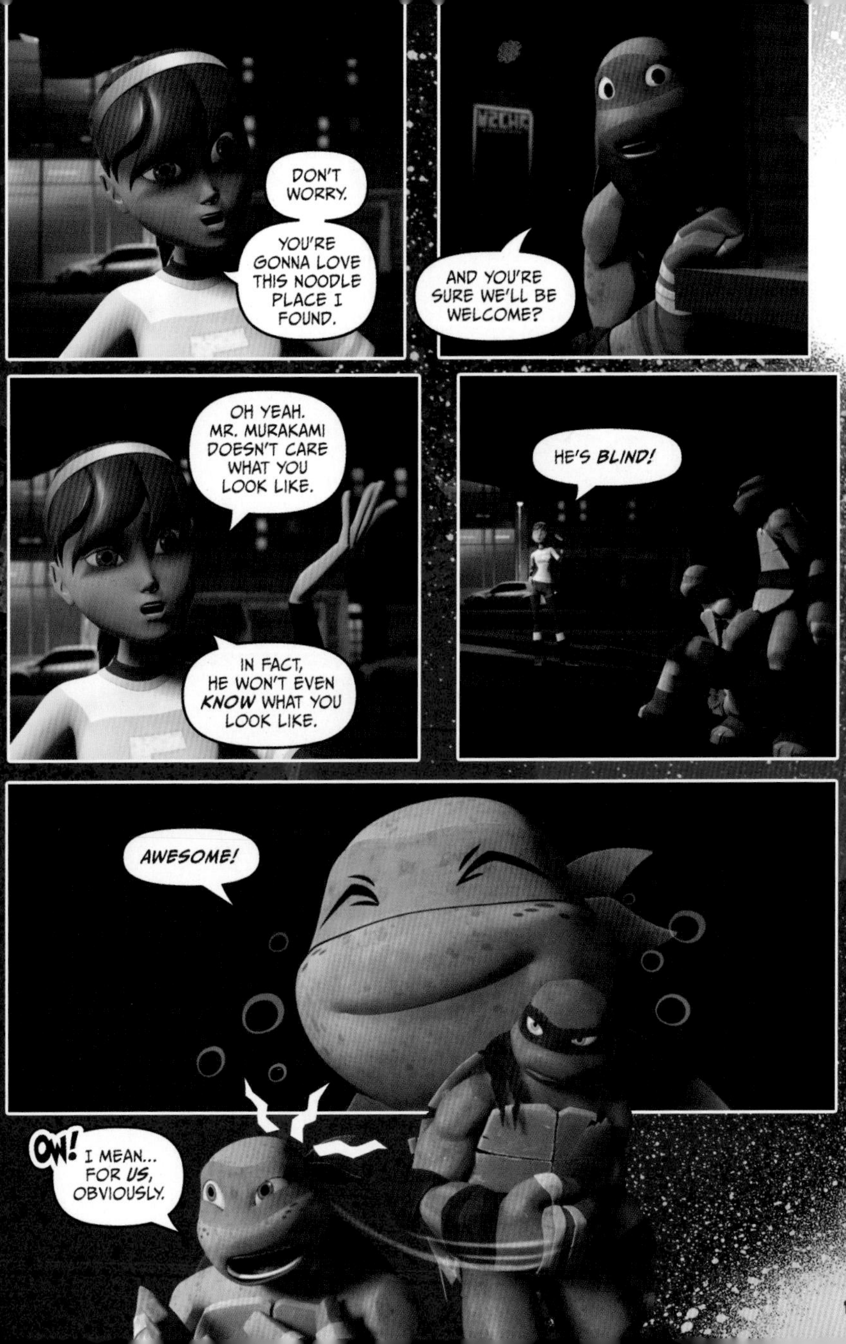

DON'T WORRY.
YOU'RE GONNA LOVE THIS NOODLE PLACE I FOUND.
AND YOU'RE SURE WE'LL BE WELCOME?
OH YEAH. MR. MURAKAMI DOESN'T CARE WHAT YOU LOOK LIKE.
IN FACT, HE WON'T EVEN *KNOW* WHAT YOU LOOK LIKE.
HE'S *BLIND!*
AWESOME!
OW!
I MEAN... FOR *US*, OBVIOUSLY.

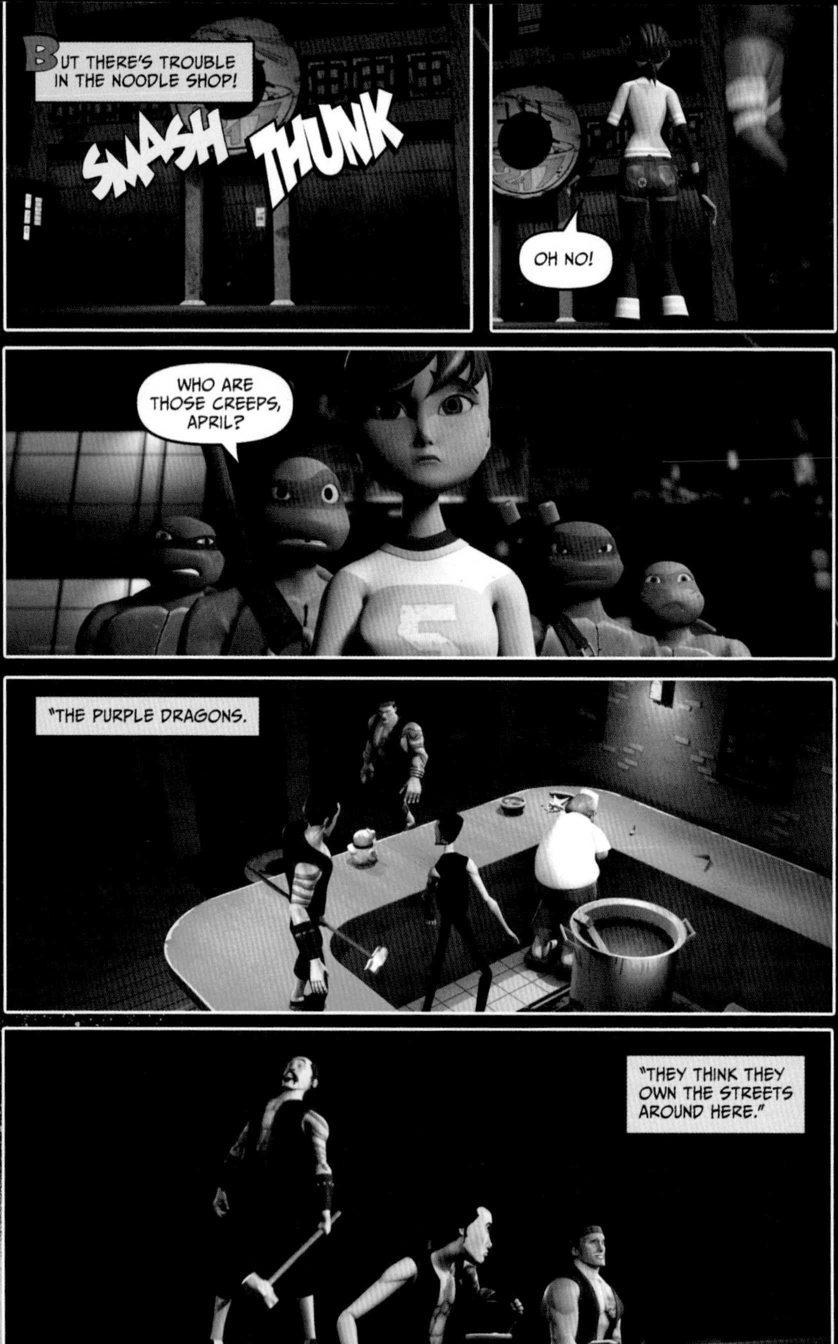
BUT THERE'S TROUBLE IN THE NOODLE SHOP!
SMASH
THUNK
OH NO!
WHO ARE THOSE CREEPS, APRIL?
"THE PURPLE DRAGONS.
"THEY THINK THEY OWN THE STREETS AROUND HERE."

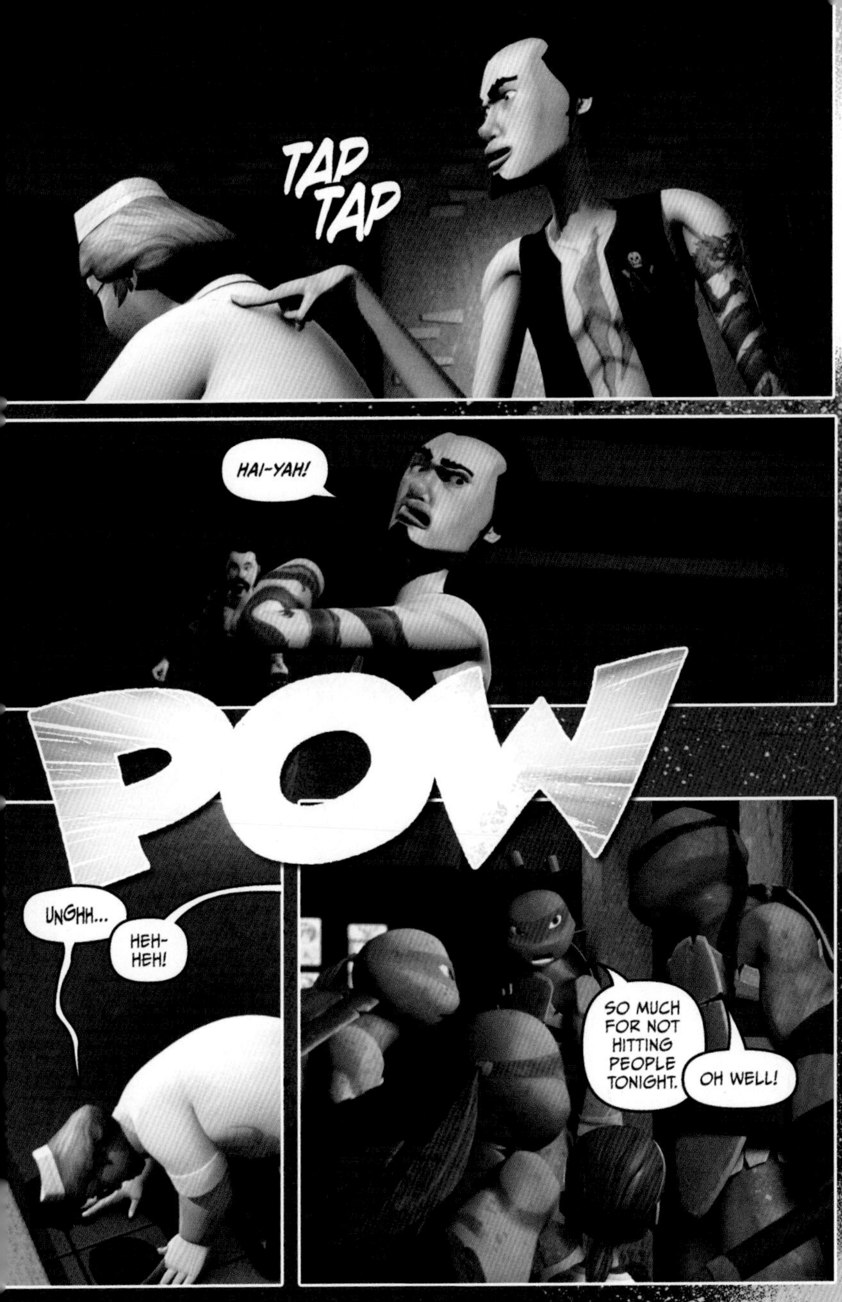
TAP TAP
HAI-YAH!
POW
UNGHH...
HEH-HEH!
SO MUCH FOR NOT HITTING PEOPLE TONIGHT.
OH WELL!

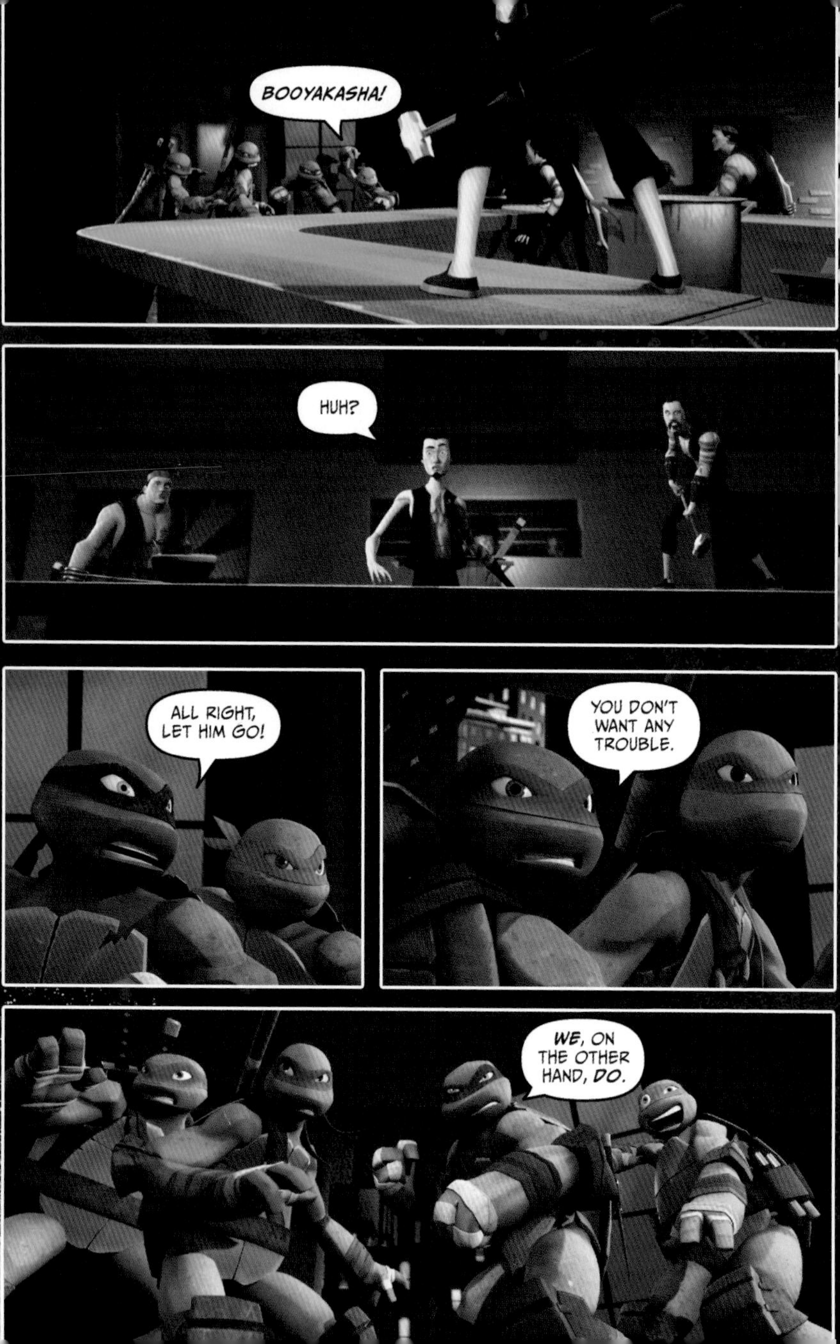
BOOYAKASHA!
HUH?
ALL RIGHT, LET HIM GO!
YOU DON'T WANT ANY TROUBLE.
WE, ON THE OTHER HAND, DO.

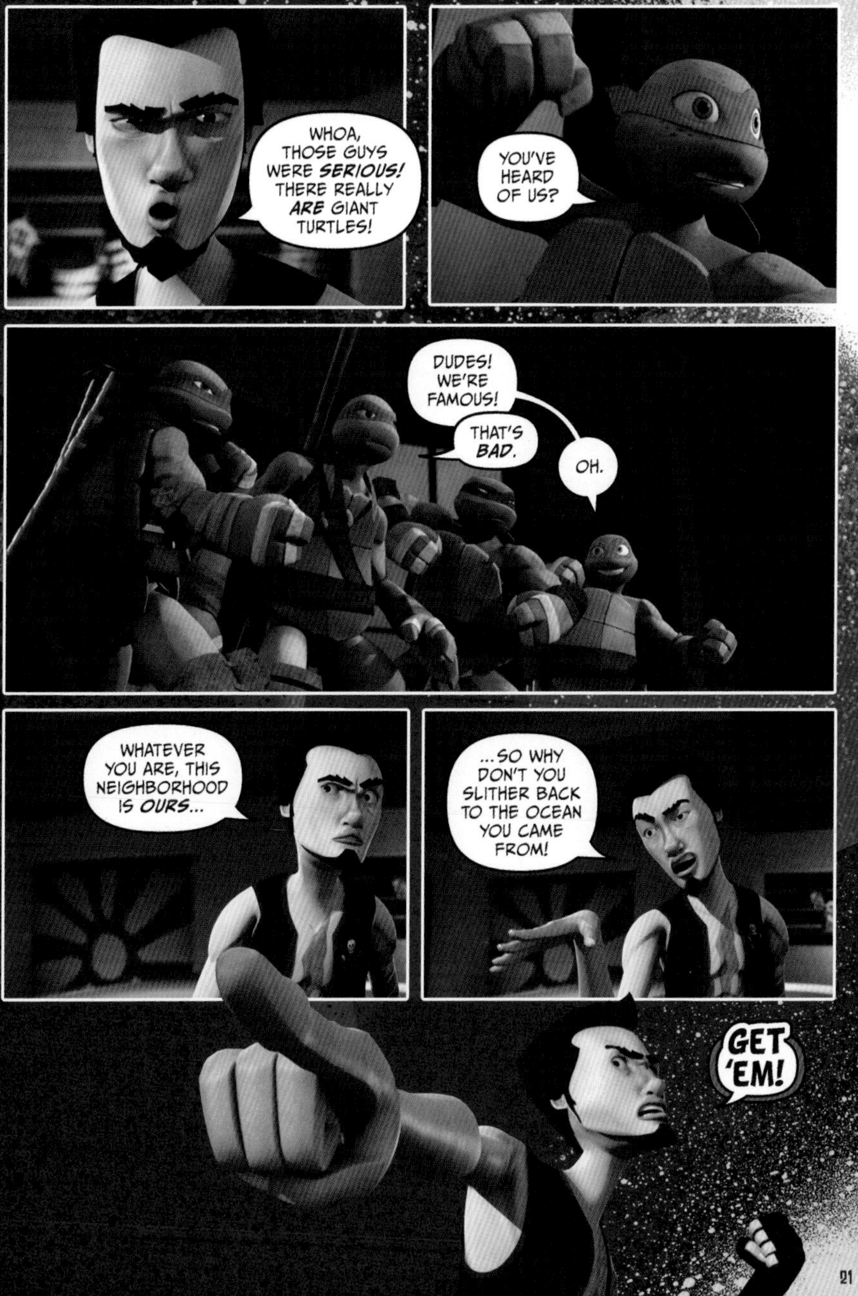
WHOA, THOSE GUYS WERE SERIOUS! THERE REALLY ARE GIANT TURTLES!
YOU'VE HEARD OF US?
DUDES! WE'RE FAMOUS!
THAT'S BAD.
OH.
WHATEVER YOU ARE, THIS NEIGHBORHOOD IS OURS...
...SO WHY DON'T YOU SLITHER BACK TO THE OCEAN YOU CAME FROM!
GET 'EM!

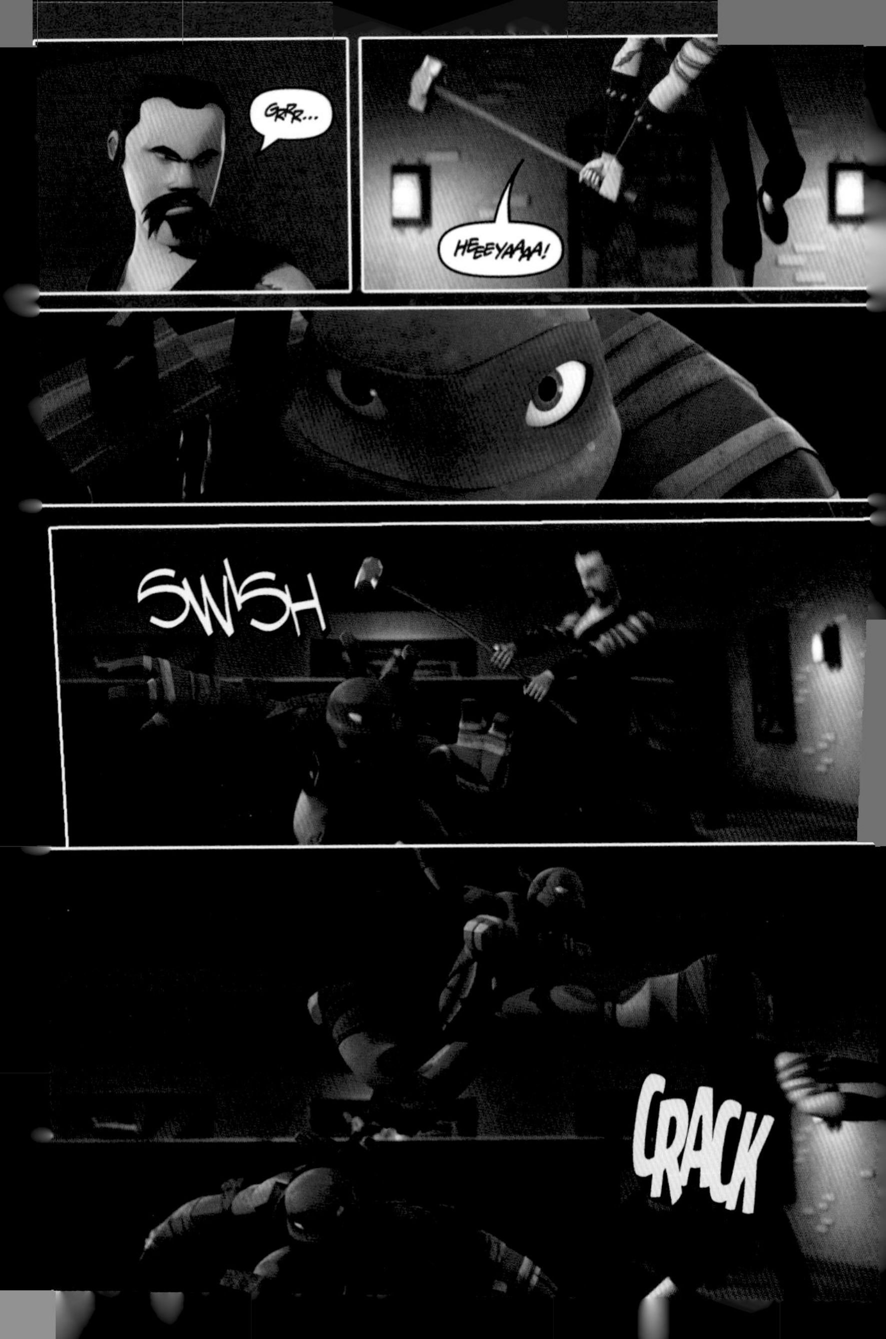
GRRR...
HEEEYAAAA!
SWISH
CRACK

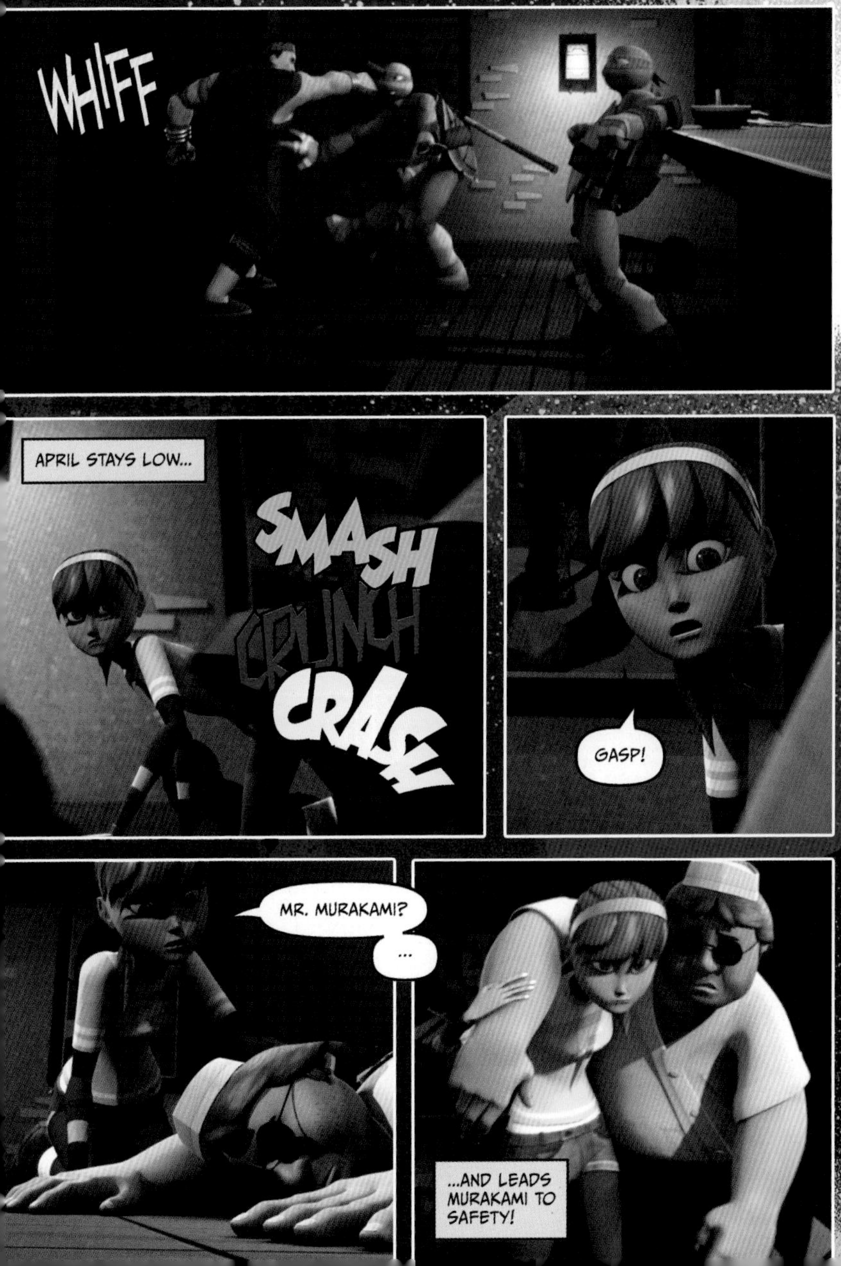
WHIFF
APRIL STAYS LOW...
SMASH
CRUNCH
CRASH
GASP!
MR. MURAKAMI?
...
...AND LEADS MURAKAMI TO SAFETY!

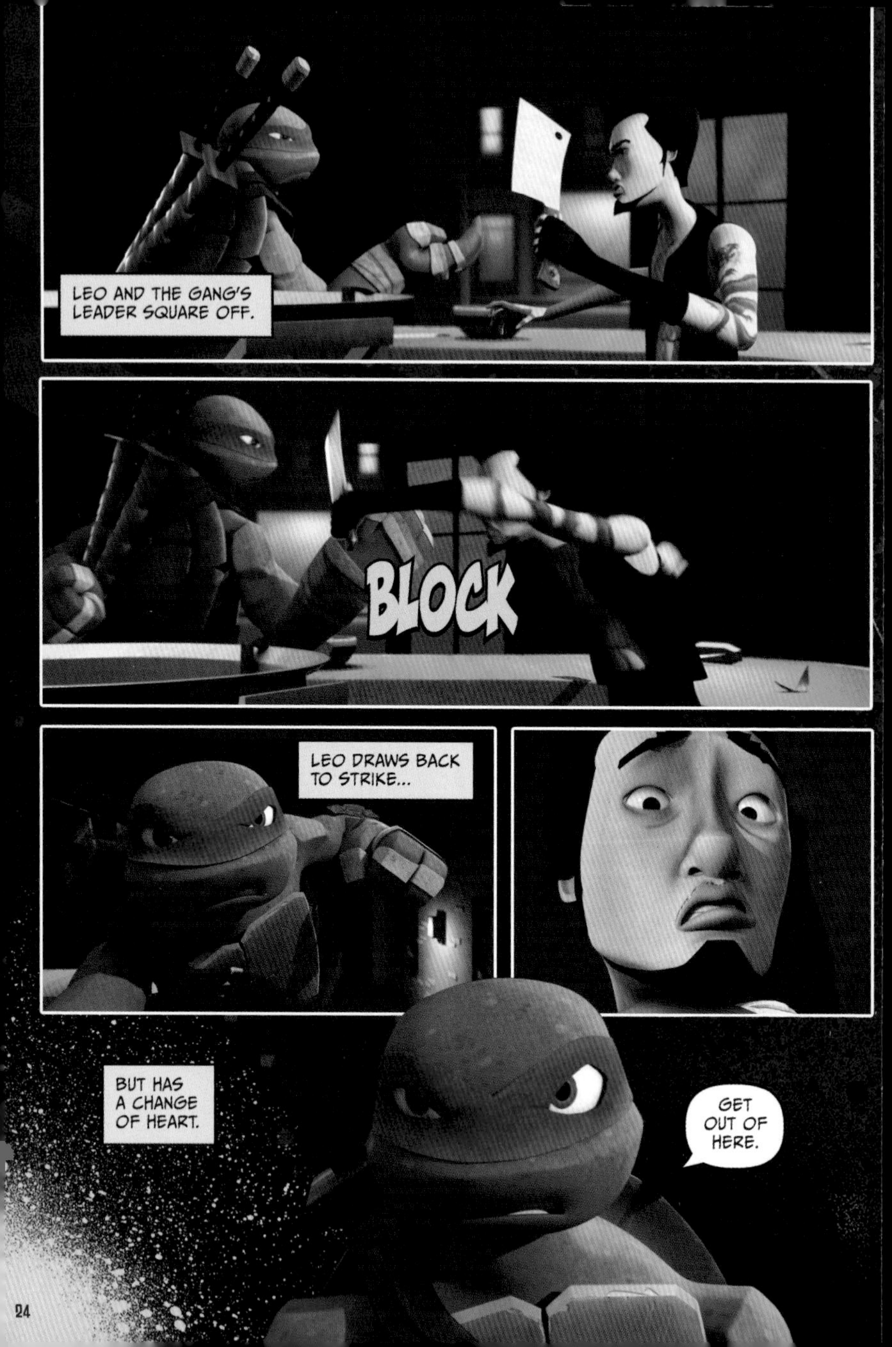
LEO AND THE GANG'S LEADER SQUARE OFF.
BLOCK
LEO DRAWS BACK TO STRIKE...
BUT HAS A CHANGE OF HEART.
GET OUT OF HERE.

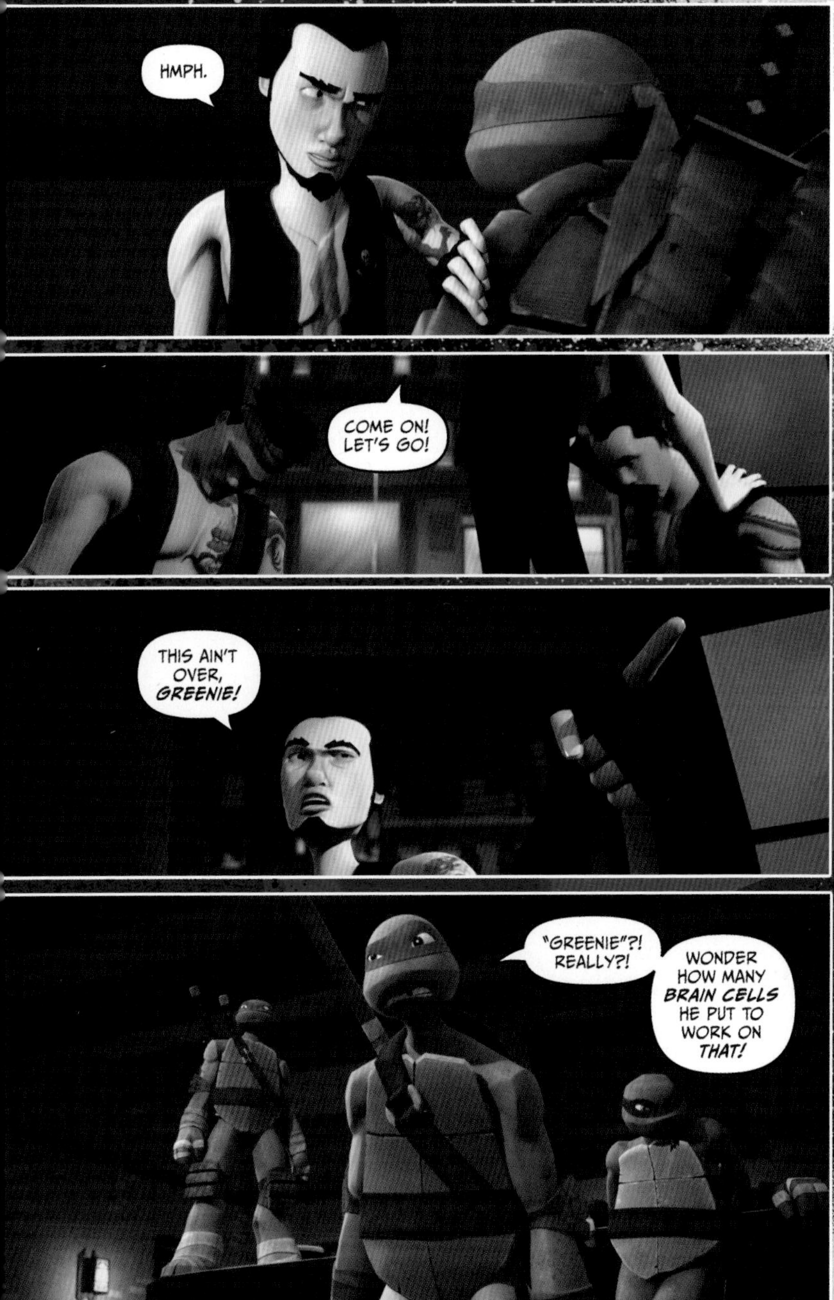
HMPH.
COME ON! LET'S GO!
THIS AIN'T OVER, *GREENIE!*
"GREENIE"?! REALLY?!
WONDER HOW MANY *BRAIN CELLS* HE PUT TO WORK ON *THAT!*

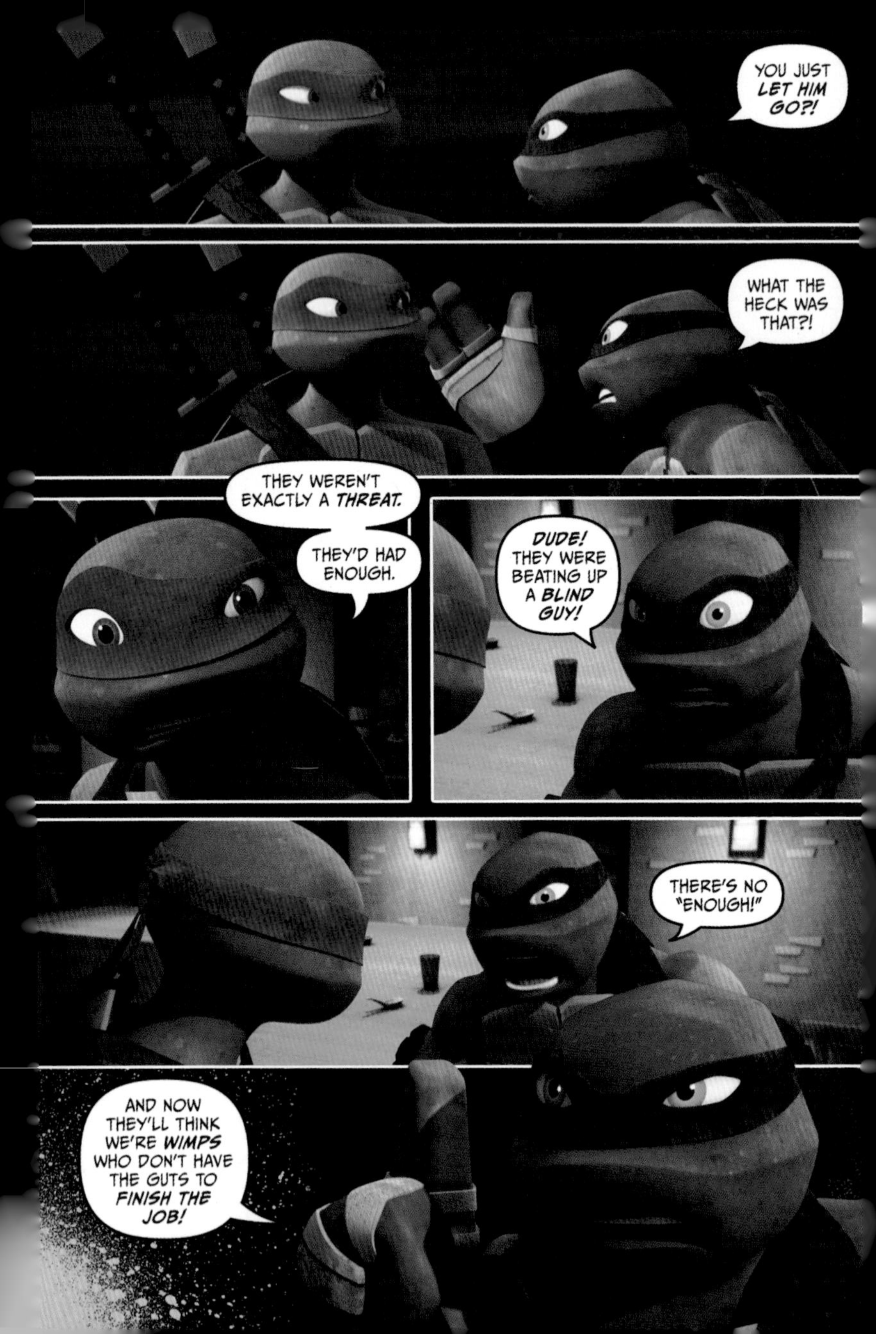
YOU JUST LET HIM GO?!
WHAT THE HECK WAS THAT?!
THEY WEREN'T EXACTLY A THREAT.
THEY'D HAD ENOUGH.
DUDE! THEY WERE BEATING UP A BLIND GUY!
THERE'S NO "ENOUGH!"
AND NOW THEY'LL THINK WE'RE WIMPS WHO DON'T HAVE THE GUTS TO FINISH THE JOB!

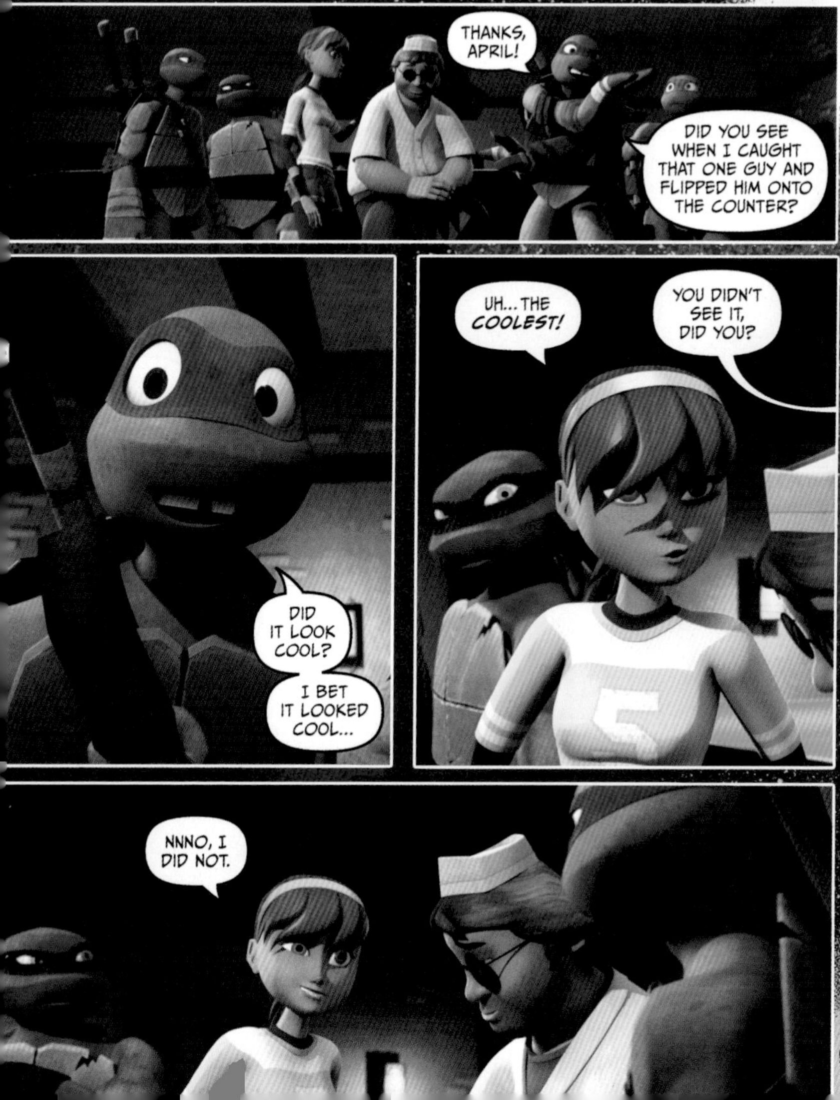
THANKS, APRIL!
DID YOU SEE WHEN I CAUGHT THAT ONE GUY AND FLIPPED HIM ONTO THE COUNTER?
DID IT LOOK COOL?
I BET IT LOOKED COOL...
UH... THE *COOLEST!*
YOU DIDN'T SEE IT, DID YOU?
NNNO, I DID NOT.

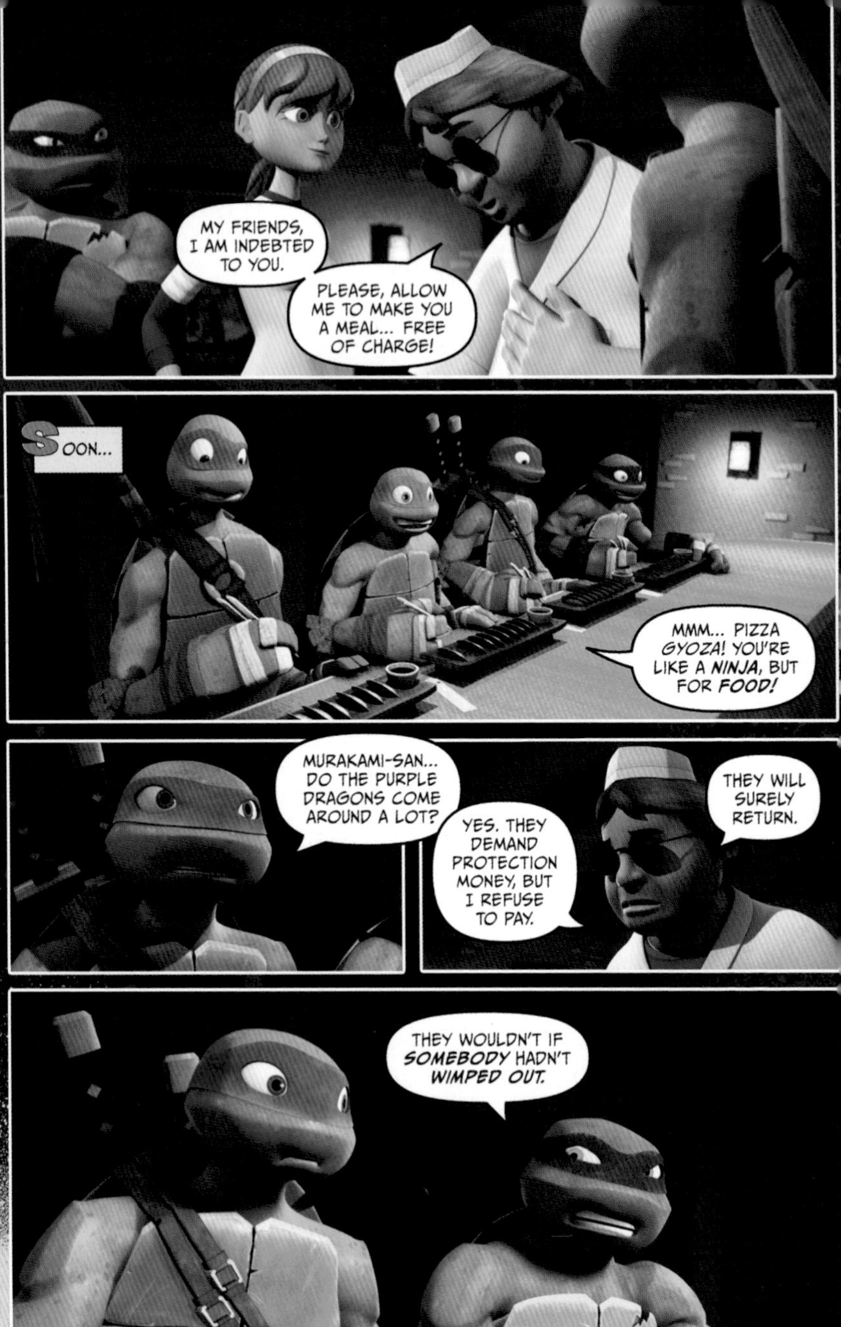
MY FRIENDS, I AM INDEBTED TO YOU.
PLEASE, ALLOW ME TO MAKE YOU A MEAL... FREE OF CHARGE!
SOON...
MMM... PIZZA GYOZA! YOU'RE LIKE A NINJA, BUT FOR FOOD!
MURAKAMI-SAN... DO THE PURPLE DRAGONS COME AROUND A LOT?
YES. THEY DEMAND PROTECTION MONEY, BUT I REFUSE TO PAY.
THEY WILL SURELY RETURN.
THEY WOULDN'T IF SOMEBODY HADN'T WIMPED OUT.

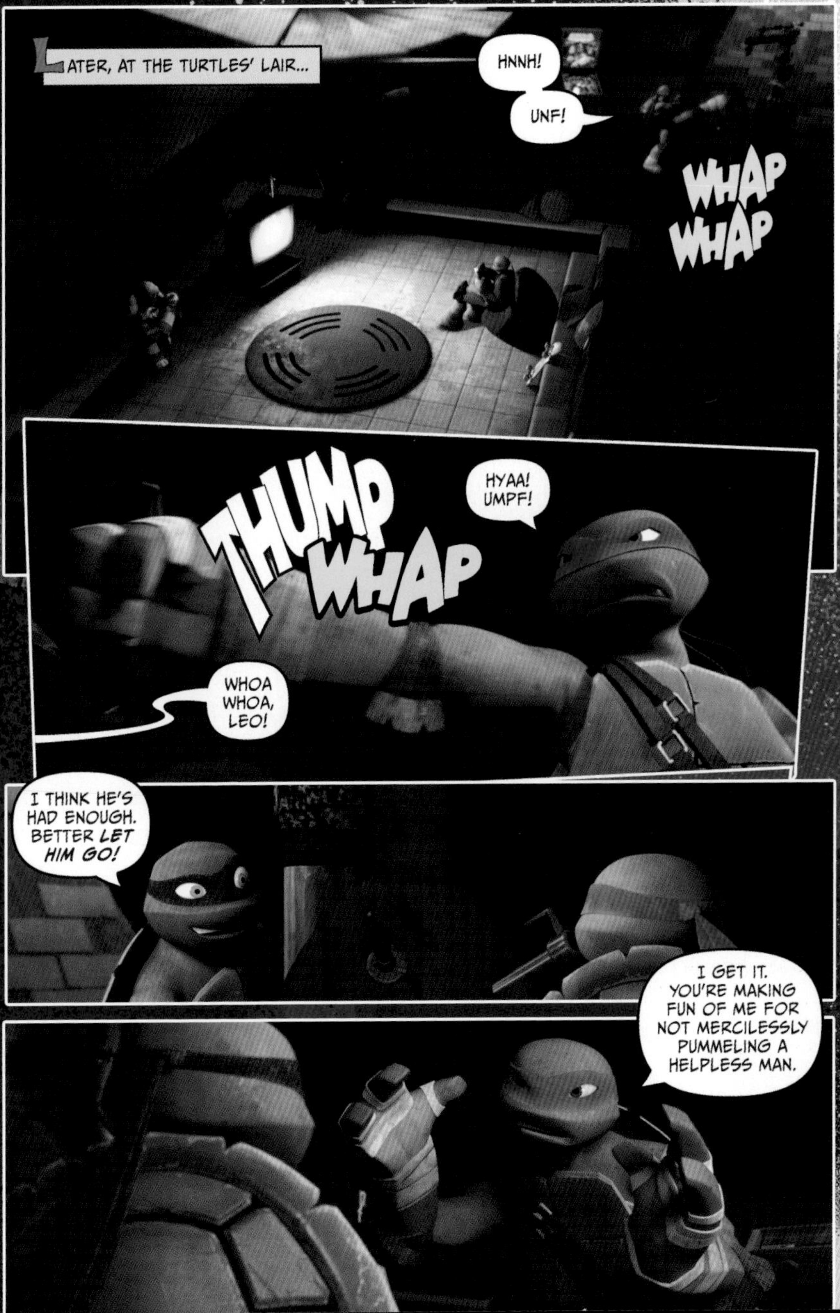
LATER, AT THE TURTLES' LAIR...
HNNH!
UNF!
WHAP WHAP
THUMP WHAP
HYAA! UMPF!
WHOA WHOA, LEO!
I THINK HE'S HAD ENOUGH. BETTER LET HIM GO!
I GET IT. YOU'RE MAKING FUN OF ME FOR NOT MERCILESSLY PUMMELING A HELPLESS MAN.

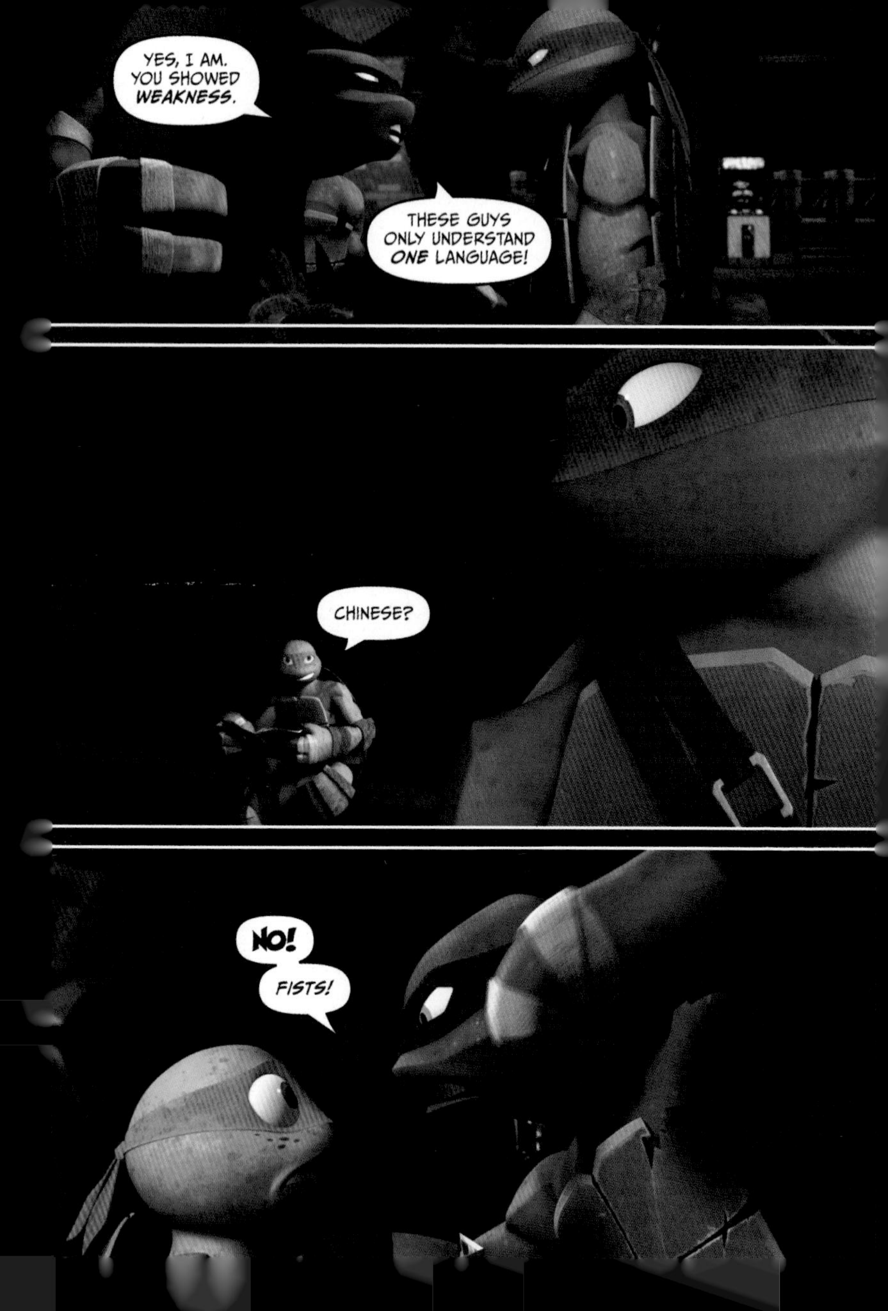
YES, I AM. YOU SHOWED WEAKNESS.
THESE GUYS ONLY UNDERSTAND ONE LANGUAGE!
CHINESE?
NO!
FISTS!

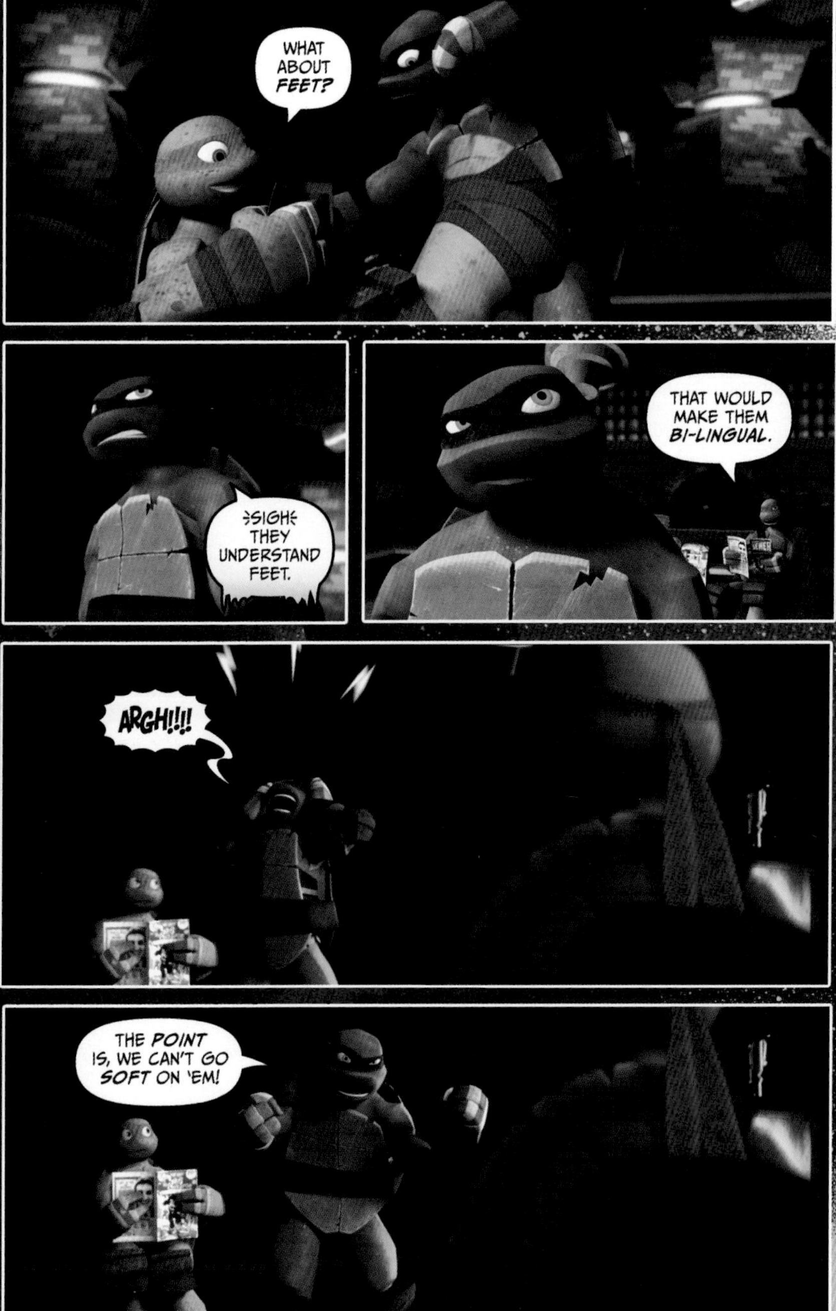

WHAT ABOUT FEET?
≶SIGH≷ THEY UNDERSTAND FEET.
THAT WOULD MAKE THEM BI-LINGUAL.
ARGH!!!!
THE POINT IS, WE CAN'T GO SOFT ON 'EM!

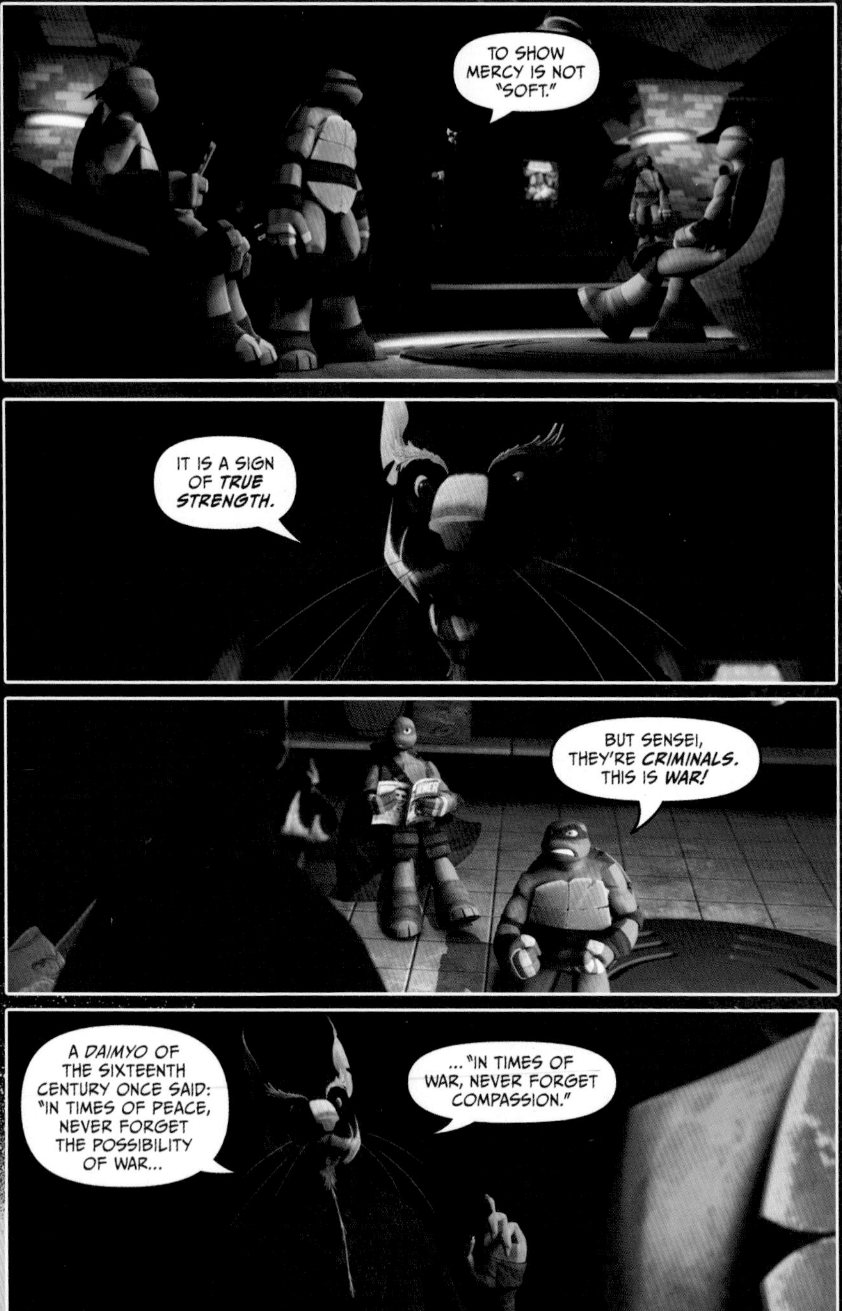

TO SHOW MERCY IS NOT "SOFT."
IT IS A SIGN OF TRUE STRENGTH.
BUT SENSEI, THEY'RE CRIMINALS. THIS IS WAR!
A DAIMYO OF THE SIXTEENTH CENTURY ONCE SAID: "IN TIMES OF PEACE, NEVER FORGET THE POSSIBILITY OF WAR...
..."IN TIMES OF WAR, NEVER FORGET COMPASSION."

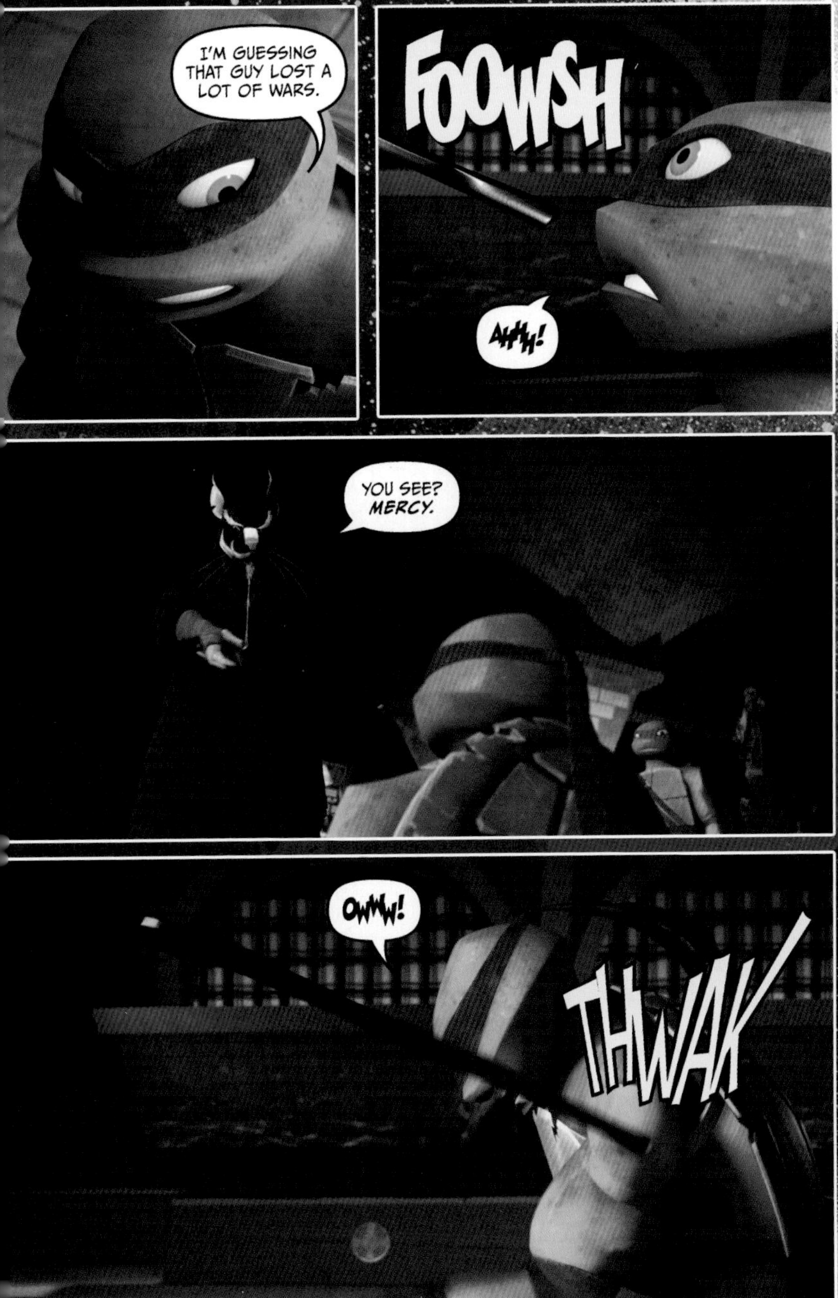
I'M GUESSING THAT GUY LOST A LOT OF WARS.
FOOWSH
AHHH!
YOU SEE? MERCY.
OWWW!
THWAK

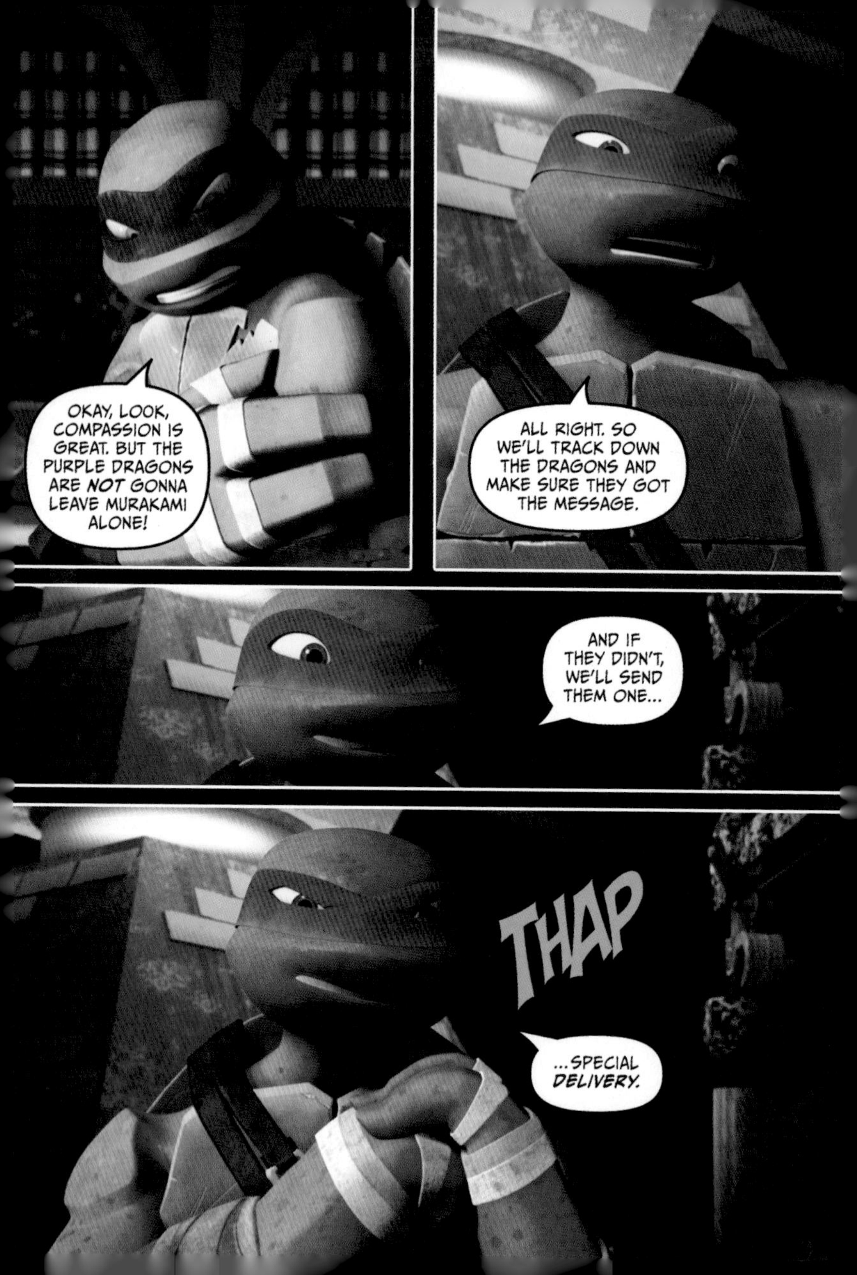
OKAY, LOOK, COMPASSION IS GREAT. BUT THE PURPLE DRAGONS ARE *NOT* GONNA LEAVE MURAKAMI ALONE!
ALL RIGHT. SO WE'LL TRACK DOWN THE DRAGONS AND MAKE SURE THEY GOT THE MESSAGE.
AND IF THEY DIDN'T, WE'LL SEND THEM ONE...
THAP
...SPECIAL *DELIVERY.*

WAS THAT MEANT TO SOUND TOUGH, OR *STUPID*?

HOW ARE WE GOING TO TRACK SOMEONE DOWN WHEN WE CAN'T TALK TO ANYBODY?

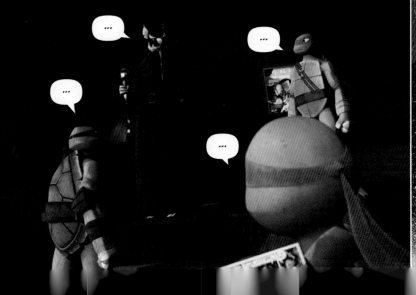

...

...

...

...

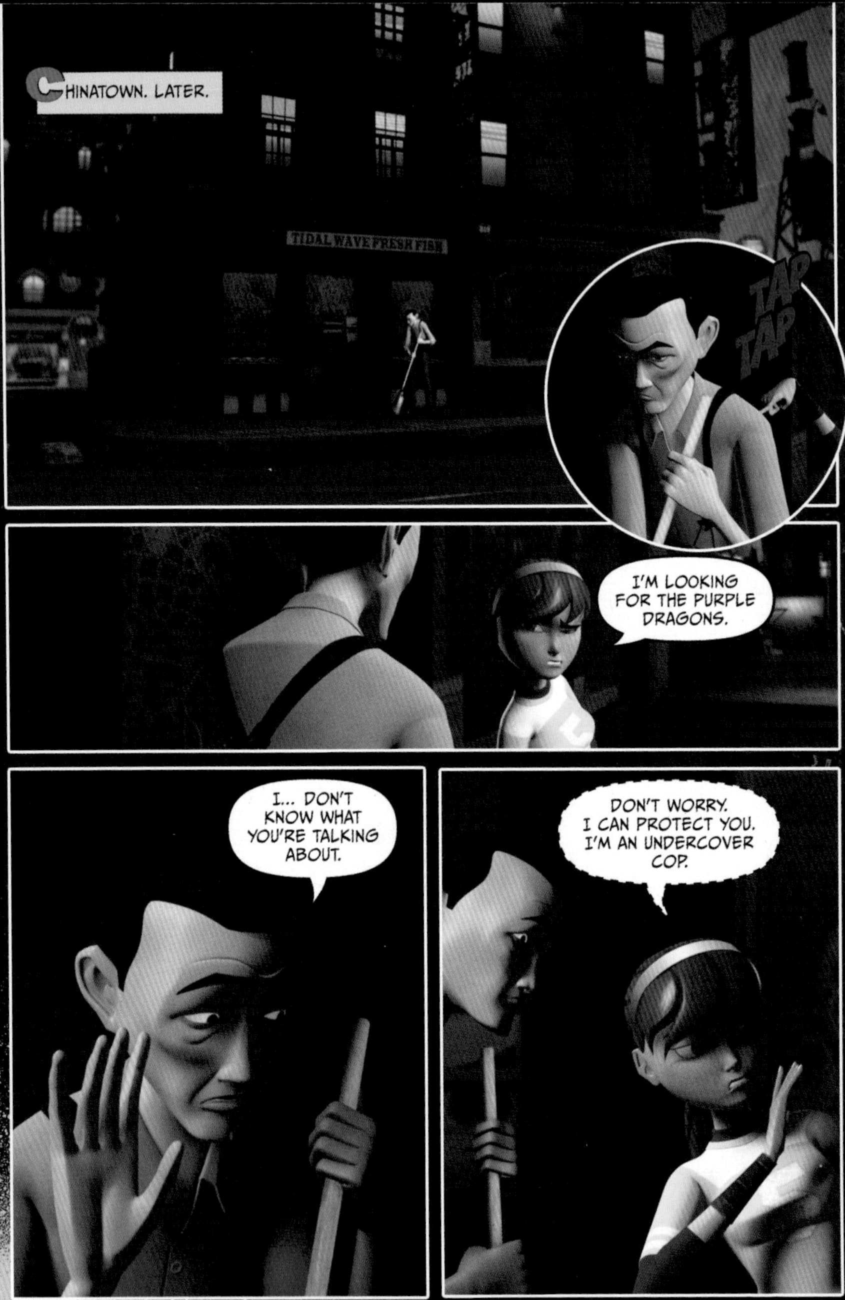
CHINATOWN. LATER.
TIDAL WAVE FRESH FISH
TAP TAP
I'M LOOKING FOR THE PURPLE DRAGONS.
I... DON'T KNOW WHAT YOU'RE TALKING ABOUT.
DON'T WORRY. I CAN PROTECT YOU. I'M AN UNDERCOVER COP.

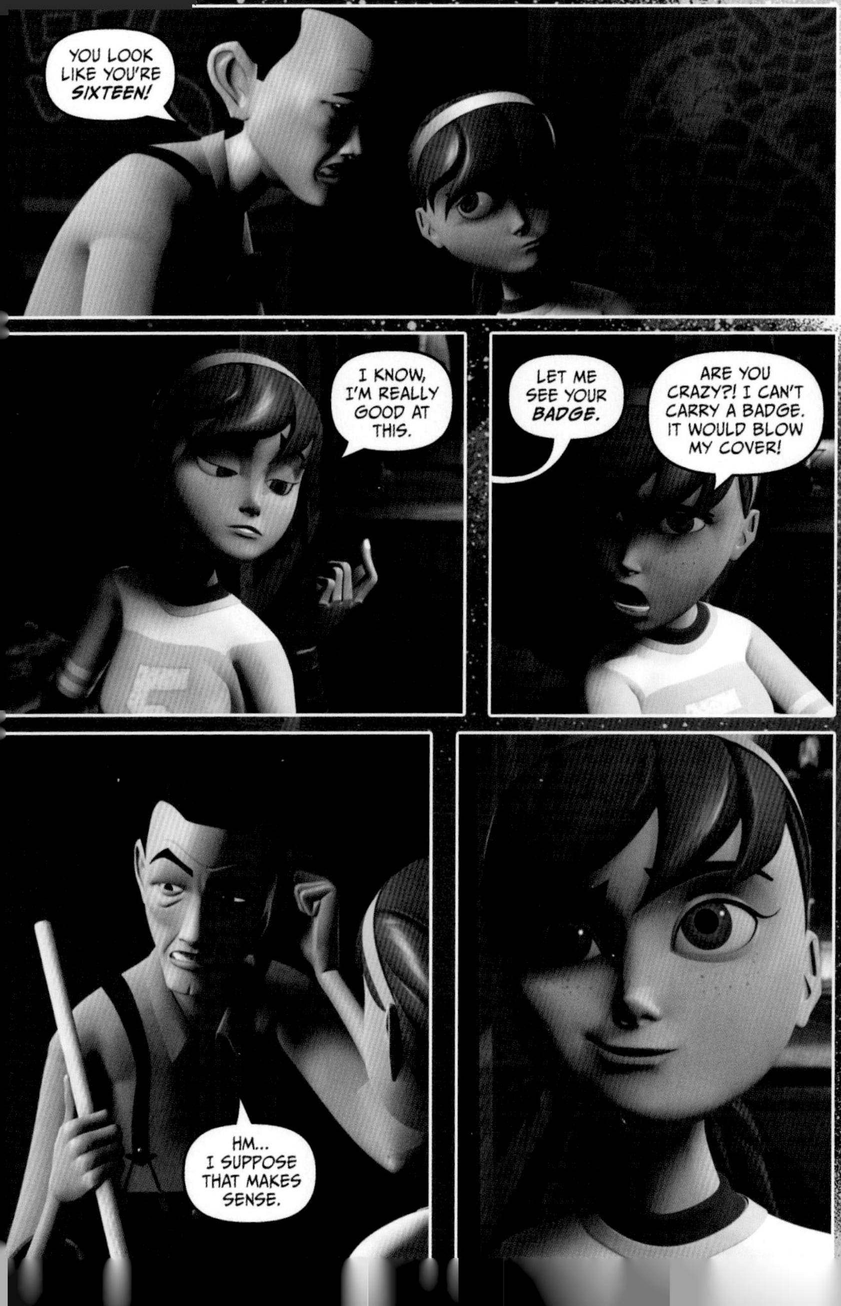
YOU LOOK LIKE YOU'RE SIXTEEN!
I KNOW, I'M REALLY GOOD AT THIS.
LET ME SEE YOUR BADGE.
ARE YOU CRAZY?! I CAN'T CARRY A BADGE. IT WOULD BLOW MY COVER!
HM... I SUPPOSE THAT MAKES SENSE.

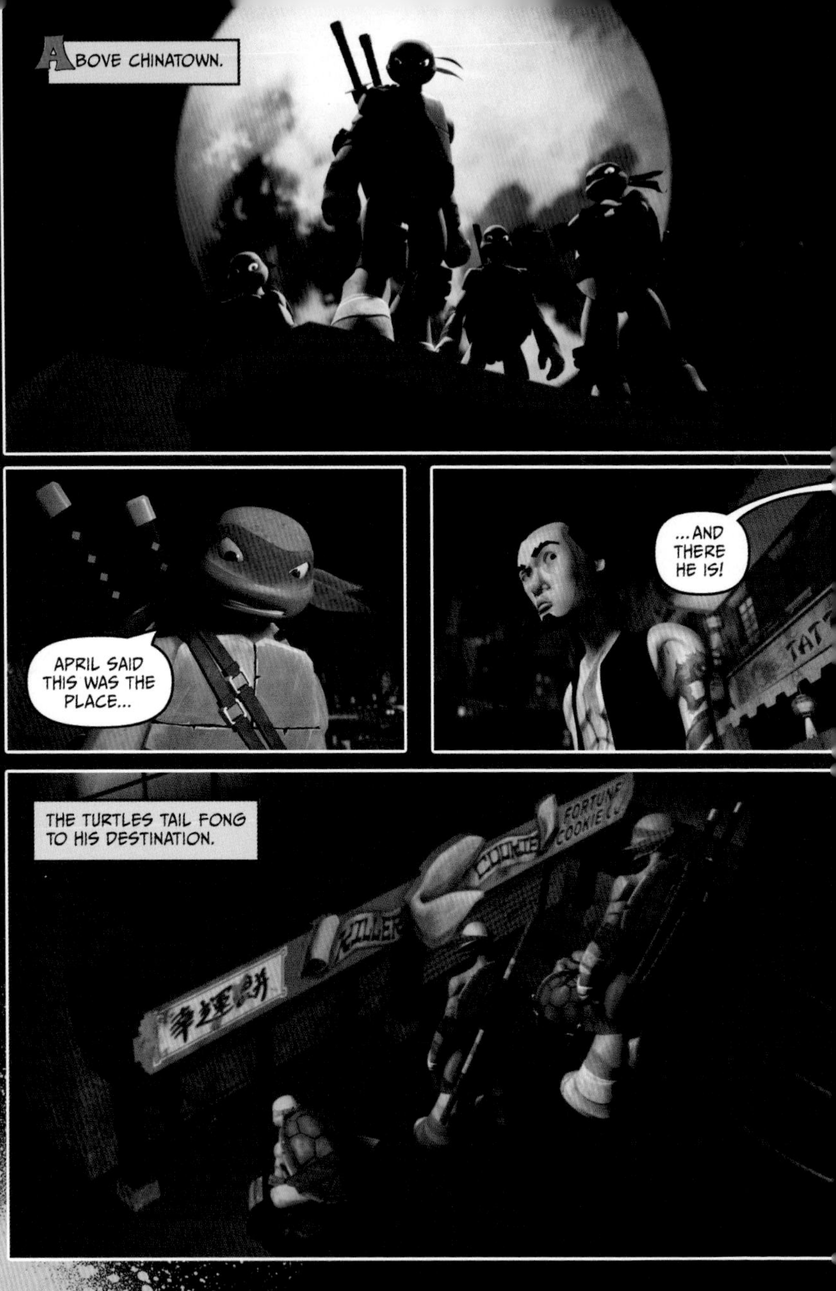
ABOVE CHINATOWN.
APRIL SAID THIS WAS THE PLACE...
...AND THERE HE IS!
THE TURTLES TAIL FONG TO HIS DESTINATION.
FORTUNE COOKIE
COOKIE

SOON...

WE SAW THAT GANG OF TURTLES YOU WERE LOOKING FOR.

AND WE'LL TELL YOU WHERE... FOR A *PRICE*.

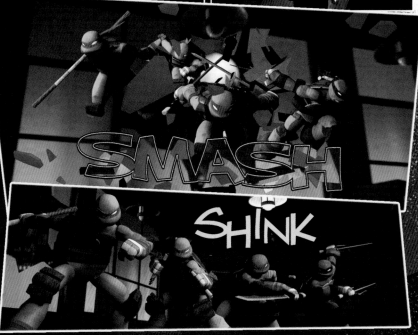

SMASH

SHINK

FREEZE, DIRTBAGS!

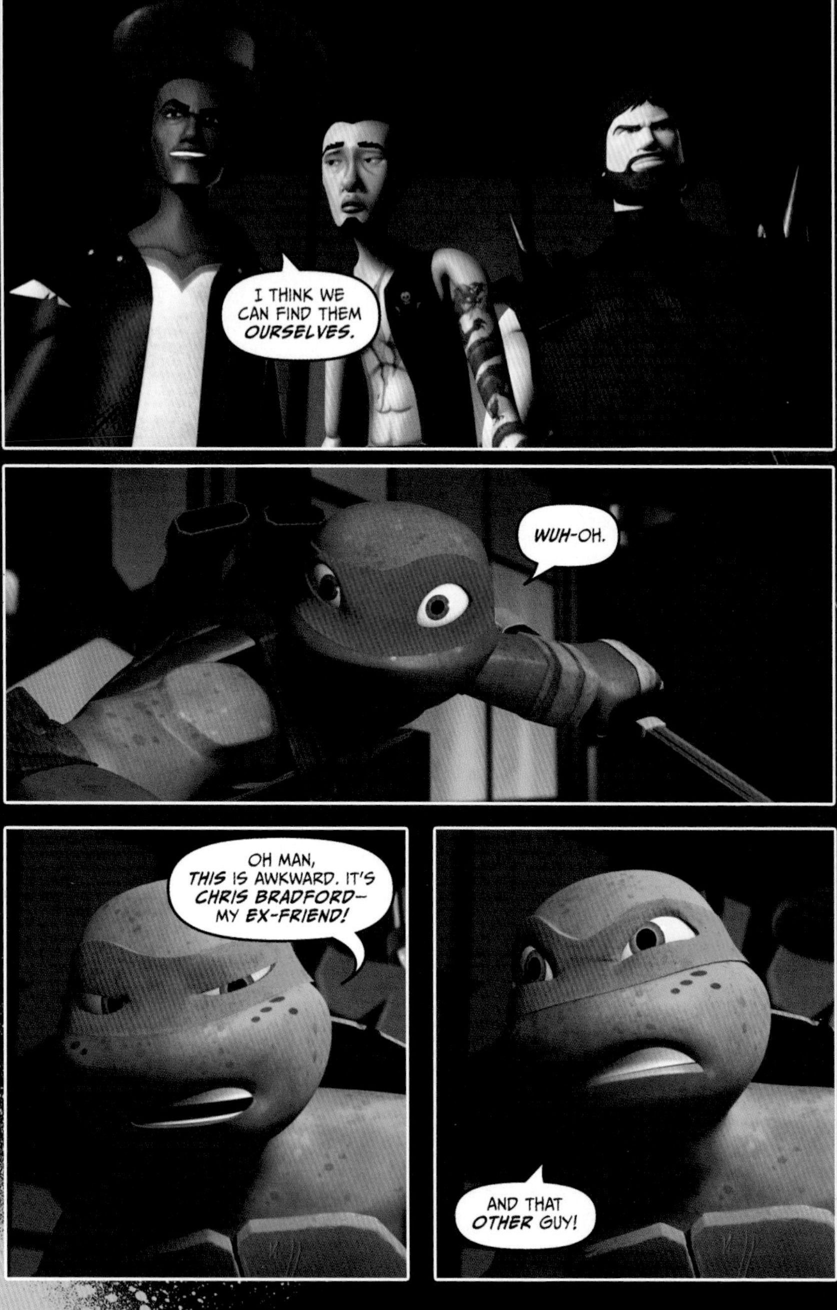

I THINK WE CAN FIND THEM *OURSELVES.*
WUH-OH.
OH MAN, *THIS* IS AWKWARD. IT'S *CHRIS BRADFORD*— MY *EX-FRIEND!*
AND THAT *OTHER* GUY!

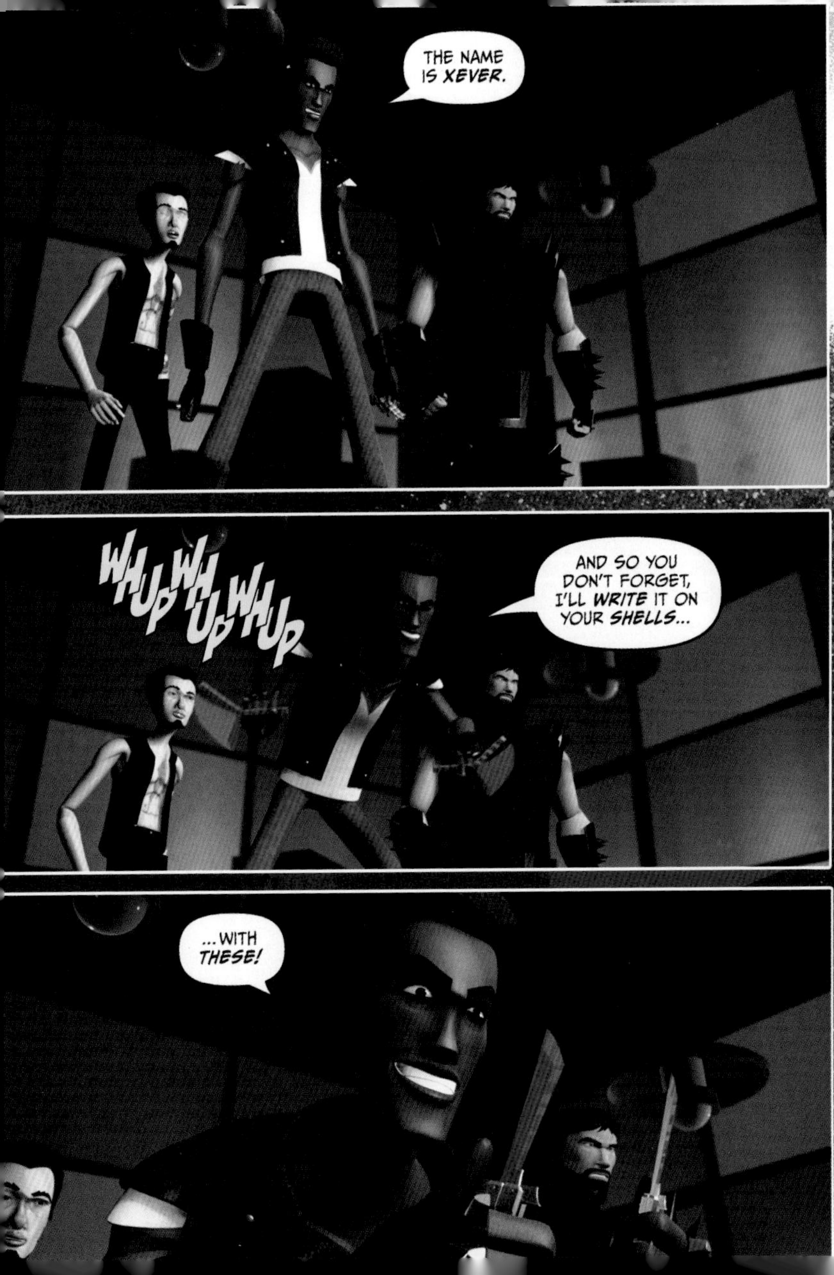
THE NAME IS XEVER.
WHUP WHUP WHUP
AND SO YOU DON'T FORGET, I'LL WRITE IT ON YOUR SHELLS...
...WITH THESE!

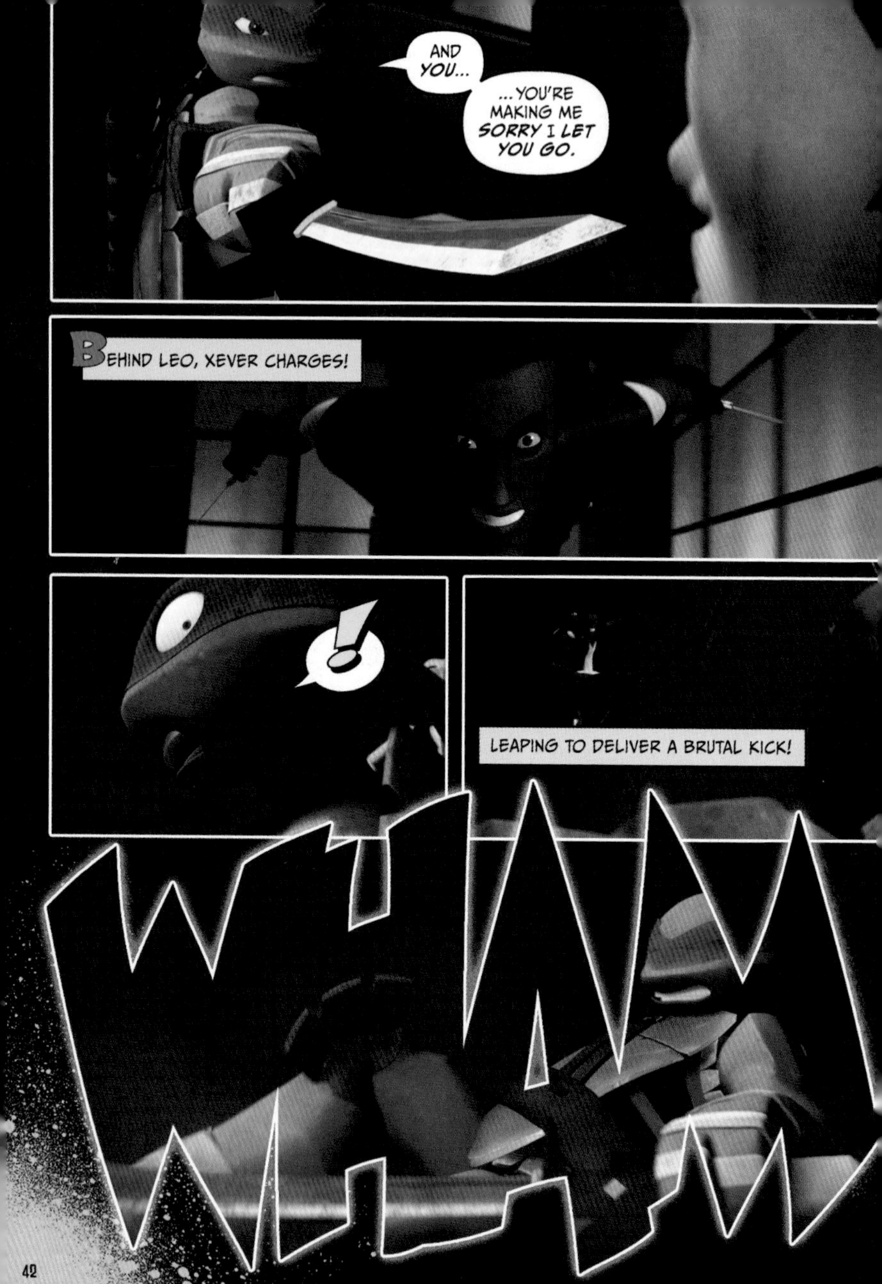
AND YOU...
...YOU'RE MAKING ME SORRY I LET YOU GO.
BEHIND LEO, XEVER CHARGES!
!
LEAPING TO DELIVER A BRUTAL KICK!
WHAM

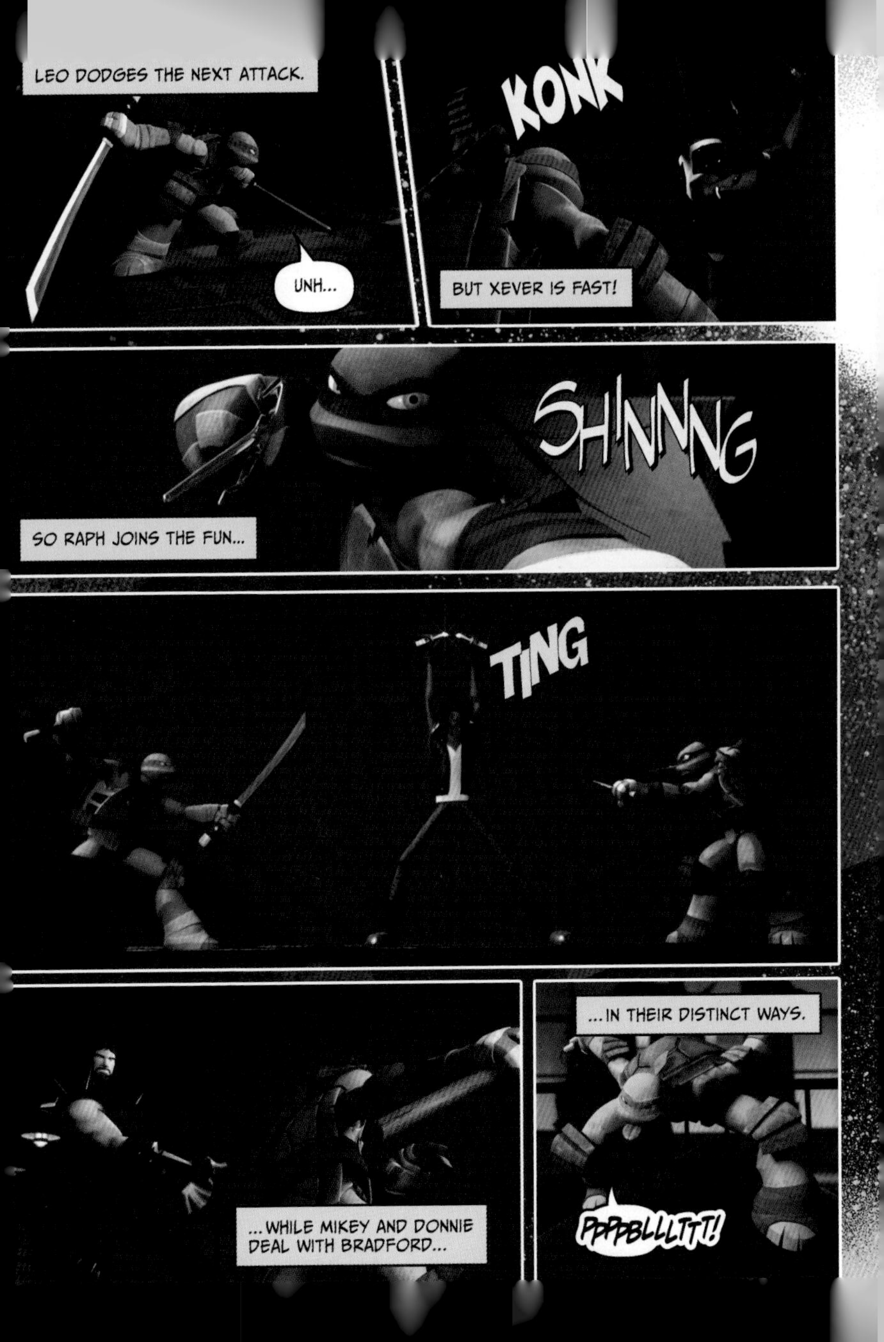
LEO DODGES THE NEXT ATTACK.
UNH...
KONK
BUT XEVER IS FAST!
SHINNNG
SO RAPH JOINS THE FUN...
TING
...WHILE MIKEY AND DONNIE DEAL WITH BRADFORD...
...IN THEIR DISTINCT WAYS.
PPPPBLLLTTT!

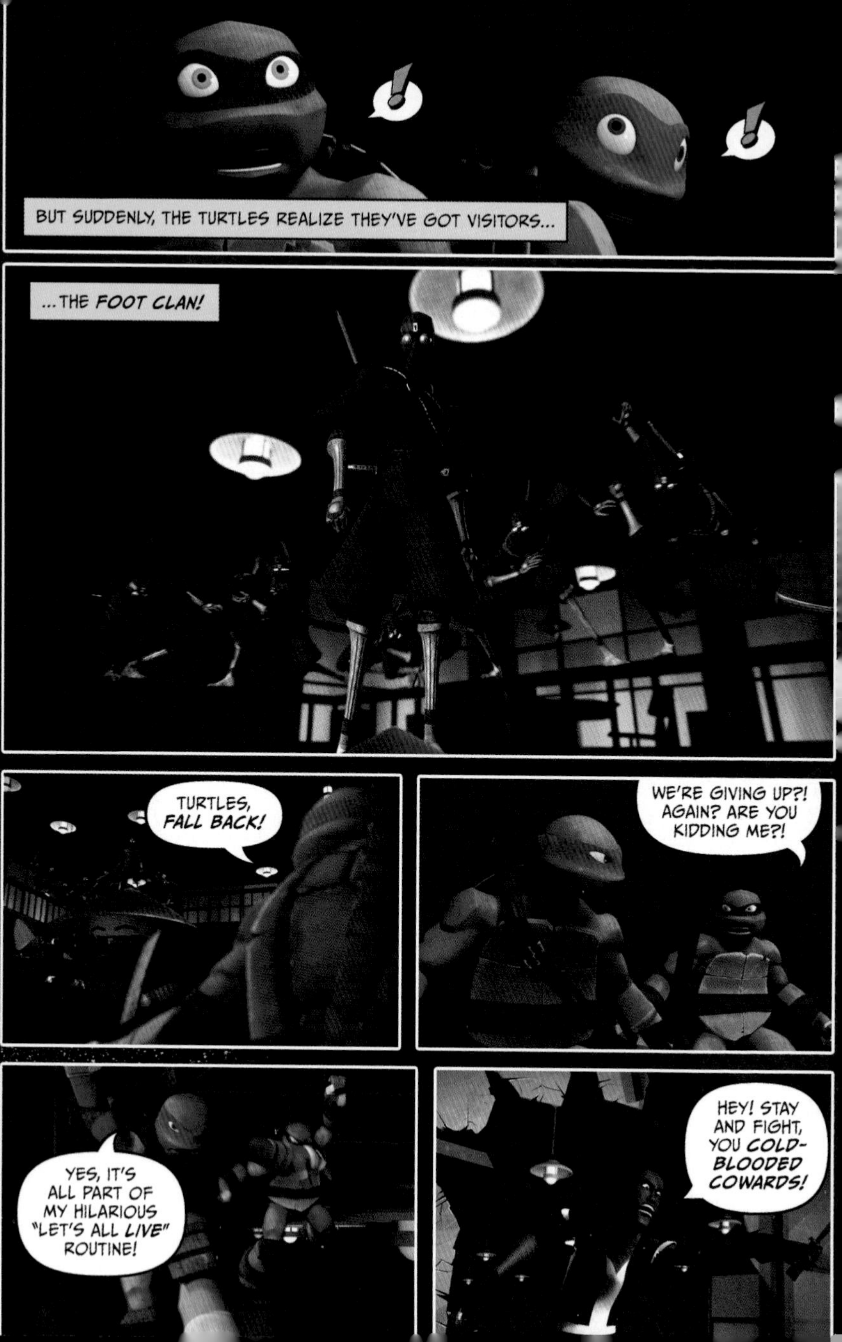
!
!
BUT SUDDENLY, THE TURTLES REALIZE THEY'VE GOT VISITORS...
...THE FOOT CLAN!
TURTLES, FALL BACK!
WE'RE GIVING UP?! AGAIN? ARE YOU KIDDING ME?!
YES, IT'S ALL PART OF MY HILARIOUS "LET'S ALL LIVE" ROUTINE!
HEY! STAY AND FIGHT, YOU COLD-BLOODED COWARDS!

BACK IN THEIR LAIR.

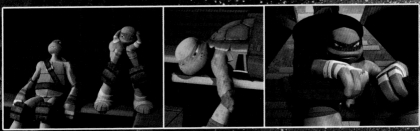

MAN, COULD THAT FIGHT HAVE BEEN ANY MORE EMBARRASSING?

SURE, WE COULD HAVE BEEN HIT IN THE FACE WITH PIES!

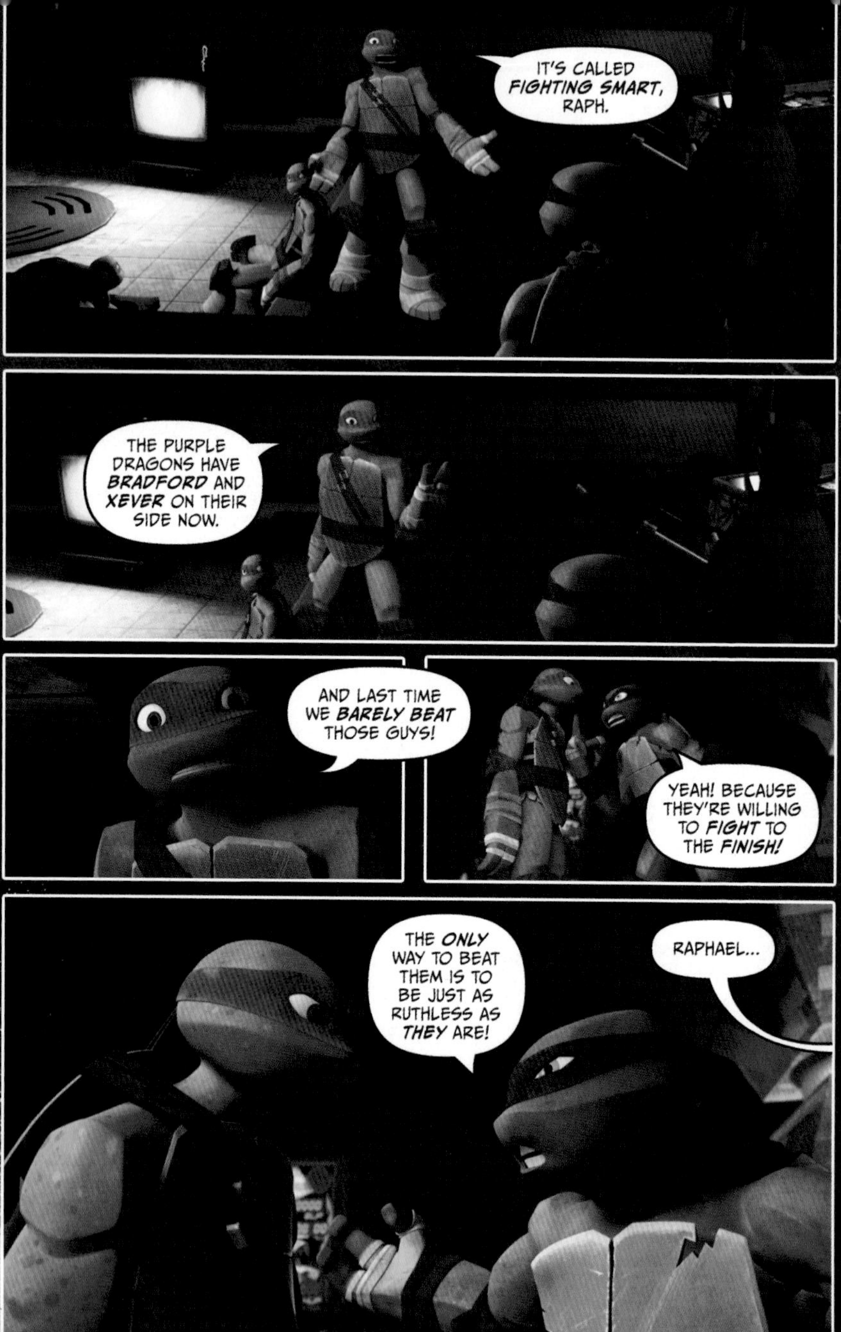
IT'S CALLED FIGHTING SMART, RAPH.
THE PURPLE DRAGONS HAVE BRADFORD AND XEVER ON THEIR SIDE NOW.
AND LAST TIME WE BARELY BEAT THOSE GUYS!
YEAH! BECAUSE THEY'RE WILLING TO FIGHT TO THE FINISH!
THE ONLY WAY TO BEAT THEM IS TO BE JUST AS RUTHLESS AS THEY ARE!
RAPHAEL...

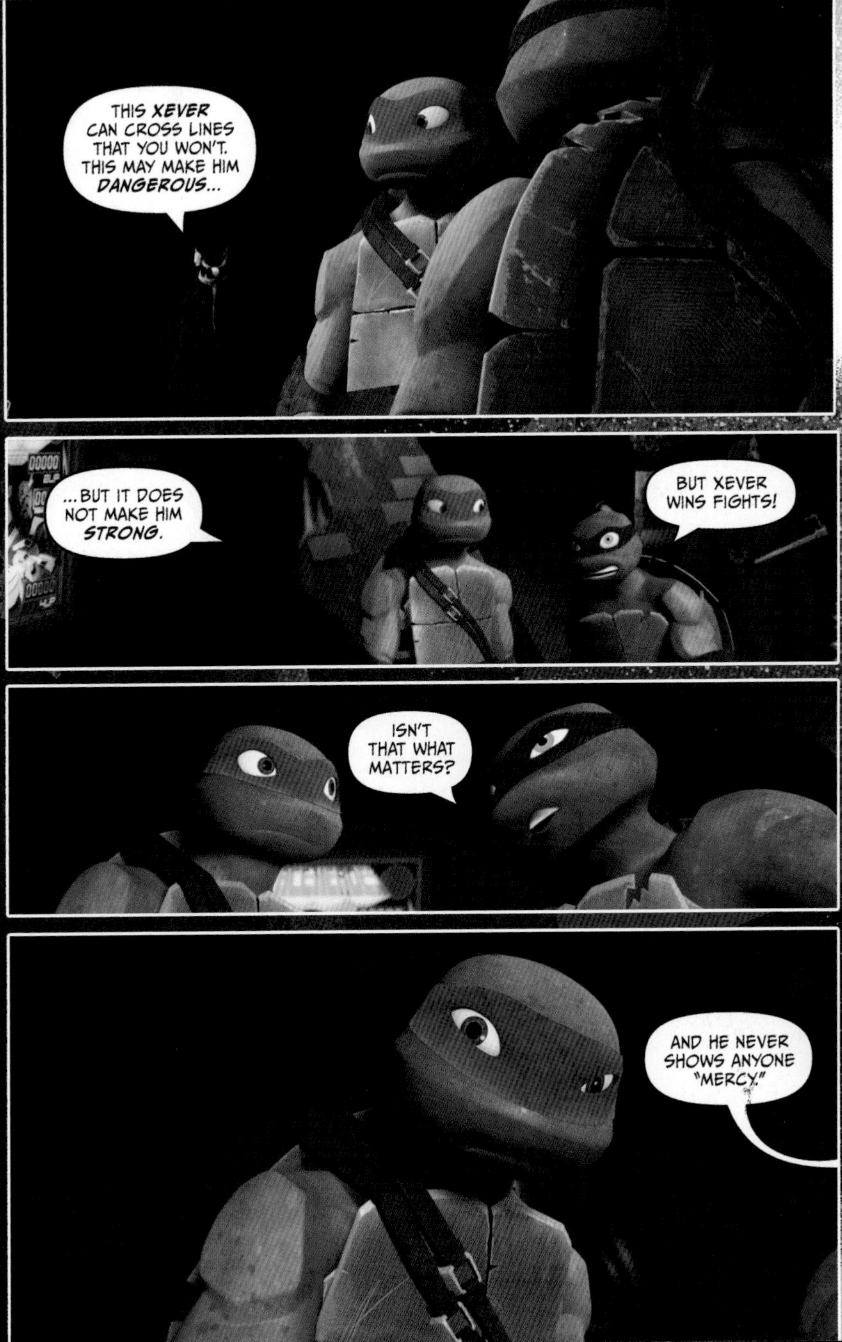
THIS XEVER CAN CROSS LINES THAT YOU WON'T. THIS MAY MAKE HIM DANGEROUS...
...BUT IT DOES NOT MAKE HIM STRONG.
BUT XEVER WINS FIGHTS!
ISN'T THAT WHAT MATTERS?
AND HE NEVER SHOWS ANYONE "MERCY."

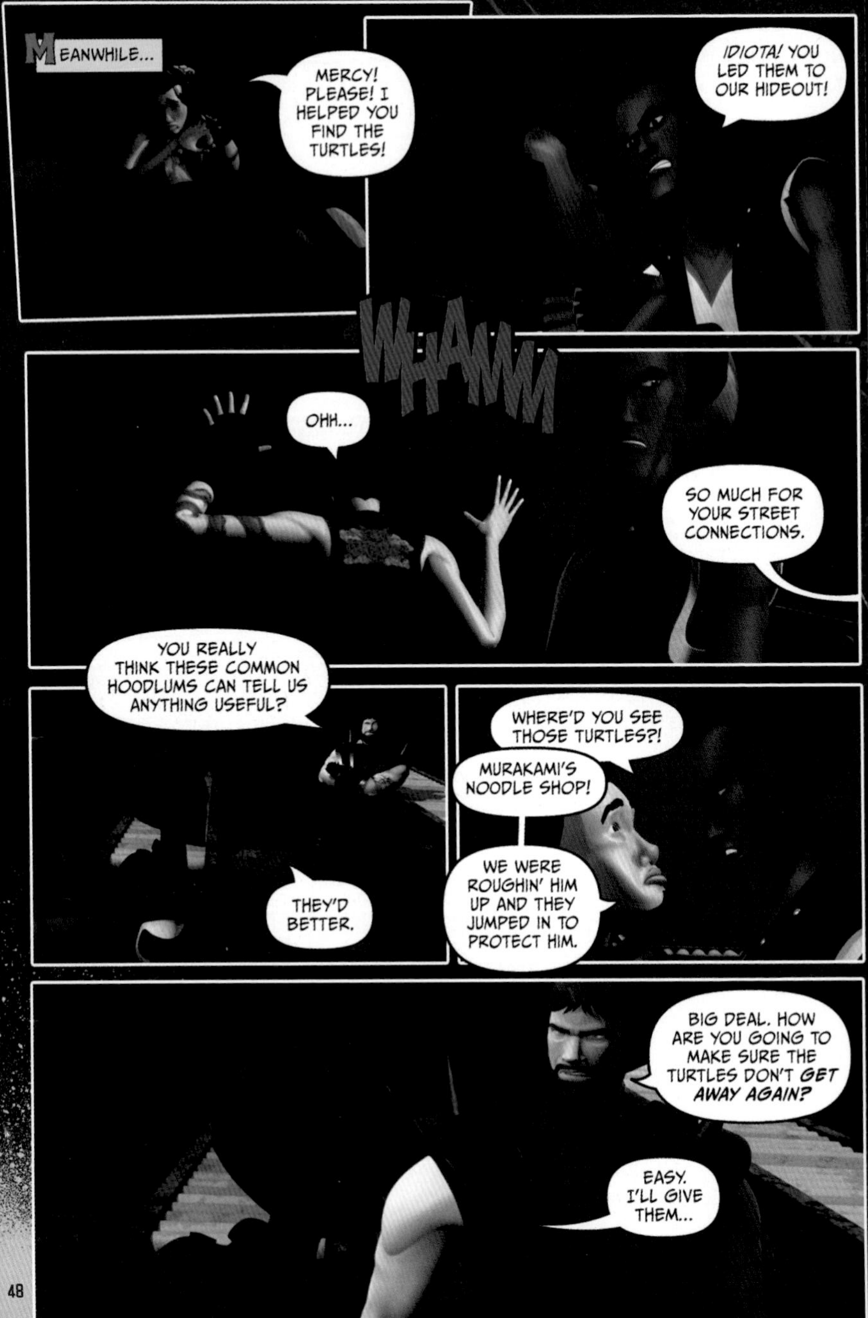
MEANWHILE...
MERCY! PLEASE! I HELPED YOU FIND THE TURTLES!
IDIOTA! YOU LED THEM TO OUR HIDEOUT!
WHAM
OHH...
SO MUCH FOR YOUR STREET CONNECTIONS.
YOU REALLY THINK THESE COMMON HOODLUMS CAN TELL US ANYTHING USEFUL?
THEY'D BETTER.
WHERE'D YOU SEE THOSE TURTLES?!
MURAKAMI'S NOODLE SHOP!
WE WERE ROUGHIN' HIM UP AND THEY JUMPED IN TO PROTECT HIM.
BIG DEAL. HOW ARE YOU GOING TO MAKE SURE THE TURTLES DON'T *GET AWAY AGAIN?*
EASY. I'LL GIVE THEM...

"...A REASON TO **STAY**."

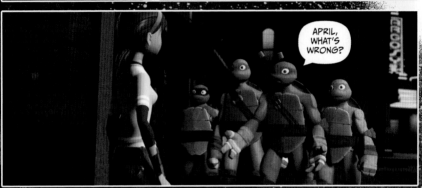

APRIL, WHAT'S WRONG?

IT'S MURAKAMI.

SOMEONE **TOOK** HIM—

—AND LEFT **THIS**.

No more running
If you want the
old man, meet us
on the roof of the
Fortune Cookie Factory.

SWEET! FREE KNIFE!

NO! THE NOTE, DUMMY!

WELL WHAT ARE WE WAITING FOR? LET'S BUST IN THERE AND SAVE MURAKAMI!

NOT SO FAST. **THINK**, RAPHAEL.

THERE'S TWO WORDS THAT DON'T USUALLY GO TOGETHER!

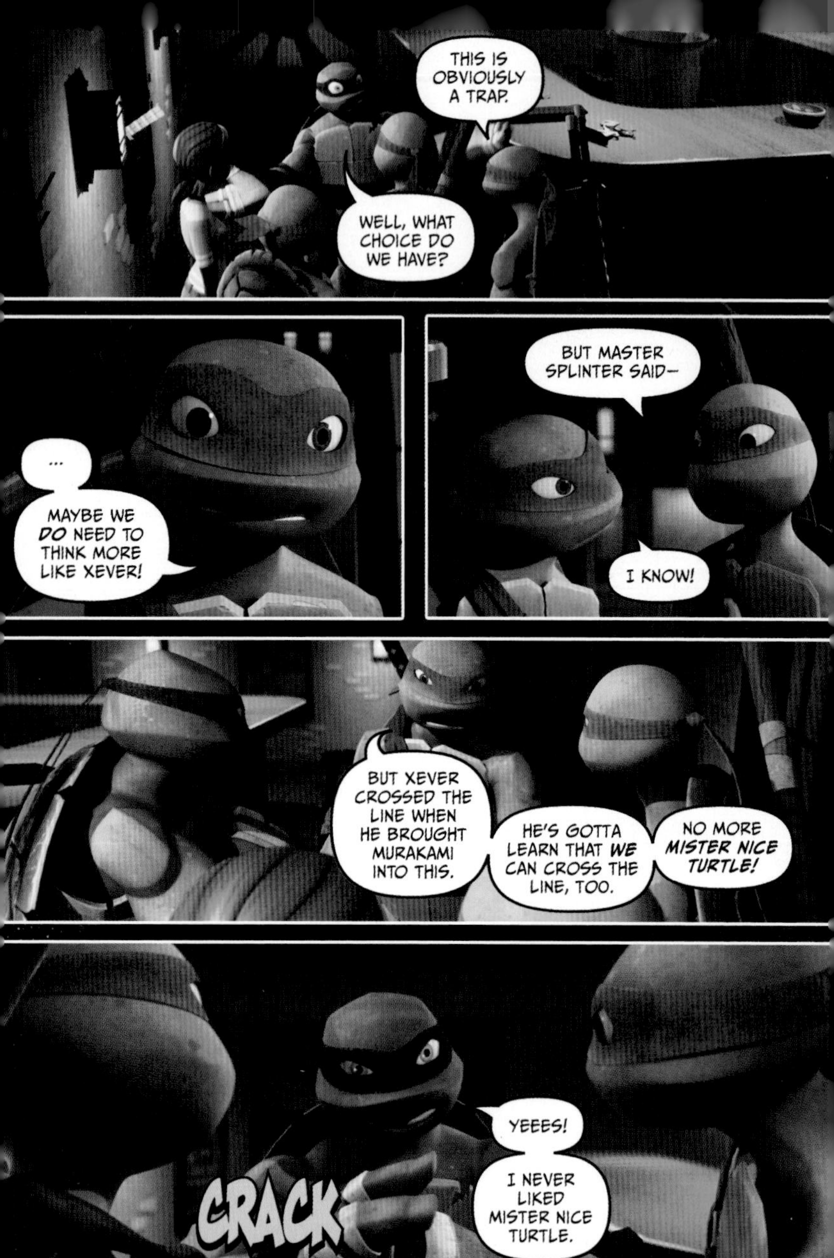
THIS IS OBVIOUSLY A TRAP.
WELL, WHAT CHOICE DO WE HAVE?
...
MAYBE WE *DO* NEED TO THINK MORE LIKE XEVER!
BUT MASTER SPLINTER SAID—
I KNOW!
BUT XEVER CROSSED THE LINE WHEN HE BROUGHT MURAKAMI INTO THIS.
HE'S GOTTA LEARN THAT *WE* CAN CROSS THE LINE, TOO.
NO MORE *MISTER NICE TURTLE!*
YEEES!
I NEVER LIKED MISTER NICE TURTLE.
CRACK

O UTSIDE BRADFORD'S DOJO...

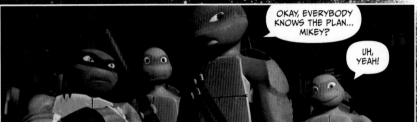

OKAY, EVERYBODY KNOWS THE PLAN... MIKEY?

UH, YEAH!

GOOD, BECAUSE THERE HE IS!

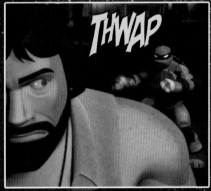

THWAP

HEY!

THAT'S WHEN LEO JUMPS...

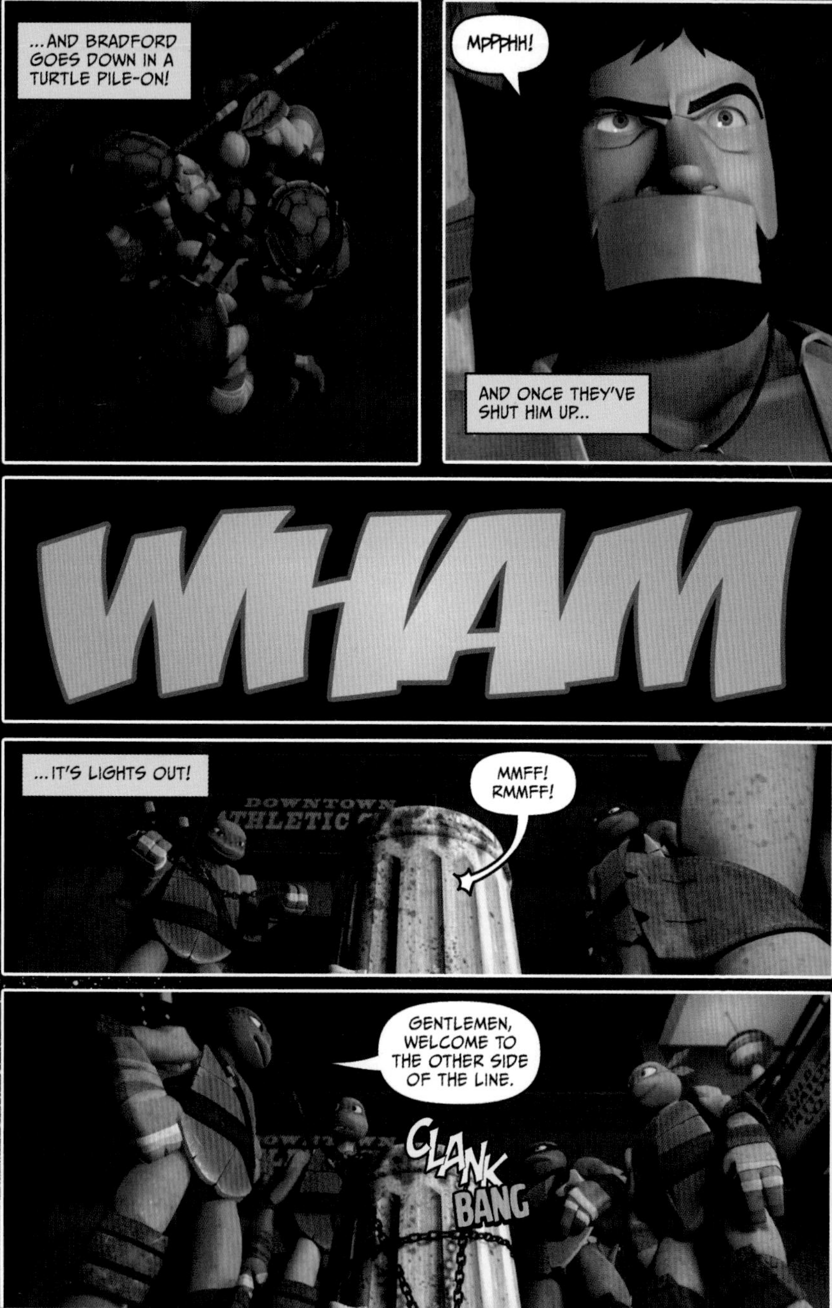
...AND BRADFORD GOES DOWN IN A TURTLE PILE-ON!
MPPPHH!
AND ONCE THEY'VE SHUT HIM UP...
WHAM
...IT'S LIGHTS OUT!
MMFF! RMMFF!
GENTLEMEN, WELCOME TO THE OTHER SIDE OF THE LINE.
CLANK
BANG

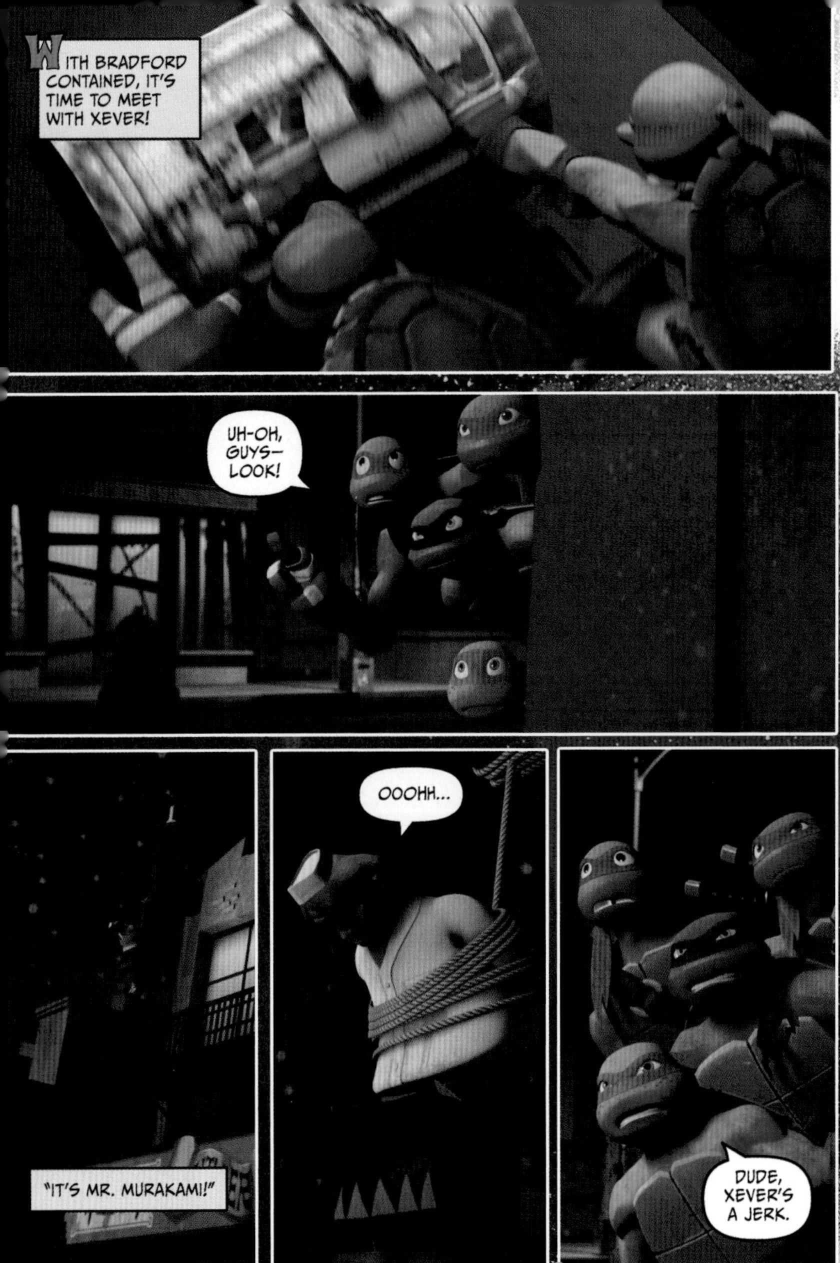

WITH BRADFORD CONTAINED, IT'S TIME TO MEET WITH XEVER!
UH-OH, GUYS— LOOK!
"IT'S MR. MURAKAMI!"
OOOHH...
DUDE, XEVER'S A JERK.

WE'RE HERE, XEVER! NOW, LET THE NOODLE MAN GO!

SORRY... ...THERE'S BEEN A CHANGE OF PLANS.

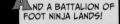

AND A BATTALION OF FOOT NINJA LANDS!

ACTUALLY, THERE'S BEEN *ANOTHER* CHANGE OF PLANS...

....YOU LET *OUR* FRIEND GO, AND WE'LL LET *YOUR* FRIEND GO.

I LOVE IT WHEN A CHANGE OF PLANS COMES TOGETHER!

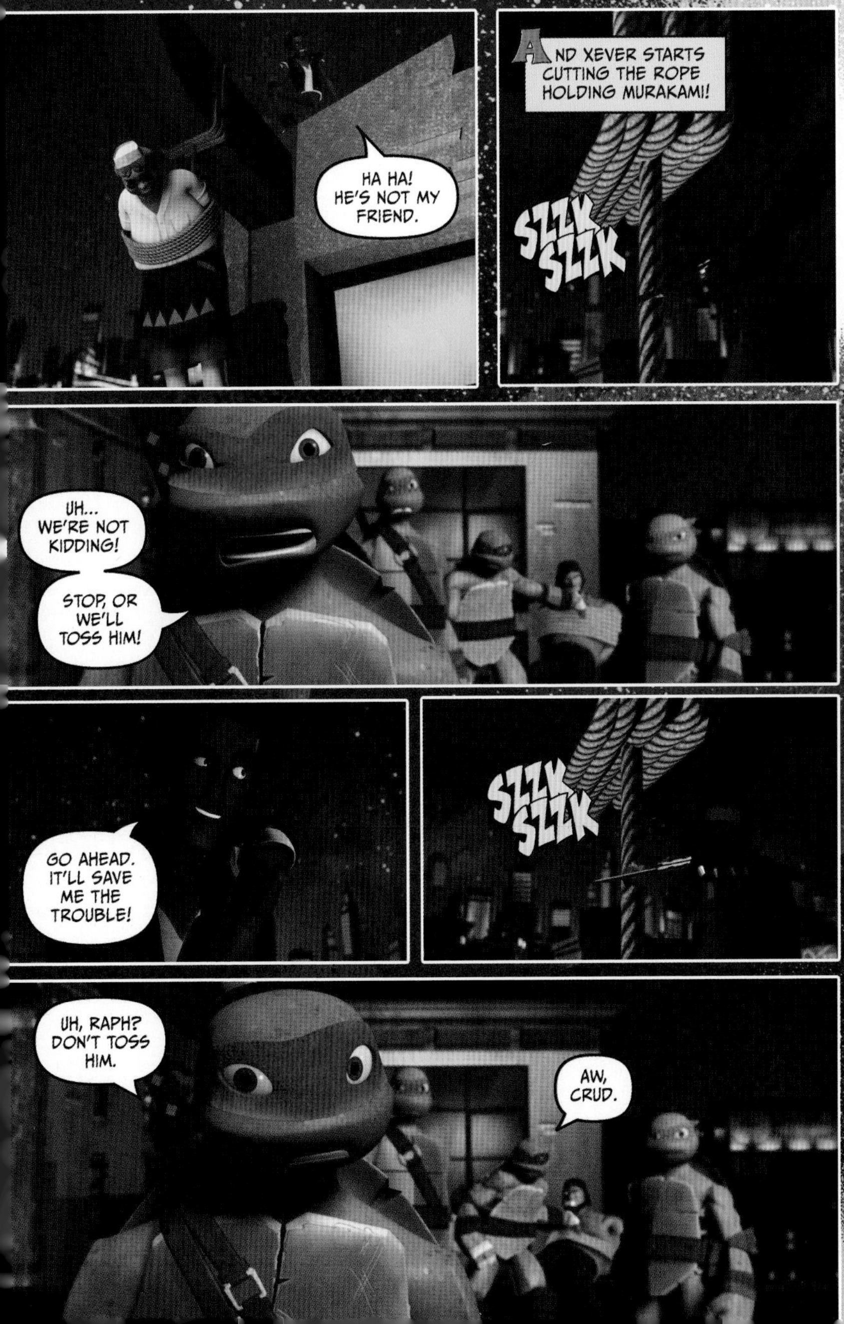
HA HA! HE'S NOT MY FRIEND.
AND XEVER STARTS CUTTING THE ROPE HOLDING MURAKAMI!
SZZK SZZK
UH... WE'RE NOT KIDDING!
STOP, OR WE'LL TOSS HIM!
GO AHEAD. IT'LL SAVE ME THE TROUBLE!
SZZK SZZK
UH, RAPH? DON'T TOSS HIM.
AW, CRUD.

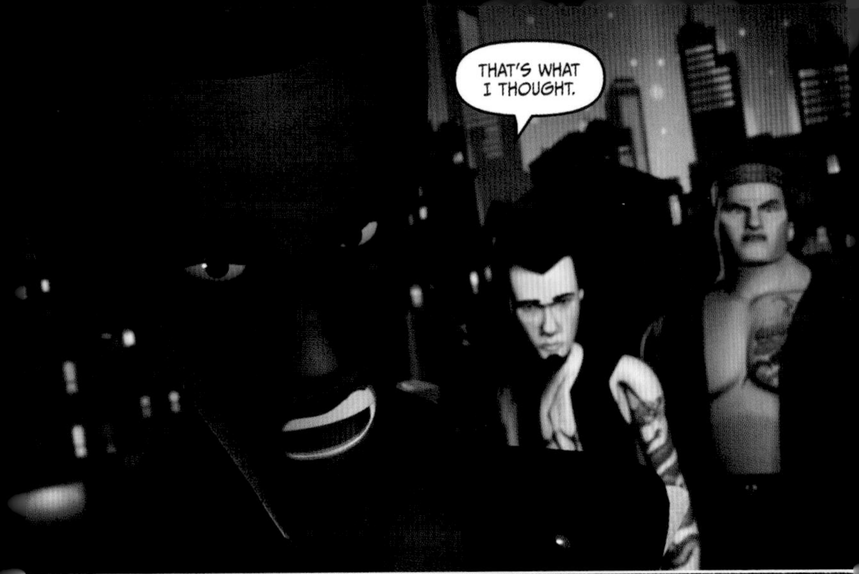
THAT'S WHAT I THOUGHT.

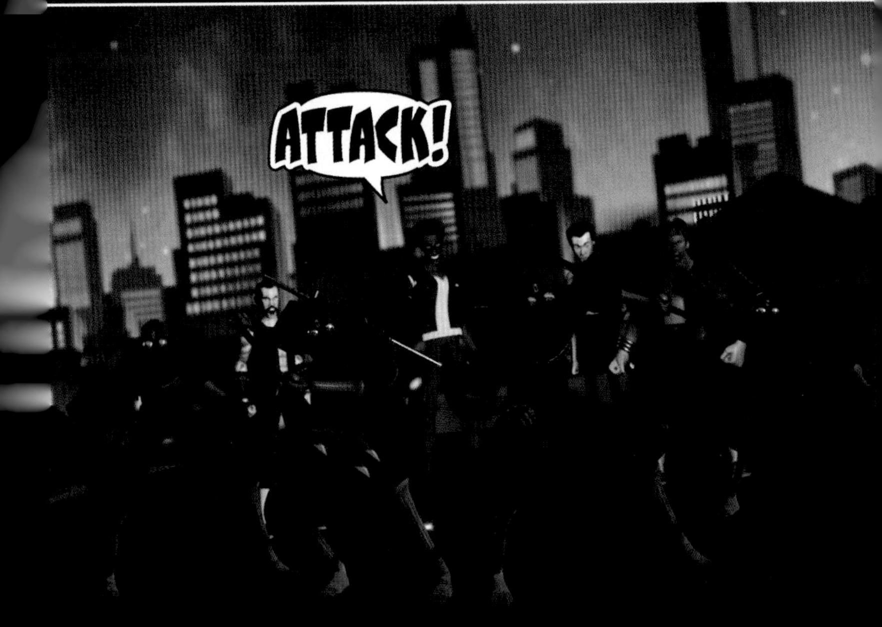
ATTACK!

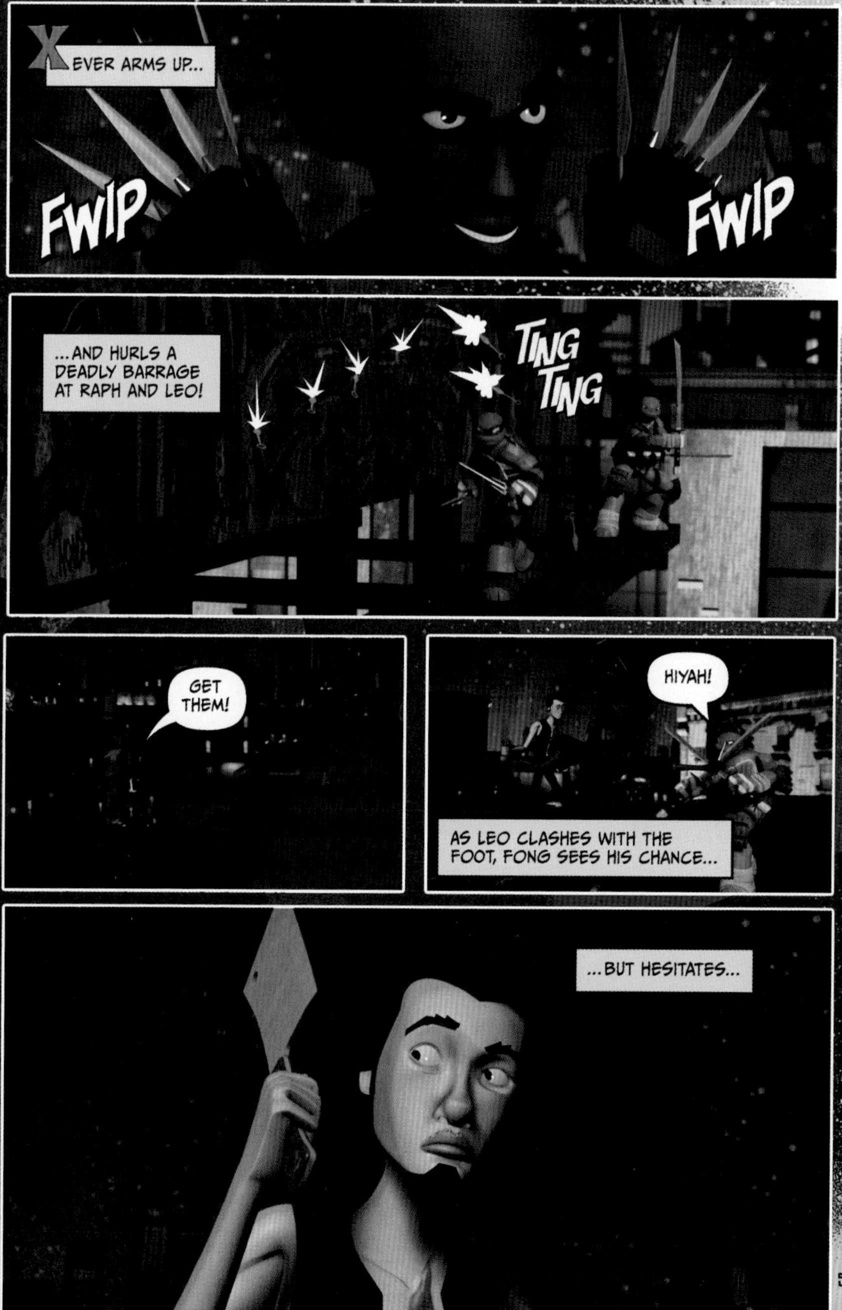
XEVER ARMS UP..
FWIP
FWIP
...AND HURLS A DEADLY BARRAGE AT RAPH AND LEO!
TING
TING
GET THEM!
HIYAH!
AS LEO CLASHES WITH THE FOOT, FONG SEES HIS CHANCE...
...BUT HESITATES...

...BEFORE GOING FOR IT!

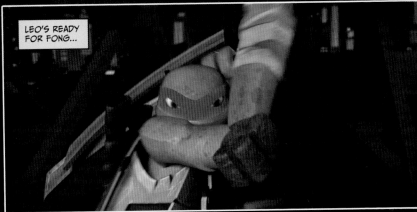

LEO'S READY FOR FONG...

SHHLING

58

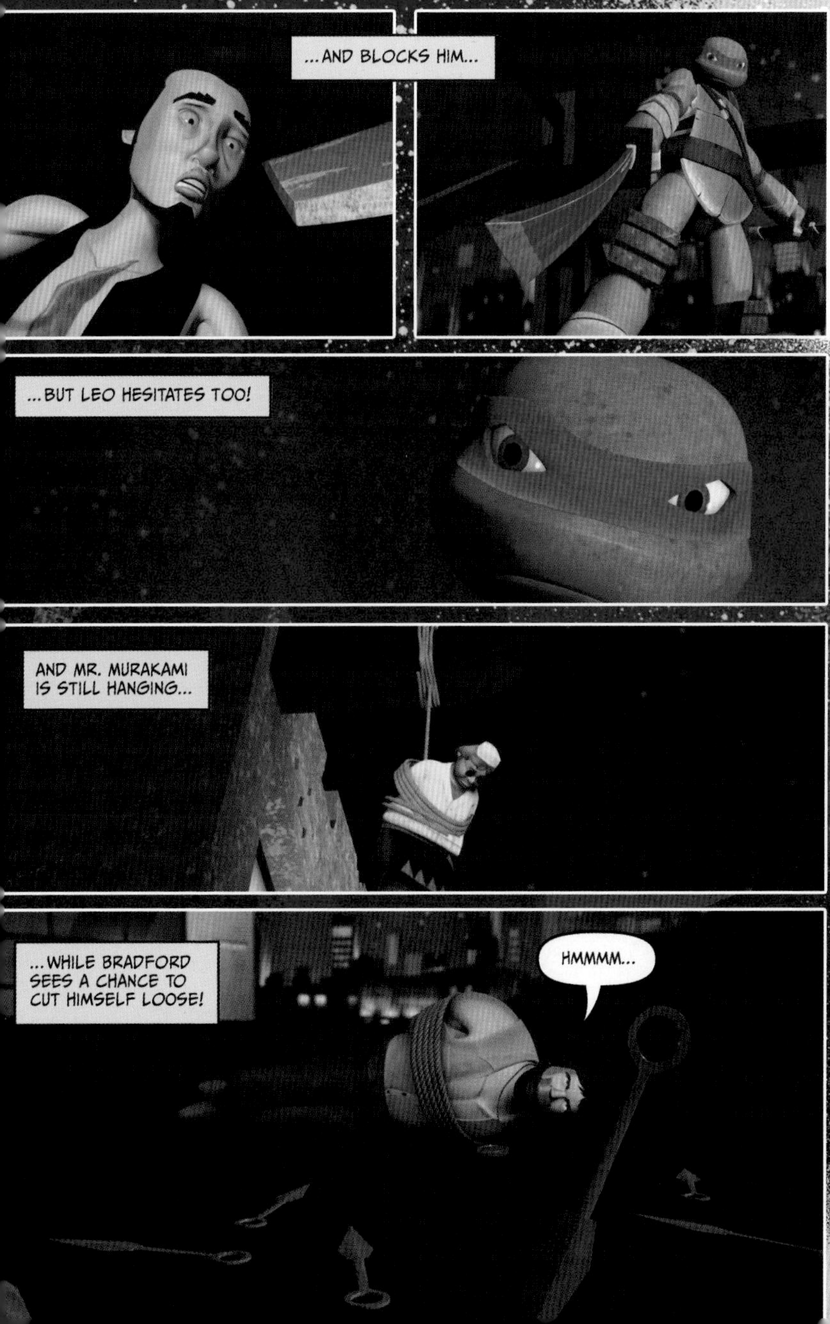
...AND BLOCKS HIM...
...BUT LEO HESITATES TOO!
AND MR. MURAKAMI IS STILL HANGING...
...WHILE BRADFORD SEES A CHANCE TO CUT HIMSELF LOOSE!
HMMMM...

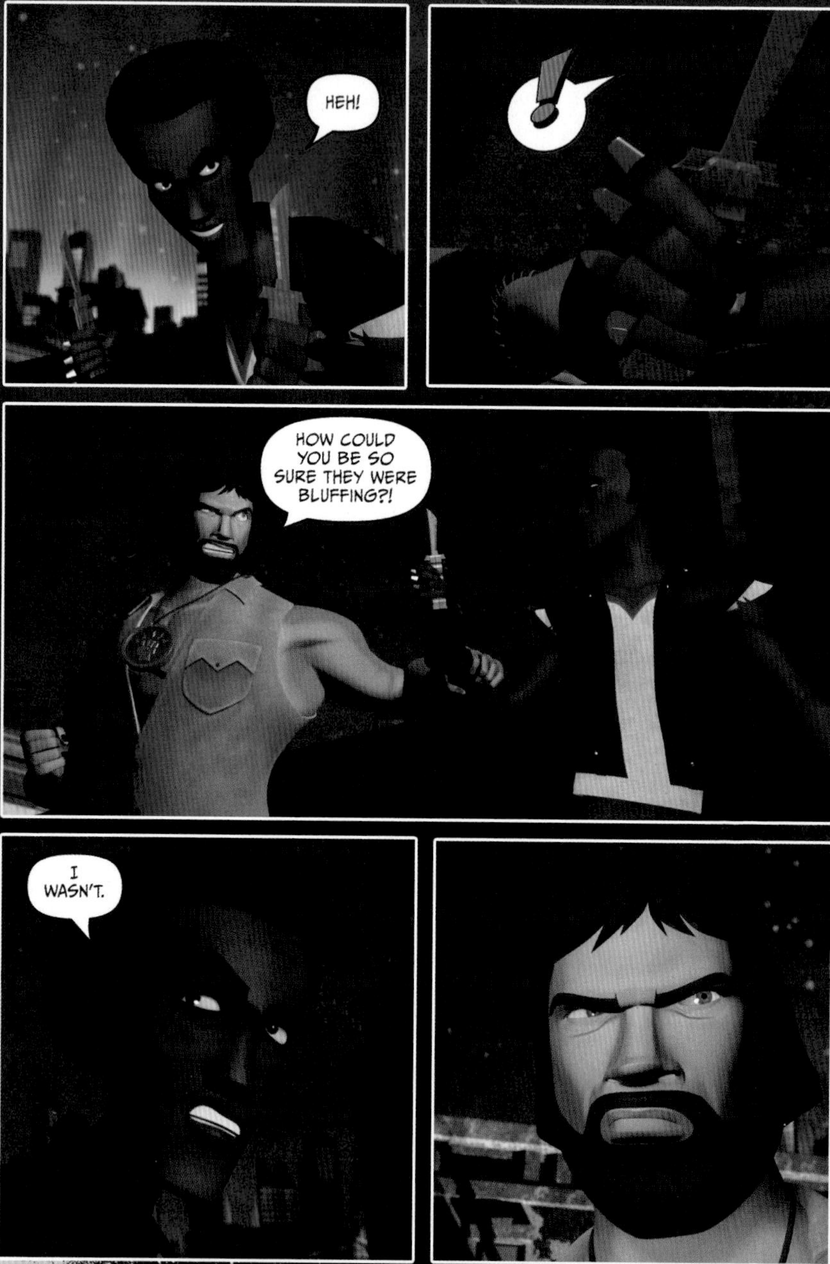
HEH!
!
HOW COULD YOU BE SO SURE THEY WERE BLUFFING?!
I WASN'T.

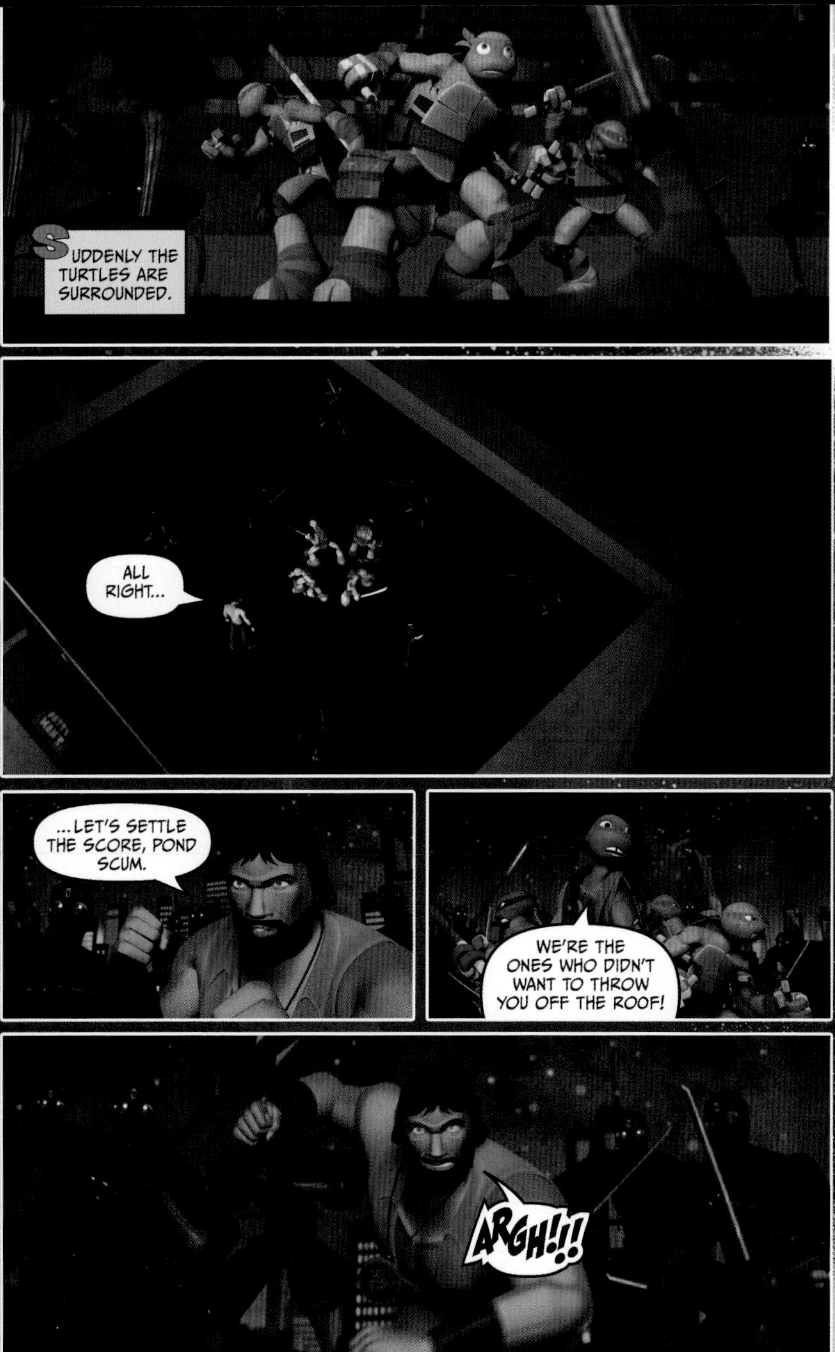
SUDDENLY THE TURTLES ARE SURROUNDED.
ALL RIGHT...
...LET'S SETTLE THE SCORE, POND SCUM.
WE'RE THE ONES WHO DIDN'T WANT TO THROW YOU OFF THE ROOF!
ARGH!!!

FWOOSH

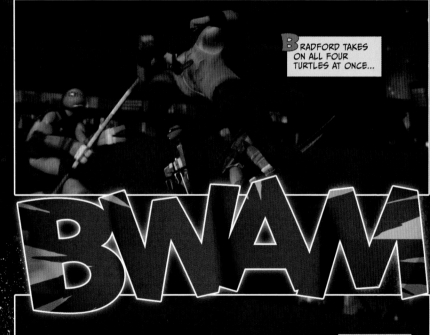

BRADFORD TAKES ON ALL FOUR TURTLES AT ONCE...

BWAM

...AND TAKES DOWN DONNIE!

THUD

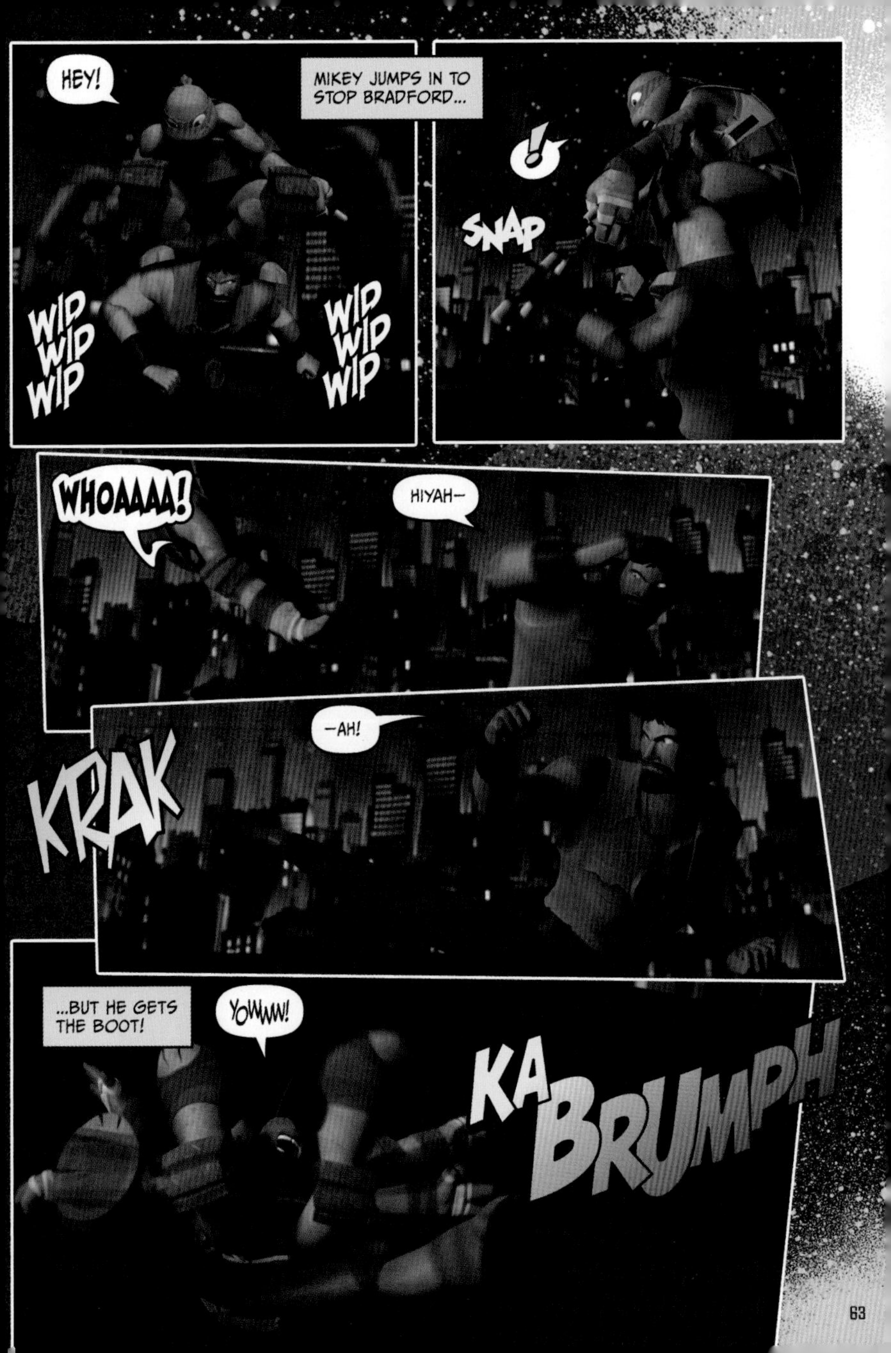
HEY!
MIKEY JUMPS IN TO STOP BRADFORD...
WIP WIP WIP
WIP WIP WIP
!
SNAP
WHOAAAA!
HIYAH—
—AH!
KRAK
...BUT HE GETS THE BOOT!
YOWWW!
KA BRUMPH

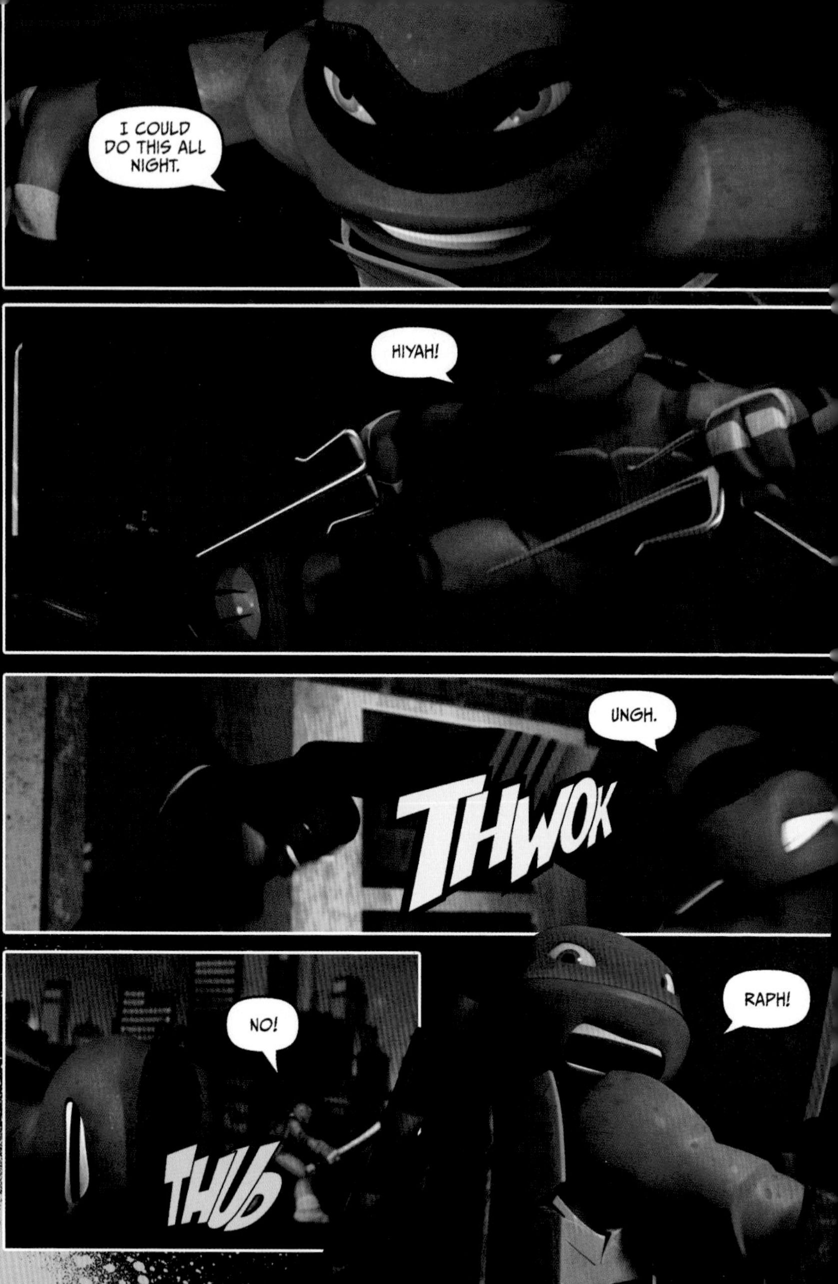
I COULD DO THIS ALL NIGHT.
HIYAH!
UNGH.
THWOK
NO!
RAPH!
THUD

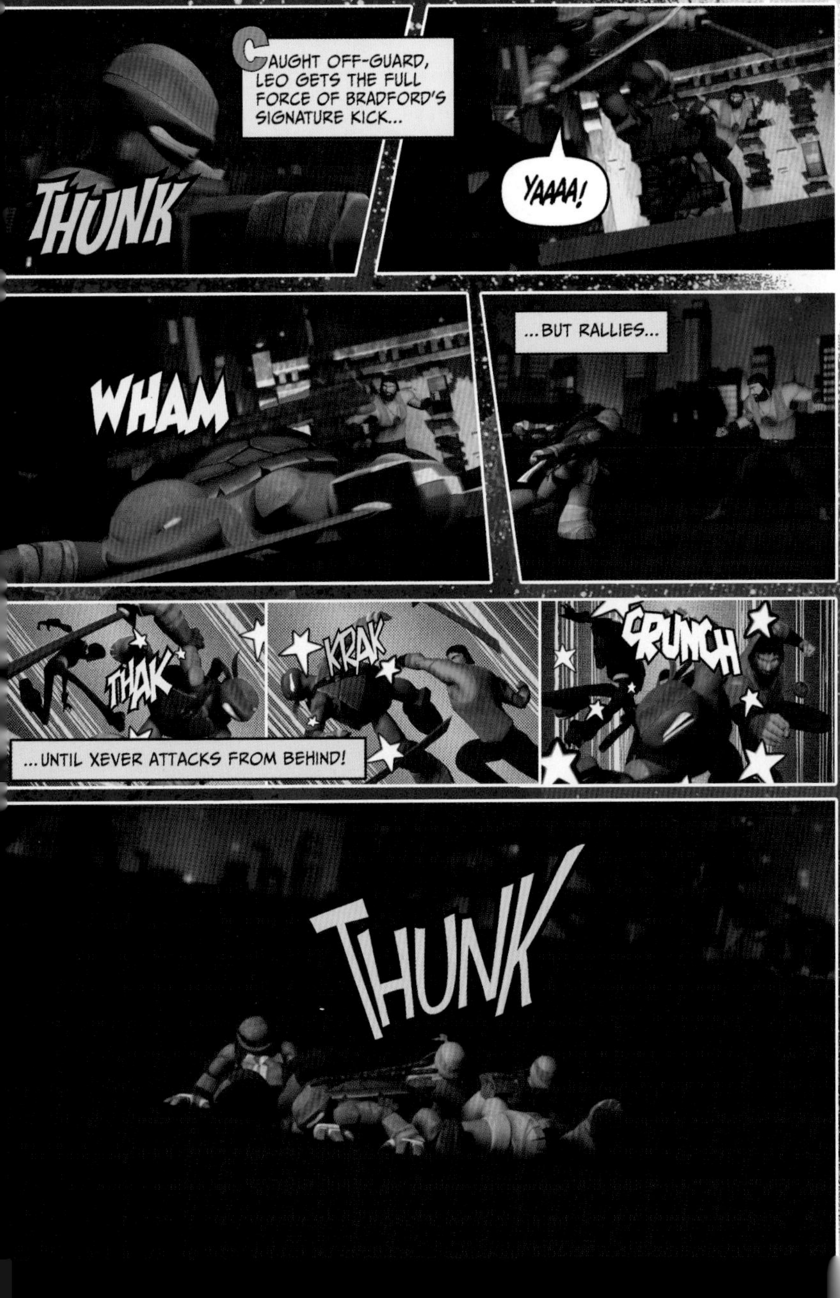

CAUGHT OFF-GUARD, LEO GETS THE FULL FORCE OF BRADFORD'S SIGNATURE KICK...
THUNK
YAAAA!
WHAM
...BUT RALLIES...
THAK
KRAK
...UNTIL XEVER ATTACKS FROM BEHIND!
CRUNCH
THUNK

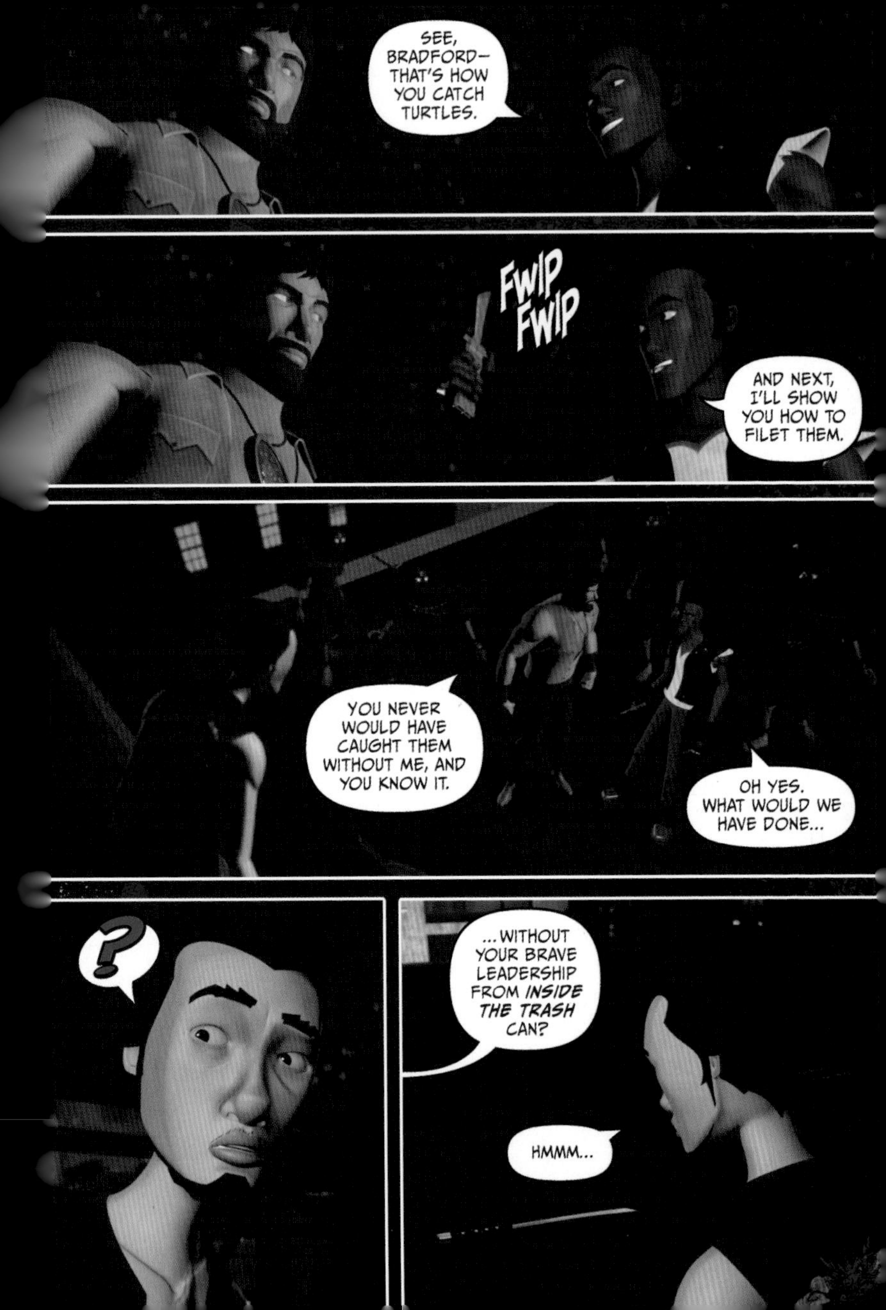
SEE, BRADFORD— THAT'S HOW YOU CATCH TURTLES.
FWIP FWIP
AND NEXT, I'LL SHOW YOU HOW TO FILET THEM.
YOU NEVER WOULD HAVE CAUGHT THEM WITHOUT ME, AND YOU KNOW IT.
OH YES. WHAT WOULD WE HAVE DONE...
?
...WITHOUT YOUR BRAVE LEADERSHIP FROM *INSIDE THE TRASH* CAN?
HMMM...

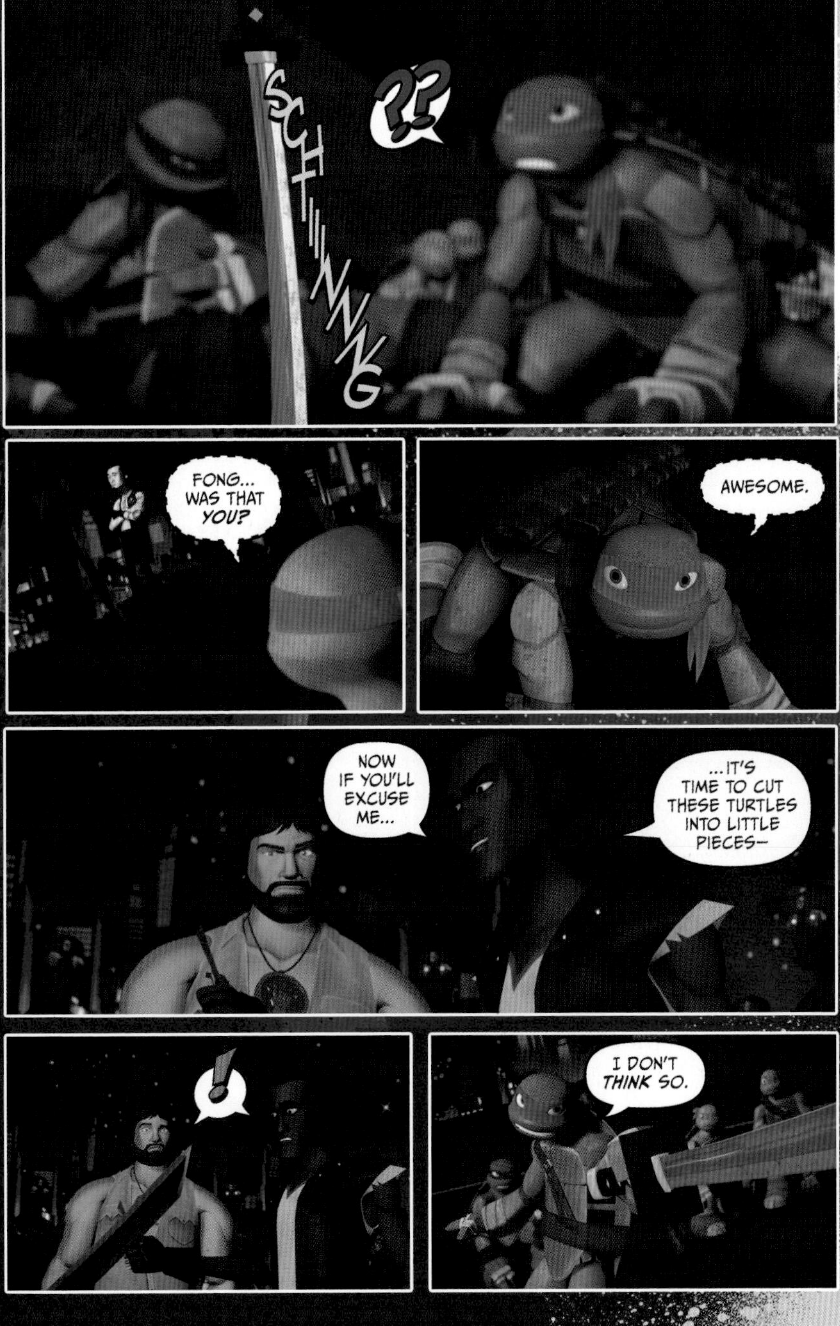

SCHIIIINNNG
??
FONG... WAS THAT YOU?
AWESOME.
NOW IF YOU'LL EXCUSE ME...
...IT'S TIME TO CUT THESE TURTLES INTO LITTLE PIECES—
!
I DON'T THINK SO.

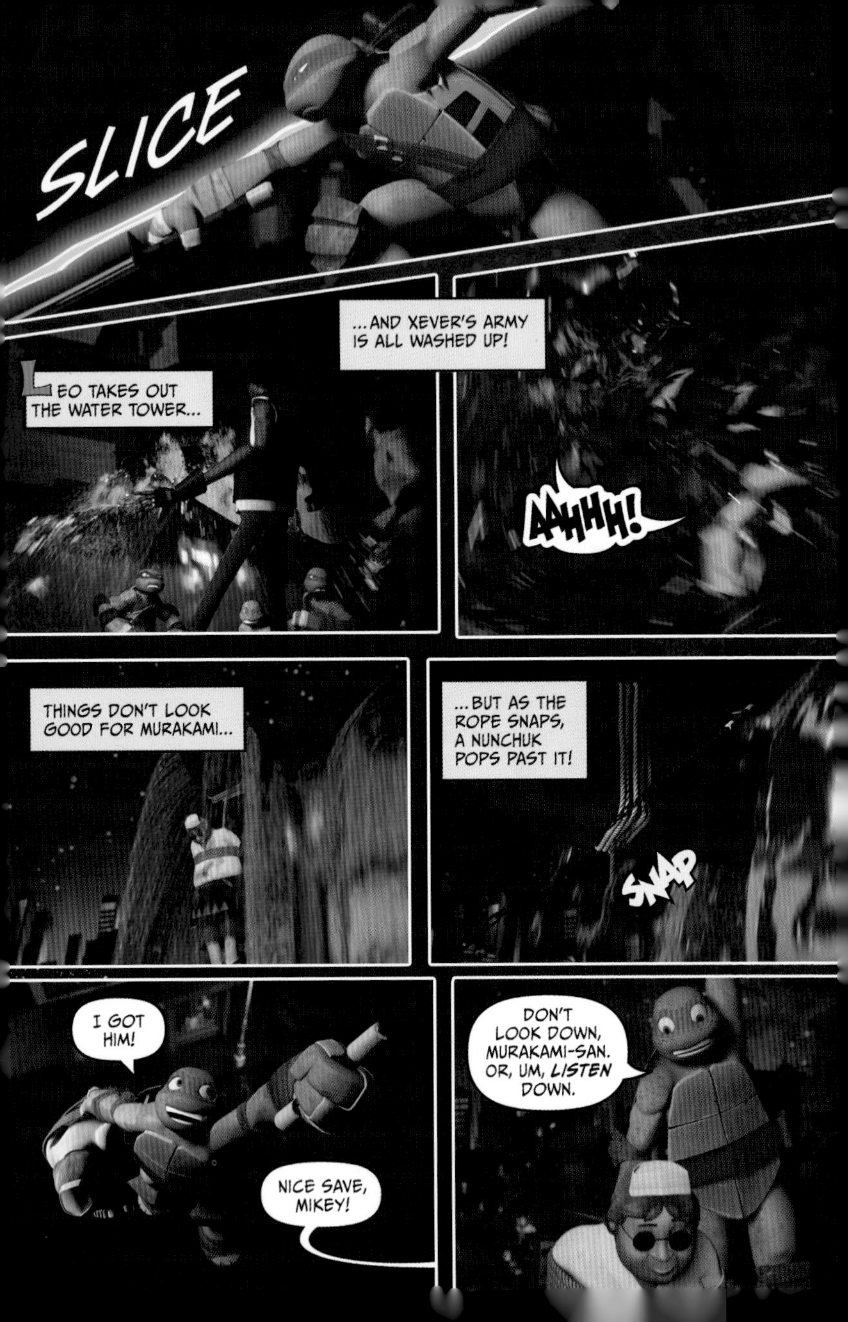
SLICE
LEO TAKES OUT THE WATER TOWER...
...AND XEVER'S ARMY IS ALL WASHED UP!
AAHHH!
THINGS DON'T LOOK GOOD FOR MURAKAMI...
...BUT AS THE ROPE SNAPS, A NUNCHUK POPS PAST IT!
SNAP
I GOT HIM!
NICE SAVE, MIKEY!
DON'T LOOK DOWN, MURAKAMI-SAN. OR, UM, *LISTEN* DOWN.

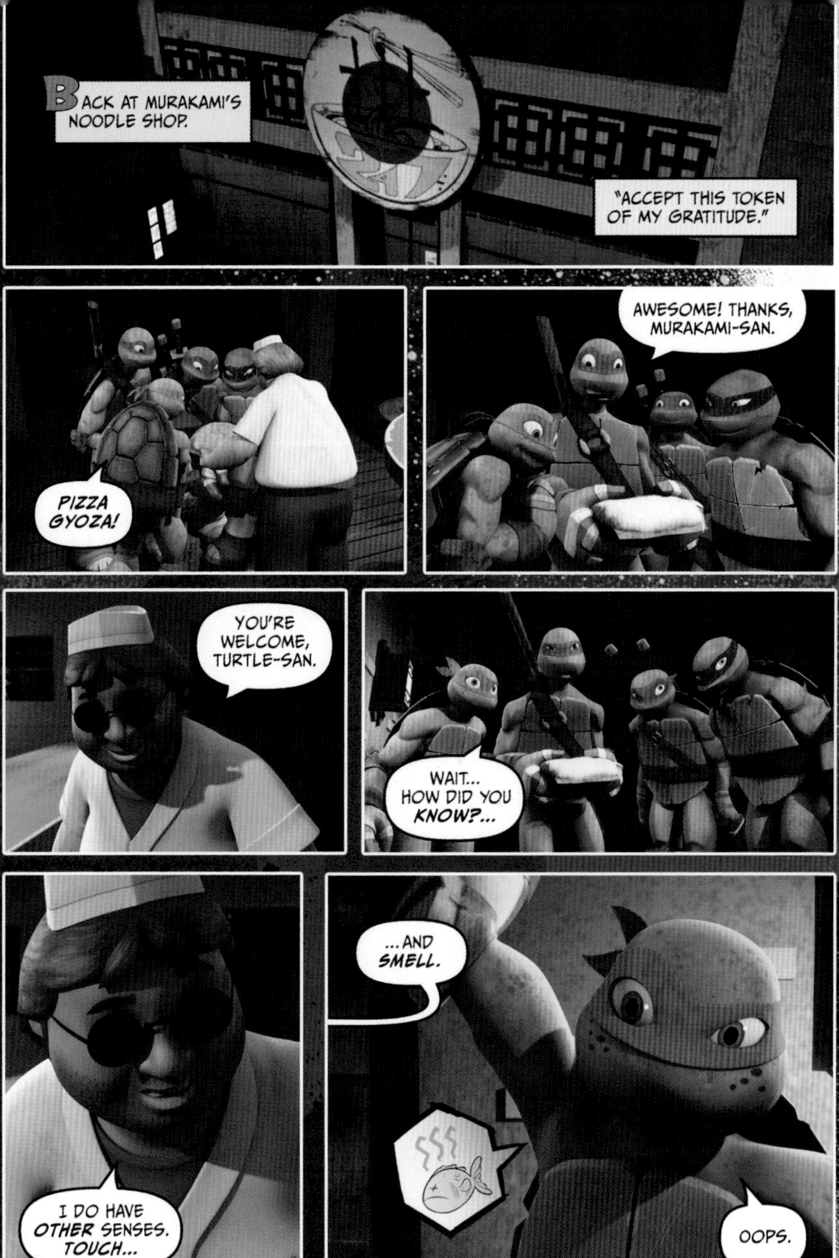
BACK AT MURAKAMI'S NOODLE SHOP.
"ACCEPT THIS TOKEN OF MY GRATITUDE."
PIZZA GYOZA!
AWESOME! THANKS, MURAKAMI-SAN.
YOU'RE WELCOME, TURTLE-SAN.
WAIT... HOW DID YOU KNOW?...
I DO HAVE OTHER SENSES. TOUCH...
...AND SMELL.
OOPS.

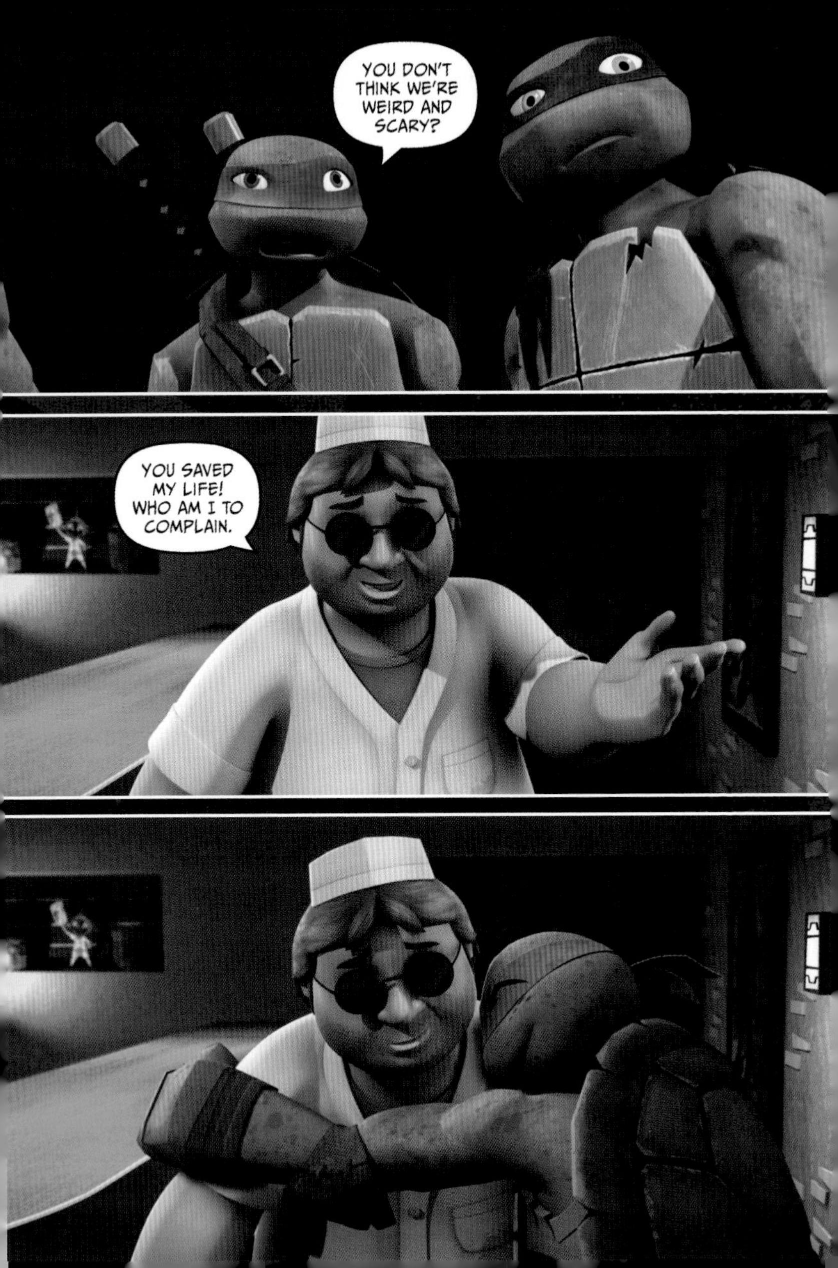
YOU DON'T THINK WE'RE WEIRD AND SCARY?
YOU SAVED MY LIFE! WHO AM I TO COMPLAIN.

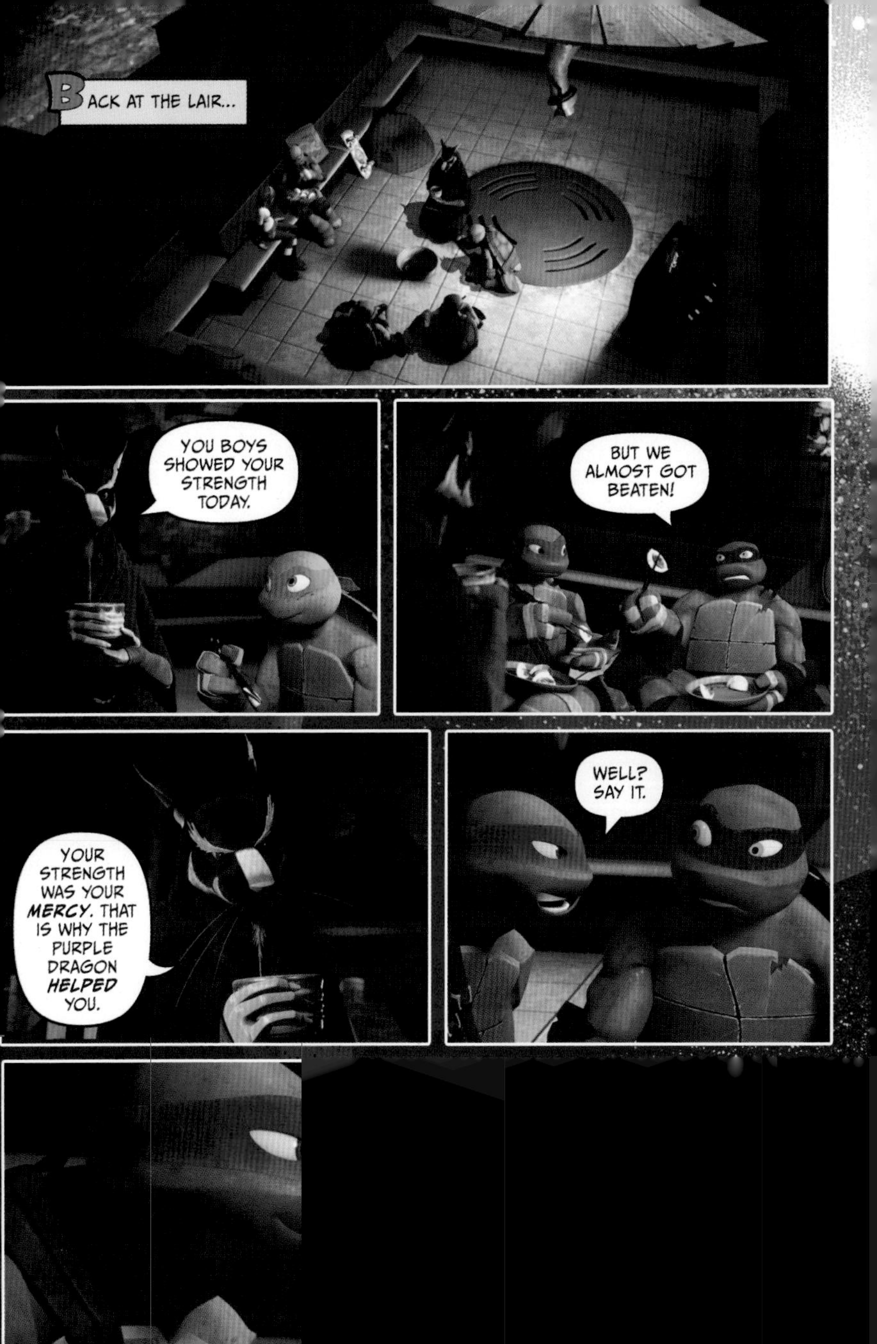
BACK AT THE LAIR...
YOU BOYS SHOWED YOUR STRENGTH TODAY.
BUT WE ALMOST GOT BEATEN!
YOUR STRENGTH WAS YOUR MERCY. THAT IS WHY THE PURPLE DRAGON HELPED YOU.
WELL? SAY IT.

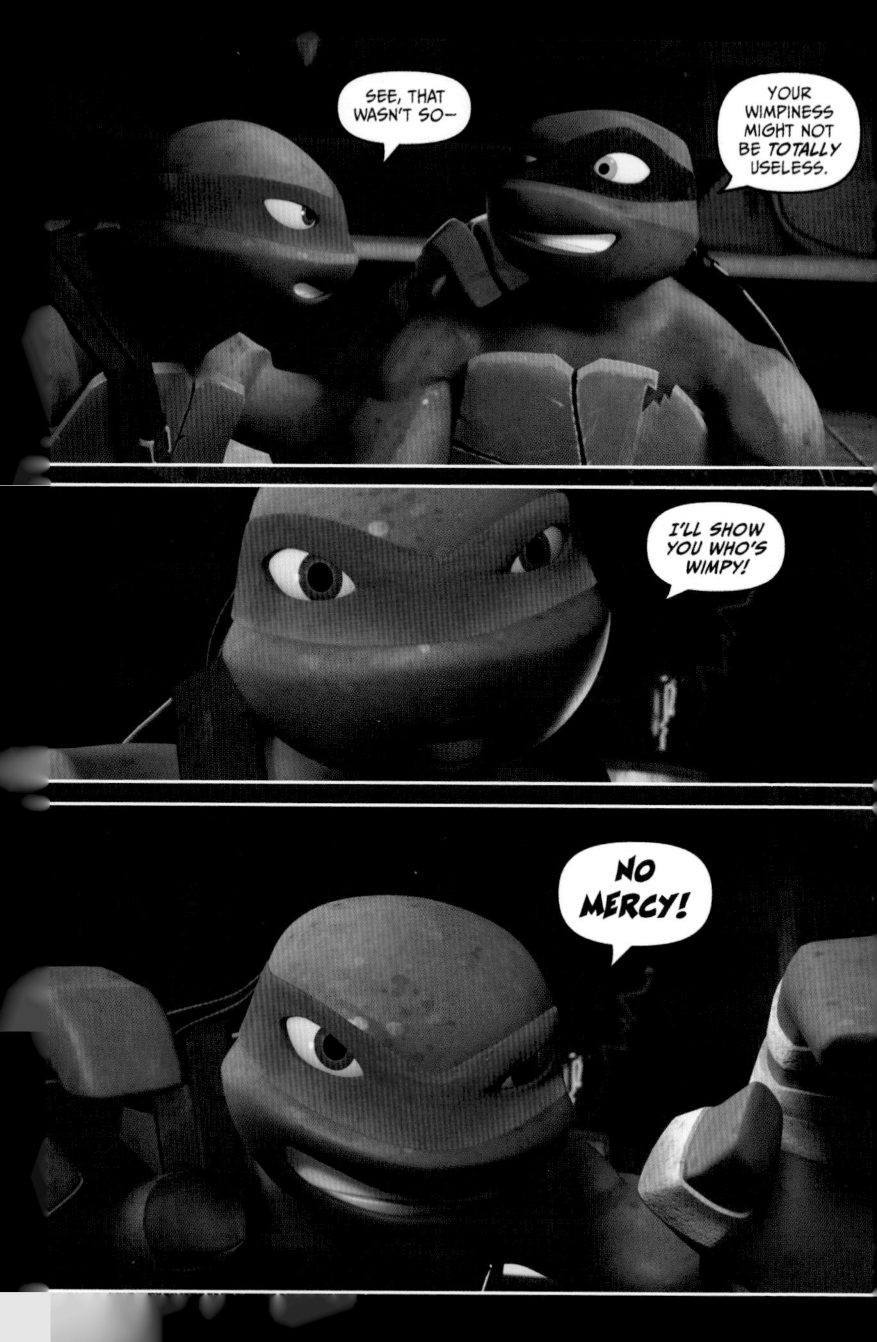
SEE, THAT WASN'T SO—
YOUR WIMPINESS MIGHT NOT BE *TOTALLY* USELESS.
I'LL SHOW YOU WHO'S WIMPY!
NO MERCY!

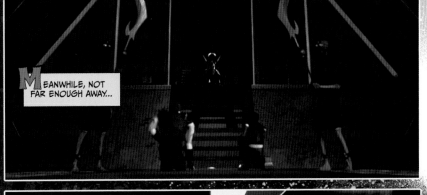

MEANWHILE, NOT FAR ENOUGH AWAY...

THIS IS UNACCEPTABLE.

HUMBLE APOLOGIES, MASTER SHREDDER.

I SWEAR, NEXT TIME WE'LL—

ENOUGH!

I WILL DEAL WITH HAMATO YOSHI'S DISCIPLES...

...MYSELF.

NOT THE END!

THE GAUNTLET

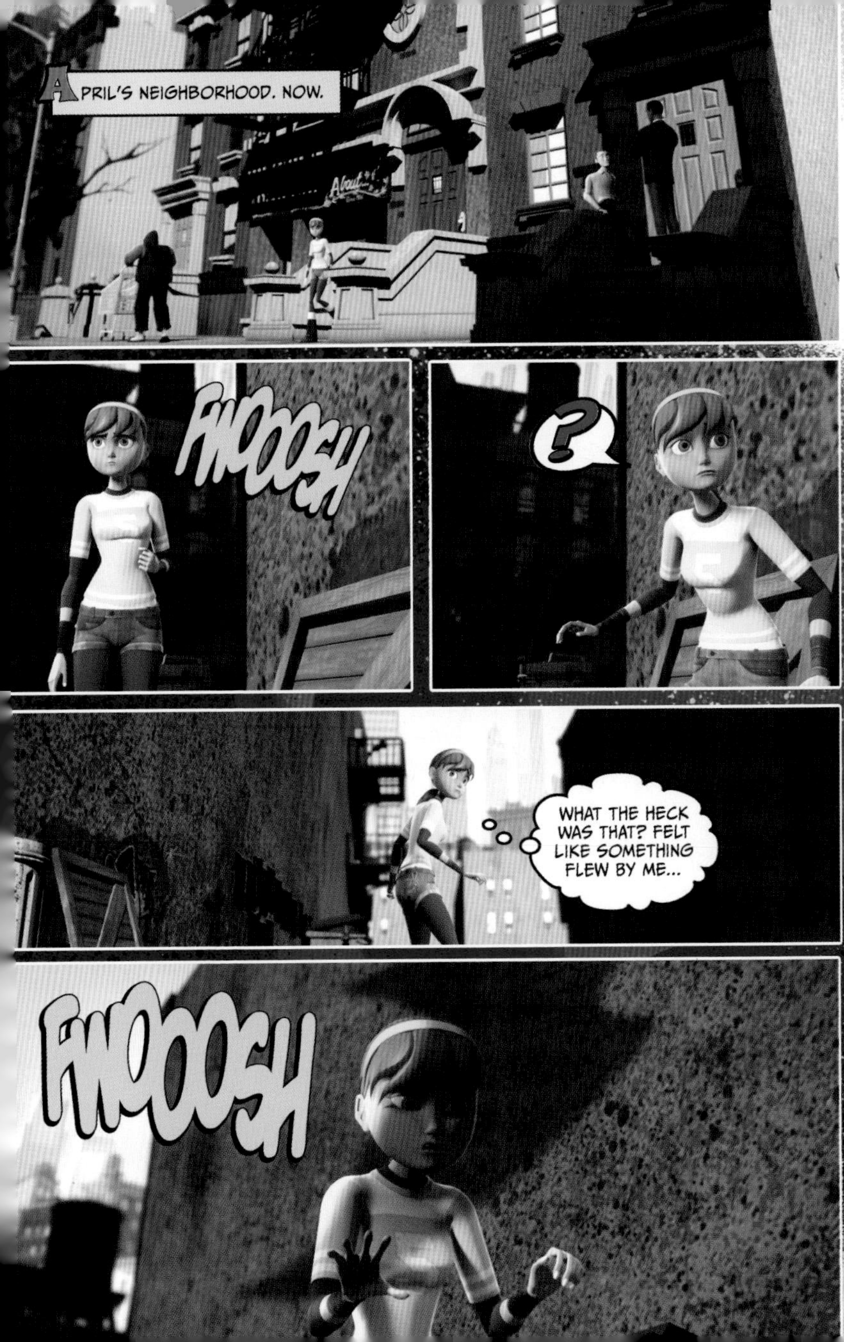
APRIL'S NEIGHBORHOOD. NOW.
FWOOOSH
?
WHAT THE HECK WAS THAT? FELT LIKE SOMETHING FLEW BY ME...
FWOOOSH

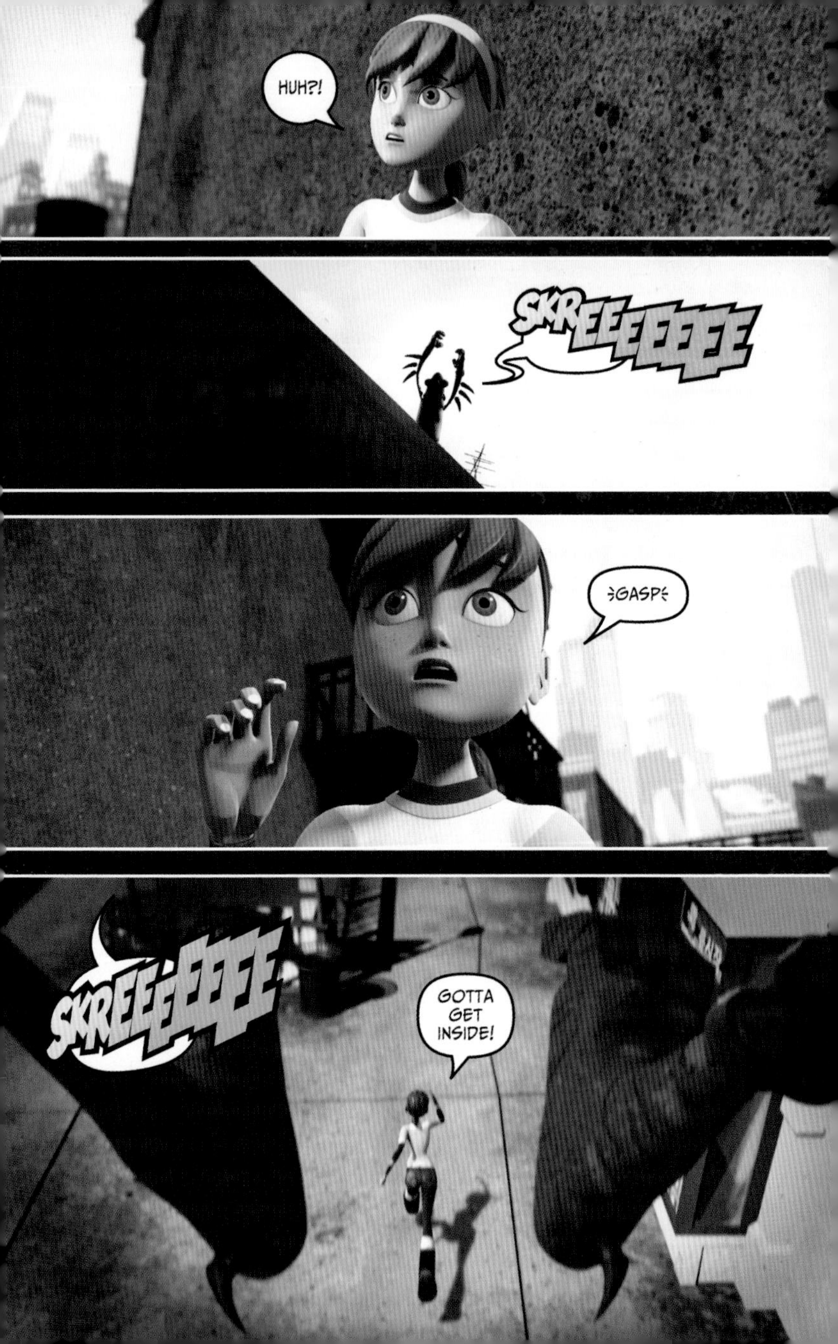
HUH?!
SKREEEEEEEE
GASP
SKREEEEEEEE
GOTTA GET INSIDE!

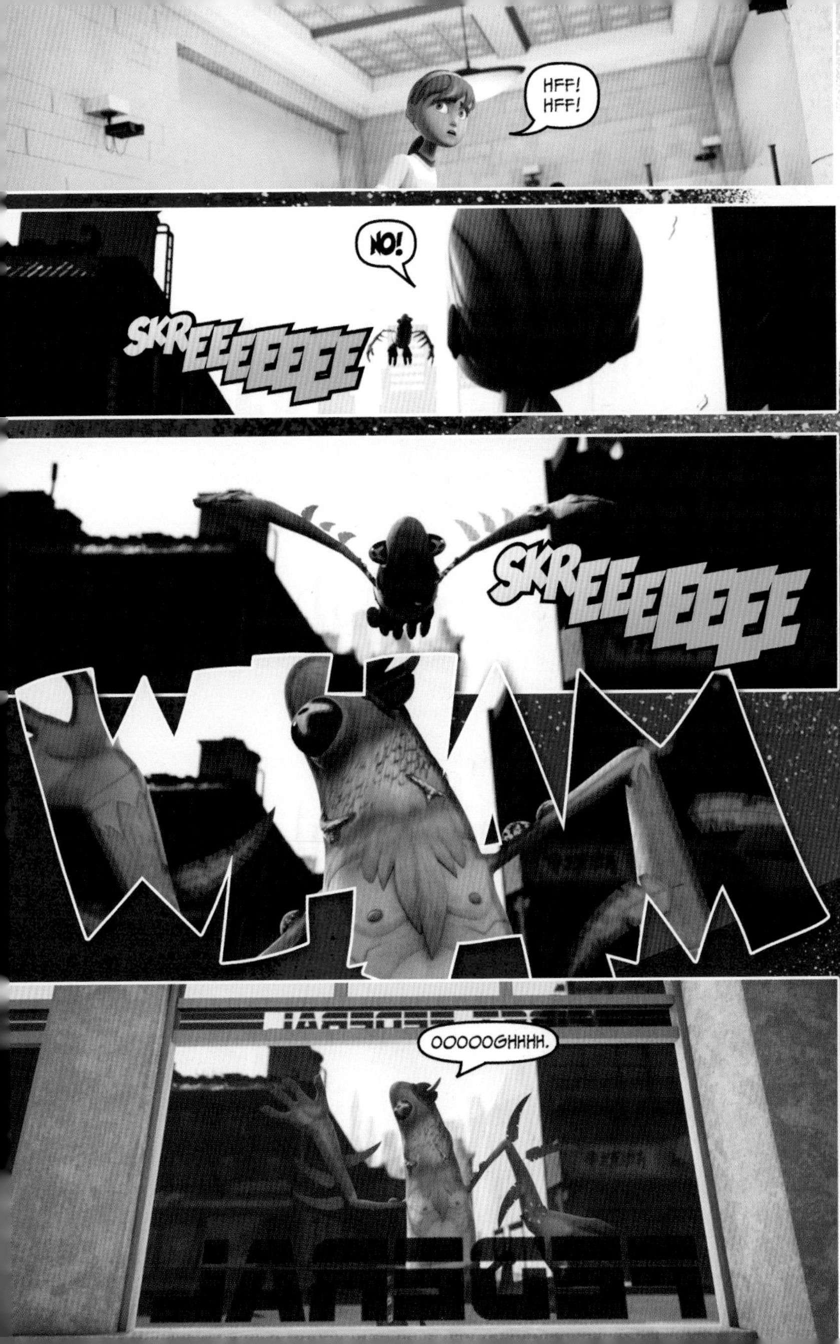
HFF!
HFF!
NO!
SKREEEEEEE
SKREEEEEEE
WHAM
OOOOOGHHHH.

WHOA...
BLINK BLINK
FLAP FLAP FLAP
MY LIFE HAS GOTTEN REALLY WEIRD.

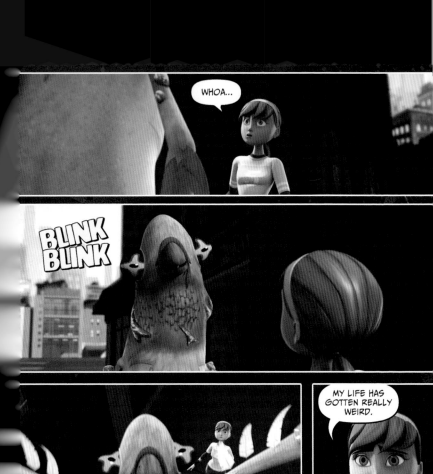

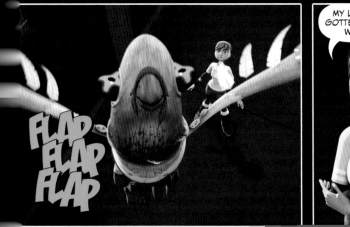

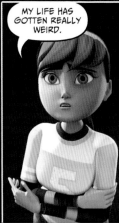

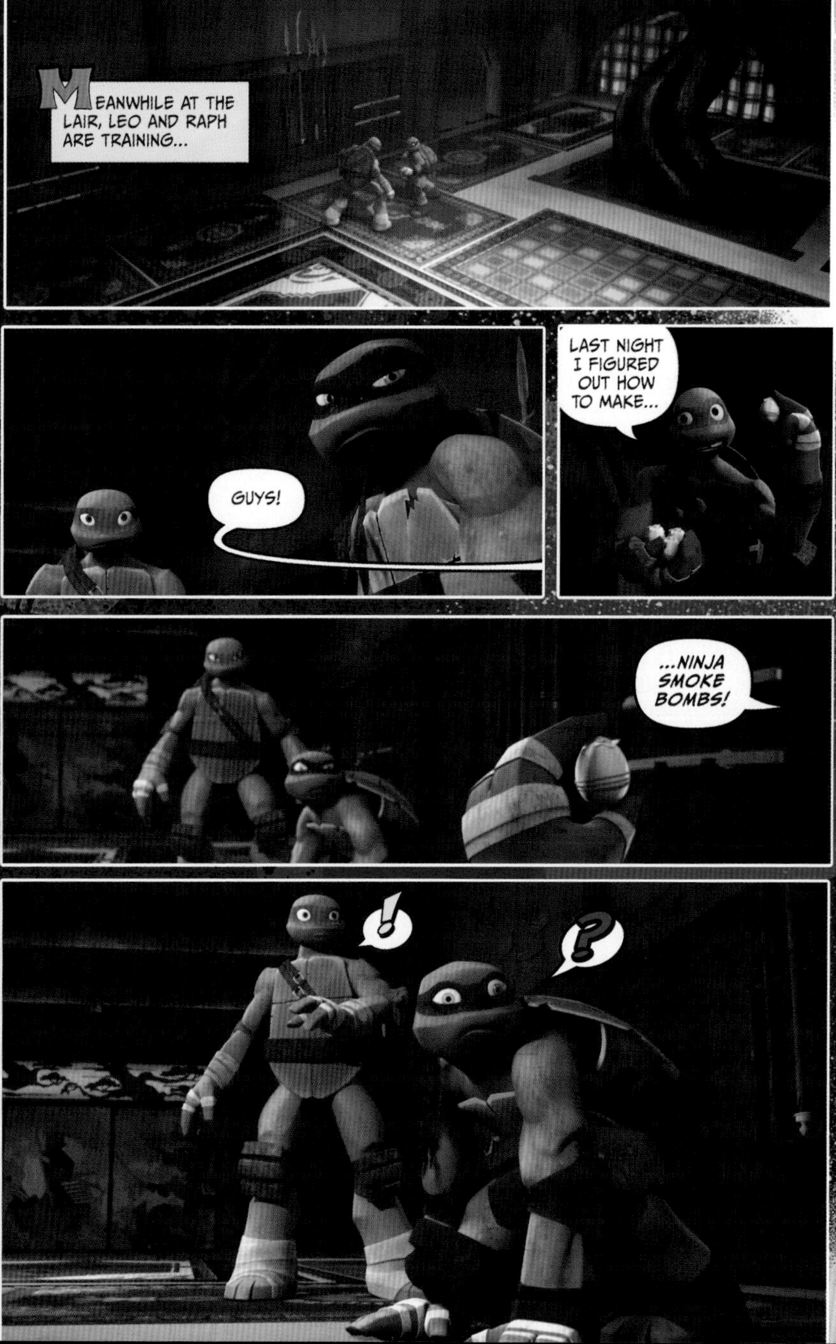
MEANWHILE AT THE LAIR, LEO AND RAPH ARE TRAINING...
GUYS!
LAST NIGHT I FIGURED OUT HOW TO MAKE...
...NINJA SMOKE BOMBS!
!
?

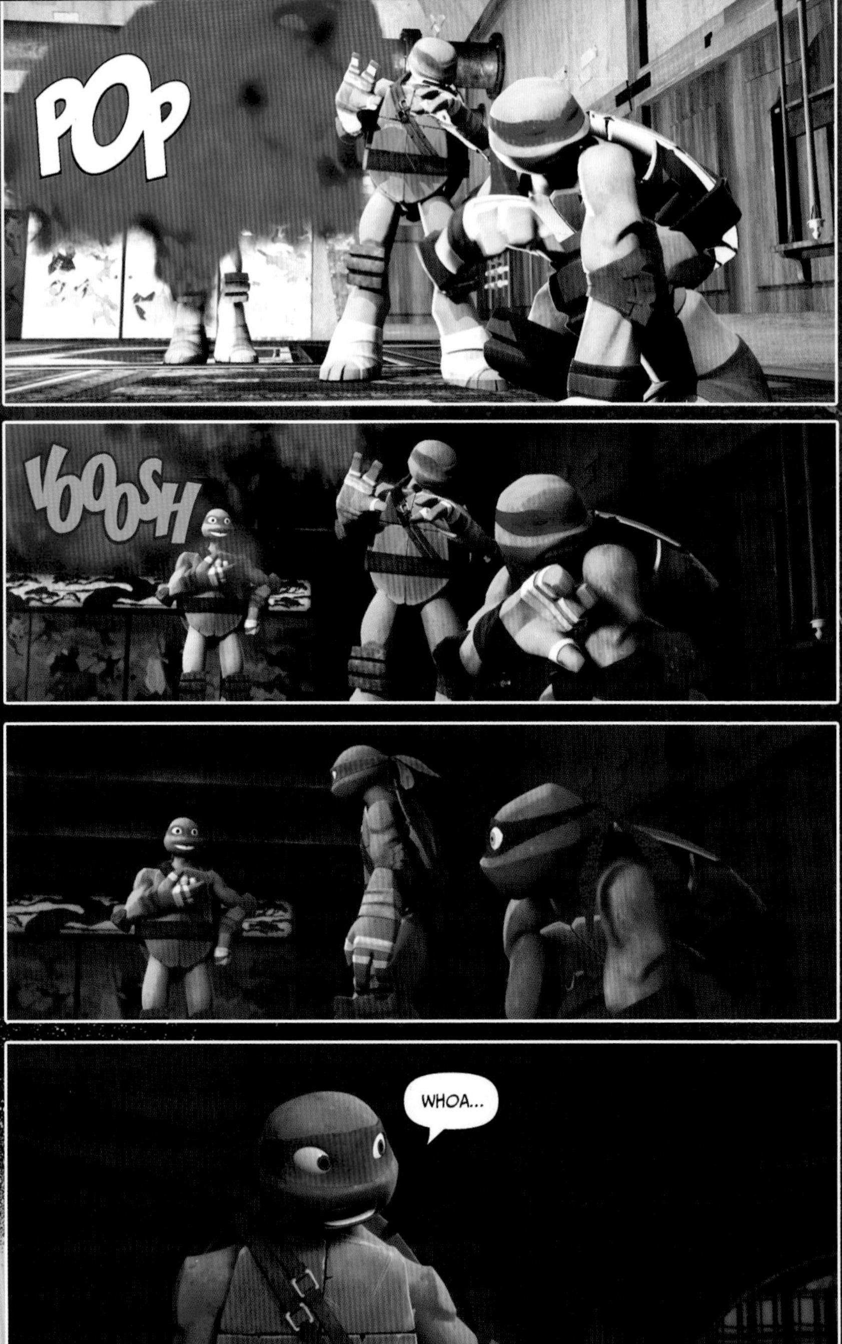
POP
VOOOSH
WHOA...

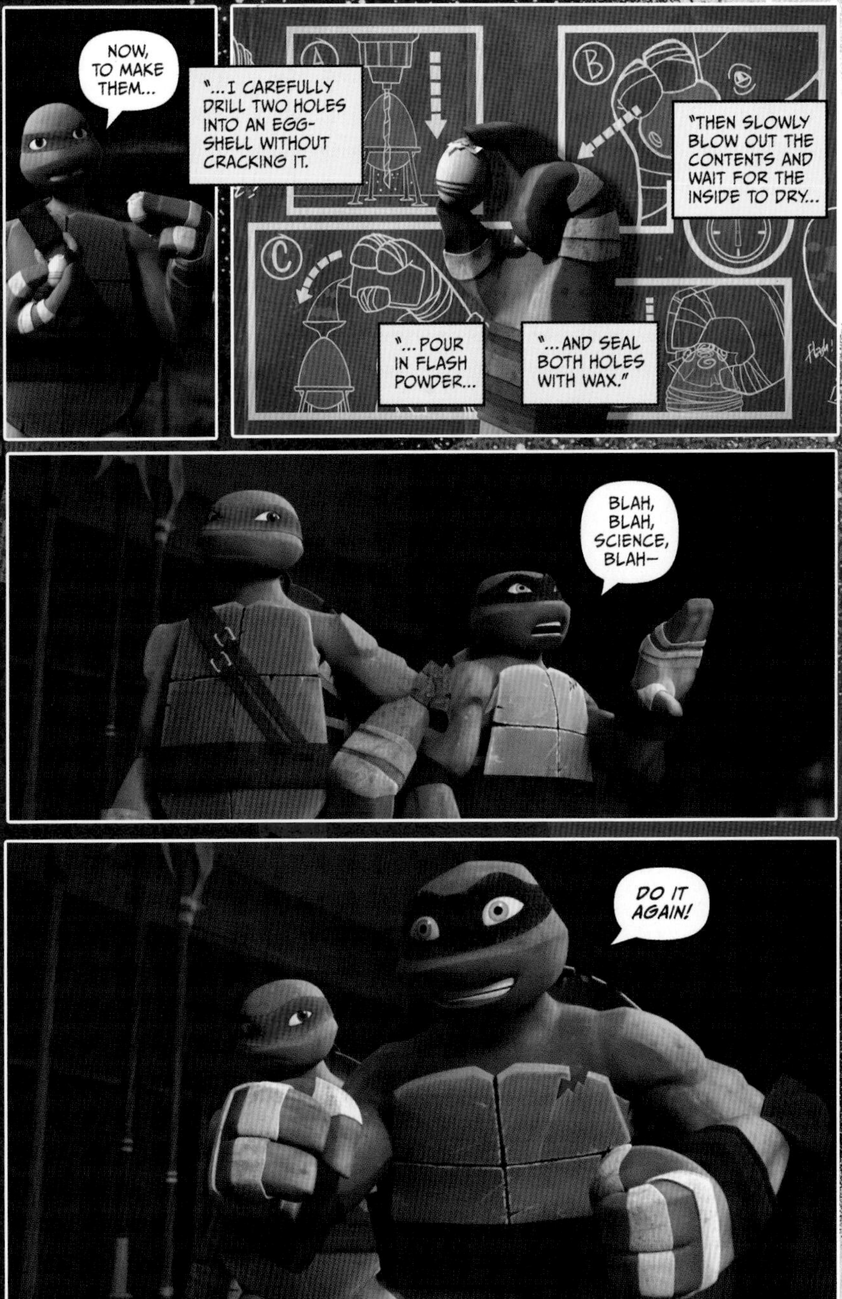
NOW, TO MAKE THEM...
"...I CAREFULLY DRILL TWO HOLES INTO AN EGG-SHELL WITHOUT CRACKING IT.
"THEN SLOWLY BLOW OUT THE CONTENTS AND WAIT FOR THE INSIDE TO DRY...
"...POUR IN FLASH POWDER...
"...AND SEAL BOTH HOLES WITH WAX."
BLAH, BLAH, SCIENCE, BLAH—
DO IT AGAIN!

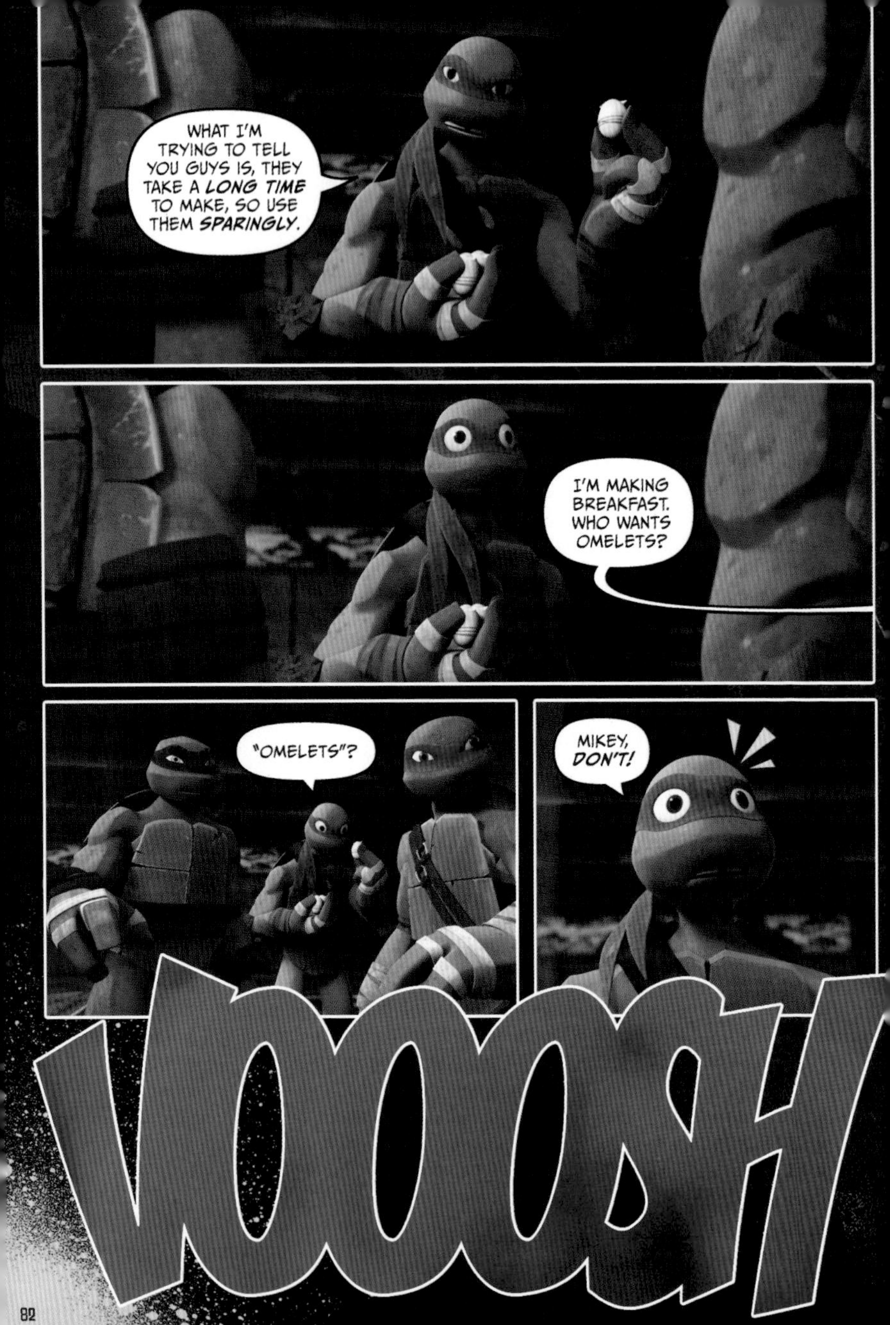
WHAT I'M TRYING TO TELL YOU GUYS IS, THEY TAKE A LONG TIME TO MAKE, SO USE THEM SPARINGLY.
I'M MAKING BREAKFAST. WHO WANTS OMELETS?
"OMELETS"?
MIKEY, DON'T!
VOOOSH

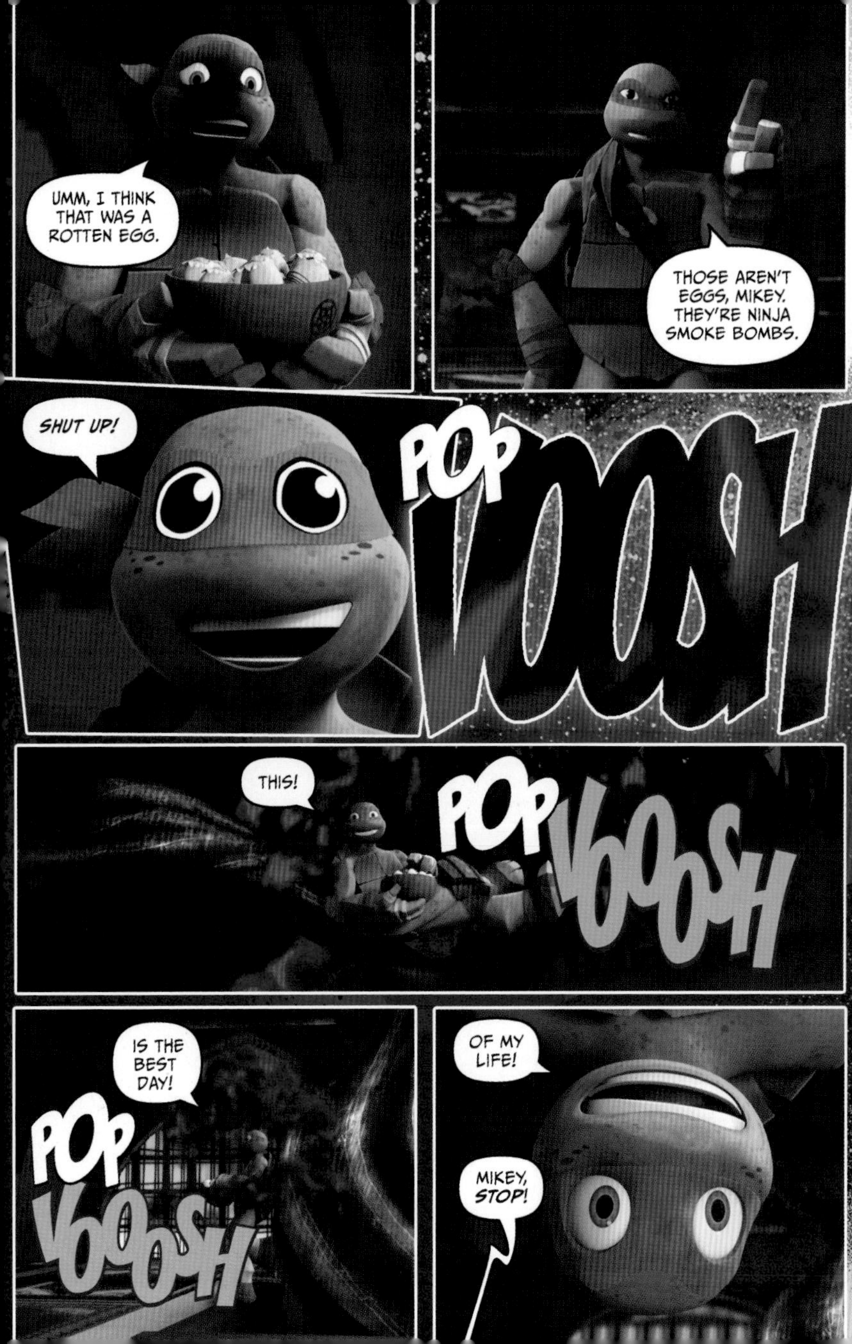
UMM, I THINK THAT WAS A ROTTEN EGG.
THOSE AREN'T EGGS, MIKEY. THEY'RE NINJA SMOKE BOMBS.
SHUT UP!
POP
VOOOSH
THIS!
POP
VOOOSH
IS THE BEST DAY!
POP
VOOOSH
OF MY LIFE!
MIKEY, STOP!

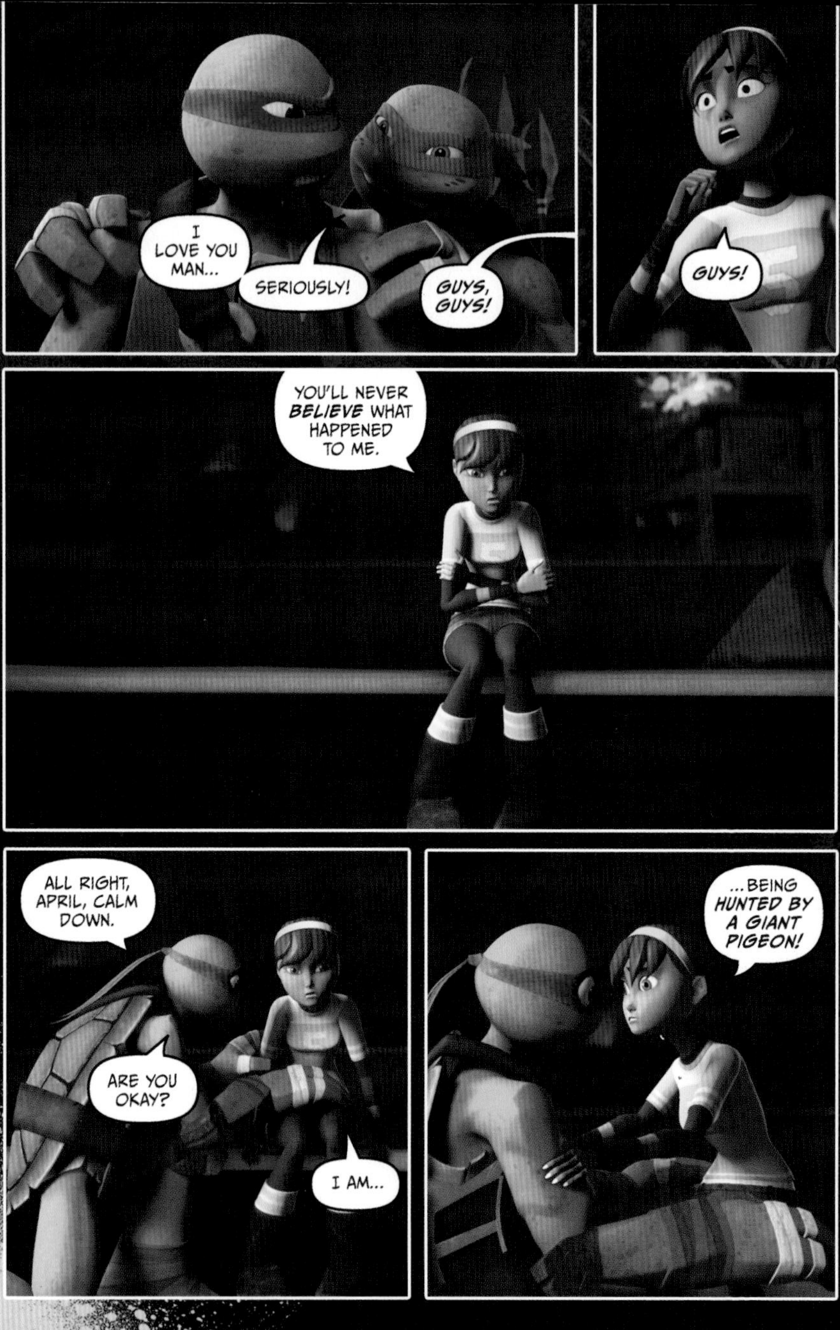
I LOVE YOU MAN...
SERIOUSLY!
GUYS, GUYS!
GUYS!
YOU'LL NEVER BELIEVE WHAT HAPPENED TO ME.
ALL RIGHT, APRIL, CALM DOWN.
ARE YOU OKAY?
I AM...
...BEING HUNTED BY A GIANT PIGEON!

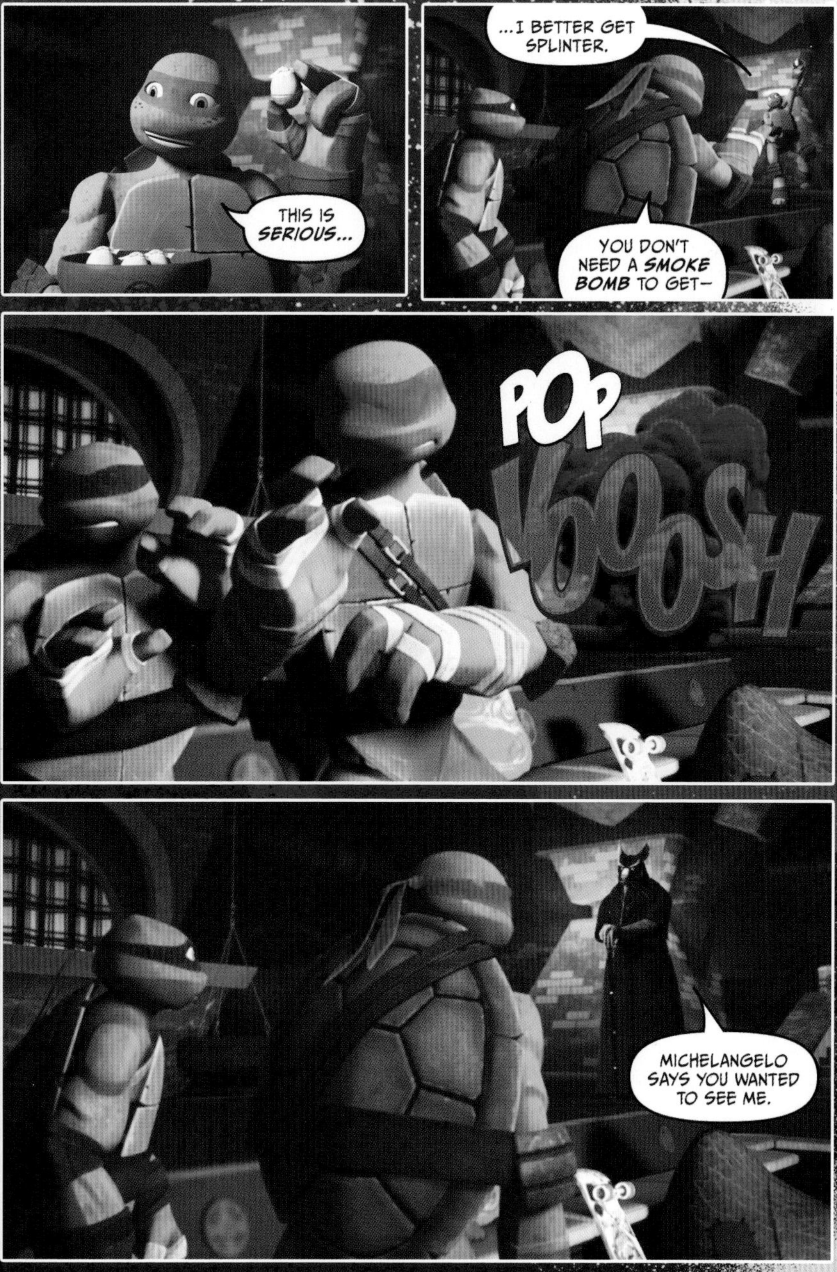
THIS IS SERIOUS...
...I BETTER GET SPLINTER.
YOU DON'T NEED A SMOKE BOMB TO GET—
POP
WOOOSH
MICHELANGELO SAYS YOU WANTED TO SEE ME.

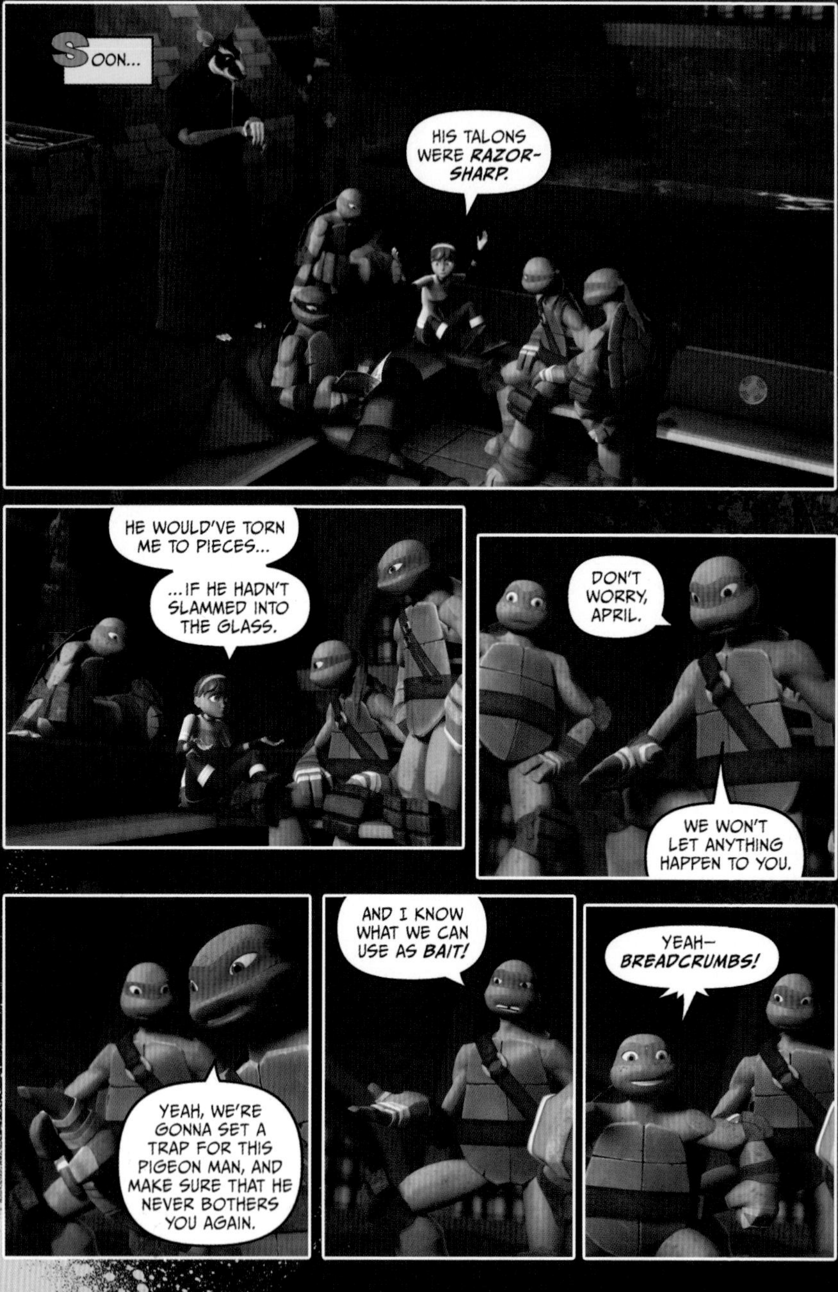
SOON...
HIS TALONS WERE RAZOR-SHARP.
HE WOULD'VE TORN ME TO PIECES...
...IF HE HADN'T SLAMMED INTO THE GLASS.
DON'T WORRY, APRIL.
WE WON'T LET ANYTHING HAPPEN TO YOU.
YEAH, WE'RE GONNA SET A TRAP FOR THIS PIGEON MAN, AND MAKE SURE THAT HE NEVER BOTHERS YOU AGAIN.
AND I KNOW WHAT WE CAN USE AS BAIT!
YEAH— BREADCRUMBS!

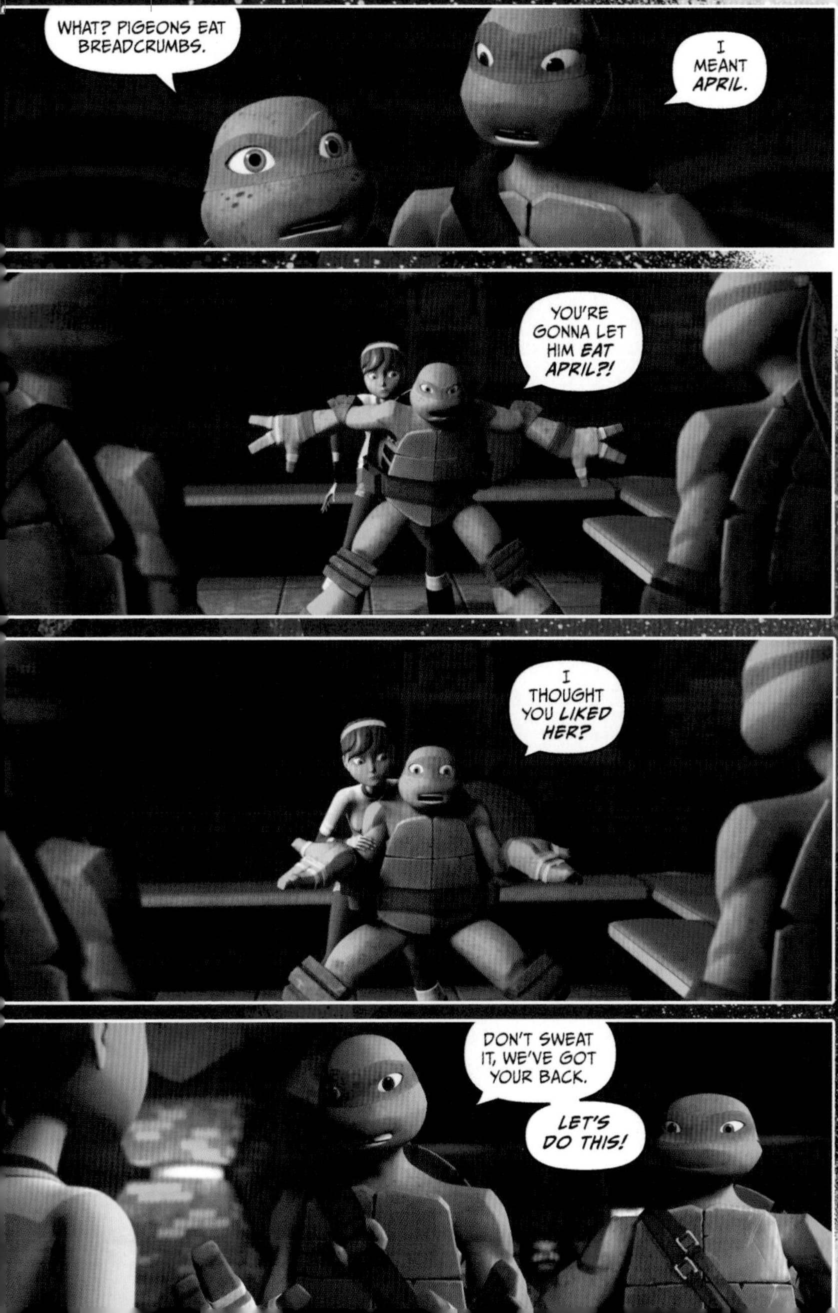
WHAT? PIGEONS EAT BREADCRUMBS.
I MEANT APRIL.
YOU'RE GONNA LET HIM EAT APRIL?!
I THOUGHT YOU LIKED HER?
DON'T SWEAT IT, WE'VE GOT YOUR BACK.
LET'S DO THIS!

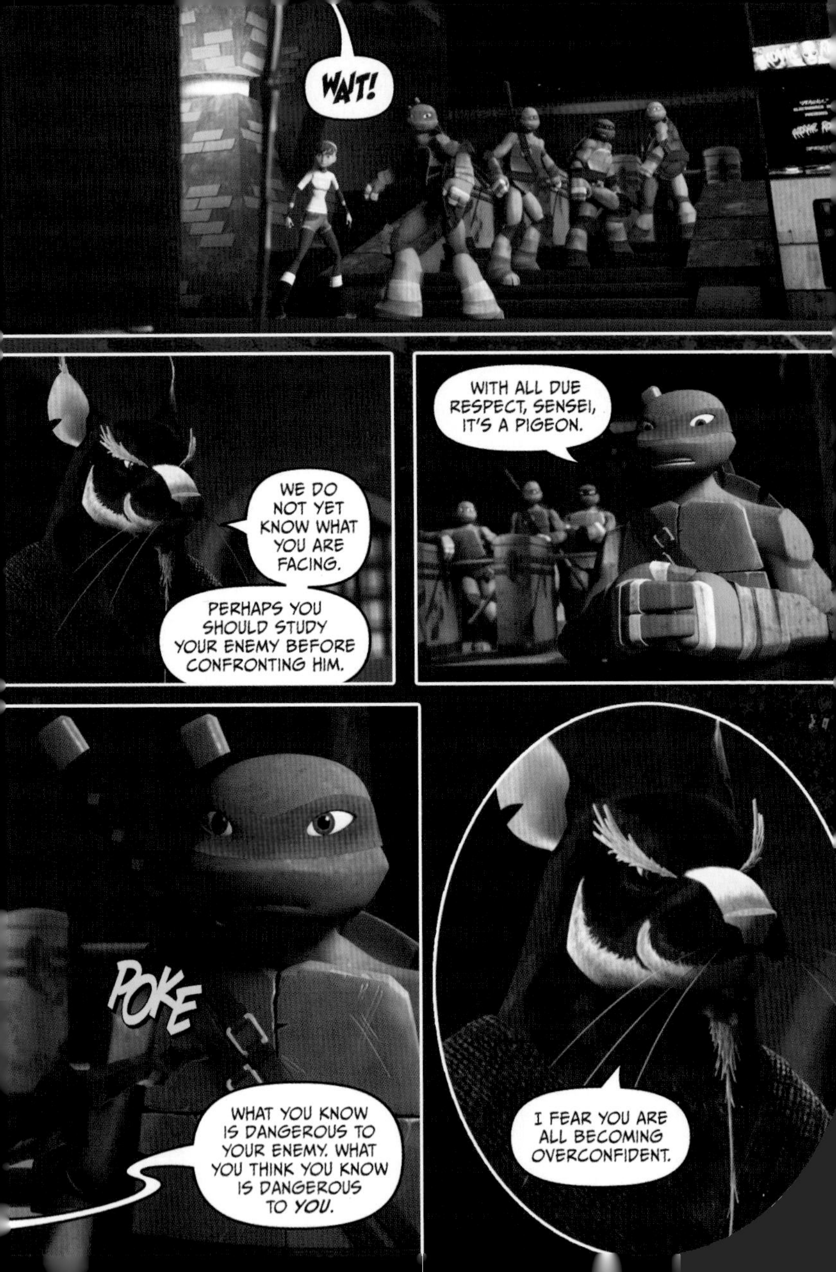
WAIT!
WE DO NOT YET KNOW WHAT YOU ARE FACING.
PERHAPS YOU SHOULD STUDY YOUR ENEMY BEFORE CONFRONTING HIM.
WITH ALL DUE RESPECT, SENSEI, IT'S A PIGEON.
POKE
WHAT YOU KNOW IS DANGEROUS TO YOUR ENEMY. WHAT YOU THINK YOU KNOW IS DANGEROUS TO YOU.
I FEAR YOU ARE ALL BECOMING OVERCONFIDENT.

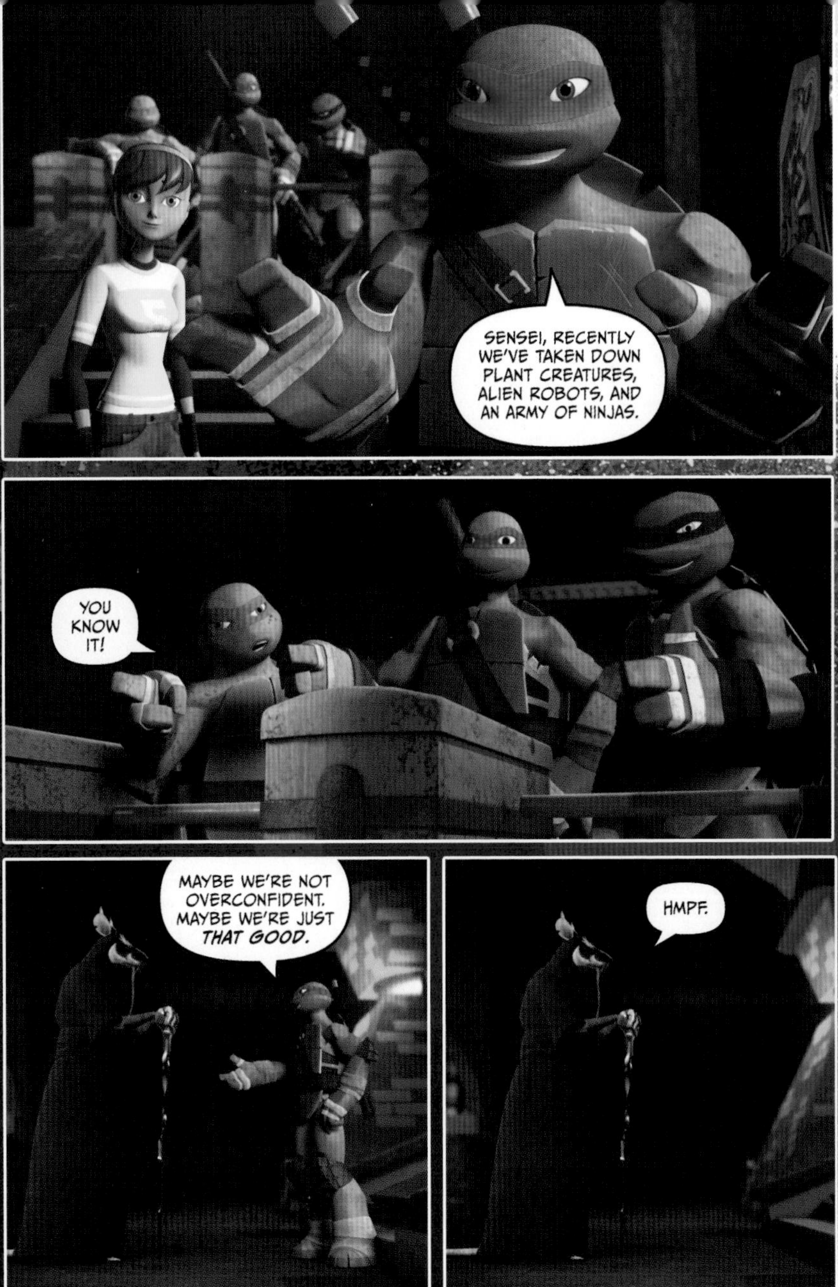
SENSEI, RECENTLY WE'VE TAKEN DOWN PLANT CREATURES, ALIEN ROBOTS, AND AN ARMY OF NINJAS.
YOU KNOW IT!
MAYBE WE'RE NOT OVERCONFIDENT. MAYBE WE'RE JUST *THAT GOOD*.
HMPF.

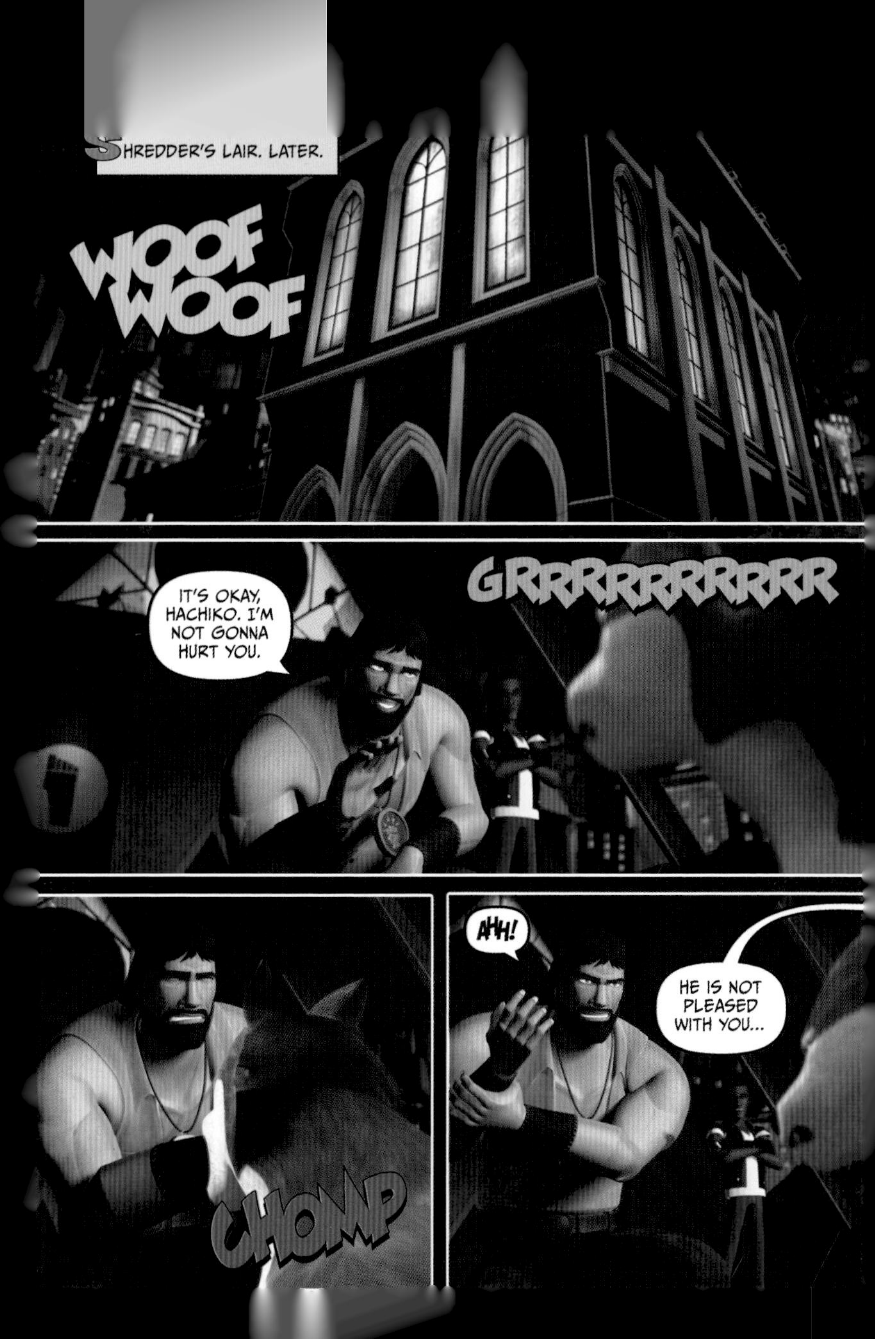
SHREDDER'S LAIR. LATER.
WOOF WOOF
IT'S OKAY, HACHIKO. I'M NOT GONNA HURT YOU.
GRRRRRRRRRRR
CHOMP
AHH!
HE IS NOT PLEASED WITH YOU...

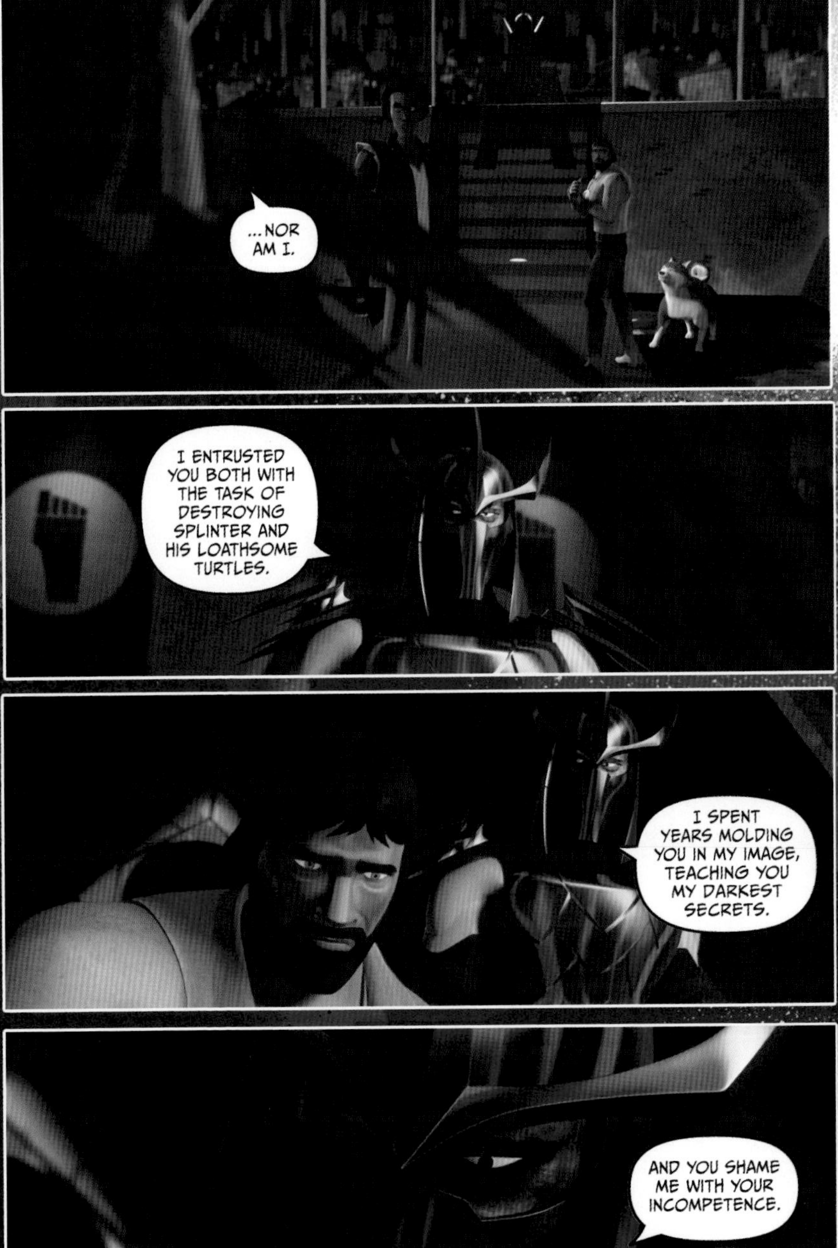
...NOR AM I.
I ENTRUSTED YOU BOTH WITH THE TASK OF DESTROYING SPLINTER AND HIS LOATHSOME TURTLES.
I SPENT YEARS MOLDING YOU IN MY IMAGE, TEACHING YOU MY DARKEST SECRETS.
AND YOU SHAME ME WITH YOUR INCOMPETENCE.

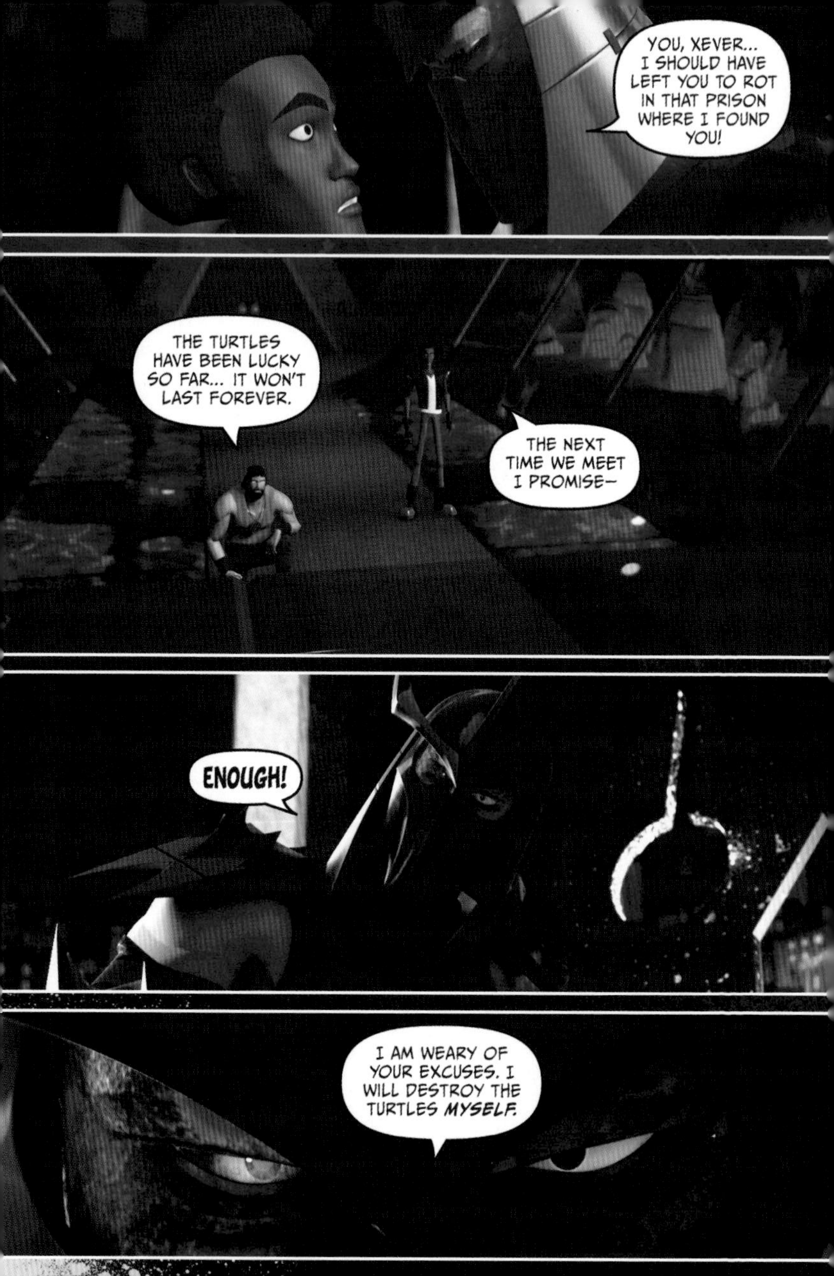
YOU, XEVER... I SHOULD HAVE LEFT YOU TO ROT IN THAT PRISON WHERE I FOUND YOU!
THE TURTLES HAVE BEEN LUCKY SO FAR... IT WON'T LAST FOREVER.
THE NEXT TIME WE MEET I PROMISE–
ENOUGH!
I AM WEARY OF YOUR EXCUSES. I WILL DESTROY THE TURTLES *MYSELF*.

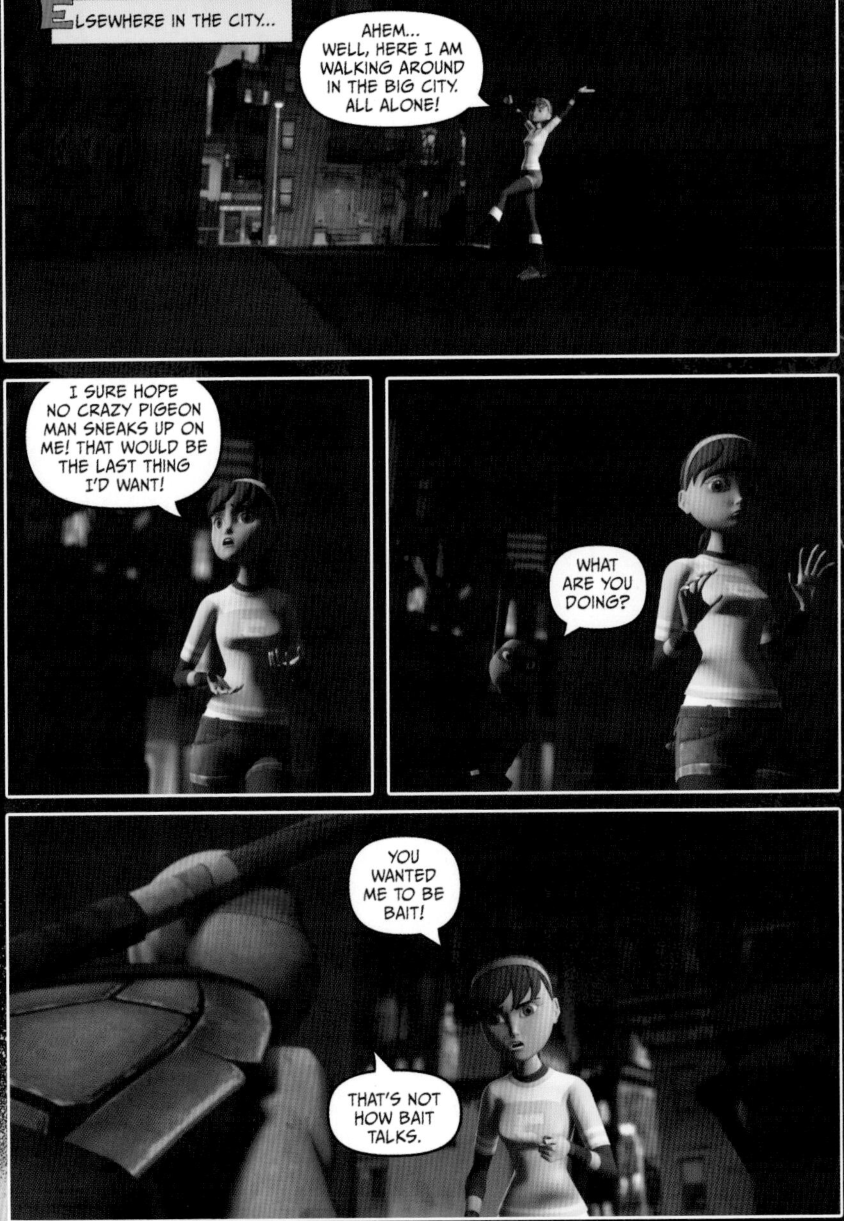
ELSEWHERE IN THE CITY...
AHEM... WELL, HERE I AM WALKING AROUND IN THE BIG CITY. ALL ALONE!
I SURE HOPE NO CRAZY PIGEON MAN SNEAKS UP ON ME! THAT WOULD BE THE LAST THING I'D WANT!
WHAT ARE YOU DOING?
YOU WANTED ME TO BE BAIT!
THAT'S NOT HOW BAIT TALKS.

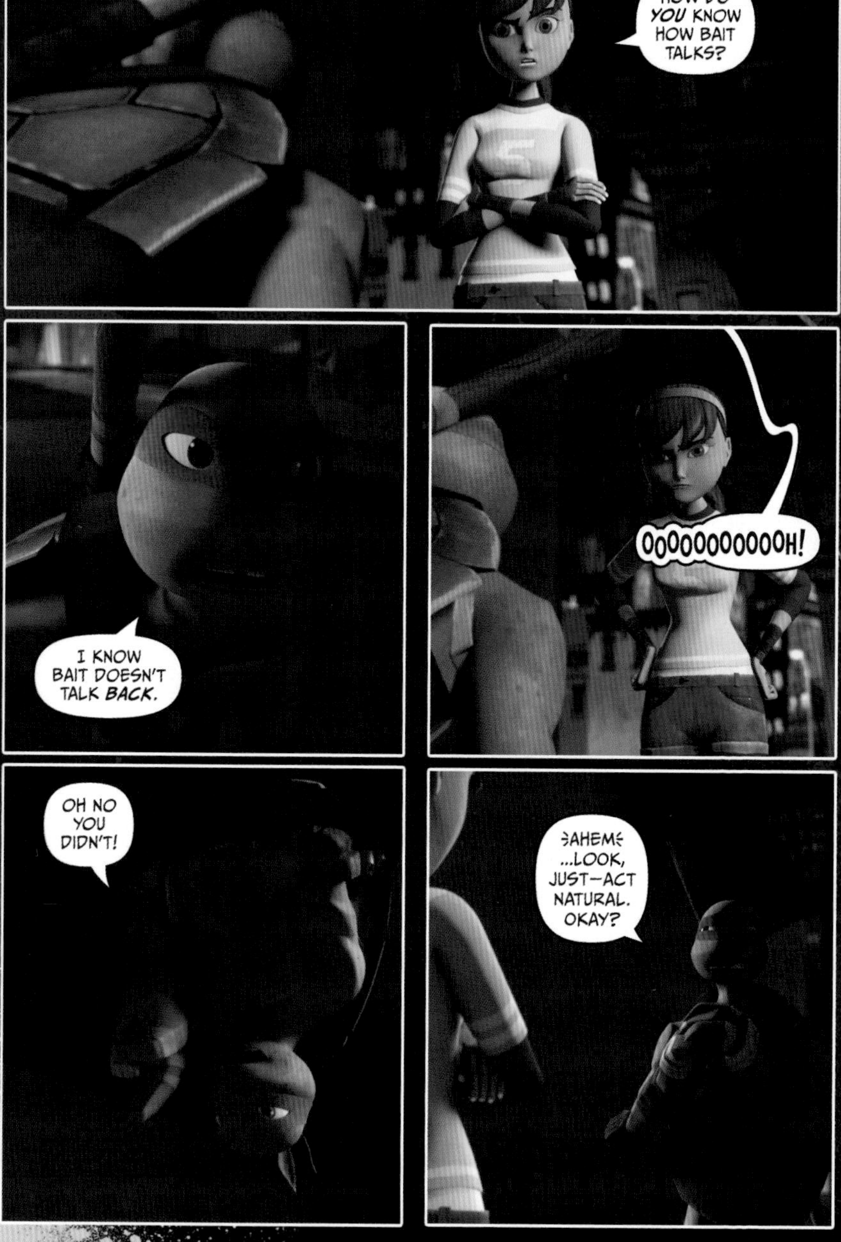
YOU KNOW HOW BAIT TALKS?
I KNOW BAIT DOESN'T TALK *BACK*.
OOOOOOOOOOOH!
OH NO YOU DIDN'T!
AHEM ...LOOK, JUST—ACT NATURAL. OKAY?

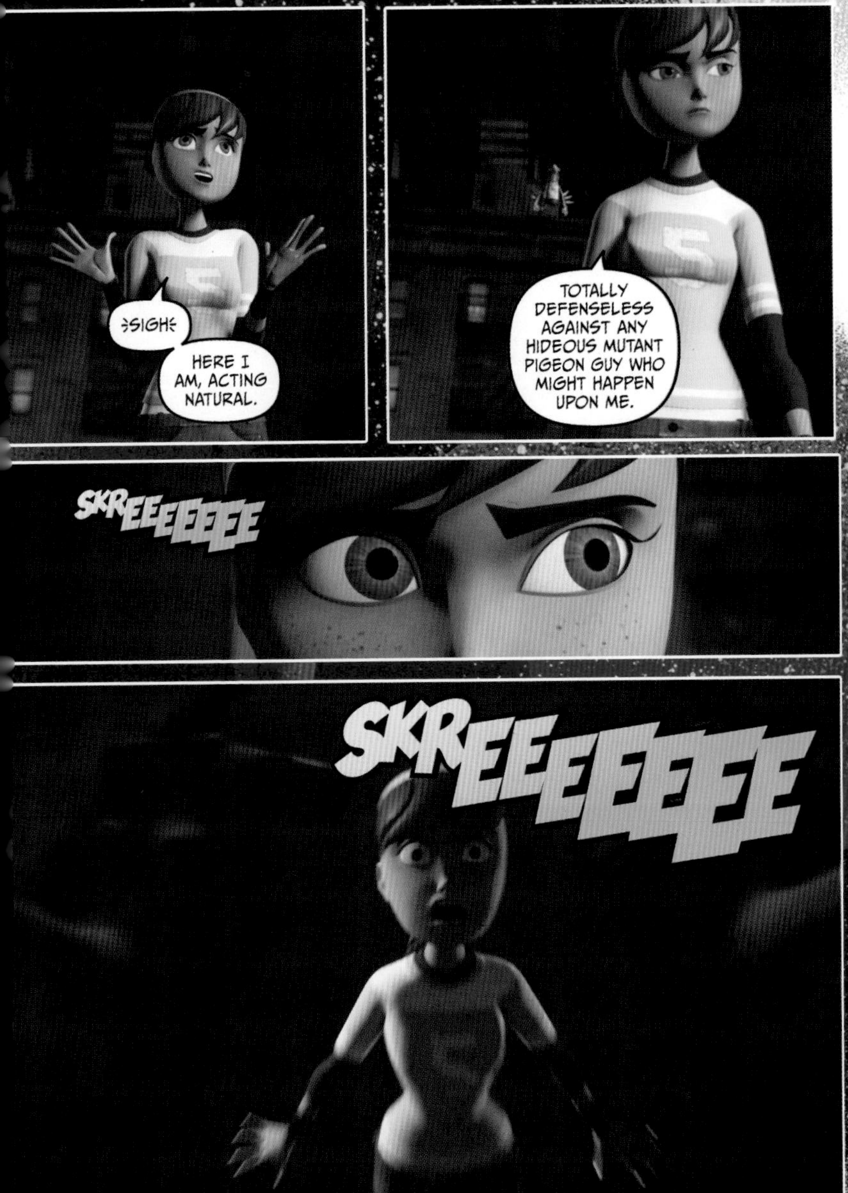

SIGH
HERE I AM, ACTING NATURAL.
TOTALLY DEFENSELESS AGAINST ANY HIDEOUS MUTANT PIGEON GUY WHO MIGHT HAPPEN UPON ME.
SKREEEEEEE
SKREEEEEEEE

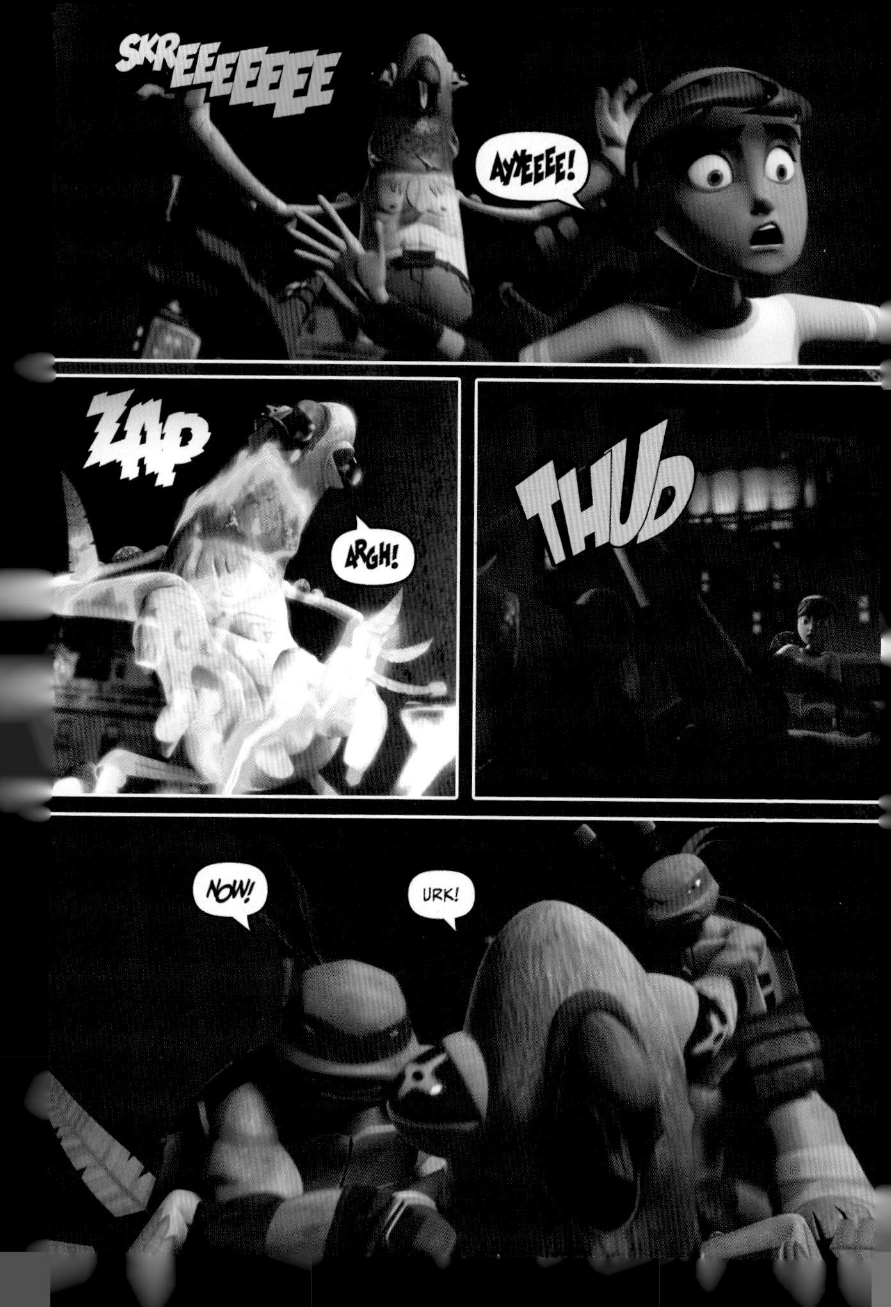
SKREEEEEEEE
AYEEEE!
ZAP
ARGH!
THUD
NOW!
URK!

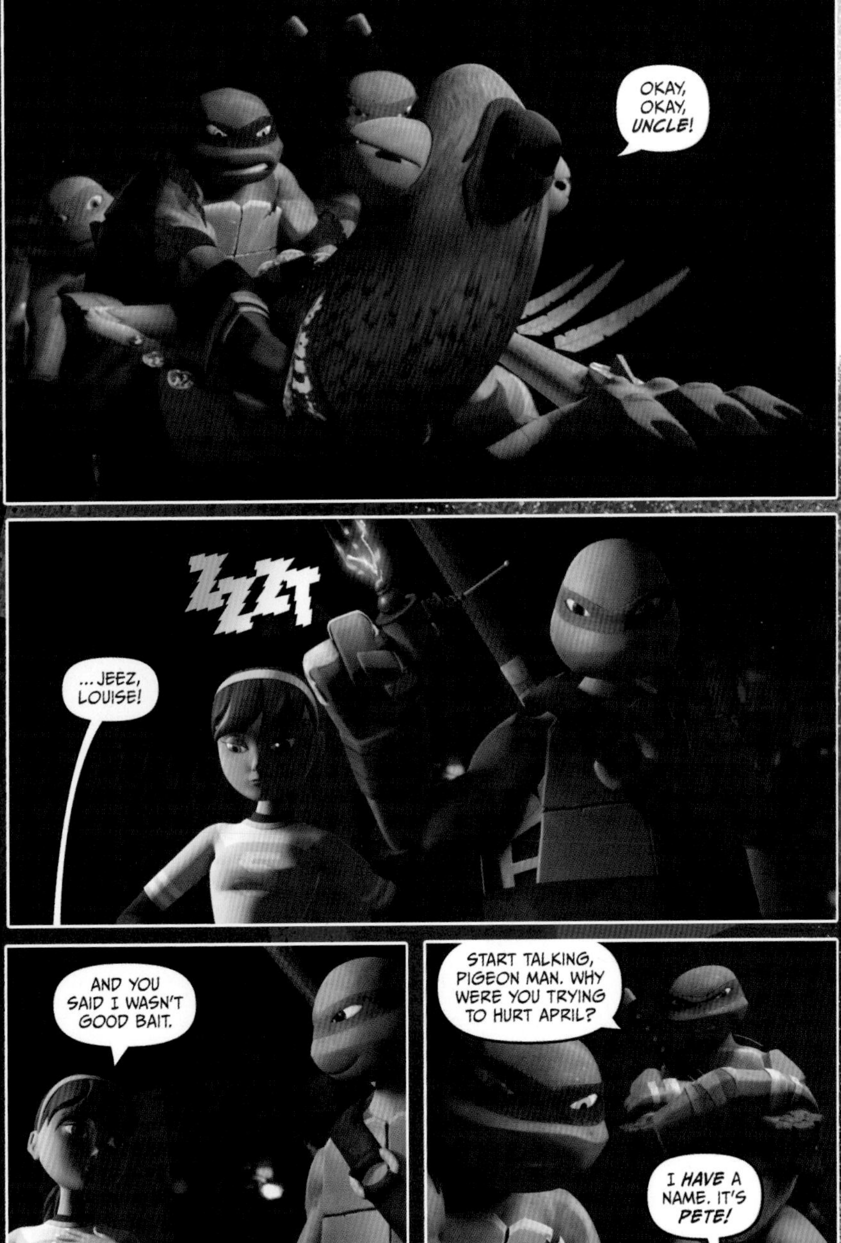
OKAY, OKAY, UNCLE!
ZZZZT
...JEEZ, LOUISE!
AND YOU SAID I WASN'T GOOD BAIT.
START TALKING, PIGEON MAN. WHY WERE YOU TRYING TO HURT APRIL?
I HAVE A NAME. IT'S PETE!

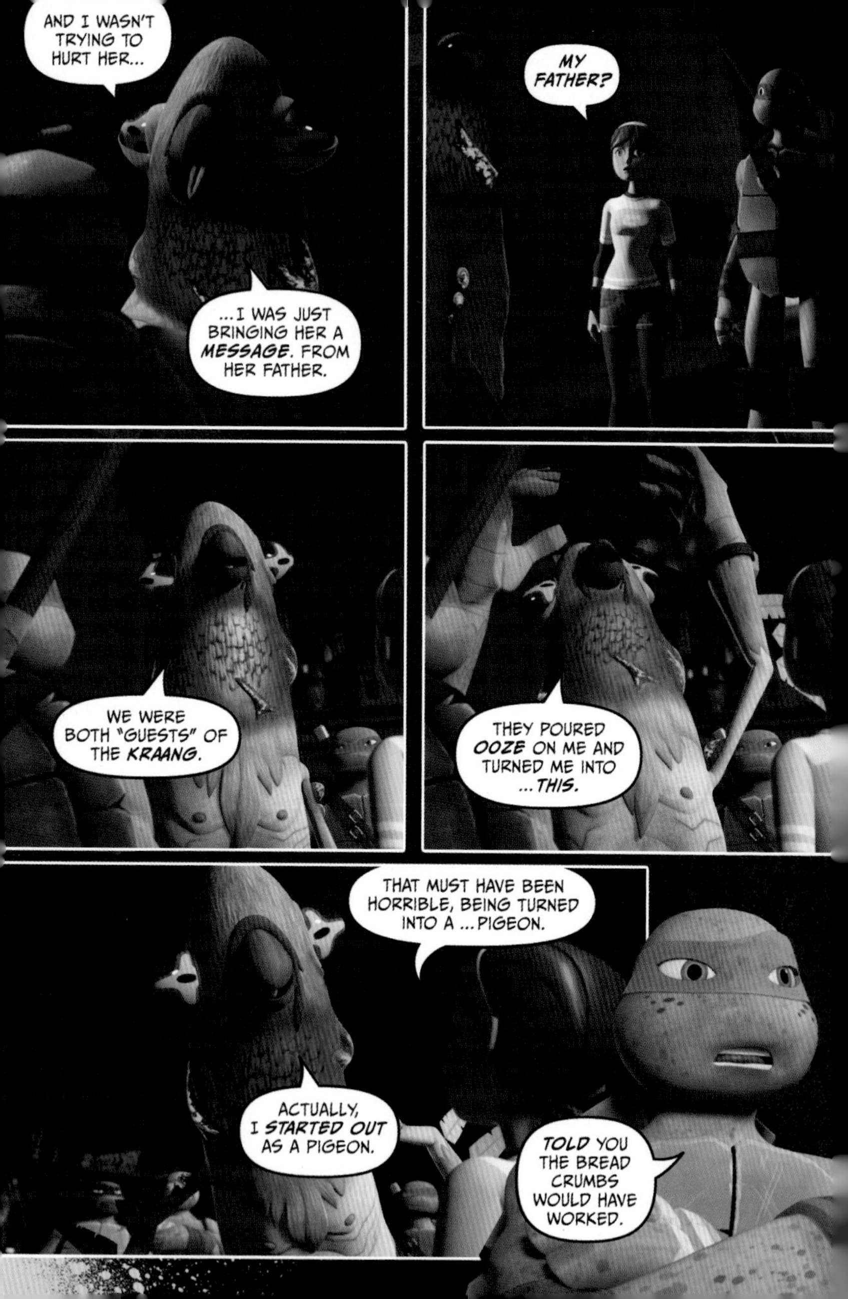
AND I WASN'T TRYING TO HURT HER...
...I WAS JUST BRINGING HER A MESSAGE. FROM HER FATHER.
MY FATHER?
WE WERE BOTH "GUESTS" OF THE KRAANG.
THEY POURED OOZE ON ME AND TURNED ME INTO ...THIS.
THAT MUST HAVE BEEN HORRIBLE, BEING TURNED INTO A ...PIGEON.
ACTUALLY, I STARTED OUT AS A PIGEON.
TOLD YOU THE BREAD CRUMBS WOULD HAVE WORKED.

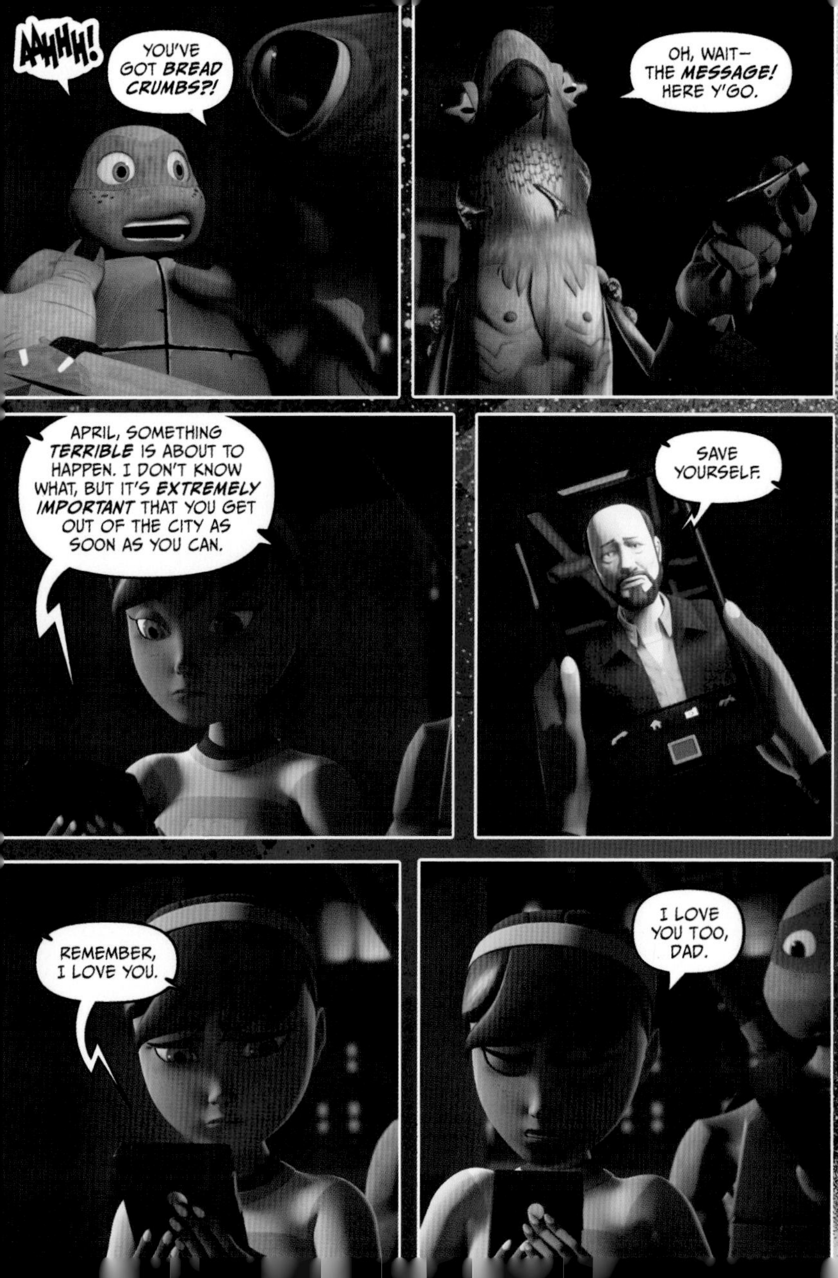
AAHHH!
YOU'VE GOT BREAD CRUMBS?!
OH, WAIT— THE MESSAGE! HERE Y'GO.
APRIL, SOMETHING TERRIBLE IS ABOUT TO HAPPEN. I DON'T KNOW WHAT, BUT IT'S EXTREMELY IMPORTANT THAT YOU GET OUT OF THE CITY AS SOON AS YOU CAN.
SAVE YOURSELF.
REMEMBER, I LOVE YOU.
I LOVE YOU TOO, DAD.

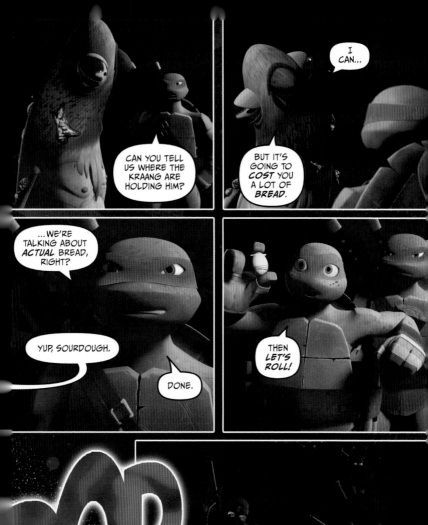

CAN YOU TELL US WHERE THE KRAANG ARE HOLDING HIM?

I CAN...

BUT IT'S GOING TO *COST* YOU A LOT OF *BREAD*.

...WE'RE TALKING ABOUT *ACTUAL* BREAD, RIGHT?

YUP, SOURDOUGH.

DONE.

THEN *LET'S ROLL!*

POP

BUT SHREDDER'S NINJA ARE WATCHING...

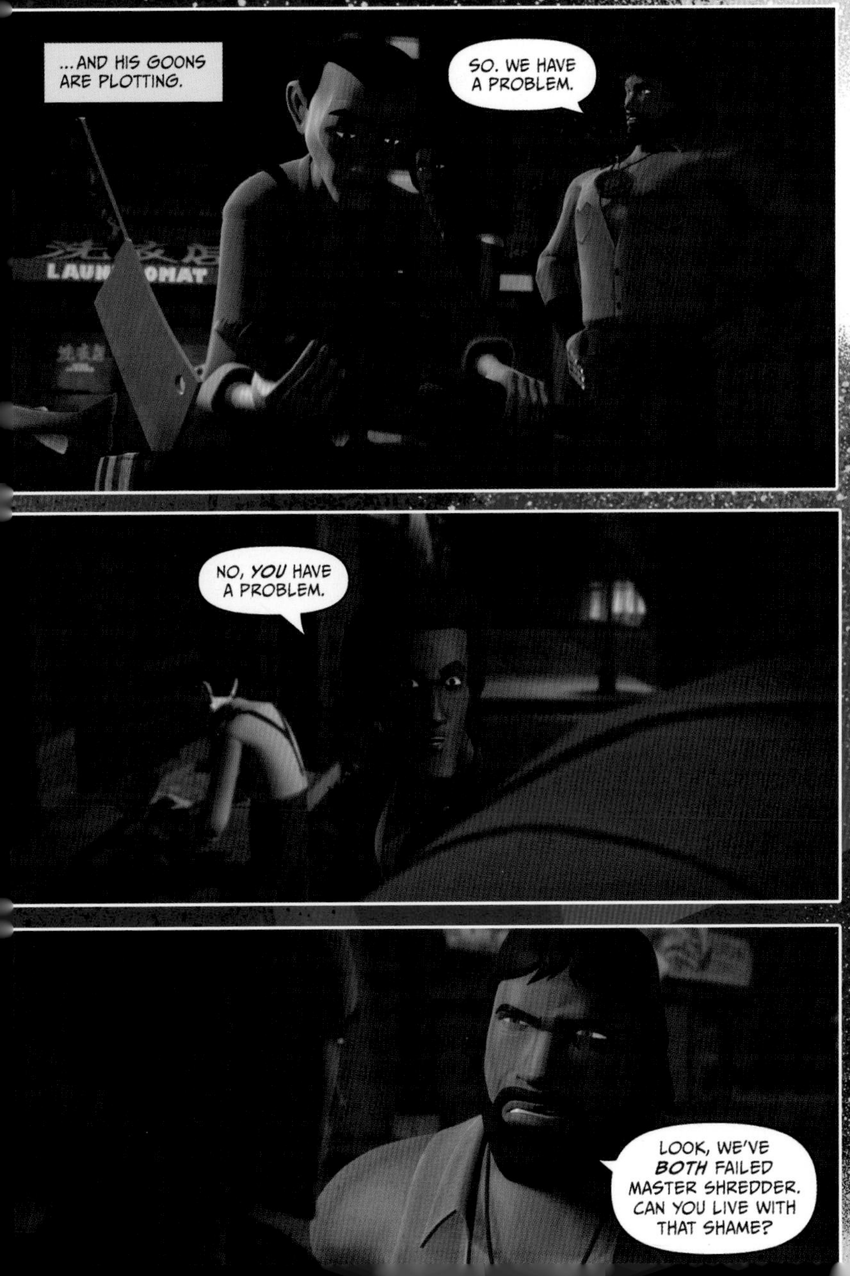
...AND HIS GOONS ARE PLOTTING.
SO. WE HAVE A PROBLEM.
LAUN OMAT
NO, *YOU* HAVE A PROBLEM.
LOOK, WE'VE *BOTH* FAILED MASTER SHREDDER. CAN YOU LIVE WITH THAT SHAME?

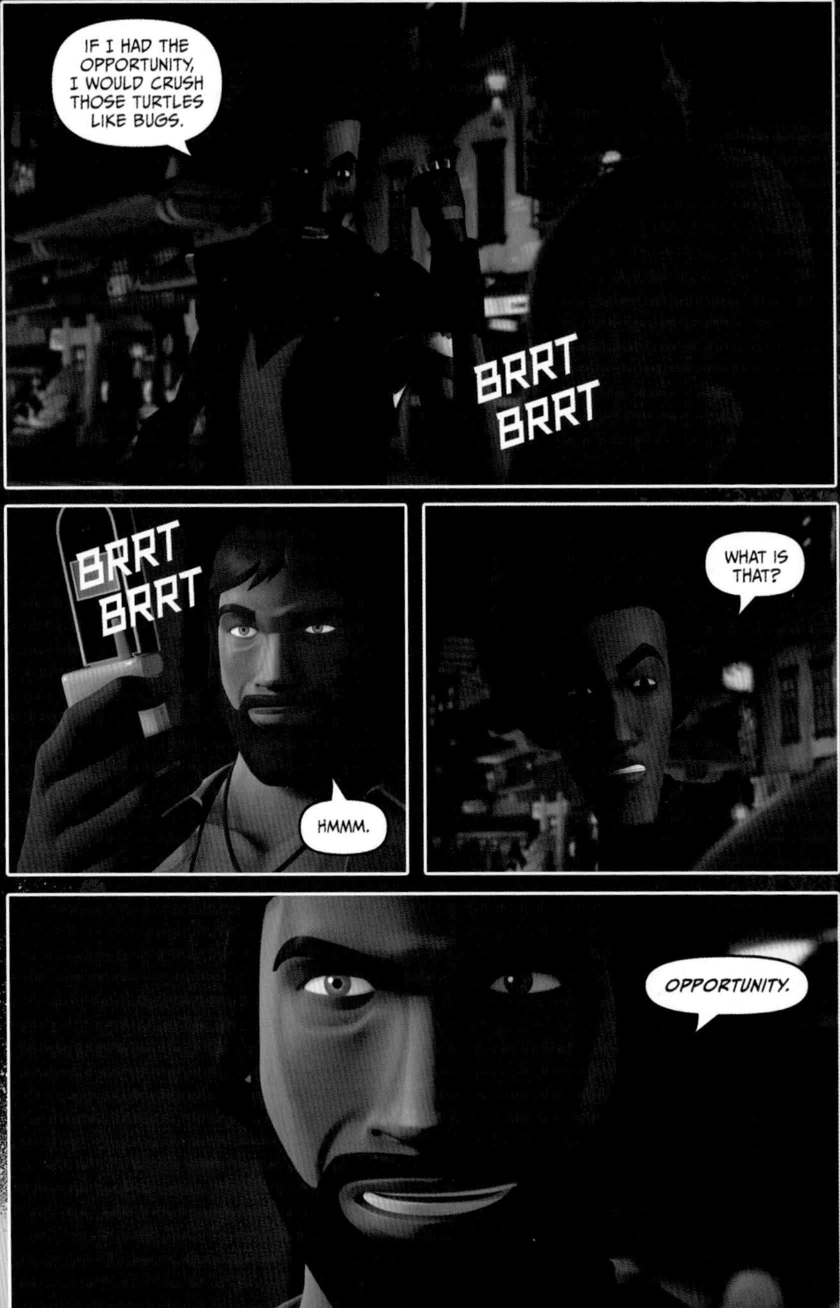
IF I HAD THE OPPORTUNITY, I WOULD CRUSH THOSE TURTLES LIKE BUGS.
BRRT BRRT
BRRT BRRT
HMMM.
WHAT IS THAT?
OPPORTUNITY.

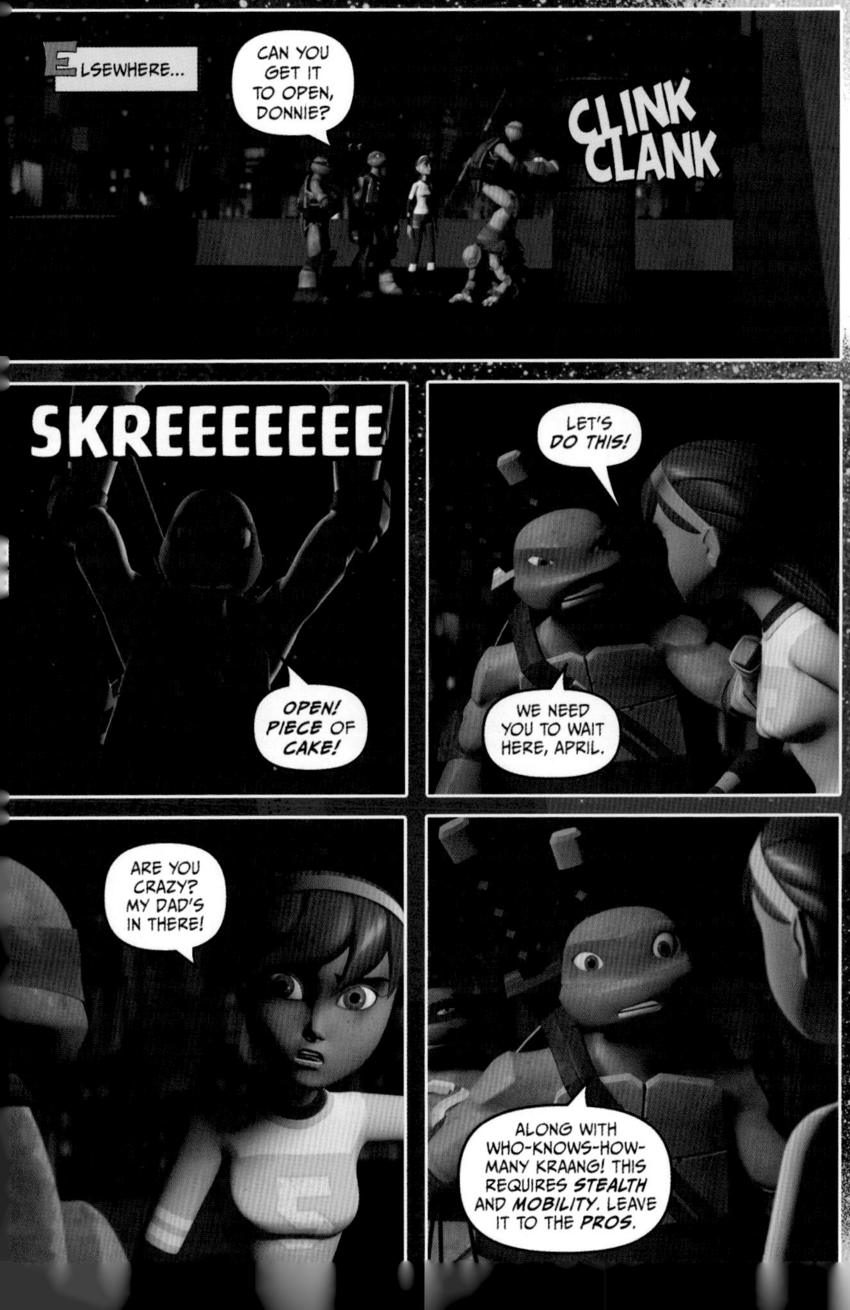
ELSEWHERE...
CAN YOU GET IT TO OPEN, DONNIE?
CLINK CLANK
SKREEEEEEEE
OPEN! PIECE OF CAKE!
LET'S DO THIS!
WE NEED YOU TO WAIT HERE, APRIL.
ARE YOU CRAZY? MY DAD'S IN THERE!
ALONG WITH WHO-KNOWS-HOW-MANY KRAANG! THIS REQUIRES STEALTH AND MOBILITY. LEAVE IT TO THE PROS.

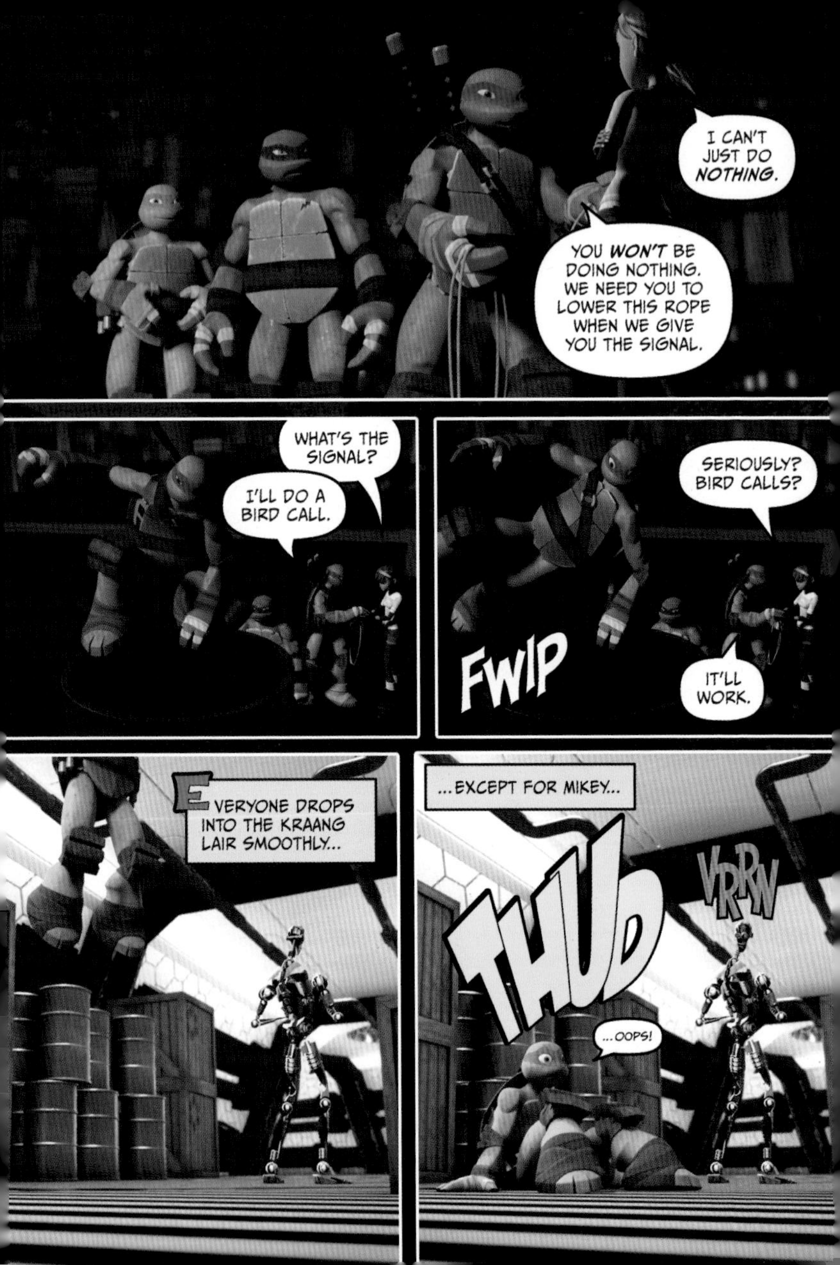
I CAN'T JUST DO *NOTHING*.
YOU *WON'T* BE DOING NOTHING. WE NEED YOU TO LOWER THIS ROPE WHEN WE GIVE YOU THE SIGNAL.
WHAT'S THE SIGNAL?
I'LL DO A BIRD CALL.
SERIOUSLY? BIRD CALLS?
FWIP
IT'LL WORK.
EVERYONE DROPS INTO THE KRAANG LAIR SMOOTHLY...
...EXCEPT FOR MIKEY...
THUD
VRRN
...OOPS!

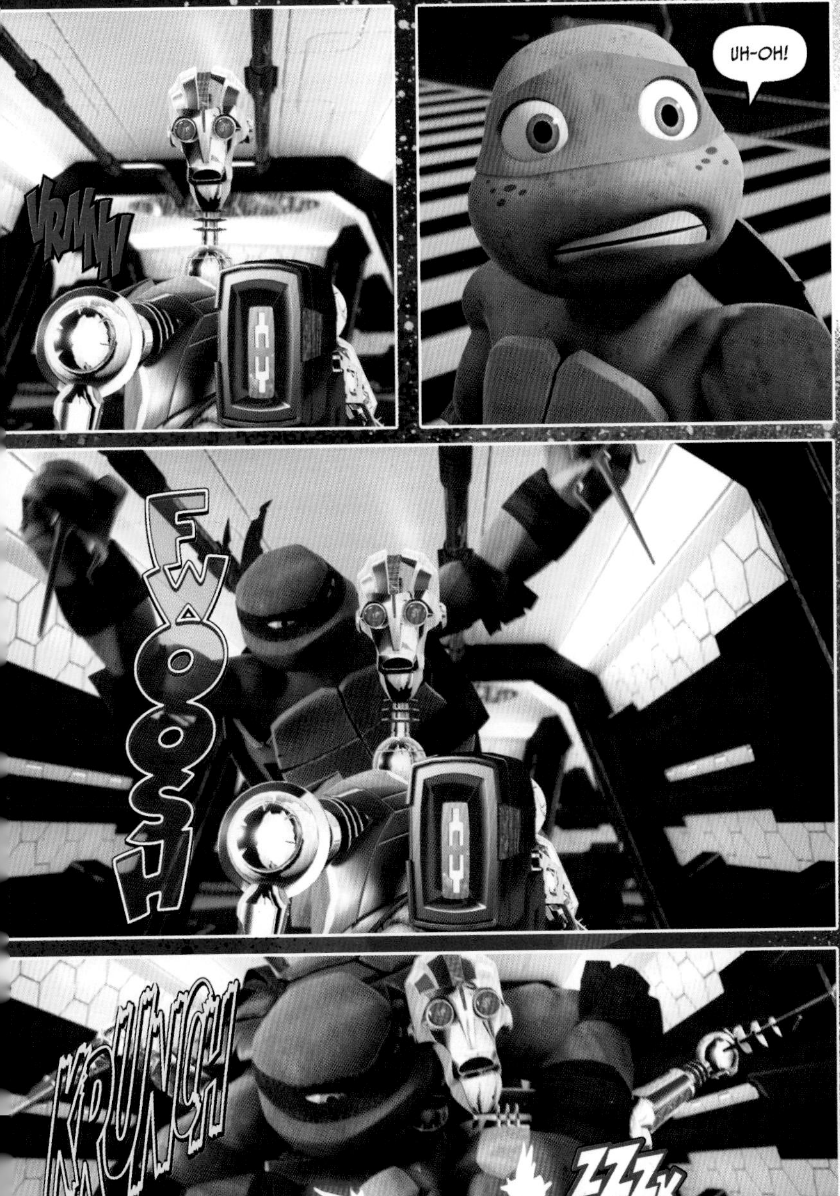
VRMMM
UH-OH!
FWOOSH
KRUNCH
ZZZK

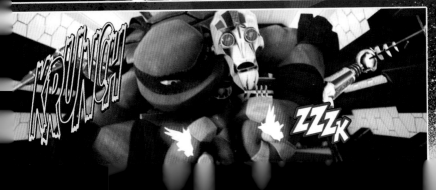

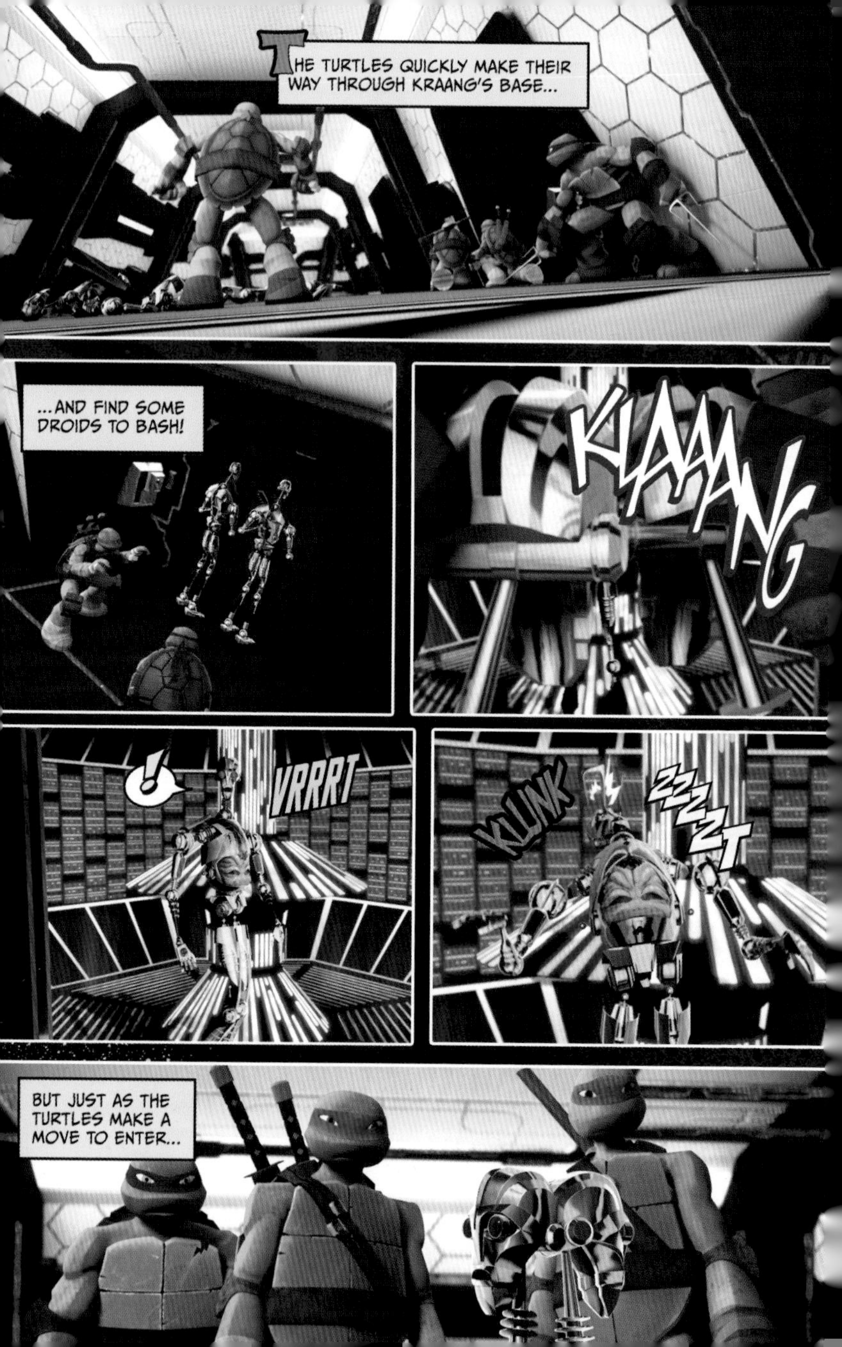
THE TURTLES QUICKLY MAKE THEIR WAY THROUGH KRAANG'S BASE...
...AND FIND SOME DROIDS TO BASH!
KLAAAANG
!
VRRRT
KLUNK
ZZZZT
BUT JUST AS THE TURTLES MAKE A MOVE TO ENTER...

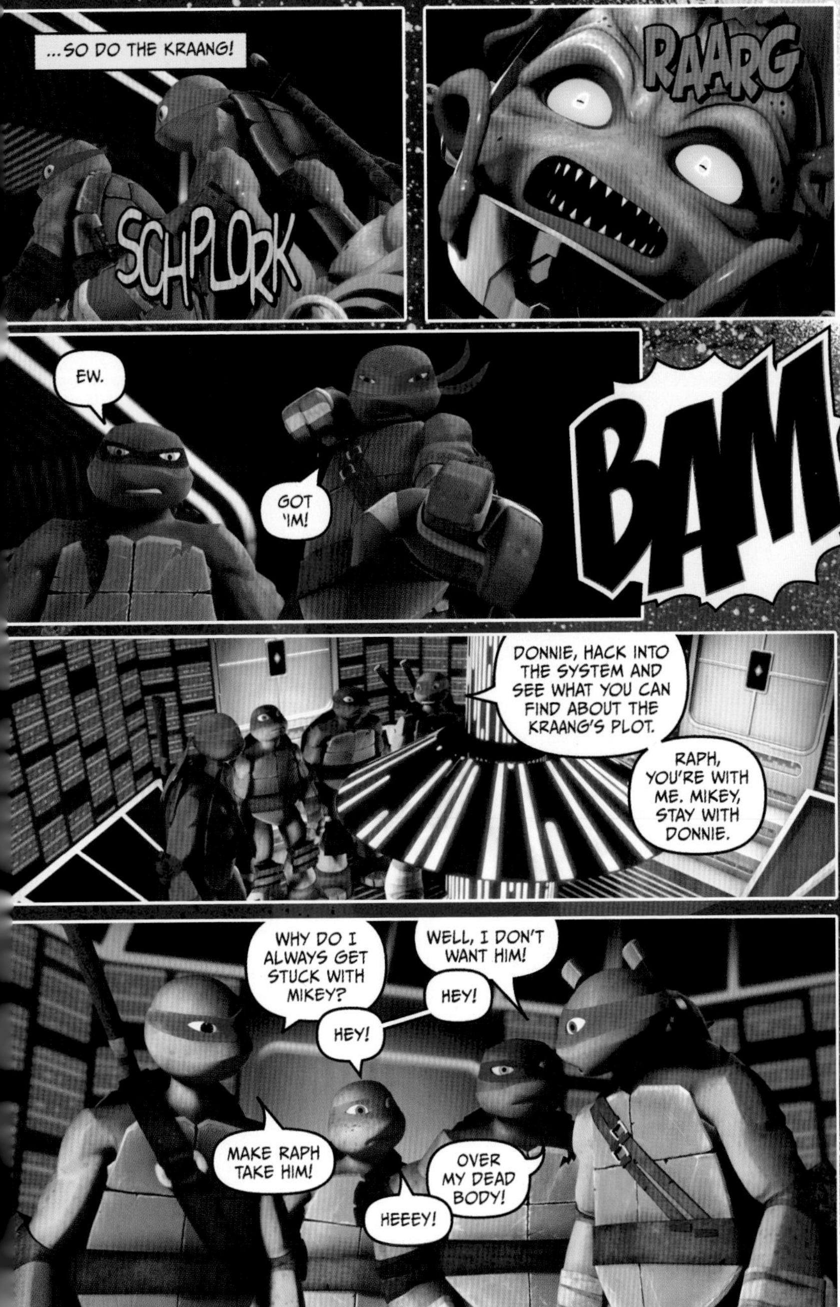
...SO DO THE KRAANG!
SCHPLORK
RAARG
EW.
GOT 'IM!
BAM
DONNIE, HACK INTO THE SYSTEM AND SEE WHAT YOU CAN FIND ABOUT THE KRAANG'S PLOT.
RAPH, YOU'RE WITH ME. MIKEY, STAY WITH DONNIE.
WHY DO I ALWAYS GET STUCK WITH MIKEY?
HEY!
WELL, I DON'T WANT HIM!
HEY!
MAKE RAPH TAKE HIM!
OVER MY DEAD BODY!
HEEEY!

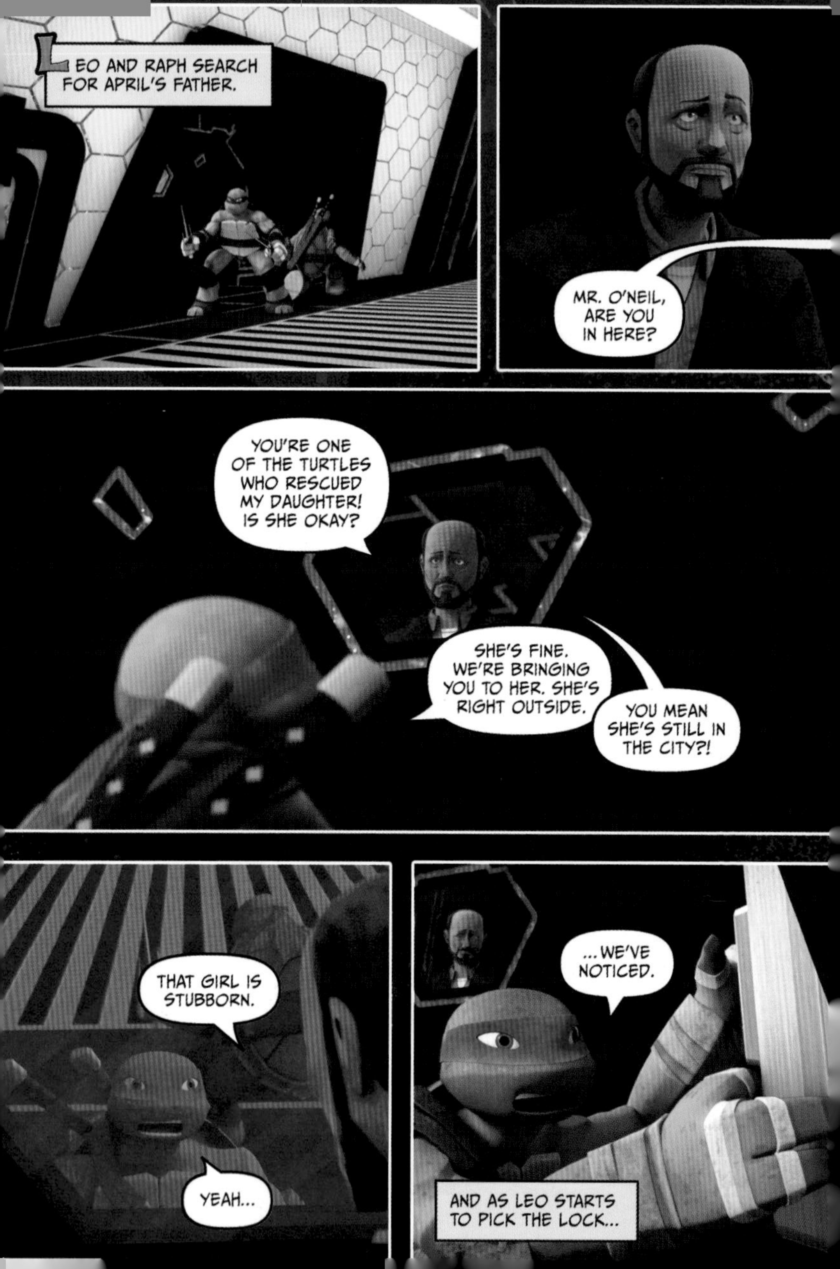
LEO AND RAPH SEARCH FOR APRIL'S FATHER.
MR. O'NEIL, ARE YOU IN HERE?
YOU'RE ONE OF THE TURTLES WHO RESCUED MY DAUGHTER! IS SHE OKAY?
SHE'S FINE. WE'RE BRINGING YOU TO HER. SHE'S RIGHT OUTSIDE.
YOU MEAN SHE'S STILL IN THE CITY?!
THAT GIRL IS STUBBORN.
YEAH...
...WE'VE NOTICED.
AND AS LEO STARTS TO PICK THE LOCK...

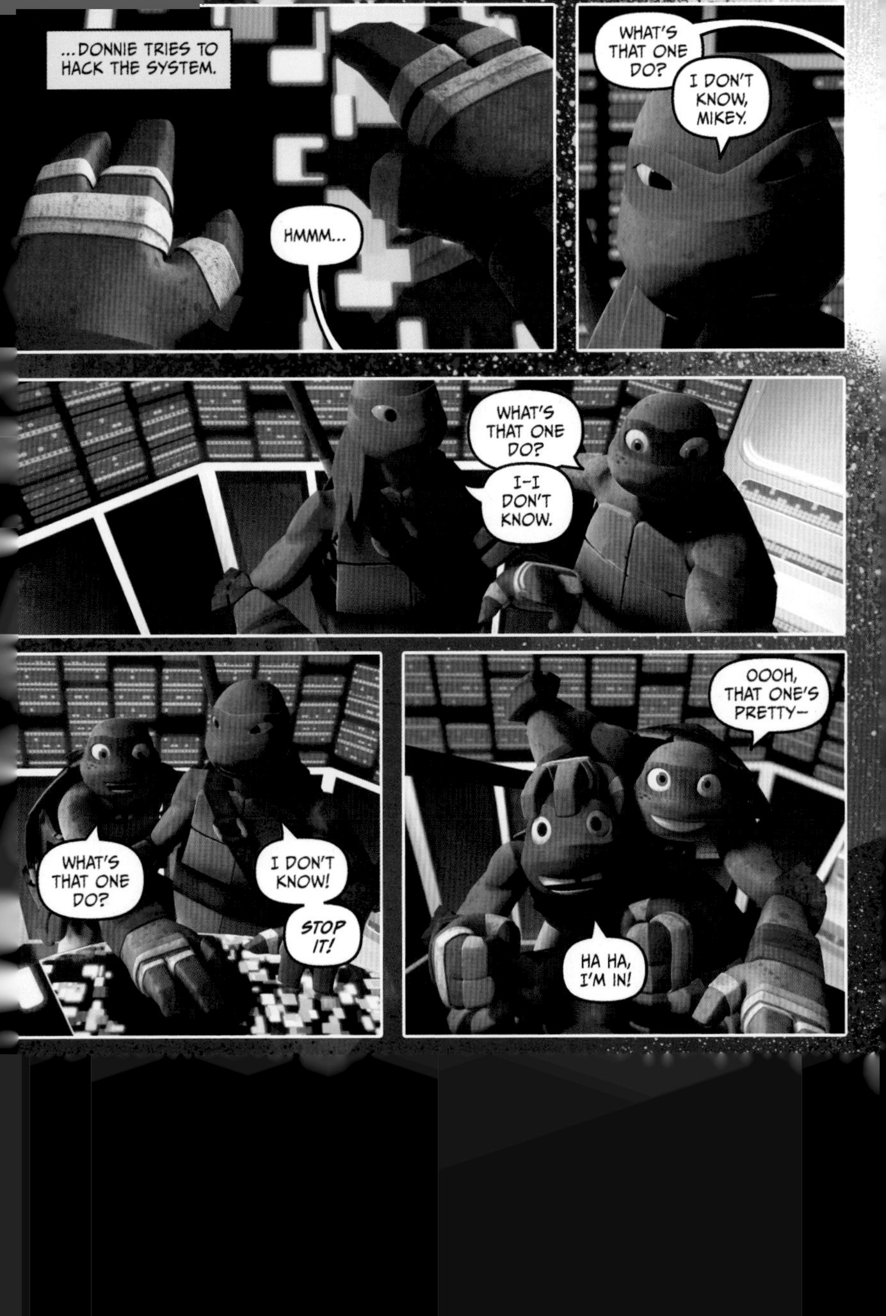
...DONNIE TRIES TO HACK THE SYSTEM.
HMMM...
WHAT'S THAT ONE DO?
I DON'T KNOW, MIKEY.
WHAT'S THAT ONE DO?
I-I DON'T KNOW.
WHAT'S THAT ONE DO?
I DON'T KNOW!
STOP IT!
OOOH, THAT ONE'S PRETTY—
HA HA, I'M IN!

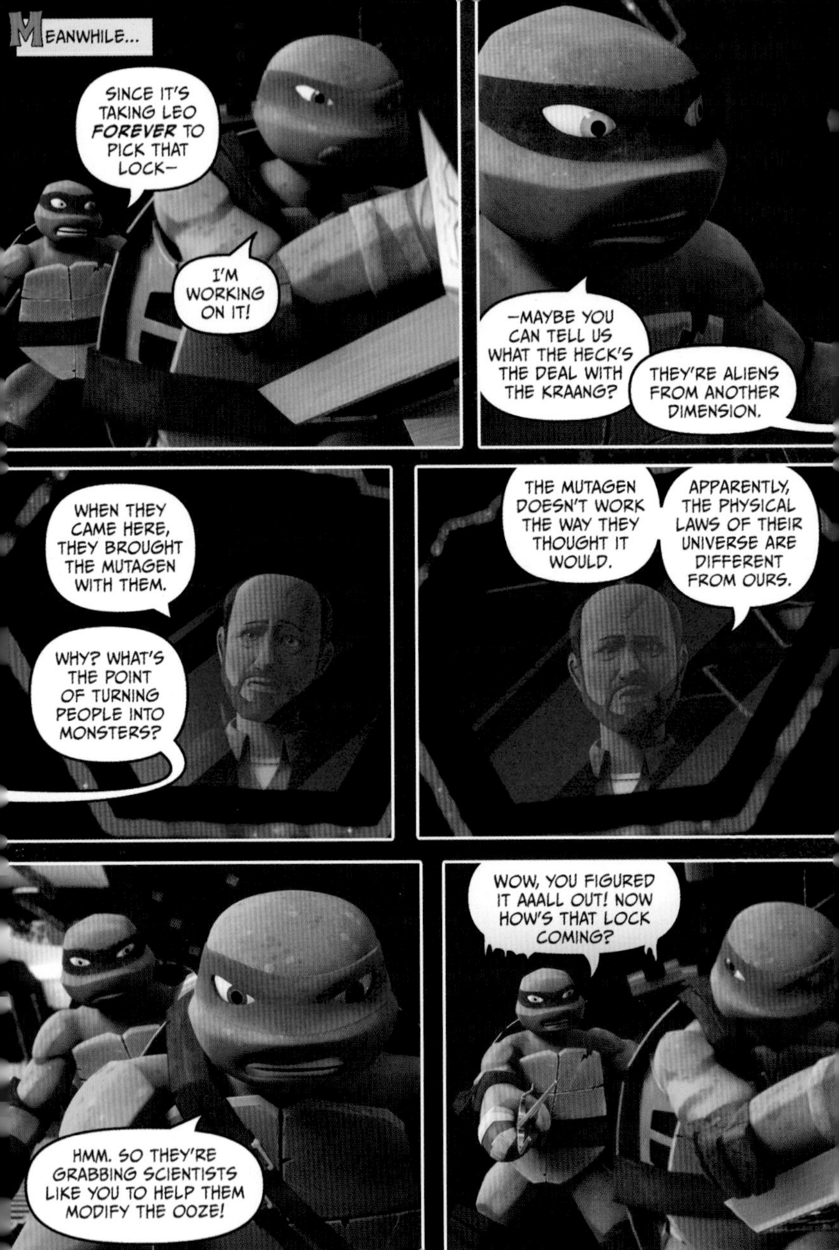
MEANWHILE...
SINCE IT'S TAKING LEO *FOREVER* TO PICK THAT LOCK—
I'M WORKING ON IT!
—MAYBE YOU CAN TELL US WHAT THE HECK'S THE DEAL WITH THE KRAANG?
THEY'RE ALIENS FROM ANOTHER DIMENSION.
WHEN THEY CAME HERE, THEY BROUGHT THE MUTAGEN WITH THEM.
WHY? WHAT'S THE POINT OF TURNING PEOPLE INTO MONSTERS?
THE MUTAGEN DOESN'T WORK THE WAY THEY THOUGHT IT WOULD.
APPARENTLY, THE PHYSICAL LAWS OF THEIR UNIVERSE ARE DIFFERENT FROM OURS.
HMM. SO THEY'RE GRABBING SCIENTISTS LIKE YOU TO HELP THEM MODIFY THE OOZE!
WOW, YOU FIGURED IT AAALL OUT! NOW HOW'S THAT LOCK COMING?

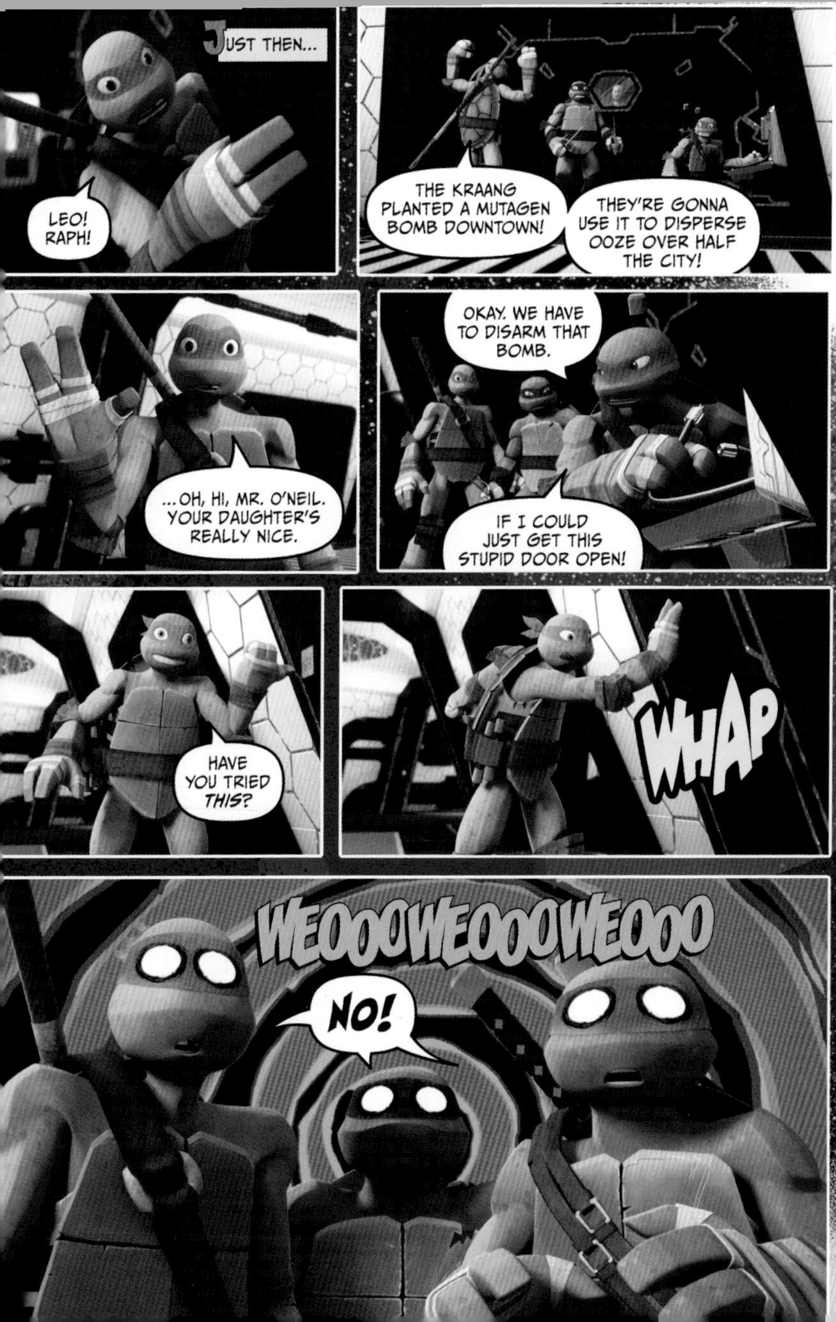
JUST THEN...
LEO! RAPH!
THE KRAANG PLANTED A MUTAGEN BOMB DOWNTOWN!
THEY'RE GONNA USE IT TO DISPERSE OOZE OVER HALF THE CITY!
...OH, HI, MR. O'NEIL. YOUR DAUGHTER'S REALLY NICE.
OKAY. WE HAVE TO DISARM THAT BOMB.
IF I COULD JUST GET THIS STUPID DOOR OPEN!
HAVE YOU TRIED *THIS?*
WHAP
WEOOOWEOOOWEOOO
NO!

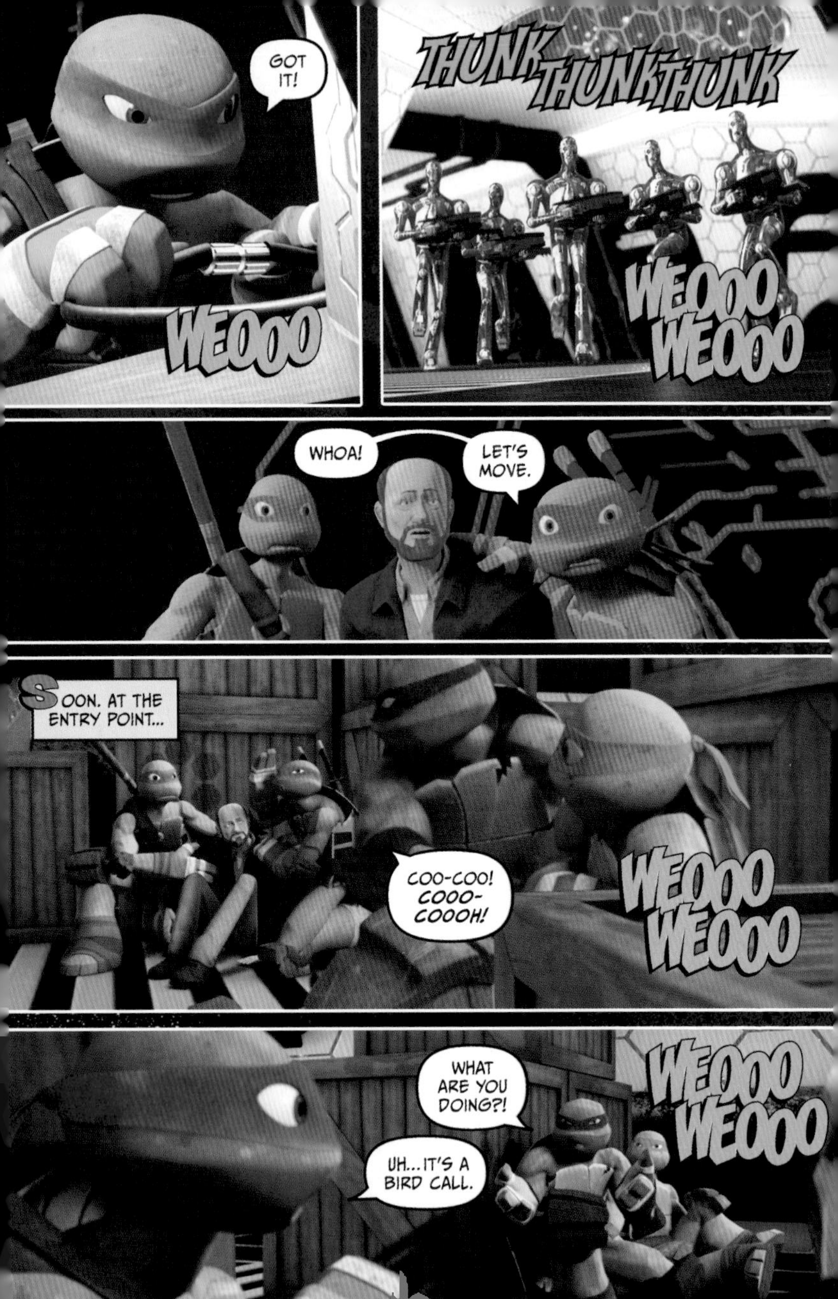
GOT IT!
WEOOO
THUNK THUNK THUNK
WEOOO WEOOO
WHOA!
LET'S MOVE.
SOON. AT THE ENTRY POINT...
COO-COO! COOO-COOOH!
WEOOO WEOOO
WHAT ARE YOU DOING?!
UH...IT'S A BIRD CALL.
WEOOO WEOOO

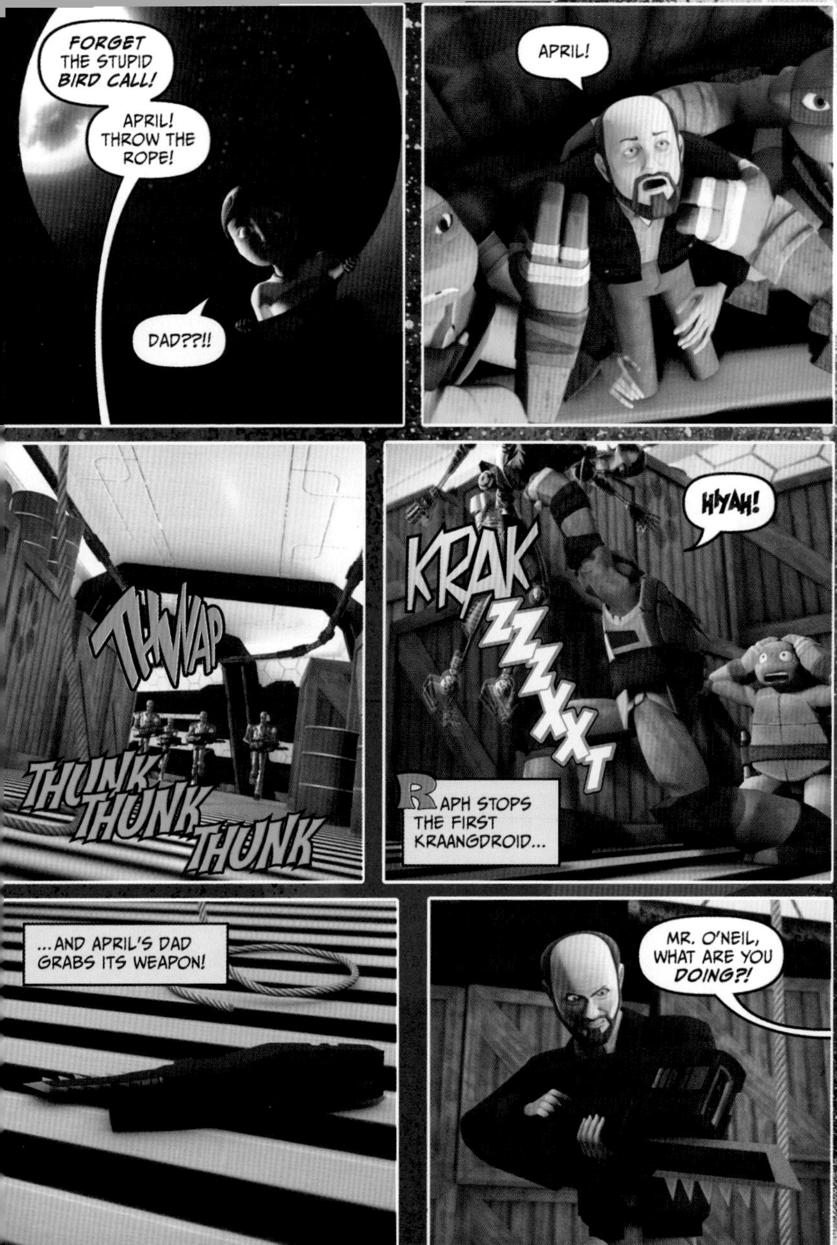
FORGET THE STUPID BIRD CALL!
APRIL! THROW THE ROPE!
DAD??!!
APRIL!
THWAP
THUNK THUNK THUNK
KRAK
HIYAH!
ZZZXXT
RAPH STOPS THE FIRST KRAANGDROID...
...AND APRIL'S DAD GRABS ITS WEAPON!
MR. O'NEIL, WHAT ARE YOU DOING?!

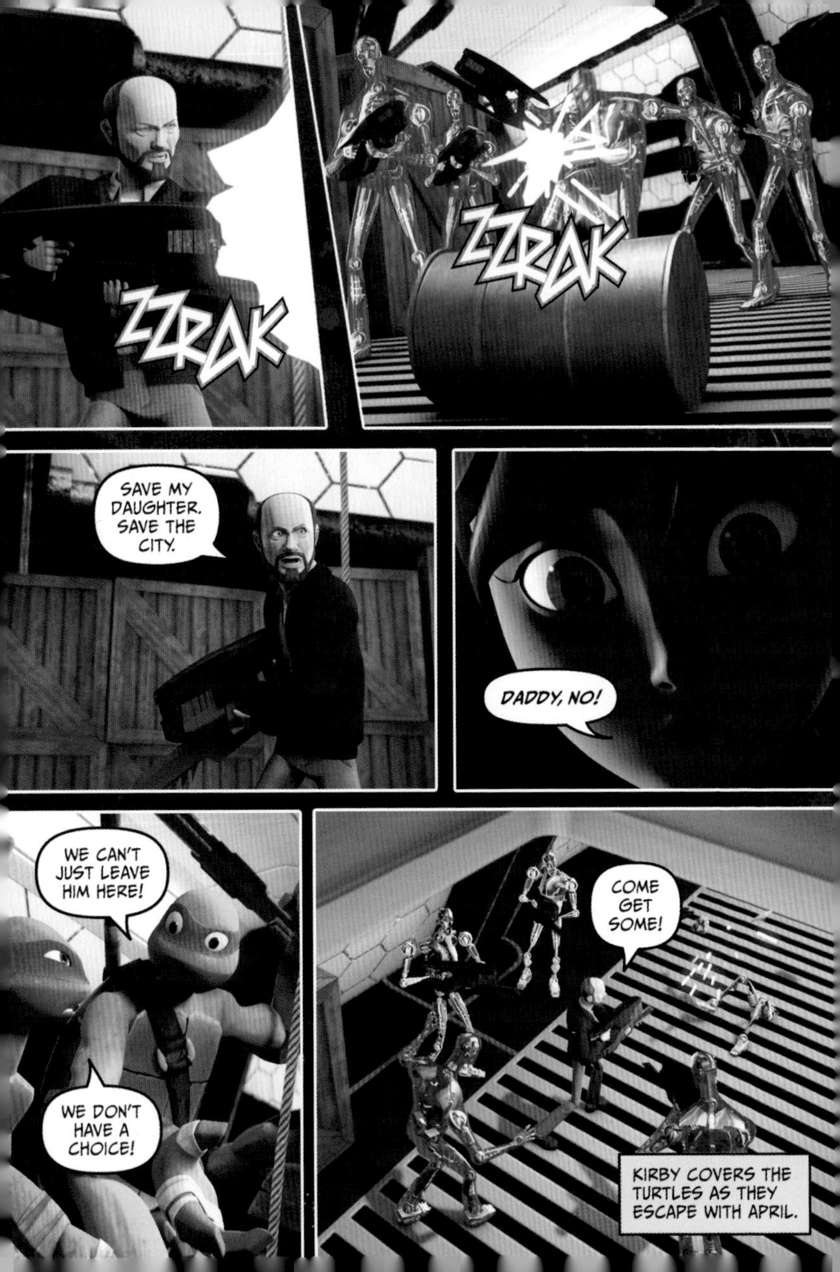
ZZRAK
ZZRAK
SAVE MY DAUGHTER. SAVE THE CITY.
DADDY, NO!
WE CAN'T JUST LEAVE HIM HERE!
WE DON'T HAVE A CHOICE!
COME GET SOME!
KIRBY COVERS THE TURTLES AS THEY ESCAPE WITH APRIL.

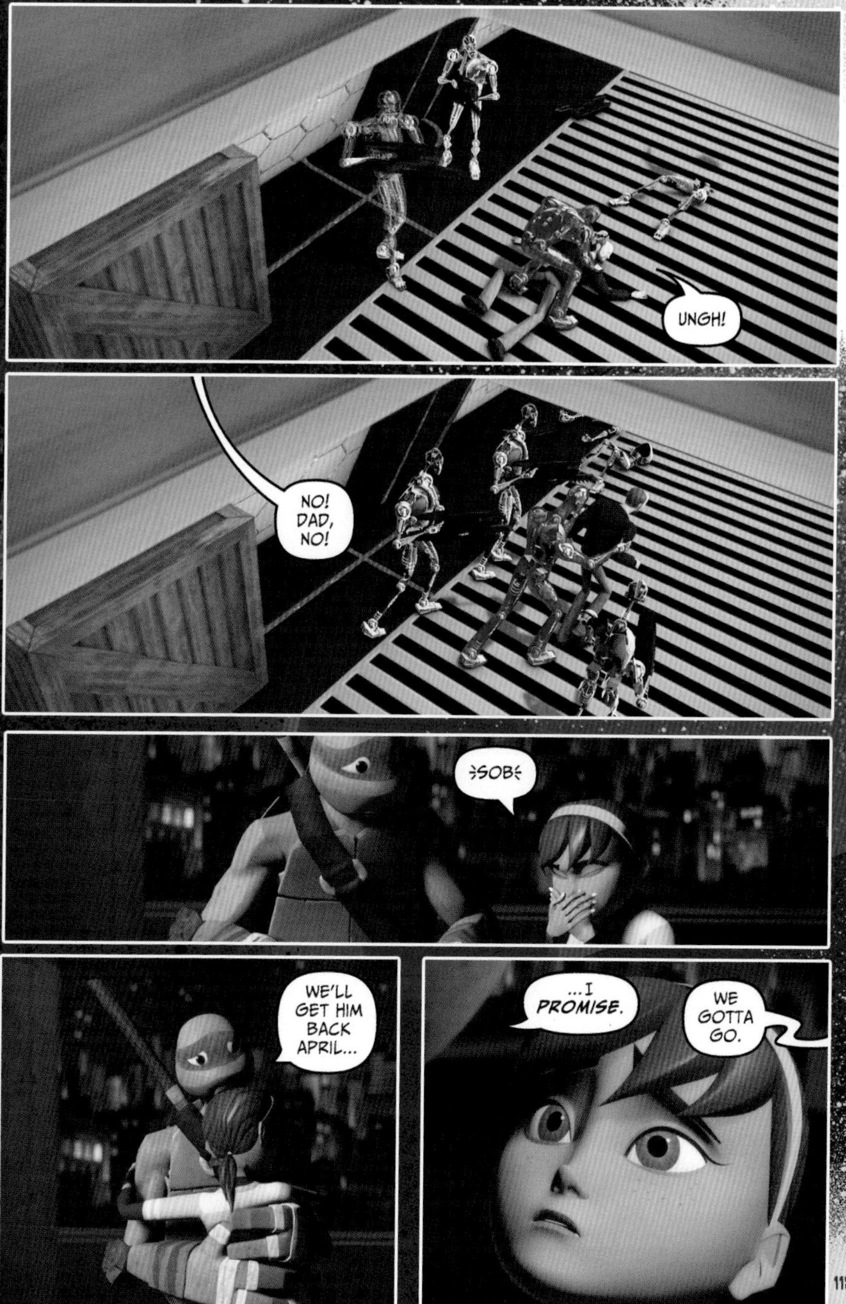
UNGH!
NO! DAD, NO!
SOB
WE'LL GET HIM BACK APRIL...
...I PROMISE.
WE GOTTA GO.

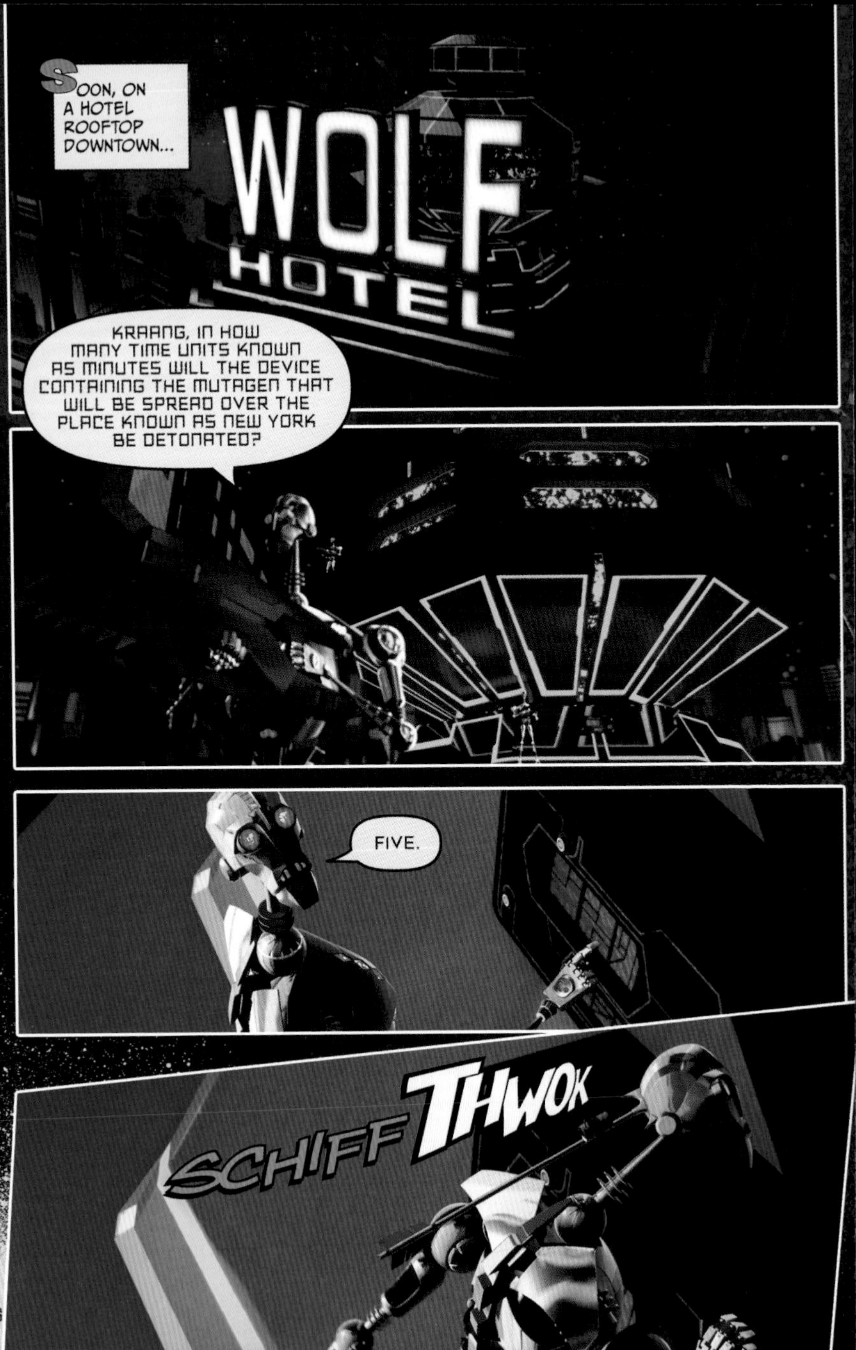
SOON, ON A HOTEL ROOFTOP DOWNTOWN...
WOLF HOTEL
KRAANG, IN HOW MANY TIME UNITS KNOWN AS MINUTES WILL THE DEVICE CONTAINING THE MUTAGEN THAT WILL BE SPREAD OVER THE PLACE KNOWN AS NEW YORK BE DETONATED?
FIVE.
SCHIFF THWOK

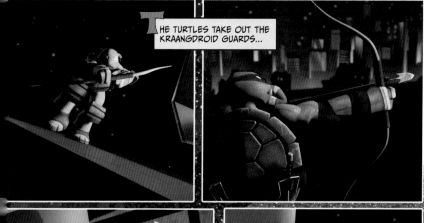

THE TURTLES TAKE OUT THE KRAANGDROID GUARDS...

THWAK

POP

THWAK

POP

SHRIEEEEK

YECHHH. THOSE THINGS ARE GROSS.

OKAY, DONNIE. IT'S UP TO YOU.

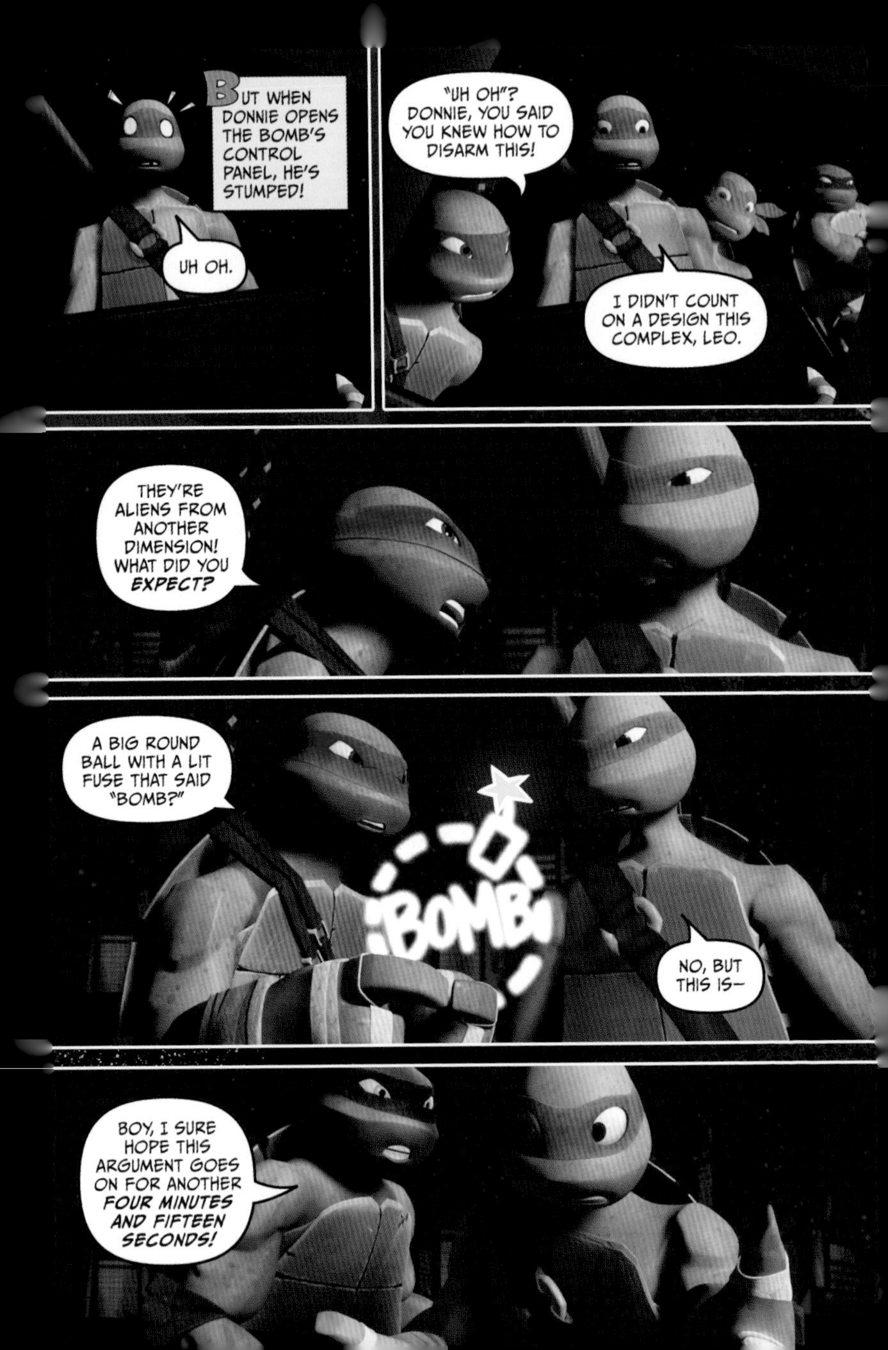
BUT WHEN DONNIE OPENS THE BOMB'S CONTROL PANEL, HE'S STUMPED!
UH OH.
"UH OH"? DONNIE, YOU SAID YOU KNEW HOW TO DISARM THIS!
I DIDN'T COUNT ON A DESIGN THIS COMPLEX, LEO.
THEY'RE ALIENS FROM ANOTHER DIMENSION! WHAT DID YOU *EXPECT?*
A BIG ROUND BALL WITH A LIT FUSE THAT SAID "BOMB?"
BOMB
NO, BUT THIS IS–
BOY, I SURE HOPE THIS ARGUMENT GOES ON FOR ANOTHER *FOUR MINUTES AND FIFTEEN SECONDS!*

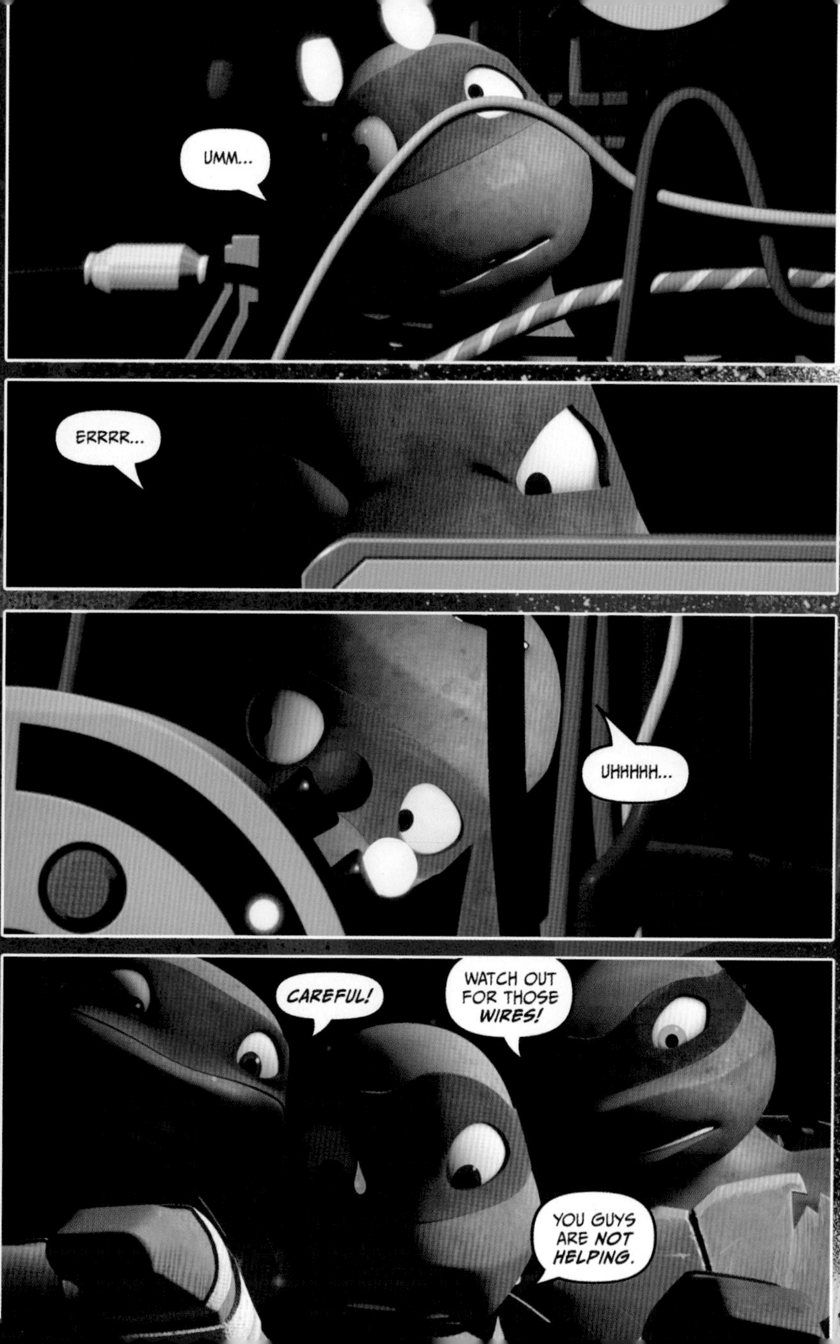
UMM...
ERRRR...
UHHHHH...
CAREFUL!
WATCH OUT FOR THOSE WIRES!
YOU GUYS ARE NOT HELPING.

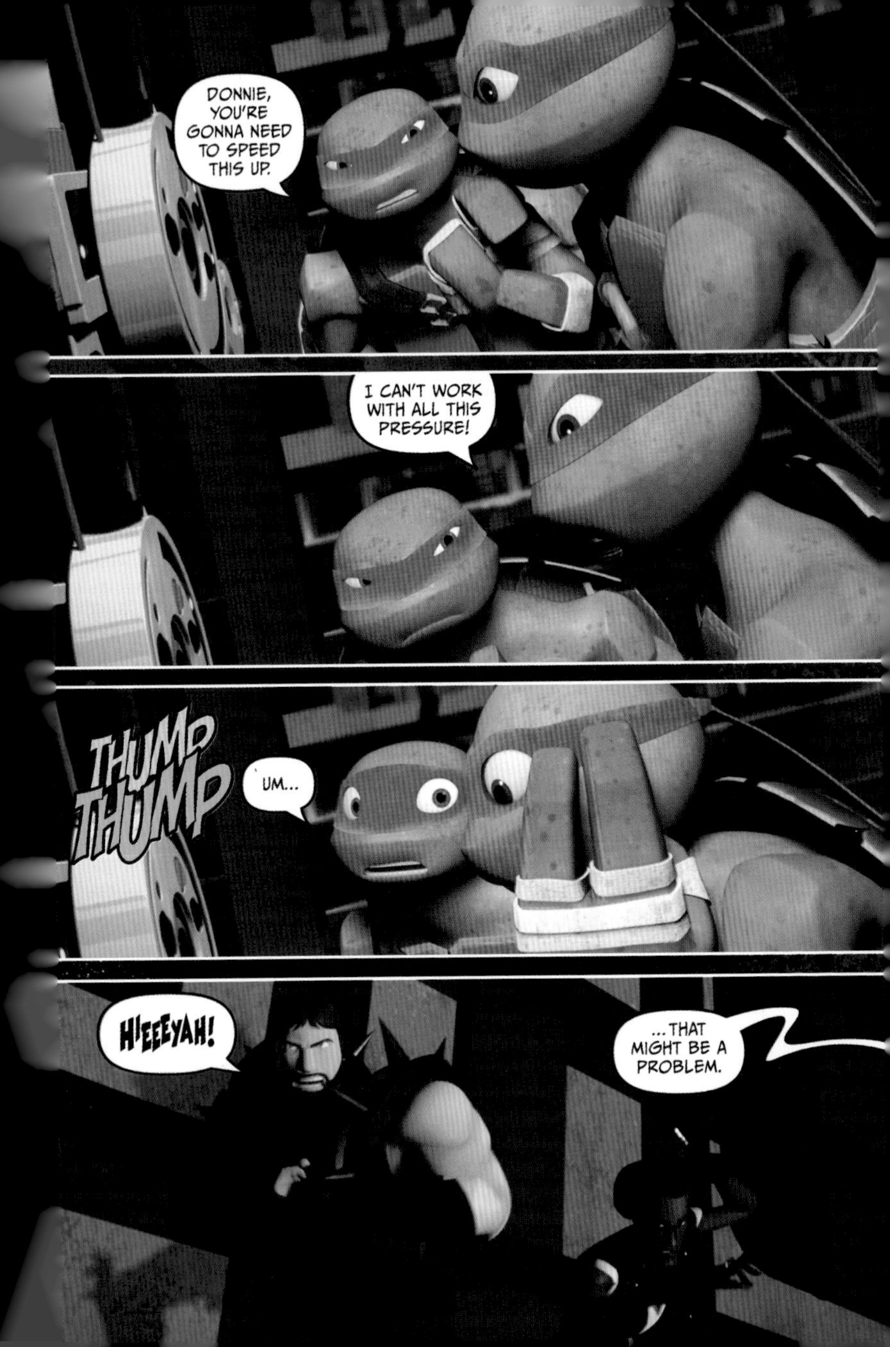
DONNIE, YOU'RE GONNA NEED TO SPEED THIS UP.
I CAN'T WORK WITH ALL THIS PRESSURE!
THUMP THUMP
UM...
HIEEEYAH!
...THAT MIGHT BE A PROBLEM.

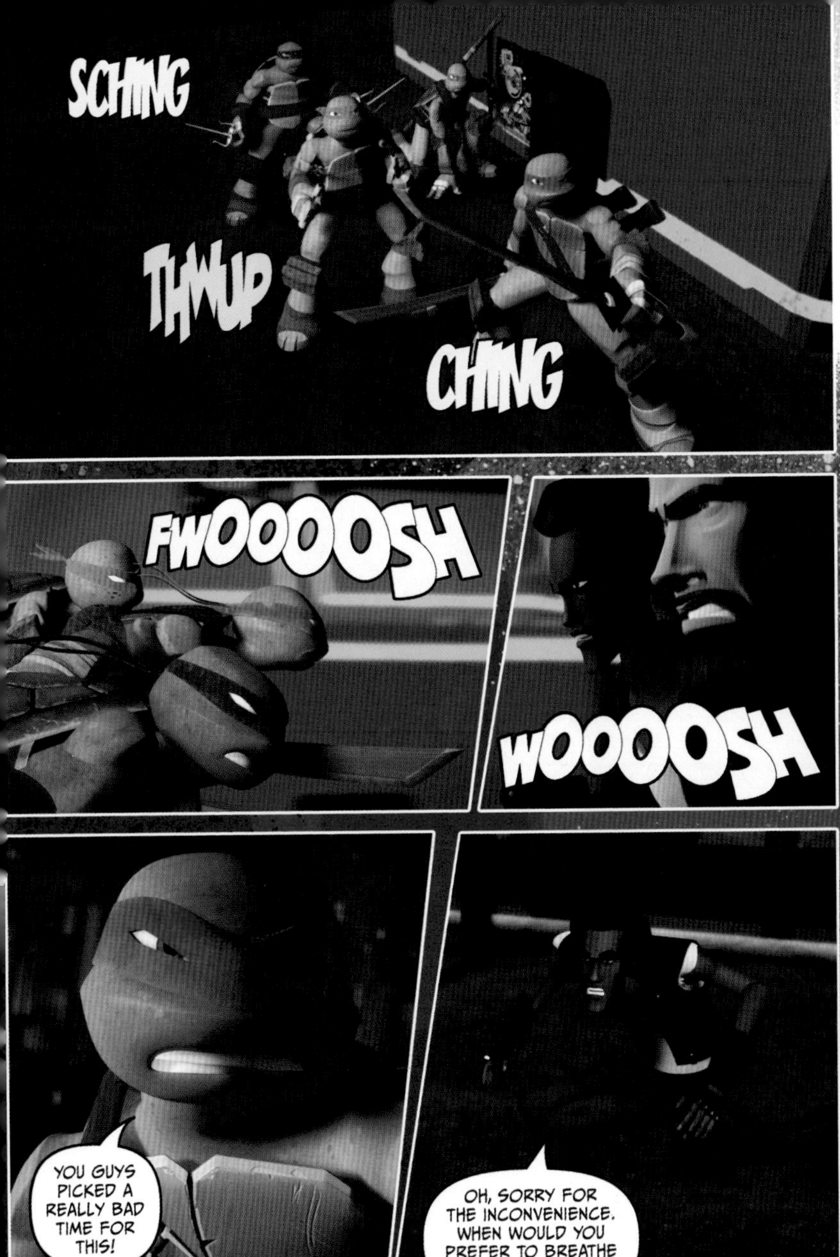
SCHING
THWUP
CHING
FWOOOOSH
WOOOOSH
YOU GUYS PICKED A REALLY BAD TIME FOR THIS!
OH, SORRY FOR THE INCONVENIENCE. WHEN WOULD YOU PREFER TO BREATHE YOUR LAST BREATH?

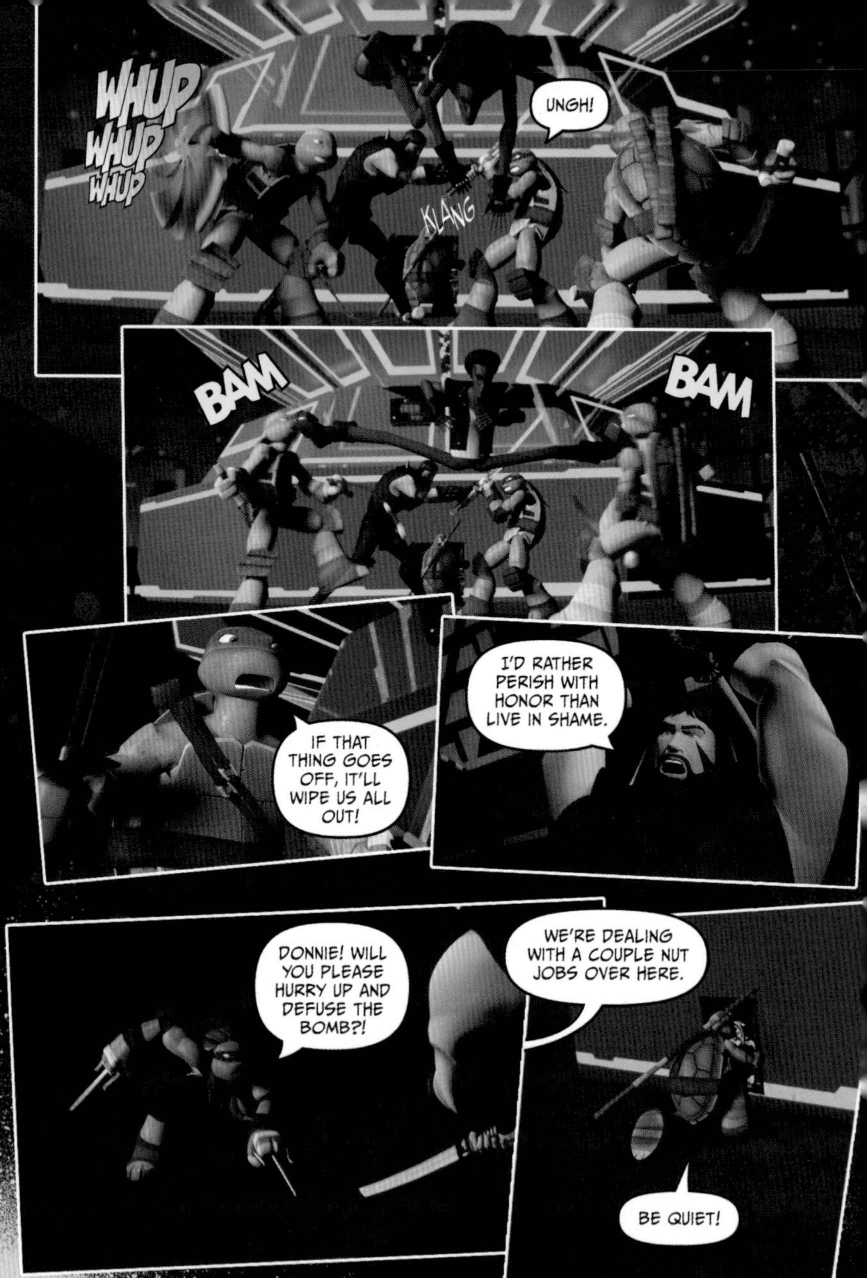
WHUP WHUP WHUP
UNGH!
KLANG
BAM
BAM
IF THAT THING GOES OFF, IT'LL WIPE US ALL OUT!
I'D RATHER PERISH WITH HONOR THAN LIVE IN SHAME.
DONNIE! WILL YOU PLEASE HURRY UP AND DEFUSE THE BOMB?!
WE'RE DEALING WITH A COUPLE NUT JOBS OVER HERE.
BE QUIET!

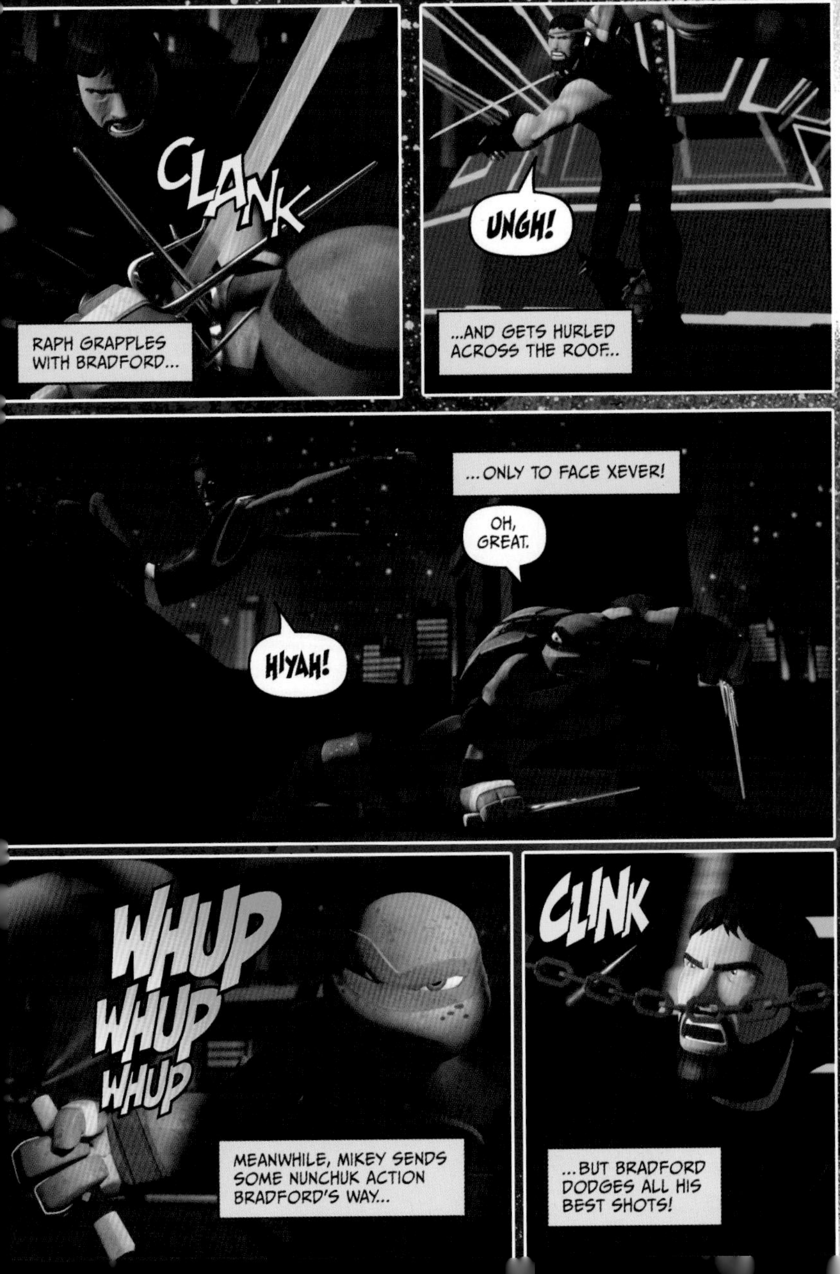
CLANK
RAPH GRAPPLES WITH BRADFORD...
UNGH!
...AND GETS HURLED ACROSS THE ROOF...
...ONLY TO FACE XEVER!
OH, GREAT.
HIYAH!
WHUP WHUP WHUP
MEANWHILE, MIKEY SENDS SOME NUNCHUK ACTION BRADFORD'S WAY...
CLINK
...BUT BRADFORD DODGES ALL HIS BEST SHOTS!

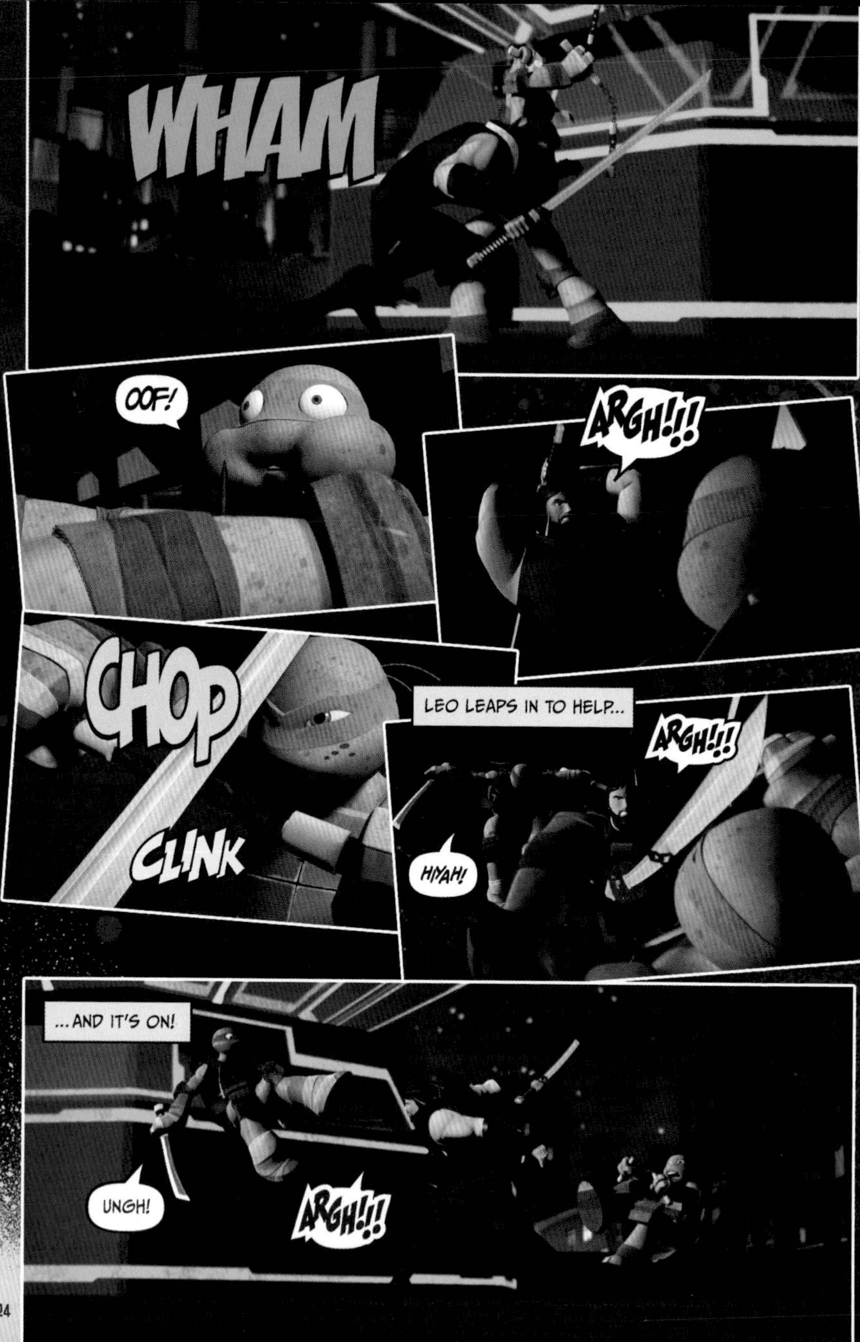
WHAM
OOF!
ARGH!!!
CHOP
CLINK
LEO LEAPS IN TO HELP...
ARGH!!!
HIYAH!
...AND IT'S ON!
UNGH!
ARGH!!!

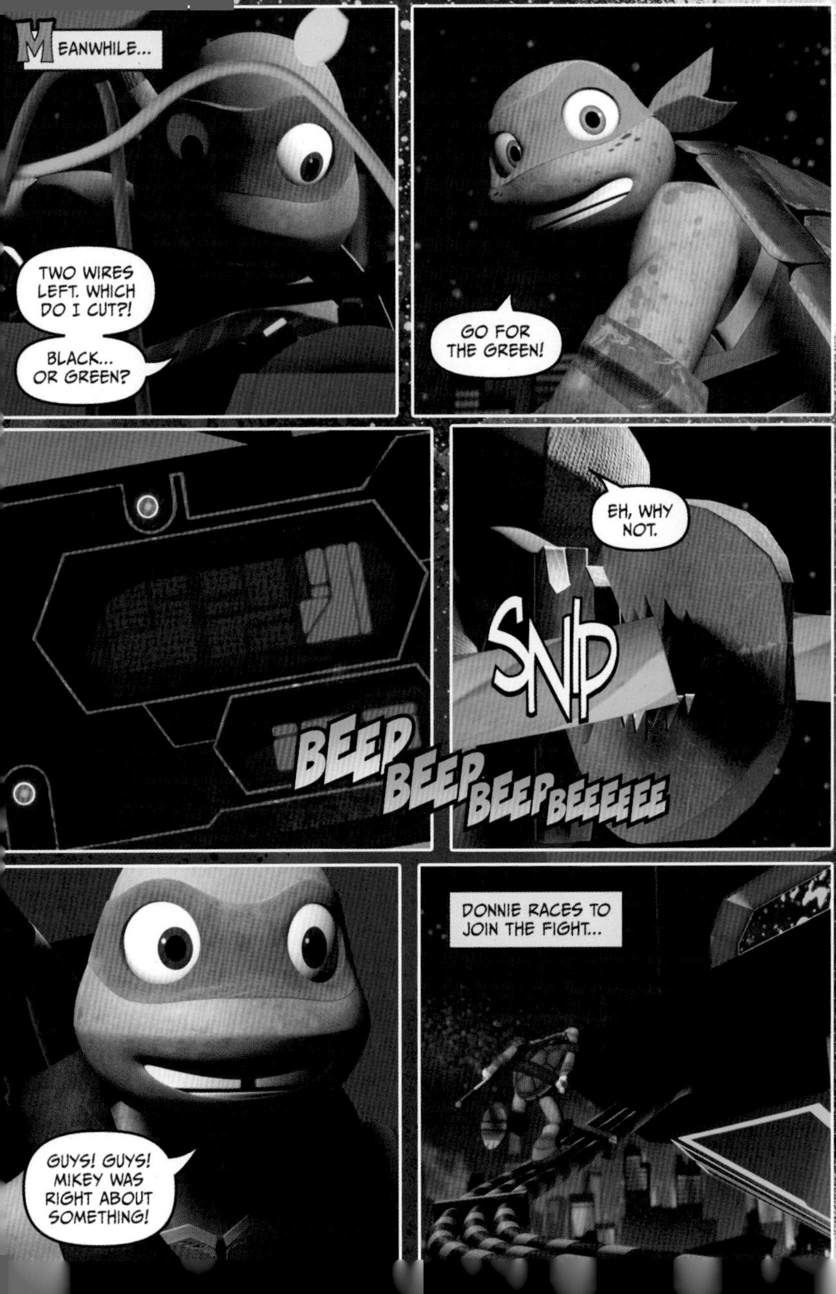
MEANWHILE...
TWO WIRES LEFT. WHICH DO I CUT?!
BLACK... OR GREEN?
GO FOR THE GREEN!
EH, WHY NOT.
SNIP
BEEP BEEP BEEP BEEEEEE
GUYS! GUYS! MIKEY WAS RIGHT ABOUT SOMETHING!
DONNIE RACES TO JOIN THE FIGHT...

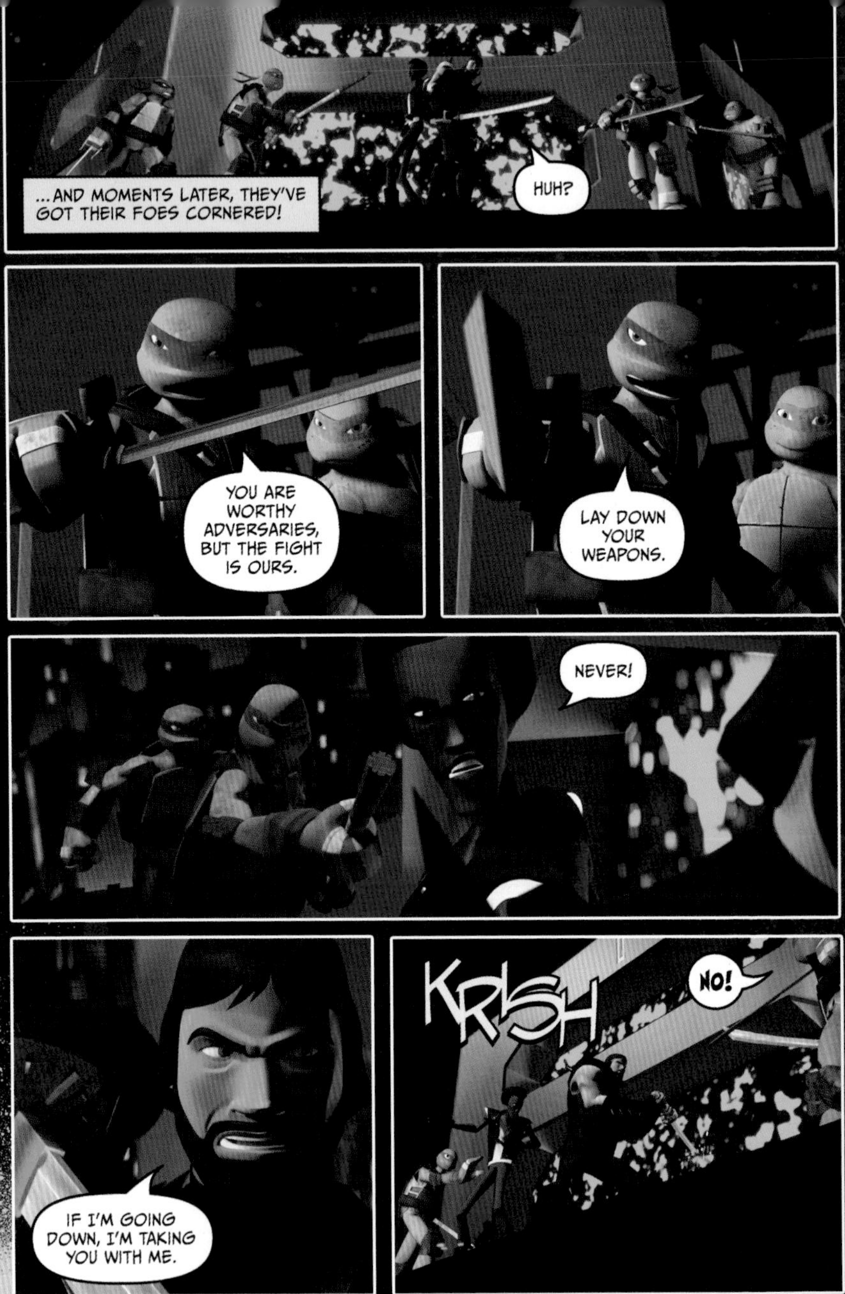
...AND MOMENTS LATER, THEY'VE GOT THEIR FOES CORNERED!
HUH?
YOU ARE WORTHY ADVERSARIES, BUT THE FIGHT IS OURS.
LAY DOWN YOUR WEAPONS.
NEVER!
IF I'M GOING DOWN, I'M TAKING YOU WITH ME.
KRISH
NO!

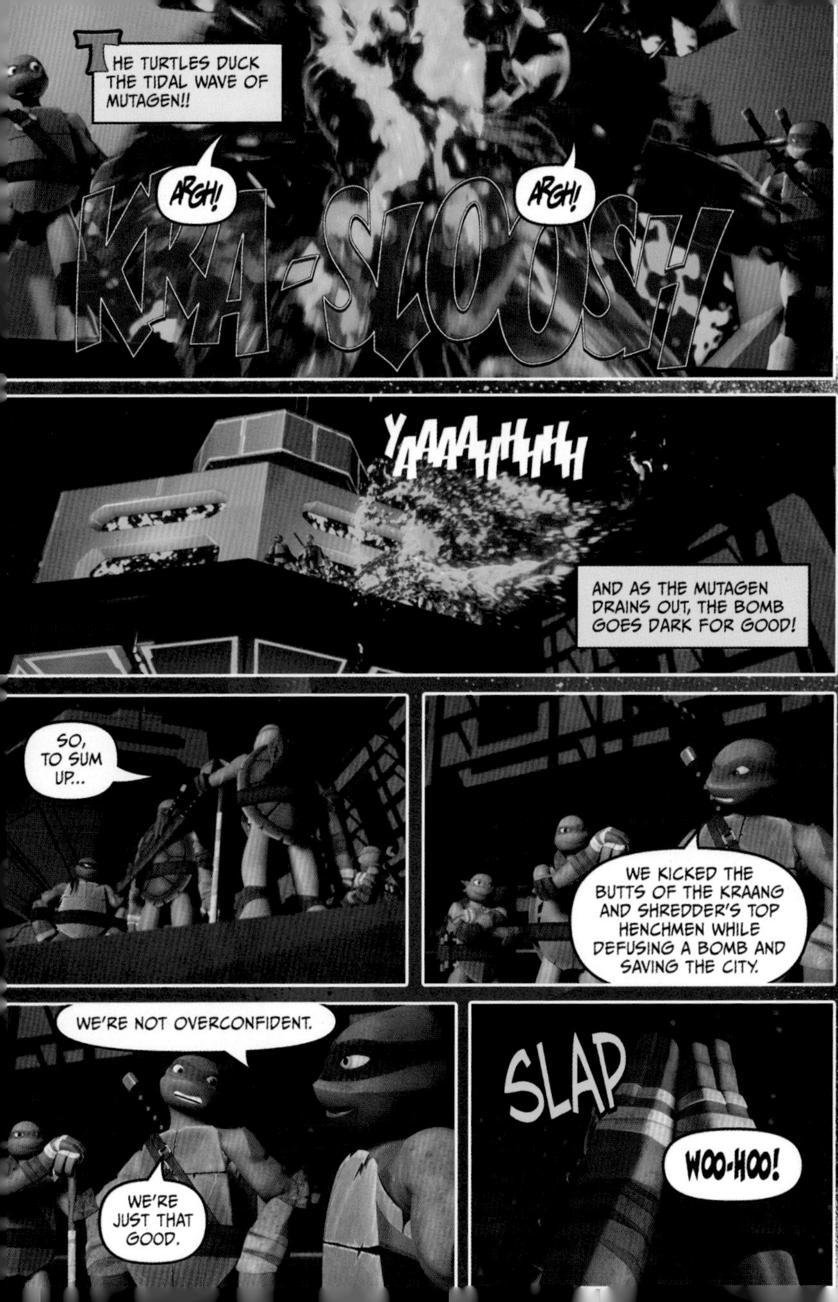
THE TURTLES DUCK THE TIDAL WAVE OF MUTAGEN!!
ARGH!
ARGH!
KWA-SLOOSH
YAAAAHHHHH
AND AS THE MUTAGEN DRAINS OUT, THE BOMB GOES DARK FOR GOOD!
SO, TO SUM UP...
WE KICKED THE BUTTS OF THE KRAANG AND SHREDDER'S TOP HENCHMEN WHILE DEFUSING A BOMB AND SAVING THE CITY.
WE'RE NOT OVERCONFIDENT.
WE'RE JUST THAT GOOD.
SLAP
WOO-HOO!

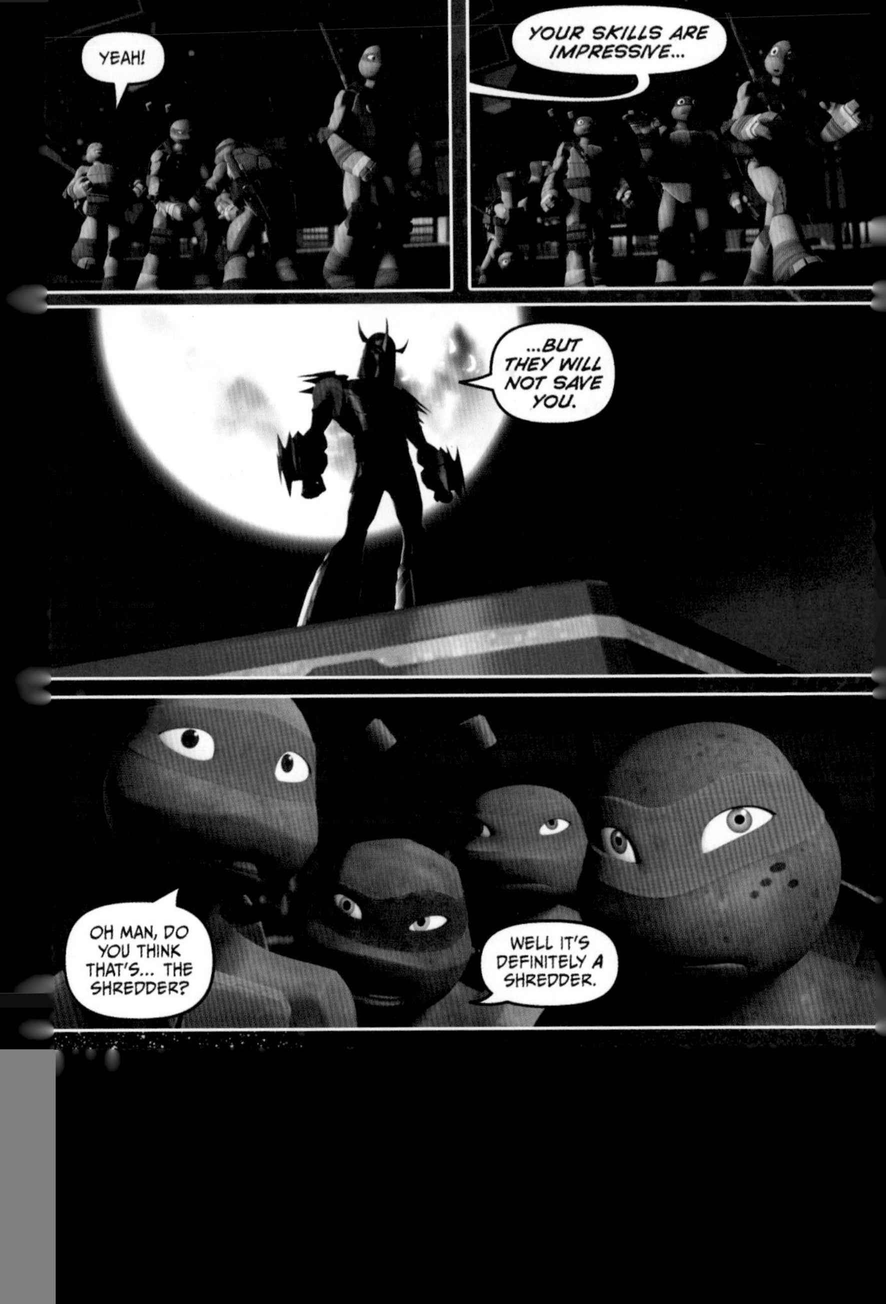
YEAH!
YOUR SKILLS ARE IMPRESSIVE...
...BUT THEY WILL NOT SAVE YOU.
OH MAN, DO YOU THINK THAT'S... THE SHREDDER?
WELL IT'S DEFINITELY A SHREDDER.

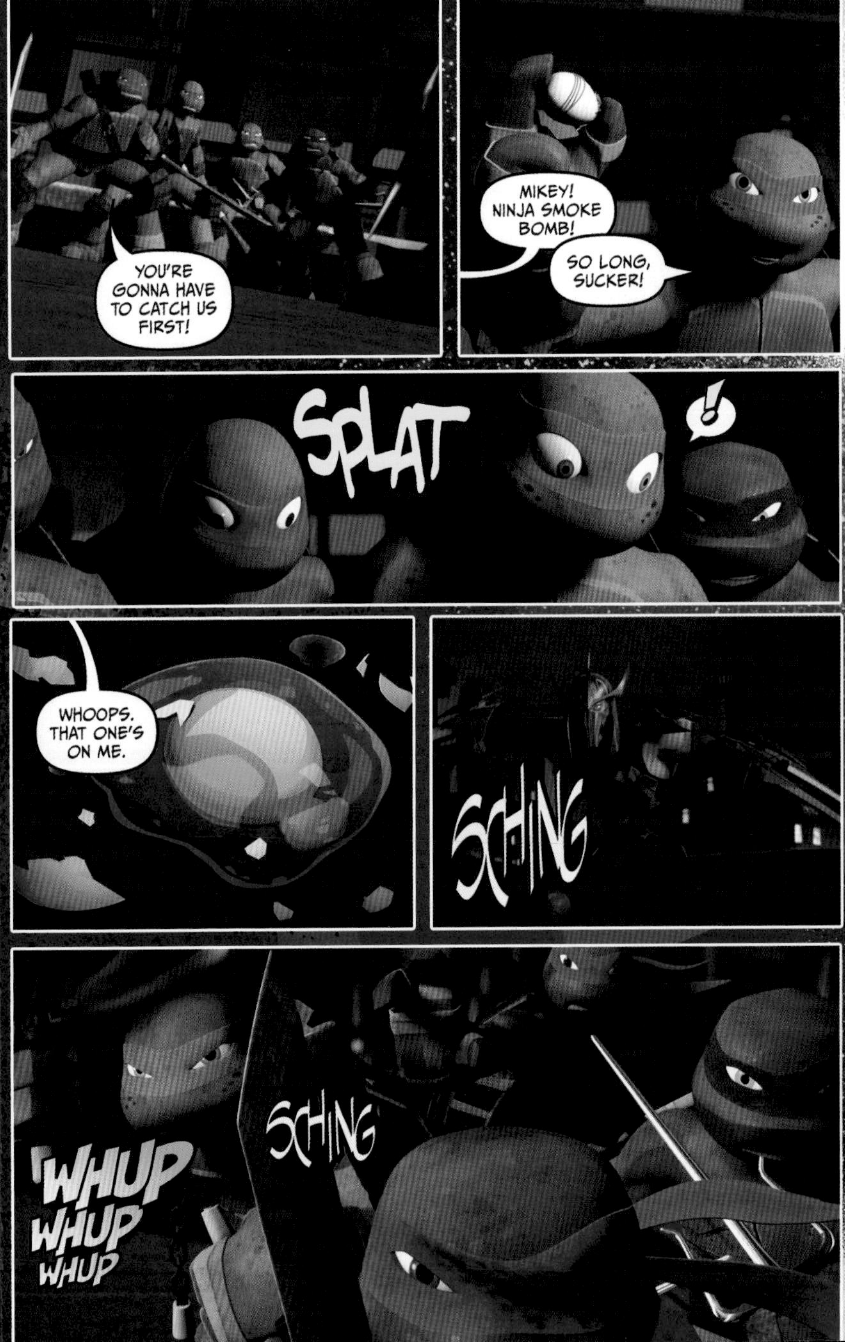
YOU'RE GONNA HAVE TO CATCH US FIRST!
MIKEY! NINJA SMOKE BOMB!
SO LONG, SUCKER!
SPLAT
!
WHOOPS. THAT ONE'S ON ME.
SCHING
SCHING
WHUP WHUP WHUP

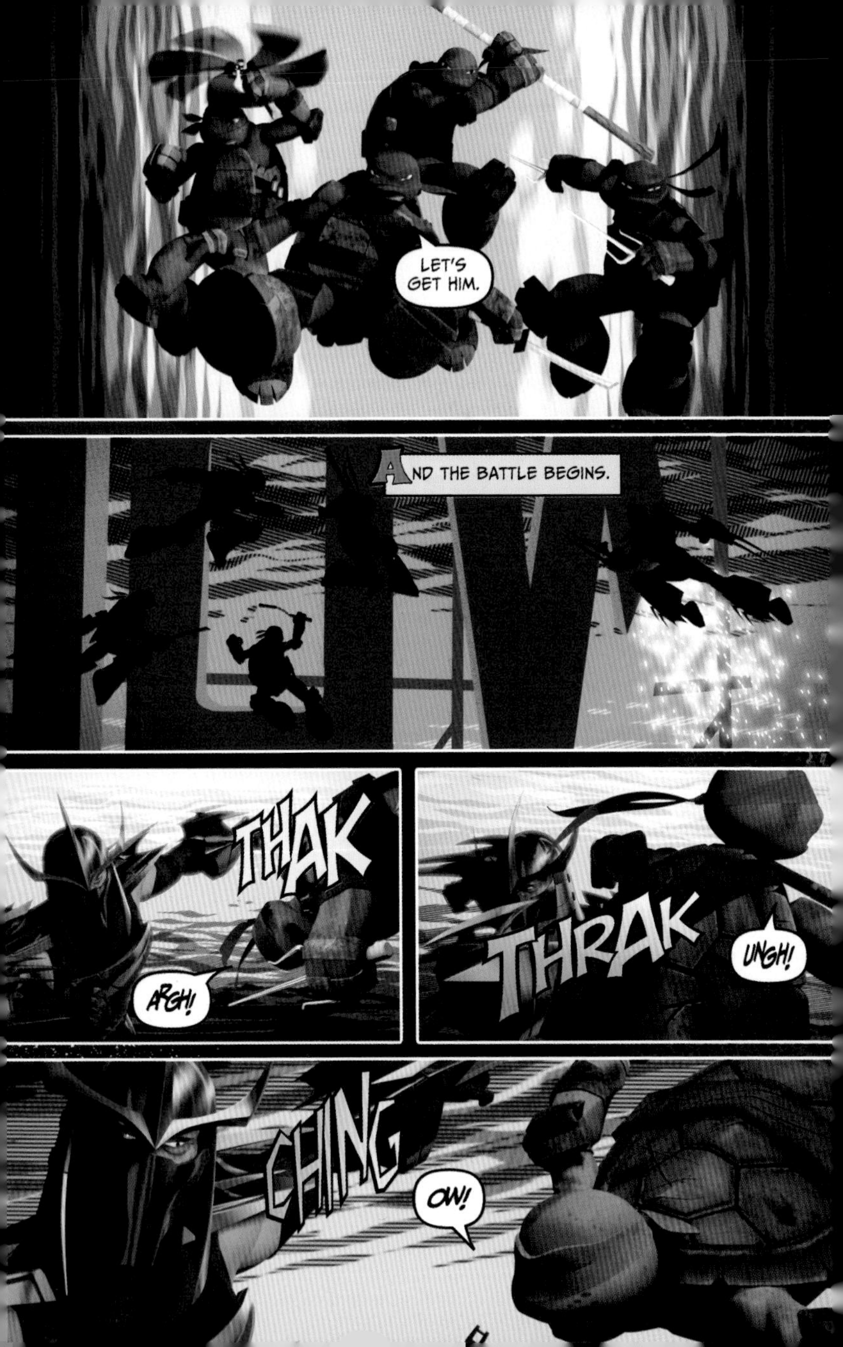
LET'S GET HIM.
AND THE BATTLE BEGINS.
THAK
ARGH!
THRAK
UNGH!
CHING
OW!

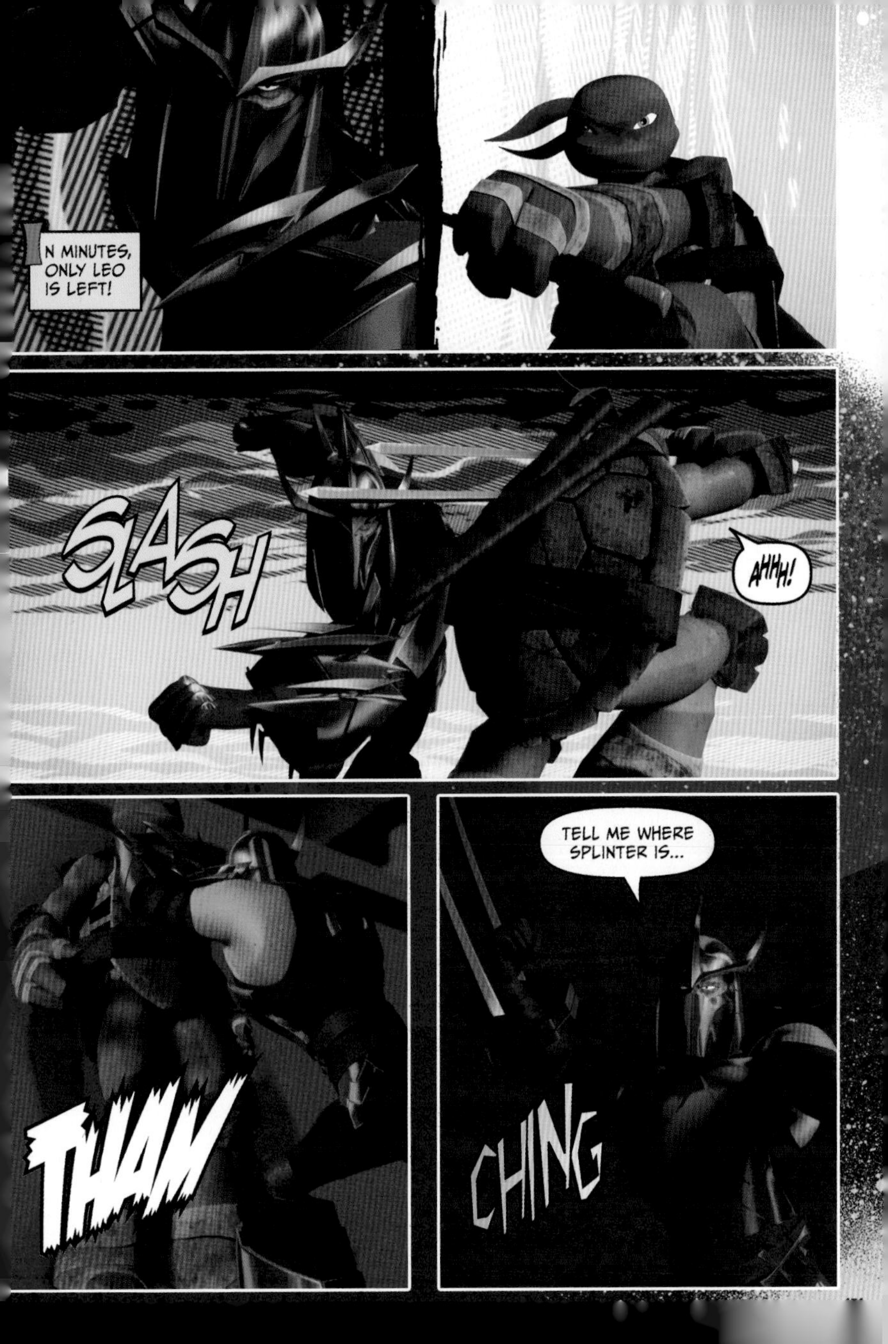
N MINUTES, ONLY LEO IS LEFT!
SLASH
AHHH!
THAM
TELL ME WHERE SPLINTER IS...
CHING

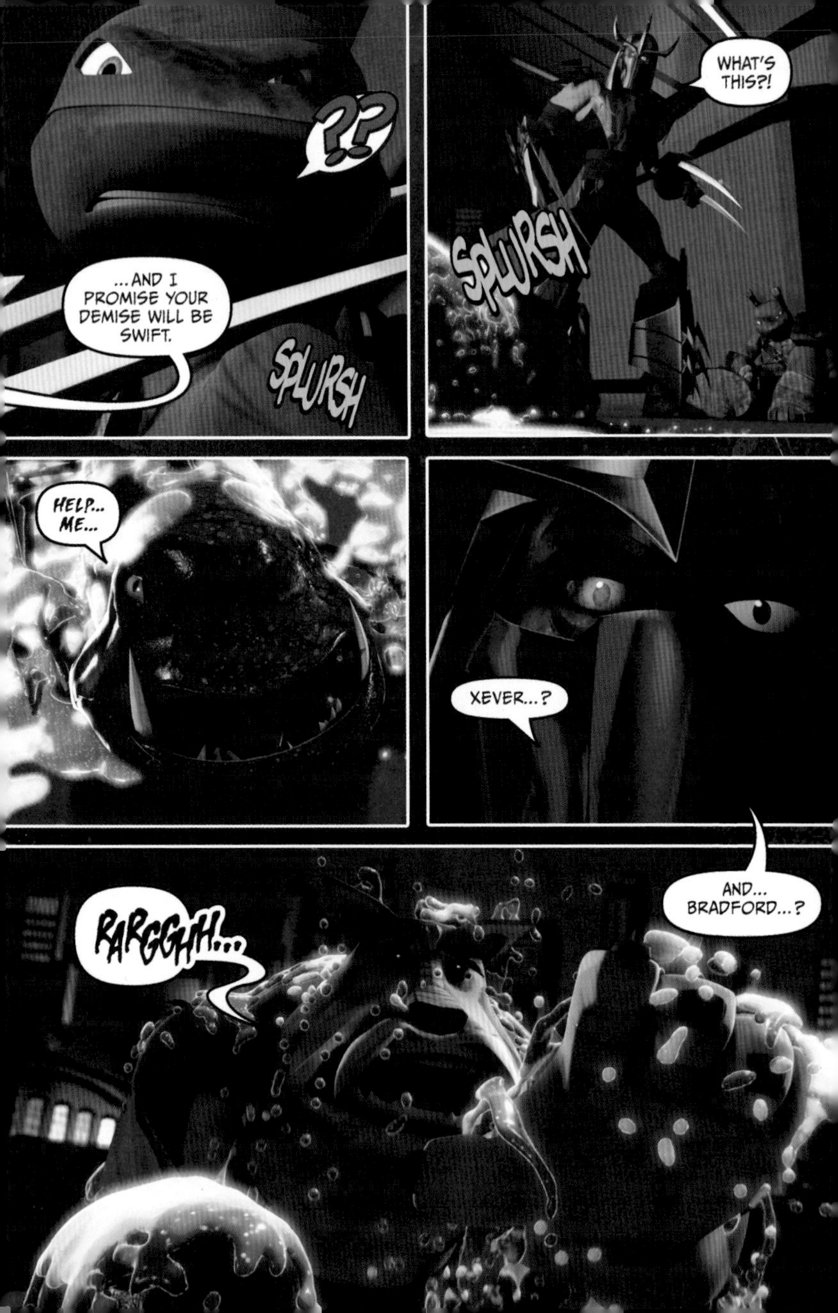
??
...AND I PROMISE YOUR DEMISE WILL BE SWIFT.
SPLURSH
WHAT'S THIS?!
SPLURSH
HELP... ME...
XEVER...?
AND... BRADFORD...?
RARGGHH...

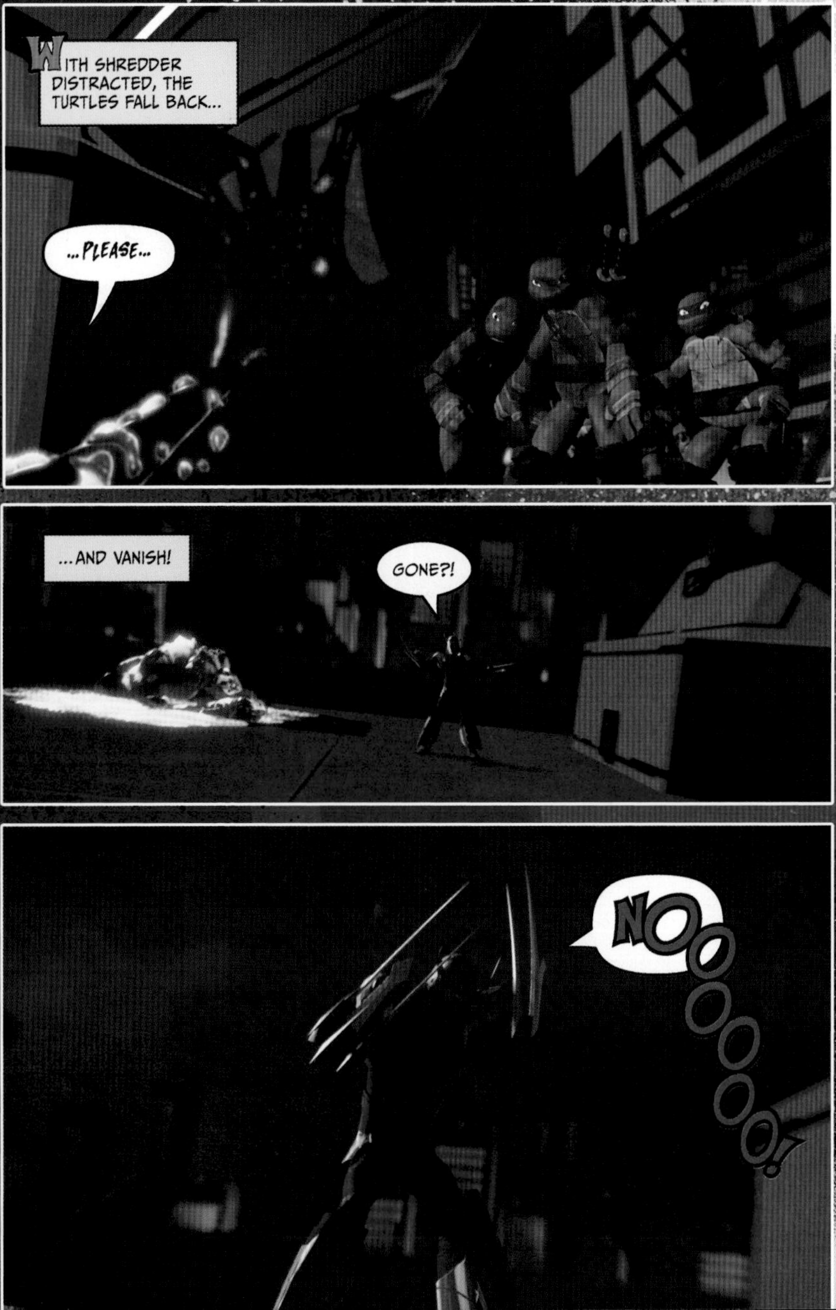

WITH SHREDDER DISTRACTED, THE TURTLES FALL BACK...
...PLEASE...
...AND VANISH!
GONE?!
NOOOOOOO!

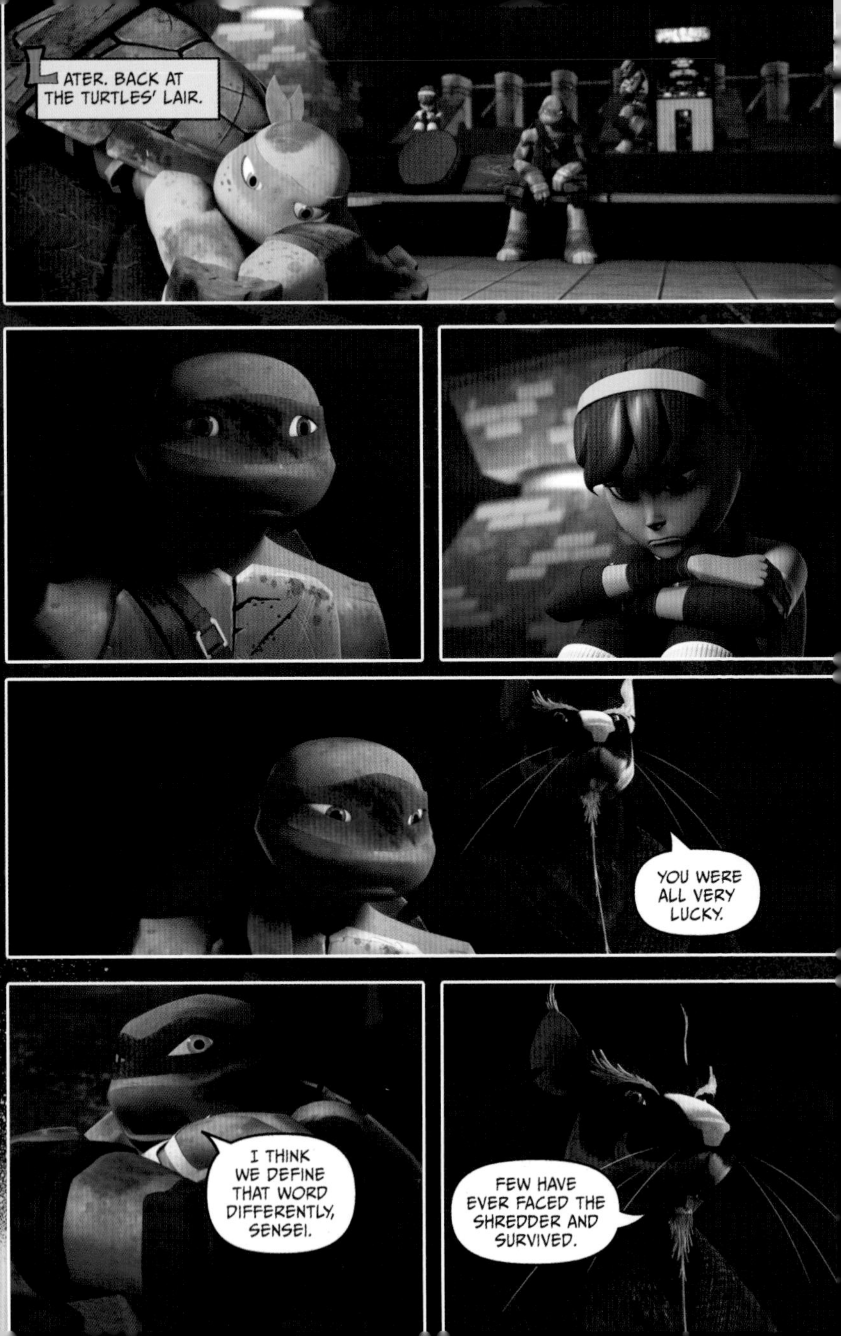
LATER. BACK AT THE TURTLES' LAIR.
YOU WERE ALL VERY LUCKY.
I THINK WE DEFINE THAT WORD DIFFERENTLY, SENSEI.
FEW HAVE EVER FACED THE SHREDDER AND SURVIVED.

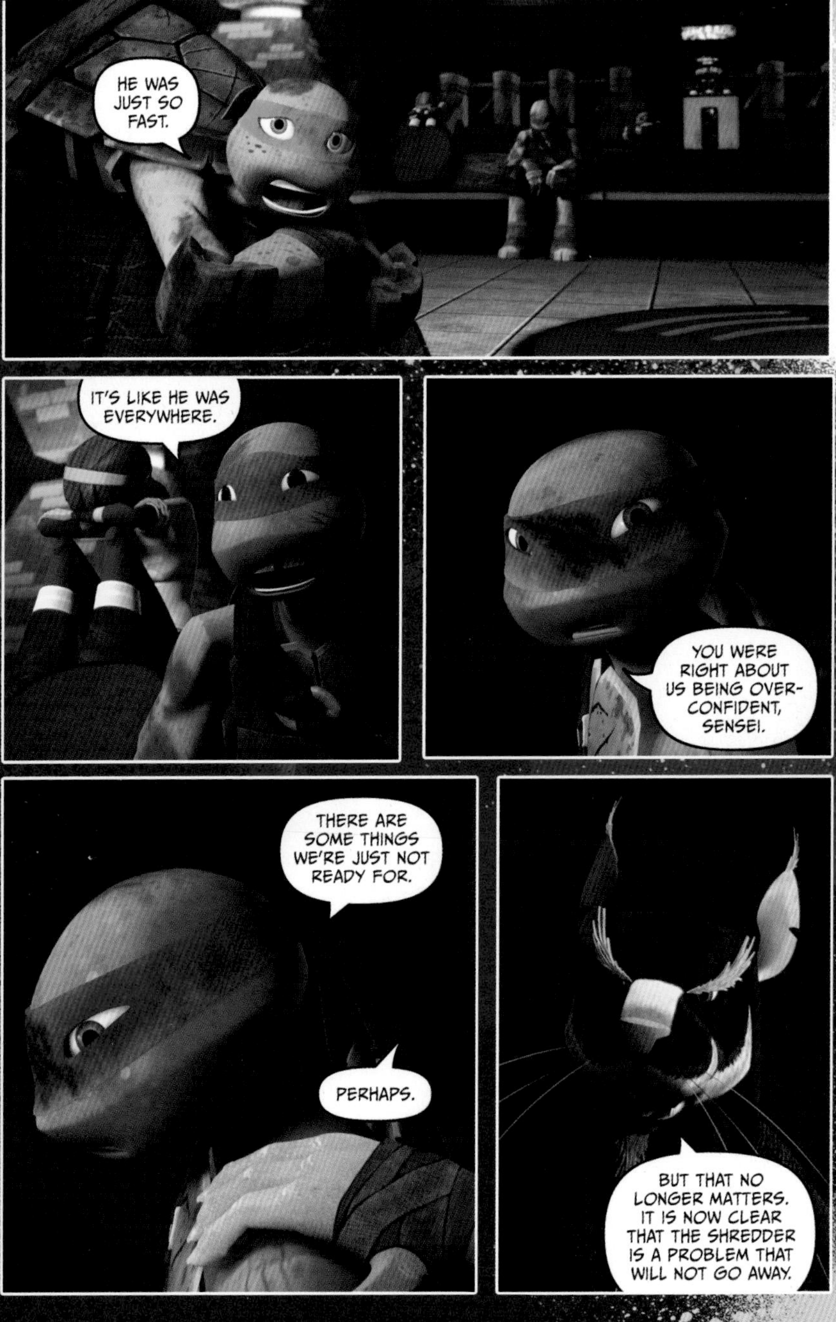
HE WAS JUST SO FAST.
IT'S LIKE HE WAS EVERYWHERE.
YOU WERE RIGHT ABOUT US BEING OVER-CONFIDENT, SENSEI.
THERE ARE SOME THINGS WE'RE JUST NOT READY FOR.
PERHAPS.
BUT THAT NO LONGER MATTERS. IT IS NOW CLEAR THAT THE SHREDDER IS A PROBLEM THAT WILL NOT GO AWAY.

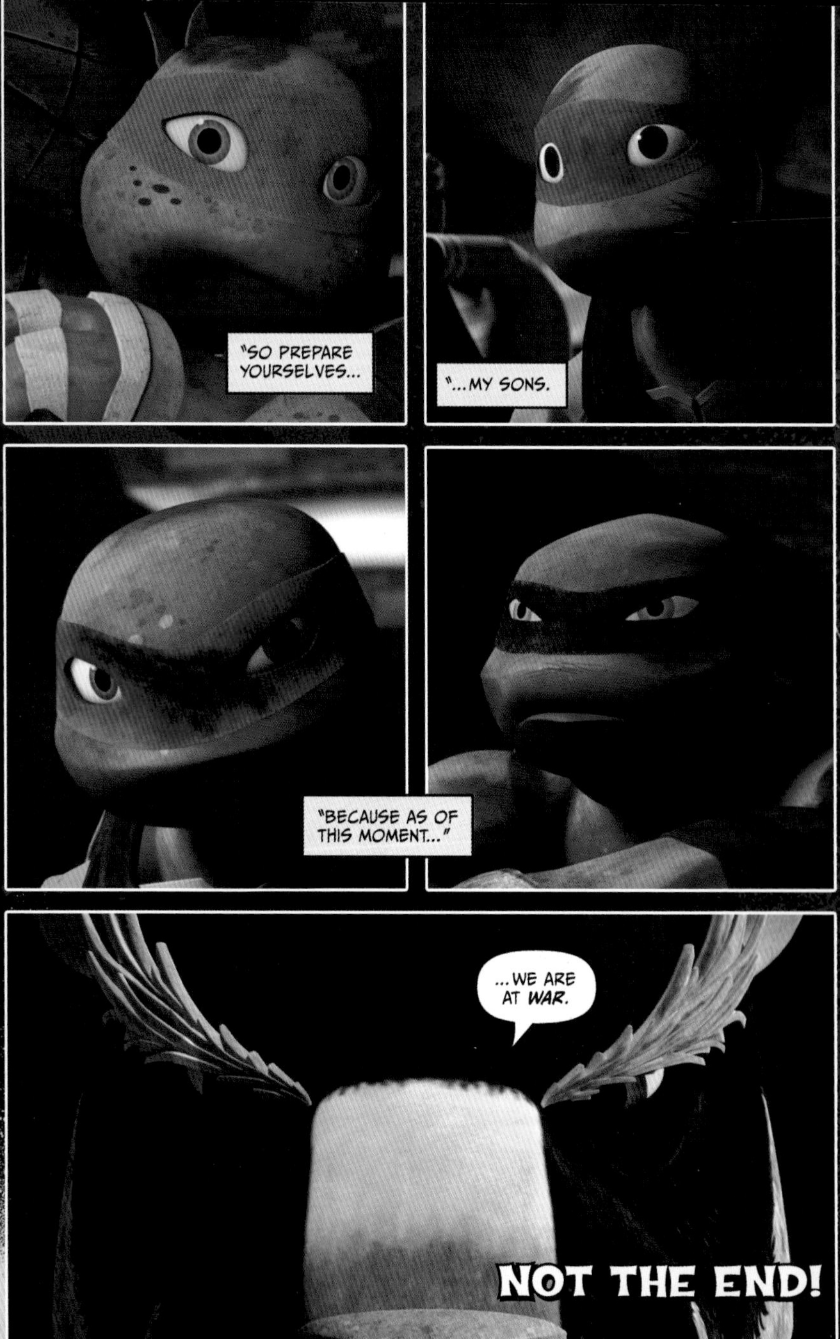
"SO PREPARE YOURSELVES...
"...MY SONS.
"BECAUSE AS OF THIS MOMENT..."
...WE ARE AT WAR.
NOT THE END!